She Lies in Wait

GYTHA LODGE

MICHAEL JOSEPH
an imprint of
PENGUIN BOOKS

MICHAEL JOSEPH

UK | USA | Canada | Ireland | Australia
India | New Zealand | South Africa

Michael Joseph is part of the Penguin Random House group of companies
whose addresses can be found at global.penguinrandomhouse.com.

Penguin
Random House
UK

First published 2019
002

Copyright © Gytha Lodge, 2019

The moral right of the author has been asserted

Set in 13.5/16 pt Garamond MT Std
Typeset by Jouve (UK), Milton Keynes
Printed and bound in Great Britain by Clays Ltd, Elcograf S.p.A.

A CIP catalogue record for this book is available from the British Library

HARDBACK ISBN: 978–0–241–36297–6
OM PAPERBACK ISBN: 978–0–241–36298–3

www.greenpenguin.co.uk

MIX
Paper from
responsible sources
FSC® C018179

Penguin Random House is committed to a
sustainable future for our business, our readers
and our planet. This book is made from Forest
Stewardship Council® certified paper.

To Ma and Pa Lodge, who not only read and gave feedback, but have been there, supporting, for the twenty years since I wrote a truly awful first book. You've got some serious stickability.

Prologue

She made her skittering, sliding way down the riverbank. Her trainers hit the flat ground at the lip of the water, and she wobbled but recovered.

'Jessie!'

She heard her name, and felt an answering buzz of adrenalin. She paused, then kicked her way on again. Just her brother, not Dad. Away up the slope. Her brother wasn't going to yell at her for wandering off.

It was quiet. Much quieter than up by the camping stove where Dad's commands were unrelenting. Her ears were full of leaves rustling, and rushes of birdsong.

She left the shadow of the trees, the sun making fierce patterns on skin already hot from scrambling. She put a hand up over her eyes to block the glare from the water. She should have brought sunglasses, and thought about going back for them. But she didn't want to risk being seen. Not when being seen meant being inspected for dirt and told to clean herself, lay the table, and put things away.

She moved into the shadows under the bank, her eyes dazzled. There were blue patterns everywhere she looked. A spreading beech tree was above her, and roots arced out of the soil like flattened croquet hoops. Her foot caught on one. She stumbled, her heart jolting as she thought she might fall into the water. The river was dirty in the shadows under the tree, ominous. But she wasn't really close enough to fall in, and she regained her balance.

In front of her was a scooped-out section of earth the shape of a hammock that made her want to nestle in it.

'Jessie!'

Great. It was her dad this time, and closer by. He was using the kind of voice that wanted an answer. But in front of her was the cool earth, and a hiding place.

She stretched one foot down into the hollow, and then the other. She felt immediately cooler, and took a seat on the slightly crumbly earth. She imagined herself as an early villager, sheltering in the woods while Vikings raided her home.

But it wasn't as soft as she'd expected. Ridges of root pressed against her pelvis and back. She squirmed left and right, trying to find a comfortable spot.

Her shorts snagged, and she felt a jab in her leg.

She pushed a hand down to disentangle the cloth, and then felt the root crumble in her hand. She lifted it and saw not old wood, but flakes of brown, and the bleach-white shapes of freshly exposed bone.

She didn't need her GP father to tell her she was holding a human finger.

I

Jonah was halfway up Blissford Hill when he felt the buzz of his phone in the zip pocket on the back of his Lycra. He was standing up on the pedals and slogging upwards. He considered ignoring it, and then had a vivid image of his mum in hospital. And following that, he had a slightly stomach-turning thought that it might be Michelle. Which was just as irrational as every other time he'd believed it in the last eight months, but he thought it anyway.

He braked with gritted teeth and stopped his grinding climb. He caught his shin on one of the pedals as he jumped down, and was savage by the time he'd rooted his phone out and seen DS Lightman's extension flashing on the screen.

'Ben?' he said, and then moved the phone away from his mouth to mask his heavy breathing.

'Sorry, chief.' Lightman didn't sound it. Never really sounded anything. Michelle had liked to call him Barbie. Exquisitely pretty and emotionless. A lot smarter than Barbie, though, Jonah knew. 'Call from DCS Wilkinson. He wants you to postpone your days off to investigate a possible homicide.'

Jonah let the DS wait in silence. He looked up at the tree-shadowed top of the hill. It was a slog away, but he wanted the slog. His legs were crying out for it. He squeezed the drop handles of his bike with his free hand and felt the sweat on his palm. He hadn't spent enough time doing this recently.

'Sir?'

'Where?' he asked, not bothering to hide his irritation.

'Brinken Wood.'

There was another silence, but this one wasn't deliberate. He felt knocked off balance.

'Recent remains?' he asked in the end, though he thought he knew the answer.

'No. DCS says not,' said the sergeant, who was too young to understand.

His day of cycling was over, but Jonah suddenly felt too old for it anyway. He couldn't remember ever feeling old before.

'Send a car to pick me up in Godshill. Bring the kitbag from behind my desk. And find someone to lend me a deodorant.'

'Yes, sir,' Lightman answered, his voice as level as ever.

Jonah slotted his phone back into the pocket of the technical top. There was sweat already cooling on him and leaving him chilled. He ought to get cycling again. It was a few more miles to Godshill.

He stayed there, unmoving, for a full minute, then swung his leg off the Cannondale and started to walk it slowly up the hill.

Hanson was in such a hurry to climb out of the car that she caught the sleeve of her expensive new suit on a protruding piece in the door and pulled a thread. It gave her a slightly sick feeling. She hadn't really been able to afford it in the first place. She'd bought three others in her first two weeks as a DC, having previously owned only jeans, tank tops and sweaters, and a few dresses for going out. Suits were bloody expensive, and she resented the money she could have been spending on her unreliable car. Or maybe on an actual social life, which she seemed to have forgotten about somewhere along the way.

She tried to smooth the plucked sleeve down while she made her way inside. She wondered if she could get her mum

4

to take a look at it, if she managed to make it to her mum's any time soon. A potential homicide might mean working through the weekend. Late nights and living off caffeine while they caught the killer. The thought made her smile.

She let herself into CID and saw Lightman's head bent over his screen. She wondered how long he'd been here, and whether he did anything else with his life. Whether there was a Lightman wife and kids that he hadn't yet mentioned. He somehow had the look of an unfaithful husband about him. Too pretty, and too closed off. Unless that was more her own recent experience warping her expectations.

Lightman caught sight of her and gave a small smile. 'I got hold of the chief. He's going to need picking up and taking to the crime scene.'

'On it,' Hanson answered immediately. 'Where is he?'

'Godshill,' he said. 'He's on his bike.'

Hanson nodded. She pretended she knew the place well, and that she wasn't about to punch it into her satnav. Two weeks into the job and she basically knew the route from home to the station and the supermarket, and from there to the dockside, where they'd been looking at some potential fraud. She missed the certainty of zooming around Birming-ham, where she'd grown up, and then worked as a constable for two years. Though she had to admit that the New Forest was a lot prettier.

'You'll need this,' Lightman said, and lifted a dark-grey kitbag from the floor. 'And despite the time constraints, I'd take him a coffee. He's not going to be that happy at having his day off interrupted.'

'OK. Just . . . a filter coffee? Not a latte or something?'

Lightman laughed. 'God no. Have you not had one of his rants on coffee menus yet?'

'No, but I'm sure it'll be great.' She put the kitbag on to her shoulder. 'OK. Anything else? Do you know what it's about yet?'

Lightman shook his head. 'Local sergeant will hand over to the chief at the scene. You'll both get a run-down, though if it's not recent, there won't be much so far.'

Hanson nodded, and tried not to smile. You shouldn't smile at news of a murder, even if it had been ages ago. But the truth was, she was delighted.

Hanson was wound up like it was exam results day. She gabbled at Jonah about the kitbag and coffee, and then without pausing for breath asked about the remains. Jonah found it somewhere between sweet and irritating.

'Ben said they might not be recent,' she said.

'I'd wait until forensics give an opinion,' he replied, taking a long gulp of coffee. 'Most people – including me – don't have a scooby what age bones are.'

Having sweated and chilled, he was cold even in the suit he had tugged on in the public toilets at Godshill. Cold, and drifting around his own thoughts of thirty years ago. He had to interrupt her to ask her to turn the heater on. The Fiat veered while she turned the dial, and then steadied.

'Sorry,' she said.

'I'm just grateful you're driving,' he said, with a slight smile. 'The coffee was a good call, by the way. You've given me at least a couple of hours of not being in a really bad mood.'

'Hmm. A couple of hours. So I've either got to find you a Starbucks before then, or get out of the way?'

'Pretty much,' Jonah agreed.

Brinken Wood was suddenly on them. There was a cluster of squad cars and uniforms in the shingle car park. He found it impossible not to remember this place as it had been back then. The car park had all been bark and mud, but it had been just as overrun by police. The haircuts different; the faces somehow the same.

Jonah levered himself out of the car once they'd pulled up, taking the coffee cup with him. He felt like he'd gone back in time. So many months had been spent here, searching endlessly.

He approached the sergeant. 'DCI Sheens. This is DC Hanson.'

Hanson had been the same rank as the sergeant two weeks ago. But to train as a detective, you had to take what amounted to a demotion, and become a detective constable. Jonah remembered not being sure who was more important when it had happened to him, and wondered if Hanson felt the same.

There was sweat along the sergeant's hairline. His eyes were over-wide and his smile brief and agitated. His police constable, a stocky twenty-something, seemed calmer.

Jonah addressed his question somewhere between the two of them: 'Who found the remains?'

The sergeant answered. 'A GP out camping with his family. Well, his daughter, but he called it in.'

'How old's the daughter?'

'Nine,' the constable said. 'Seems fine, though. It's the father who's taking it hard.'

'They're still here?'

'We've kept them at their campsite. It's not within view of the remains.'

Jonah nodded, and let the sergeant lead the way, though he knew where he was going. It was where seven kids had bedded down thirty years ago, but only six of them had got up in the morning.

*

Dr Martin Miller was sitting apart from his family. The doctor's wife was watching the boy play on an iPad. The girl was kicking up dust around the edge of the camp.

It was the mother Jonah approached.

'DCI Sheens.' He smiled at her. He'd had to learn how to smile when his mind was full of complicated, dark thoughts like crazed glass between him and the world. 'Would you mind if I talk to your daughter for a few minutes?'

'Jessie!' It was a call from the father. His voice was high-pitched and irritable. 'Stop kicking like that. You're making a mess.'

The girl was halfway upset and halfway rebellious. She scuffed over to her mother and Jonah, sat down quickly, and looked up at him, her knees up near her chin.

The mother slid an arm round her in a brief hug. 'You don't mind talking to the police, do you, Jessie?' she asked her daughter.

Jessie shook her head.

'We don't need to ask much,' Jonah said, steadily. 'Just a few details about what you found.'

'Sure.'

'She doesn't know anything,' her slightly older brother interrupted scathingly. The disdain of older siblings had always seemed uniquely intense to Jonah.

He glanced over at the boy, who was now watching them both a little sullenly. He thought about asking him to move away, but decided to let him be.

He crouched close to Jessie. 'So, a few questions for you.'

The girl gave him another wary look, and then her gaze wandered away and she picked up a pebble, threw it off to the side, repeated it with another.

'Jessie, for goodness' sake!' The father again. Much closer.

'Stop throwing things, and look at the policeman when he's talking to you. This is important.'

Jonah tried to smile up at the doctor. 'It's OK, don't worry.'

'Jessie!'

Jonah might as well not have spoken.

The girl gave her father a truculent look, and then did her best to look up at Jonah through her straight brown fringe. Jonah tried not to become irritated at the father's interruptions, which had nothing to do with helping the police, he thought, and everything to do with control.

'Are you an inspector?' Jessie asked quietly.

Jonah grinned. 'I am. Detective chief inspector, in fact.'

Jessie's eyes were still a little wary. 'So you're in charge?'

'Yes.' She seemed happy enough with that, so he went on. 'Could you tell me what you were doing when you found the bones?'

Jessie glanced at her father, and then said quietly, 'Hiding.'

Jonah saw the mother grimace, but she didn't try to deny it.

'Hiding can be fun,' he said. 'That hollow under the tree. That was already there? You didn't have to dig it?'

Jessie shook her head. 'I just got in and sat down. There was something poking me, so I pulled it out.'

Jonah nodded. 'Naturally. And it came out easily?'

'Yes. I thought – I thought it was a root, and then maybe a plant because I grabbed a handful. But then I realized it was a finger.'

'Well done,' he said, nodding. 'Not everybody would have realized.'

Jessie nodded, gave a small smile, and stood up. Her mother pulled her into a brief hug.

'I'd like them not to talk to their school friends about this for a few days,' Jonah said to Mrs Miller, once she'd let go of her daughter.

'It's OK, they're not seeing any for a few weeks. We thought we'd carry on the holiday, but somewhere else.'

Privately educated kids, he realized. They were already on holiday, a good month before the state schools broke up.

'Good. It would be better if this wasn't talked about just yet.'

'Of course.'

He heard Dr Miller's footsteps.

'Are we done? It's a beautiful day and I don't think we have much to add.'

'Yes, we're all done. Thanks for your patience.'

As Jonah stood, the doctor was already giving his children orders to get packed up.

He hurried them over to the tent, and Jonah found himself watching until Mrs Miller rose and began to pick up a few half-eaten packs of raisins and a cup.

'I'm sorry your holiday got interrupted,' he said.

'It's fine,' she said, with a brief wave of her hand, and glanced at her husband. 'Martin's just . . . It's not great for him.' This in a low voice. 'This was supposed to be a holiday where he could forget . . . He's been very unwell. They only gave him a fifty per cent chance of living past Christmas.'

Jonah nodded, wondering whether she was used to apologizing for her husband. But he understood that she meant cancer; that those bones had been a little handful of mortality. He felt a trace of sympathy.

An hour and a half of excavation. Dozens of photographs. A tent set up and eight bags of carefully labelled bone fragments.

Everyone was getting hot and irritable. Jonah's mouth was beginning to taste like bitter, hours-old coffee. His feet were fractious, impossible to keep still. And he had the kind of energy-sapping hunger that made it hard to focus.

'Anything yet?' Hanson asked, after wandering up to the car park and back a few times.

Excitement had turned into boredom, the one reliable constant in the emotional range of every detective.

'I think it'll be a while,' Jonah said. 'It's an old corpse . . . time-consuming job.'

'Is there anything we can be . . .?'

'We can be here when they want to talk to us,' he said with a half-smile.

Some twenty minutes later, Linda McCullough, the scene of crime officer, stepped carefully up out of the dip and approached him. He was glad it was McCullough. You needed someone obsessively careful on a site that would have only the barest traces of data left.

'How goes it, Linda?'

'We're going to be bagging this up for some time.' She lifted her mask and let it sit on the top of her white hood. Her weathered face was wet with sweat, as anyone's would have been if they'd been wearing overalls in that weather. But McCullough seemed not to notice it. 'But as initial feedback, it's a pubescent female, in an advanced state of decay.'

'How advanced?'

'Rough estimate only, but more than ten years. Fewer than fifty.'

Thirty years, he thought. *Thirty.*

He found it hard, momentarily, to believe that so much time had passed. A feeling that he must be Rip van Winkle, and have slept through much of his life, ran through him.

Rip van Winkle must have felt this strange mixture of anger and guilt, too.

'Linda!'

McCullough turned, shielding her eyes from the sun. Another white bio-suit was leaning out of the tent to call to her.

'I'm uncovering other materials. Can I get your opinion?'

'Sure.'

She replaced her mask and climbed carefully back to the site, disappearing into the tent.

'So if it's murder, it's an old one,' Hanson said, and Jonah was half blinded by the white of the paper as she flipped her notebook to write in it. She sounded disappointed. Unaware of the huge implications behind those numbers. 'And a teen-age girl.'

'It's thirty years old,' he said. 'And it's Aurora Jackson.'

2. Aurora

Friday, 22 July 1983, 5:30 p.m.

Light, dark, light, dark.

Every tree was a shadowy pulse as they flashed past it. It was a soothing rhythm. She rested her head on the car door and watched her hair flicking and snapping out. She thought about drifting on the hot wind, away from here, to somewhere the light was golden-orange all day.

'Where were you last night? I tried calling your house a few times.' It was Topaz, sunglasses pushed up into her dark hair as she leaned forward from the back seat. She wasn't talking to Aurora, of course.

Aurora wished Brett hadn't been kind to her and let her ride shotgun. She could tell that Topaz wanted to be there. Her sister was angry that she'd been relegated; angry with Aurora. Connor had been angry, too. He didn't like that Brett had offered to drive the three of them while he'd been left to cycle with the others.

'Huh? Oh. I went to a film.' Brett shifted gears as he spoke. His hand brushed Aurora's flimsy skirt. 'Sorry,' he muttered.

Aurora moved a little, shrugging. 'My fault. I'm in the way.'

'What film? Something scary?' Topaz asked, almost over the top of her.

'*Blue Thunder.*'

'Again?' Topaz laughed, and pushed his shoulder lightly. 'You must have seen that twenty times.'

'Just three,' Brett replied. 'It's a great film. It knocks a lot of the stuff this year out of the water.' A brief pause to overtake a caravan. 'What kind of films do you like, Aurora?'

'Huh?'

It was a knee-jerk response. The pretence of being elsewhere. It happened so often that even though she'd been listening, she couldn't help it. She heard Topaz mutter, 'Airhead.'

She looked at Brett, who was smiling warmly enough.

'What kind of films do you like watching?'

'I don't know. Anything . . . where I get to see another world, I suppose. Things set in strange countries, or space, or fantastical places. I like romance, too.'

She heard Coralie snort, and wondered if she should have lied and told him she liked action movies. Topaz always pretended to be into them, and rolled her eyes at 'girly girls' who only liked soppy films. Aurora had always let her do it, even though she knew Topaz's favourite films were all period dramas or romantic comedies.

'So you must like *Star Wars*, then?' Brett asked. 'That's got all of that. Have you seen *Return of the Jedi* yet?'

Aurora shook her head. 'I was going to wait till it was out on video. My parents didn't like the last one . . .'

'Ah, you have to see it in the cinema,' he said, shaking his head. 'All the effects, the Star Destroyers, the rumbling that comes from the speakers – and it's going to be ages till the video. We should sort that out, Topaz.' He glanced in the rearview mirror. 'Go as a group.'

'Sounds good,' Topaz said, and Aurora could tell from the set of her mouth that she wasn't happy.

I shouldn't have mentioned our parents. She told me not to talk about them.

Aurora felt a knot of tension in her stomach. She never knew what to say in front of Topaz's friends. Whatever she came out with was always the wrong thing. And getting it wrong in front of Brett was worse. He was the older one everyone crushed on. The star sportsman who could draw a dozen girls as an audience just by turning up to train in the school pool.

Her feelings about being here were such a mixture of gratitude and anxiety. Everyone in her year – everyone in the school really – would have killed to be sitting here. Brett Parker was right next to her, close enough to touch. And more than that, she was with *the group*. With Benners' gang of strange, anarchic, brilliant and beautiful friends.

It was a group she didn't fit into at all; one she had only been invited into because of her sister. And, in one of those ironies, Topaz didn't want her there at all.

She looked back at the trees and the sunshine, imagining that she could be lifted by that breeze and placed gently in a pair of strong arms. She gave the arms an owner and a head of dark hair.

She imagined him speaking to her. *I've never met anyone like you before. You're all the world to me.*

'Hey.' Coralie was leaning forward to point. 'That's where you pull in.'

She added a strange little laugh on to the end of it. It was a habit of hers. It made her seem even more childlike. Another thing to add to the pink clothes and the wide eyes and the cultivated confusion at the world.

The car slowed and Aurora watched, regretfully, as the flickering subsided into a slower rhythm and then became just the shadow of overhanging trees. She tried to hold on to that feeling of being cradled and lulled, but Coralie was opening her door, and Brett pulling the keys out of the ignition.

Reluctantly, she climbed out of the car and watched Topaz get out and walk round towards Brett, who was unloading a few sleeping bags and backpacks. Topaz stretched upwards, her crop top riding up to show her tanned stomach, and then turned round to face away from him. She leaned forward to touch her toes.

Aurora saw Brett's eyes drop to Topaz's backside, where some of her buttocks and the very bottom of her lace under-wear were visible.

'I'm soooooo stiff,' Topaz said. She straightened up slowly, and looked at Brett over her shoulder. 'Coming?'

'Uhhh . . . Sure.'

Coralie hurried round the car and took Topaz's hand. The two of them swayed ahead down the forest path.

3

Jonah took Hanson with him to the Jackson house outside Lyndhurst. He could have left informing next of kin to a couple of community support officers, but he felt a powerful need to be there. Perhaps to comfort; perhaps because he'd waited thirty years for a conclusion.

The Jacksons had never left the New Forest. It was the more common outcome in disappearance cases. Where a murder often drove a family away, an unresolved missing person bound them to the place where the missing one had been. There was always that dwindling hope that they would one day arrive back home again.

The half-mile driveway was almost impassable now. The sand-and-hardcore surface had disintegrated into a mine-field of potholes. Hanson swore when the front-left tyre dipped deeply enough into a pothole that the bottom of the car scraped the hard-baked mud. She pulled the wheel sharply to avoid another, and Jonah steadied himself against the dashboard.

'Doesn't the council resurface this?' she asked.

'Private road,' Jonah replied. 'The Jacksons have never believed in tarmac. They're a bit alternative. Though I'm not sure if it's about a love of nature or just laziness, to be honest.'

'I don't mind nature when it keeps its hands off my car,' Hanson muttered.

She pulled up in a half-cleared area in front of a single-storey house. Jonah opened his door over a dried-mud crater.

Stepping into it, he felt corners of stone press into his foot through the sole of his shoe.

He had half emerged from the car when the battered front door opened. A round, uncertain figure in a thick-knit cardigan and home-dyed dress stood in the doorway, blinking into the sun.

'Good morning, Mrs Jackson. Sorry for bothering you, but is it all right if we come in?' he said, as neutrally as he could.

'I – Yes. Yes, I suppose so.' She emerged further from under the shadow of a scorched-looking wisteria. Then she stopped. 'It's not Topaz, is it?'

Jonah shook his head, but Hanson answered for him.

'Your daughter's just fine, Mrs Jackson.' She said it with a warm smile, and Jonah was glad he'd brought her along.

'We just wondered if we might chat about some developments in Aurora's disappearance,' he added.

Joy Jackson's head turned back towards the house briefly, and her hands reached for her cardigan pockets.

'Yes. Yes, of course. Why don't you –'

She stood shifting as Jonah and Hanson navigated the overgrown stones of the path. Two of them tipped under Jonah's feet.

Up close, Joy was ruddier and more lined than he'd remembered her. Round cheeks underscored by webs of red; eyes that constantly shifted in creased sockets.

Lavender came off her clothes as she turned. 'Come in. I'll find Tom. Tom!' Her voice was shrill as she dipped into the shadow of the hall. 'Tom!'

The hallway floor was barely possible to walk along. Most of it was covered with assorted coats, shoes, boxes and eclectic outdoor items. Joy picked her way past without looking at her feet, long practised at this arrangement.

'Come into the kitchen. I'll put some tea on. Tom!'

The kitchen was no less cluttered. There were two or three spare feet of clear space at one end of the huge oak table, and a mountain of newspaper, letters and shrapnel on the remainder.

'Don't trouble yourself over tea unless you want one,' Jonah said, as Joy opened three cupboards in turn before finding a box of tea. She turned round with it, and came to a stop again.

He moved around the edge of the table and let his eyes scan the kitchen. The work surfaces were under a layer of visible grime, with dirty crockery spread out like ornaments. Larger objects interspersed them at intervals. An old piece of plumbing. A table-tennis racquet. A hammer.

The stooped figure that emerged from a doorway brought Jonah up short. If it hadn't been for the wild grey beard and hair, he would never have known him for Tom Jackson, the arrogant, well-bred, decidedly Aspergic oddball. He could barely see any traces of the argumentative man who had clattered in and out of Lyndhurst in his battered Volvo, and who had engaged in periodic feuds with the council or post office. This was no more than a fragment of him. A poor sketch.

'Police, is it?'

The voice was lifeless too. Jonah remembered the fury of him after Aurora had gone. The aggressive finger-stabbing as he told them what they were doing wrong, and why they couldn't find her. Perhaps thirty years of fury could burn the life out of a man.

'Yes, Tom.' Joy had begun moving again, filling an ancient stovetop kettle from the sink. 'Will you . . .? I'll make a pot.'

Tom pulled a wooden carver out. He sat heavily in it and looked first at Hanson, then at Jonah. He seemed to lose interest in both, and began to gaze at a dim painting of the sea on the uneven wall.

The silence as the kettle boiled stretched into awkwardness. Jonah's patience wore through before it had finished.

'We wanted to speak to you first. There's been a development this morning.'

There was a flurry of activity from Joy. She shoved cups down and turned, reaching into her pockets for something, her hands coming up empty.

'They've got some news on Aurora, Tom,' Joy said.

'Yes. I assumed so.'

Jonah met a gaze from Tom that was full of profound disinterest. He found himself looking away.

'Although formal identification is to follow,' Jonah said, 'we've discovered remains not far from the campsite where Aurora disappeared. The age and gender are right, and they look to be thirty years old.' He waited for a response. Tom only flicked a strand of hair out of his eyes, while Joy waited with her gaze on Hanson for some reason.

'We believe it's your daughter,' Jonah finished as gently as he could.

Joy stared with her mouth hanging slack for a moment, and then reached to put a cup down, clumsily.

'She – Oh, Tom.' She drew in a noisy breath, and then sobbed. She turned away, hiding her face. 'Tom. Oh, Tom. She's –'

Hanson moved immediately to put a comforting arm round her. Tom Jackson remained motionless, that empty gaze on his wife now.

'Well, she wasn't going to be alive, was she?' he said, his

voice harsh. 'Thirty years of not a blasted word. Of course she's dead.'

Eight forty on a Sunday. Connor Dooley should be taking his weekend, but he'd still had to come in early for marking, and to prepare for their inter-departmental meeting. It happened increasingly: holidays and weekends being gradually absorbed into meetings and paperwork and conflict resolution. And his rooms were being absorbed, too. Once pristine mahogany was now hidden beneath folders and envelopes, its occasionally revealed corners dusty and dull.

Today, he was preparing himself to fight. It was a frustrating, unnecessary fight based on the intractable tightness of the bursar. A new post had been created a year ago out of need. The history fellows had long been overloaded; the college taking on ever more PhD and MPhil students. Even with the extra support of that new post, they were eight per cent below target contact time with their students. However, he'd thought this fight at least partially won until Lopez had taken a professorship at Glasgow, and the bursar had announced no plans to reappoint. He'd told Connor point-blank that the extra fellow had been a luxury they could no longer afford. That the existing three history fellows could cover the extra work between them.

So Connor was here, on Sunday morning, before the coffee shops along West Nicholson Street were even open, ready to print out tables and charts of the time commitments of his faculty. Ready to beat the bursar down with facts. If that tactic failed, he might just invite the man home for dinner. Fighting was sometimes rendered unnecessary when his wife moved towards a colleague wearing a little black dress.

The buzz of his phone was halfway welcome. It was an

excuse to postpone the data-trawling. A reason to put off thinking about grabbing the bursar by his jowly neck.

Topaz. Was she calling to tell him she couldn't come for lunch with him? He half remembered being in bed this morning at fuck-knew what time, and her kissing him good-bye with her hair scraped back and her sports kit on.

He tried to remember what she'd been doing. Training earlier than usual, obviously. She'd been going to a coffee or something afterwards. One of those meet-ups that was half-way between a business meeting and a social chat.

'Hey, T,' he said. 'All OK?'

'They found her.'

It was an odd moment. He heard emotion in her voice, but couldn't pinpoint it. He knew who she meant without needing to be told. He imagined, with a lurch, that Topaz was about to tell him she'd been alive all this time and in hiding.

'She's –'

'She never left the campsite.' He could hear the edge to her voice then. 'They found remains near the river. It's her. She's –'

The pause was long and awful. No chance for him to comfort her in any meaningful way. But he tried anyway.

'Oh, Topaz,' he said. And then: 'I'll come and pick you up.'

A watery breath.

'Sorry . . . yes. Please. We should go down there. There will be flights . . .'

Connor hesitated, thinking of the bursar and the fight he would inevitably lose if he left now. Then, cutting through that thought, there was a memory of a hot, hazy summer and a girl with a halo of blonde hair.

'Sure. I'll cancel tomorrow's meetings. We should go.'

He hung up, and stood unmoving for a while.

So she was by the river . . .

He thought about what that meant. Then he closed his laptop and started gathering his belongings together again.

4. Aurora

'We found it last summer, when we were out here for Benners' birthday.' Topaz was picking her way down the crumbling riverbank. Coralie was in her automatic place just behind her, tripping along on her skinny legs like a foal, always on the verge of falling but never quite doing it. Benners and Connor and Jojo hadn't arrived yet, but Topaz couldn't seem to wait to show Brett around.

Brett seemed happy enough to be given the tour. He was close enough on their heels to reach out and touch them both if he'd wanted to. Aurora thought he probably did want to. They all did.

Aurora trailed further back, drunk on heat and sunshine. She was following for the sake of following. She tripped on something on the lip of the bank and stumbled.

Brett turned, remembering her. 'You been here before?'

'No.'

'Aurora –' She heard the sharpness of her sister.

Coralie looked at her, and whispered, 'Great, the love child's here . . .'

Topaz had turned to face them all, her body blocking the way uncertainly. Behind her was a huge spreading beech tree, its roots plunging into the glittering river.

'You don't say a word about this to Mum and Dad, all right?' Topaz said.

'Why would I tell them anything?' Aurora looked up at the tree, and smiled at it. 'It's pretty.'

'I mean it.'

She looked at her sister's hard blue eyes. She had the quality of sharpened rock just then. Like something carved out of unforgiving stone. Chiselled and sculpted and weathered.

'Of course I won't tell them anything.'

'Come on, then.' Brett stepped forward and put a hand on Topaz's dark-bronze shoulder. She yielded, and turned again.

'This way.'

She ducked her head under a spray of glossy leaves, vanishing into the gloom. Aurora let Coralie and Brett go ahead, and reached out to touch the slick green foliage.

'It's hot here.' She leaned in to whisper to the tree. 'Are you thirsty?'

She ducked under, too. In the tree's shade, the soil was bare and loose and pale brown. There was just the earth, and the smooth roots, and a single shrub-like offshoot of the tree at its base.

'Here.'

Topaz pulled two branches of the sapling aside. There was a dim space behind it, where the bank beneath the roots had been hollowed out.

'Nice!' Brett said, stepping forward.

'Take a look,' Topaz said. 'There's only room for one at a time.'

Aurora watched Brett's broad shoulders tilt sideways as he squeezed his way into the opening.

'What's in there?' Aurora asked. It looked like the work of animals. Badgers or rabbits. Maybe an otter.

'Private things,' Topaz said immediately. 'Things you need to keep quiet. All right?'

Aurora shrugged. 'All right.'

And then Brett was re-emerging, his face alight and smudged with mud.

'Jesus. That's some stash. Where did it come from?'

Topaz grinned at him.

'Friend of Jojo's brother. He had a deal that didn't come off, and he owed his supplier. Benners bought it all for, you know, cost price.'

'With what money?'

'He asked his parents for it. They didn't have a clue.'

'He said it was for a new car,' Coralie chipped in. 'So he bought a heap of junk for fifty quid and the rest went on this.'

'Fuck me.' Brett laughed, and rubbed at his face. 'That's a lot of partying.' His eyes fell on Aurora. 'You need to have a look.'

'No, she doesn't,' Topaz answered. Her arms were folded across her body, her gaze on her sister.

'Come on. She's not going to tell your parents. She'd be in as much shit as you. She's here with us, isn't she?'

Aurora looked between them, and then saw Topaz wave her hand.

She dropped to her knees on the earth and crawled in, her skirt picking up soil. There was the tiniest bit of moisture in the air as she entered the darkness. The earth was soft under her hands, feeling fresh-turned, grave-like.

It was a small space. There was just enough room for her to sit, or to kneel. Ahead of her, there was something that gleamed in the dimness. She squinted at it, held out a hand and ran it over the wall of dull silver. She realized that these were piles and piles of carefully folded foil packets held in dozens of clear plastic bags.

26

She didn't need to know what was in them. Drugs of some kind, she thought. Nothing she wanted to know about.

It was a shame they'd filled so much of this space up. There was a slight animal smell here, and Aurora guessed that whatever had made the hole had been frightened away. She could imagine being a creature and living here. Sleeping here for the winter. Looking after young, safe from predators.

Slowly, she backed out, and stood up, dusting her skirt down. Some of the mud still clung to the gauze, ground in by her knees.

'What did you think?' Brett asked her.

She gave him a small smile.

'It's nice in there.'

She heard Topaz's noise of disgust, even under Brett's booming laugh.

5

McCullough angled the jaw towards him.

'Here.'

They were in the forensic department, in the bowels of the station. McCullough had rung him an hour after he'd returned from the Jacksons' house. It was a much faster turnaround than he'd been expecting. ID'ing a body could take days.

He leaned in, thankful for the age of the body and the mask. McCullough used a finger to hover over the jaw.

'That's the filling there. Look at the inside of the second premolar.'

'And . . .'

'And the chipped second incisor. Definite ID. No question about it.'

Jonah nodded. He hadn't needed confirmation, but it was official now. It was Aurora.

'Her records show she was fourteen when she died,' Linda added.

'Any cause of death?'

'Nothing solid yet.' She rested the jawbone back on the cloth covering the trolley. 'Initial visual examination of the skeleton hasn't come up with knife wounds, or evidence of bullet travel, but that might come down to digital analysis from forensic anthropology. We'll have that in the next few days.' She gave a frustrated sound. 'I'd dearly like to have enough material for a tox analysis, but decomposition is pretty complete.'

'Why a tox analysis? Any particular reason?'

'Yes, significant traces of a reason.'

She moved over to a covered workbench and pulled the tarp away. There was a dusting of soil, and within it the outlines of foil-wrapped shapes.

'Dexedrine.' Her gloved hands opened a plastic-wrapped package. She removed one of the foil packets, which had been opened. Off-white powder within. Spongy-looking, like crumbling plaster. 'It was in several foil-wrapped packets with sheeting around it, close by the body. The chemist's taken samples, but he says it looks medical-grade. There are traces of more in the soil, and it looks like some of the ground has been excavated close by. Possibly some of it's been removed, though whether by animals or not, it's hard to tell.'

Jonah dipped his latex-sheathed forefinger into the powder, trying to remember those amphetamine-touched years of the eighties. Had it been Dexedrine behind those many expensive deaths in penthouses? Or speed? Or crystal meth? Hard to distinguish between the older ones and the more recent. So many bodies; so much powder and crystal and muck.

'Can you try and find some tissue to test for traces? If she was buried with all this stuff, it's more than possible it's connected.'

'Thank you,' McCullough said drily. 'That hadn't occurred to me.'

Jonah gave her a slight smile. 'Anything else on the body?'

'Well . . .'

He dusted his finger on the plastic overalls and then followed her to the table again.

'Nothing indicative. The body's been submerged at some point. But I'd say well after death.'

Jonah thought about the flooding that the sergeant at the site had talked about. 'So she didn't drown,' he said.

McCullough gave him a level look. 'She might have drowned.'

'All right.' He gave her a small smile. 'But she was also, separately, submerged. And you haven't found evidence of drowning.'

'No, but don't rule it out until I'm sure.'

'Noted. Anything else at the scene?'

'Assorted buried items that we're searching through. There's likely to have been some previous contamination of the site, and there are items that might have been carried in by floodwater. So far, nothing exciting. Crisp packets, a crushed beer can, a rubber ball, some unidentified plastic remnants. No weapons. So nothing for you to get hopelessly excited about. Sorry.'

Jonah shook his head, thanked her, and let himself out of the morgue. He felt a mixture of relief at the natural light outside and discomfort at the sudden arrival of sticky heat. He met Hanson on the stairs, files held to her chest a little self-consciously. It looked like she was still working on the docks investigation, which was pretty committed when there was a murder to excite them all.

She turned to walk up the stairs with him. 'Chief'd like an update.'

'I'm on my way.'

Hanson nodded, waited a few steps, and then said, 'Is it definitely a murder?'

'It looks likely.'

'Was she shot?'

Jonah glanced at her, slightly startled by the question. 'Possibly. No sign of it so far. But more significantly, she was found alongside the remains of a stash of Dexedrine. So it's possible that she overdosed, but it's also possible that she found something she shouldn't have done.'

30

He saw Hanson's small smile. The dilated pupils.

'So it might have been the other kids, either killing her or hiding her death.'

'Definitely a strong possibility.'

'Fucking hell.'

This in a complaining tone from DS O'Malley, oldest member of Jonah's team, as the two Intelligence officers deposited four boxes of case files on to the table at the front of the briefing room. His slightly florid face was slack with surprise.

'Don't use up all the swear words just yet,' Jonah said drily. 'This is just the locally stored stuff.'

'No, this is the first load of the locally stored stuff,' Amir, one of the slightly awkward Intelligence staff, said, pulling at his tie. 'These are from 1983. Then there are another five covering the years from eighty-four to ninety-eight, when it was officially declared a cold case. The more recent stuff – which from what's logged on the system looks like it's mostly disproved sightings and phone calls from the parents – is on the database.'

Lightman lifted a hand. 'Sorry, but . . . eighty-three? That's –'

'Aurora Jackson, Ben. Missing person. Domnall's probably the only one old enough to have heard of her.'

Amir excused himself, and Jonah glanced at his team. Lightman with his total calm in the face of this, as everything; Hanson and the eagerness that made her shift in her seat; and O'Malley, whose face was thoughtful.

Jonah pulled the plastic folder off the top of one of the boxes and opened it. The glossy-printed photo on the top looked strangely new. Aurora, smiling slightly crookedly at the camera in a school photograph. Blazingly beautiful in this picture, though Jonah could still remember her before she'd emerged from the chrysalis of childhood. He remembered the slightly chubby, frizzy-haired girl whose clothes were always a mess. The ugly younger sister of the girl everybody wanted.

He tacked the photo to the whiteboard.

'Seriously?' O'Malley glanced around at Lightman and Hanson. Hanson was wearing a slightly smug expression. She'd known the punchline. 'That's . . . it's the biggest missing persons case I can remember.'

'It's no longer a missing persons.'

Jonah tacked a photo of the remains McCullough had dug up alongside the school photo.

'Aurora's body was found buried under a tree next to the river less than a quarter of a mile from the campsite. Buried with her are some foil packets of Dexedrine, and it looks like there might have been more.'

He saw Lightman taking notes on an A4 pad. He might as well be writing a Christmas card for all the emotional reaction. O'Malley was sitting back, looking between him and the images, his lined forehead creased up further. Jonah recognized the expression. It was the struggle to match up snatches of memory with the reality of the find. A legend come to life. Except that she was in no way alive.

'I want us to acquaint ourselves with the original investigation in full. I want notes and a summary of interviews, along with anyone and anything you feel has been missed. If you think there's some evidence that's not been followed up, note it. If you think they've done a piss-poor job, note that too.'

Only Lightman managed to conceal his dislike of this

plan. Or perhaps he didn't dislike it. He was fond of facts and figures.

'Alongside that,' Jonah went on, 'we're going to be doing a full investigation from scratch. Redoing every single interview, focusing this time on those drugs, and who moved them, and how she ended up overlooked despite being a few hundred yards from the camp.'

He could see O'Malley's smile. This was more his cup of tea. He liked to interview, did former Captain O'Malley.

'For today, Juliette gets to come on interviews. I want to see the group who were out camping. Juliette, you can compile a list of addresses while I look at the Intelligence overview. I'd like Domnall and Ben to start going through the original case notes.'

O'Malley gave an audible sigh. 'Thanks for this, chief. I'd been feeling like my life's lacking paperwork.'

Jonah smiled in response, but didn't apologize.

'Were you part of the original investigation?' Hanson asked, glancing between Jonah and the board.

'Only just,' Jonah answered. 'I was a fresh-faced constable back then. But I wanted to be involved. She was at school with me, even if I didn't really know her.'

He glanced at her photo. Looking at Aurora's glowing beauty brought back to him an uncomfortable feeling. She was a reminder of a particular night; of a confused series of actions that he'd been desperate to forget for thirty years.

He looked away from the photo. Remembering that now wouldn't help him, or any of them.

Lightman put his pen away in his pocket and started to rise. 'So this has priority over the docks investigation.'

'For the next forty-eight it has,' Jonah answered. 'I'll keep you posted after that. Look for mentions of substance abuse, or anything related,' he added to Lightman. 'If any of them knew about that drugs stash, I want to know. And then I want to grill them again on everything they saw and heard. Because if she died three hundred feet from them, all those public appeals they made and all the searching for her look like a thirty-year charade.'

6. Aurora

Benners, Jojo and Connor had met them as they made their way back from the beech tree. They looked hot and irritable, a mood that stepped up when they realized where Topaz had taken everyone.

It was mostly Benners, which surprised Aurora. She'd never seen him angry before. Topaz was always tetchy, and Connor not infrequently aggressive. But Benners had been brought up in the calm of benign, well-moneyed neglect. He was Titus Groan, or Sebastian Flyte with a bit more sense of self.

He sent Jojo and Brett to find firewood, and then turned on Topaz.

'You shouldn't have told him,' he said, his voice low, but spiking into volume erratically. 'There's more at stake here than you impressing your latest crush.'

'That's not what this is about.' Topaz's cheeks grew red.

Benners ignored the reply. He looked down at her from his rangy six foot three. 'We don't *know* him, Topaz. Not like we know every other person here.'

'I've known him for years!' Topaz retorted. 'I trust him.'

'This isn't about who *you* trust!' Benners said, and then lowered his voice with an effort. 'That stash is not your secret to share. It's mine. And it'll be me in the shit if this gets out.'

'It's not going to get out.'

Connor lifted his head, his hands still in his pockets and his eyes hard. 'I'd break his fucking arm if he talked. You can tell him. Tell him I'd break his fucking arm, and I'd enjoy it.'

Topaz rolled her eyes. 'For god's sake . . .'

Benners gave a sigh. 'All right.' He was still angry. Still upset. Trying to be the calm one. 'He doesn't need threatening. Just let him know that we're . . . all in this together. OK?'

'Fine.'

Topaz turned and stalked off, with Coralie at her heels. Her ever-present, childlike shadow. Aurora knew her sister was about to launch into a rant. She'd heard it often enough out in the orchard at home, though it hadn't usually been about Benners or Connor. During warm weekends, Topaz's anger about someone who had offended her, and Coralie's chiming in, had floated up through her bedroom window until Aurora had closed it or left the room.

Connor wasn't trying so hard to be calm. 'Brett's got a fucking nerve, poking his nose in like that.' He kicked at the dry earth. His hands were clenched so that his forearms had ridges of tendon and muscle and vein on them.

'He's just out for a good time,' Benners said. He rubbed his hair, which stood up in sweat-spikes. 'I'm sure he won't let on. He's not an idiot.'

'He is an idiot.'

Benners laughed. 'I'm not talking educationally. I mean . . . he's not going to get himself in trouble if he can help it.'

Connor grunted.

Benners glanced at Aurora, and away. It made her feel unusually awkward.

'You know . . . you know I won't tell anyone, either, don't you?' she said.

Benners gave her a frown. 'Of course I do. I'm not worried about you.'

It gave her a warm feeling. That trust of his.

'Good.'

'We should get the rest of the stuff unloaded.' Benners had resumed his cloak of practicality. The calm older brother. The scout leader. Only he'd always been too cool for scouts. 'We can leave food till later, as long as we have a tent up and all the cooking gear out.'

'All right. Better than fucking around in the dark trying to do it once we're drunk,' Connor agreed.

Benners started towards the car. Connor nodded for Aurora to go ahead. He was still angry, but old-dog angry. And he wasn't as intimidating as he liked to think.

'We should swim,' he called a few moments later. 'Did you bring swimming stuff, Aurora?'

'No . . . but I have some things . . . I can sort something out.'

'You can't not swim. It's the best bit. Moonlight and cold water.' He looked up at her under his eyebrows when she turned. She smiled at the sudden poetry in his voice; at the way his accent stepped up into full-on West-Coast-of-Ireland. Connor reacted with embarrassment. 'Sure one of the other girls can lend you. Not Jojo. She doesn't have any girls' clothes.'

They emptied Brett's car and the panniers of Benners' bike in two loads. Altogether, there were three tents as shelter in case the weather changed. Seven sleeping bags and thick foam mats. Blankets. A battery-powered radio. Shopping bags of food and bottled water. Cases and cases of beer bottles and cans. Pillows, two camping stoves and four torches, because Benners' parents had outbuildings full of that kind of stuff.

They pitched a single tent as a quick retreat in case of rain, and it was already sauna-hot in there by the time Jojo and Brett had returned from their wood-finding expedition. They'd tied the wood into bundles and were dragging it with ropes. Jojo's idea, Aurora guessed. Jojo, who virtually lived outside and was browner in her vest top than any of the boys, despite her fair hair.

'Do not go left along the riverbank,' Brett announced. 'There's a dead animal over there and it fucking stinks. I mean, stinks like the smell you'd get if you opened up a grave.'

'Recently dead?' Aurora asked.

'Three or four days, I think,' Jojo answered, straightening up and rubbing her arm across her forehead. 'Three or four really hot days. It's kind of impressive how much it smells.' She gave a sudden grin. 'Hey, maybe we should put it in Topaz's sleeping bag.'

'Maybe not the right time,' Benners replied, bent over to fiddle with a guy rope. 'Did you find the other two?'

'No. Did they come our way?' Brett squinted back in the direction they'd come.

'Theoretically. Topaz isn't exactly top at orienteering.'

'But they know the place, though, right?' Brett started tugging off his T-shirt, unembarrassed at having an audience. The top was drenched with sweat, and the well-honed body underneath was glistening with it. 'They'll be all right?'

'I'm sure they will,' Benners said.

Aurora felt suddenly flustered at Brett's bare skin. She wanted to look, but was worried about being caught. She glanced away and saw Connor's furious expression. She felt a moment of sympathy for him.

'Ahh,' Jojo said, as she straightened up from untying the

firewood and saw Brett's chest. 'Doing that without asking is like visual assault.'

Connor gave a brief, snorting laugh, but Brett just grinned at Jojo.

'But the kind of assault where you actually aren't saying no,' he said, balling up his T-shirt and chucking it towards one of the tents. 'I need a drink. Where am I looking?'

'Here,' Aurora said, pushing one of the double-bagged six-packs of Kestrel towards him with her foot.

He crouched down over the bag. 'Ah, not beer. Where's the hard stuff?'

He hunted around in the other bags, and pulled out a litre bottle of vodka and a couple of plastic cups. Aurora watched him pour a measure into each, and then top the cups up with orange juice.

'Are you fucking serious?' Connor asked, laughing un-necessarily loudly. 'Vodka and orange?'

'I'm a bloody athlete,' Brett said. 'I can't have a beer gut.'

'So you're watching your weight,' Connor said, still grinning.

Brett didn't answer. He held one of the cups out to Aurora. She shook her head quickly.

'Oh. Sorry, I don't . . . I don't want any. Thank you.'

'Really?' His face showed momentary confusion. 'Aren't you thirsty?'

'Yeah, I am. I'll just have some orange juice.'

She took the bag from him, found a clean cup, and held her hand out for the carton of juice.

'If you're worried about the taste,' he said quietly, as he passed it, 'it's actually quite sweet. Kind of thing you can drink without having to like drinking. You know?'

'She's fourteen,' she heard Connor say behind her. His

39

voice was a lot angrier than it needed to be. 'And she doesn't drink.'

There was a brief silence, and then Brett said, with that same half-smile directed across her towards Connor, 'I thought your family liked their drink. You, your dad . . .'

There was a hot, heavy silence, and then Connor moved quickly towards him. Benners was just as quick. He got in the way, while Brett straightened up slowly, still smiling slightly.

'What did you fucking say?' Connor spat.

'Come on, come on,' Benners said loudly. 'Don't rise to it. Don't rise to it.'

Benners had his arm across Connor's chest, hand gripping his shoulder, and although he was taller he was losing ground to Connor rapidly, his feet sliding in the dry earth.

Brett was shaking his head. 'You don't want to fight me, dude.' It wasn't even a threat, the way he said it. Just a statement of fact.

'Seriously,' Benners said, and then to Brett, 'Just tone it down. We're supposed to be chilling with friends, not . . .'

It was Brett who took a step backwards. 'All right. All right, that was . . . OK. I'm sorry. Being a dick. Let's have a drink, and feel better. Here.'

He pulled one of the cans of Kestrel out and held it out to Connor, who clearly had fight still pulsing through him.

'Come on, Connor,' Benners murmured. 'Don't bother.'

Aurora stepped over to Connor, her heart pounding. 'That was my fault. I . . . I should have just drunk it. Sorry, Connor.'

Connor looked at her, and his expression relaxed a little. 'No, you shouldn't.' There was another one of those heavy silences, where Aurora could feel sweat beading up on the skin of her back. And then Connor lifted his hands and stepped back, shaking his head. 'All right.'

He took the beer from Brett, and Aurora saw the condensation standing on the can like a mirror of the sweat on his skin.

'Sorry, man,' Brett said. And he lifted his cup in a salute.

7

It was a strange feeling to be writing case notes based on intelligence when Jonah knew all of this himself. He knew the people he was writing about, too, though not well enough to help him.

Though this group and occasional others had used the area to camp in before, it was not an official site and was accessed through the woods by a winding, unclear path.

He didn't need to read the notes to help him describe the place. He hadn't even needed to see the site again. He had memories of tramping the same paths over and over in a search that had only widened in the tiniest increments. He remembered, too, his strange optimism that he would find somewhere that nobody else had looked. It had turned into a desperate sort of determination and had driven him to carry on the search during his leave, and long into the night when he should have gone off-duty.

The summary of events was simple, yet strange.

Seven adolescents had gone camping just after the end of term. Three of them had been fifteen, two sixteen, one eighteen and one – Aurora – just fourteen. None of them had turned in until midnight, and Aurora had gone first. She had taken her sleeping mat a little way from the campsite to avoid being disturbed by the others, who had been drinking and were talking and laughing loudly. She had been well outside the ring of light cast by the fire, and invisible to them.

The others had gone to bed later in dribs and drabs. They

thought they had seen Aurora still in her sleeping bag, but none of them were quite sure. They had heard nothing to indicate any violence.

When early morning came, Connor Dooley, fifteen, had woken up thirsty, and gone to get himself some water. He found Aurora's sleeping bag empty, and guessed she had gone to find a quiet spot to relieve herself. But after some time, he became concerned, and on investigating the sleeping bag found that it was cold and dewy on the inside.

Connor woke the missing girl's sister, Topaz Jackson, fifteen. A search ensued that gradually brought in all six of the remaining teenagers. After half an hour, Daniel Benham, sixteen, stated that he would cycle to Lyndhurst to raise the alarm. The one driver, Brett Parker, eighteen, was still intoxicated. He and the other five continued searching while Daniel cycled to Lyndhurst.

Local police logged a call from Daniel Benham at 07:09, after he discovered Lyndhurst police station to be closed and knocked on an adjacent door to use the phone. A squad car arrived at 07:48. By 09:17, a full search team had arrived and the nearby community was alerted shortly afterwards. The active search went on for almost two weeks, with more and more of the nation becoming alerted.

Like so many stories of beautiful young girls snatched away, it became a rallying call and a subject of huge speculation. Hours and hours of television and reams of paper were devoted to her.

And then, gradually, the story became old, and tired. Thirty years passed, and Aurora was never found.

At four, he received a brief email from the DCS, checking in. It was a relief to receive it. He'd been expecting a visit to make sure things were happening and although Wilkinson was easy to work with, firing off a quick summary of his plans was much easier than going through it all in person right now.

Ten minutes later, he received a reply.

All fine. Do the press briefing first thing and we can chat after that. I won't expect you at the senior management meeting tomorrow.

That was the kind of message Jonah liked, and showed one of Wilkinson's very best qualities. He believed that his best officers should be directly involved in cases, and he would duck, dodge and weave behind the scenes to keep them from the endless meetings most DCIs were expected to attend.

He ducked out of the station to eat at just after 18:30. A day of grazing on sugar-packed convenience foods and riding from high to high had left him feeling sickly and in desperate need of something savoury.

He'd offered to take Hanson along, but she had declined with a smile. Possibly equal parts not wanting to be stuck having dinner with the boss, and wanting to impress him with how hard she was willing to work.

He told her to be ready for their first house calls on his return. The plan he had put to the chief super had been to visit as many of their list of connected people as possible before the story leaked and they were forewarned. Surprise was a powerful thing, and he wanted them all shaken to hell.

The air was still heavy with heat on Southern Road. The traffic had become sluggish with shoppers leaving the retail park, making it easy for him to jog across the road. He made his way down the cut-through beside the Novotel and struck out towards TGI Fridays, where there would be a greasy cheeseburger to demolish. This was his one regular vice. He could have stayed in the station and picked up a wrap or a piece of cottage pie at the canteen, but he liked to reward himself when he'd done a good run of desk work.

He had never enjoyed being in his office and working through notes. It made him fractious and claustrophobic to be trapped indoors for hours. He sometimes imagined this was the traveller blood in him. But then, who really did enjoy being stuck behind a desk?

He asked the waiter to make it as quick as possible, and sat drinking a Diet Coke while he waited. He lost himself a dozen times in the memories of his newly qualified nineteen-year-old self, and was shocked back into the present by noise.

It was mostly that group of seven who occupied his thoughts. The ones everyone at school knew, and to some extent wanted to be.

It had been Daniel Benham – Benners to everyone back then – who had formed the centre of the group. He had been the big philosopher, the kind of free-thinking, argumentative student that teachers had either loved or hated, depending on how threatened they felt. He had also been sultry and attractive, decidedly well off, and a talented guitarist and singer. Popularity had come easily.

Topaz and Benners had become an item early in secondary school, drawn together, presumably, by their shared attractiveness and by their love of rule-breaking. The romance had gone nowhere, but they had remained close friends after it fizzled out. And Coralie, Topaz's pretty but slightly vacuous best friend, had been a willing participant in all their activities, and a loyal follower.

Connor and Jojo had been drawn in pretty soon afterwards. It was hardly surprising. Connor was at least as smart as Benners, if not brighter, and was even more anti-establishment. Jojo was as opinionated and quick-thinking as either of them, and probably a good deal wilder.

The end result had been a group of five that had attracted constant attention. They had been frequently engaged in battles with the school authorities, but had equally been the school's star students in debates, music and arts and science competitions. They had maintained their serious cool by holding parties that had become legendary, helped in no small way by the financial backing of Benners' parents, and Coralie's.

And then there had been their sex lives. Benners had dated most of the desirable sixth-form girls by the time he'd turned fifteen, and was known to have spent the night with several of them. Jojo had messed around with some of her older brother's friends, and then there had been Topaz and Coralie, who had been in a league all their own.

The two of them had been hot property from the moment they had swung their rolled-up skirts through the school's main doors. Perfectly turned out, and fully aware of their power, they had been rumoured to have done some very sordid things with some very lucky boys.

The five of them had only grown more fascinating after Aurora Jackson had disappeared. Their ranks had briefly opened. They had expanded to encompass Brett, whose athletic body and handsome face had suited them.

But he was the only outsider ever to be let in. After Aurora, they shut themselves off completely. They held no more parties, and barely exchanged words with anyone else at the school. If they had enjoyed the attention before, they now

46

shunned it. He remembered only ever seeing them at a distance after that, their heads together in some private conversation, their body language hostile.

Jonah let out a sigh, knowing that he would have to pull them apart to get answers. Although thirty years had passed, he strongly suspected that they would present as much of a united front as ever.

He found O'Malley and Lightman still reading at their desks, Lightman's files all in neat, straight-edged piles. O'Malley's looked more like a series of rejected novels, a dozen or so opened and then cast aside. The Irish sergeant sat surrounded by them, his greying head bent and his expression lost.

'Anything so far?'

O'Malley glanced up at him. 'Nothing in particular,' he said. 'Only a general feeling of doubt about what all the kids said. No drugs, no sexy business, hardly any beer . . . I'd expect more from a religious gathering.'

'It's unconvincing?'

'They were teenagers having a party,' O'Malley replied. 'What would you say?'

Jonah nodded. There were many reasons for hiding things like that. The simple fact that they didn't want to get in trouble was one, and guilt at having a good time when Aurora had gone missing. But then there were other reasons, too, like knowing full well what had happened to her and trying to conceal it.

'Any thoughts yet, Ben?' he asked his other sergeant.

'Ah, give him a while. He's had to organize his pens, poor lad . . .' O'Malley said with a grin. Lightman glanced up and shook his head at him wryly, and then went back to reading.

Jonah grinned. It was true that O'Malley was quicker, because he dispensed with organization and chose instead instinct and a swift ability to make connections. It was hard to imagine how he must have survived in the army, this irreverent, undisciplined, fiercely intelligent man who was in a constant battle with the temptation to obliterate himself with drink.

Hanson materialized at his elbow clutching a drink in a disposable cup. He gave her a grin.

'Ready to go, Juliette?'

Hanson nodded, and pulled her bag off the back of her chair.

'I'm leaving the two of you to hold the fort,' he said to his sergeants.

'Kind of you.' Said by O'Malley, and with deep sarcasm, of course.

'Don't stay past ten unless anything significant comes up.'

'Tom Jackson phoned while you were eating,' Hanson told him once they were in the car. 'It got patched through to me. He wanted to know if the press would be involved soon. I said you'd have to answer that.'

He nodded. They were leaving Southampton and striking out west into the New Forest, the sun full in their faces and uncomfortably bright.

'I'll give him a ring this evening,' Jonah said.

'He also wanted us to know that their elder daughter had arrived from Edinburgh. She's got Connor Dooley with her. She married him, did you know that? Even though she calls herself Jackson still.'

Jonah nodded. He had known. Had followed the stories of all of them to a greater or lesser extent. It had been impossible not to watch them as they traced their lives out over the years.

'A bit easier if they've come here, isn't it?'

Jonah smiled. 'It is. But a shame we don't get a trip to Edinburgh. I love those crappy motels they find.'

He'd hoped to break the news to the Jacksons' surviving daughter himself, but knew that had been optimistic. He'd talk to them tomorrow anyway, after the press briefing. This evening's schedule included Brett Parker, Daniel Benham and Jojo Magos. Coralie Ribbans was in London and would have to wait, too.

He wondered if Topaz was still on good terms with Coralie. He knew that the relationship had changed gradually. Their claustrophobic, slightly manipulative pairing had suffered when Topaz and Connor had become an item.

Jonah had been surprised when Topaz and Connor got together. Connor had been the silent, resentful admirer most of the way through school. And Topaz had known. Of course she had. She'd played up to it and then retreated, over and over. She liked, of course, having him panting after her. Doing everything she wanted. Making her life easy.

It had been hard for Jonah to like the fifteen-year-old Topaz.

But over the year after Aurora's disappearance, something had changed. *Loss does strange things to people*, he thought. Or maybe Topaz had just started to grow up.

'So you were at school with all of them, then? Topaz Jackson, Daniel Benham . . .'

'Yes, I was,' Jonah agreed.

'Were you friends?'

Jonah instinctively disliked the question. He wasn't ready to talk about his own experiences. Particularly not about a particular experience.

And it would have sounded odd to her if he'd told her the truth, that he'd been fascinated by them. By their air of mystery and sensuality, and by the stories about Topaz and Coralie.

And at the other end of the spectrum of teenage girlhood, Jojo, who he had watched skateboarding at the park in a tank top with no bra, her stomach on display and a pair of Calvin Klein boxers riding up above her low-slung jeans.

But there had been Aurora, too, who had turned thirteen and suddenly grown out of gawkiness into an ethereal beauty. None of them had been quite sure how to approach her after that.

None of this was useful.

'We weren't really friends,' he said in the end. 'I was a few years older than Topaz and Benners and Connor. Aurora was only starting the secondary school when I started sixth form, and I was a PC by the time she died. I had a few friends who knew them better because they had siblings in Topaz's year, or Aurora's.' And, to a man, they had lusted after Topaz and been fascinated by Aurora.

'Did you have any? Siblings?' Hanson asked.

'No.'

Jonah made it clear that the conversation was not going to turn to him. He wasn't willing to talk about his family. He didn't want her sympathy or her morbid curiosity.

Hanson took the hint and kept quiet until she had followed the satnav through Lyndhurst and southwards. A mile short of Brockenhurst, they turned off down a private driveway that Jonah had often wanted an excuse to drive down. He wasn't alone. The press liked to come here, whether invited for interviews or not. Brett Parker's following had been significant for almost a decade.

There was a gate, of course, and an old lodge that looked like it was occupied. But nobody came out to ask them who they were. An etched sign asked them to press the buzzer, and so Hanson angled the car as carefully as she could, wound down the window, and pushed the button.

A brief pause and then a crackling pick-up. 'Can I help?'

It was a female voice. Slightly harried, Jonah thought.

'I'm Detective Constable Hanson. I'm here with my DCI. We need to talk to Mr Parker.'

'You're from . . . Oh.' Another brief pause. 'Of course. I'll buzz you through.'

The gates opened painfully slowly, and Hanson tapped her short nails on the steering wheel.

'It's a bit pretentious, isn't it? The gates and the buzzer.'

'I guess they're used to unwanted visitors.'

'Brett Parker . . . what was he? A writer?'

'An athlete,' Jonah replied. Time was passing. He'd thought everyone in the country knew Brett's name.

Hanson revved the engine slightly before the gates had finished opening, and drove past the neat 10 mph signs at about thirty. There were mature trees to each side, and the driveway followed a gentle uphill incline before reaching a crest a quarter of a mile along.

'Bloody hell,' Hanson said, as the large, solid, but undeniably elegant stone house swung into view. It made Jonah smile, the hungry look she gave the house. It wasn't quite so pretentious now, evidently.

It was Brett Parker who let them in, and not the unidentified woman on the intercom. For Jonah it was a strange meeting. He had somehow expected Brett, the slightly uninspiring jock, to have become ever more self-satisfied. He had also expected a retired athlete to be a little overweight; a little over-indulged.

Instead he was faced with a slim, gracious, self-deprecating host in a beautiful blue suit and open shirt. He looked tanned and fit, and ten years younger than Jonah.

'Come in, come in,' he said stepping back from the door. 'It's too hot to hang around out there. I'm glad they don't make you wear a uniform.' This with a warm smile. 'If it's a chat, shall we have it on the terrace? It's in the shade now. I'll get Anna to bring some drinks.'

'Thank you,' Jonah said with his own, smaller smile. He looked over Brett's elegantly tousled gold-and-brown hair. He realized it was dyed, and felt a little better.

The terrace was still bright. Reflective patterns moved across the perfectly rectangular swimming pool a few steps below. Further down was a lawn with a stream working its way through it. There were orderly plants in containers and in two semicircular flower beds with not a fallen leaf or petal to interrupt the prettiness.

Jonah wondered whether the garden was Brett's space or his wife's. 'This is lovely,' he said, gesturing to the grounds. 'Landscaped?'

Brett gave him a brilliant, white-toothed smile. 'I'm afraid so. But done by a friend of mine. I can give you her card, if you like.'

Jonah gave a slight laugh as he took a seat. 'I'm afraid my garden's a small patio with some tubs on it. Not worth anyone's time.' He looked at the pool, not without a touch of envy. 'Do you still swim triathlon distances?'

'Well, yes, but not in there.' He gave a slightly wry smile. 'It's too small. I can't stand turning round fifty times a session. And for triathlon, you want to train wild or it's a shock when you have your head submerged in murk. I usually go up and down the brook a few times.' He gave Jonah the glance that often moves around groups of sport-lovers. One that assessed physique and fitness. 'Do you compete?'

Jonah shook his head. 'I'm into cycling, and to a certain extent running, but like a lot of people I've never been a swimmer and can't be bothered to try it. I can see the appeal of triathlon, though. I like sports that take you somewhere.'

'I couldn't agree more. I used to hate indoor athletics championships. Why on earth would you run without fresh air around you?'

Jonah could see him becoming more at his ease. It was hard to believe you were in trouble when confronted with friendly chatter.

Jonah was ready to unsettle him, but not yet. 'How's business going?'

'It's going well. As far as I know.' He smiled. 'Anna is the business-woman. I just turn up and speak nicely.'

Jonah nodded. He could tell that this was a well-rehearsed line.

He caught a light clinking of ice on glass and turned. He was faced with Anna, who had a loosely tied head of blonde hair, a floral dress and pearls, white-heeled sandals and sinewy brown legs.

'Thank you, darling.' Brett stood to help her unload the tray. 'This is my wife. Anna, these are . . . Sorry, I don't think I . . .'

'DCI Sheens,' Jonah said, holding his hand out. Her slim fingers in his were ice-cold and wet from handling the glasses. She rubbed them lightly on her dress with a self-conscious smile. 'And DC Hanson.'

'Is it something business-related?' Anna asked. 'If so, I'd better be here too.'

There was something of the fractious butterfly about her. She moved over to stand behind her husband. She brushed her fingers over his shoulder and then moved to a chair that she hovered over.

'No, no, nothing about the business,' he said with a smile. 'Please do stay, though. Nothing secretive or embarrassing.'

Anna smiled and dipped down to perch on the chair. She put her hand on her husband's leg. Brett sat back, at ease.

'Earlier today, a body was found in Brinken Wood,' Jonah said. 'We have reason to believe it belongs to Aurora Jackson.'

His eyes were on Brett. Anna's sudden turn of the head towards her husband was in his peripheral vision, but his focus was on the man who had driven Aurora to that campsite.

He saw the slackening of Brett's face, and then the sudden increase of tension. Jonah knew shock when he saw it. Brett hadn't expected this, whatever else he might be thinking.

'Aurora? Really? I always . . .' He broke off, and rubbed at his forehead with his thumb.

'Sorry?'

'I-I always thought she'd be found alive somewhere.' He shook his head, his eyes fractionally reflective. 'Jesus Christ. She was in the woods? How did we miss her? We combed it.'

'She was underground,' Jonah said, his voice absolutely flat. 'Buried along with a stash of Dexedrine in a hollow under a tree.'

Brett sat forward in what was more a collapse of his abdomen than a straightening up. 'Oh shit,' he said, an arm going across his body in an instinctive defensive gesture.

Jonah smiled very slightly. However much Aurora's discovery had surprised Brett, he'd known damn well about the drugs.

8. Aurora

Aurora was overcome by restlessness while the others began frying up hot dogs and tearing open bread rolls and beer cans. She felt distanced from it all. She also felt like time was draining away. There wasn't much sunlight left and she wanted to be out of the shade of the trees, bathing in it.

Topaz still hadn't returned from her deliberate absence, and nor had Coralie. Aurora was tensed against her sister's return. But she still felt out of place without her. All of Topaz's friends were kind enough, but none of them were her own friends.

Jojo called to her. She was crouched over the firepit she had dug. She was now setting a frame of branches over it. Aurora had seen her curled lip at the sight of the gas-fired stoves, all shiny and unused, and the way she'd turned her back on them.

Aurora went over, expecting an errand. Heard, instead, Jojo murmur an apology.

'This isn't very interesting. You can swim if you want. If you go straight towards the river that way, there's a sandbar and you can see the bottom.' She glanced up at the boys, who were each a few cans down. 'I've got a costume in my bag there. If you go now and don't tell them, you'll get away without them "accidentally" seeing you changing.'

Aurora half laughed. She wasn't sure if Jojo was joking.

'Thank you. I'd love a swim.'

Jojo nodded, and smiled slightly. 'We'll all jump out of trees and get on the rope swings tomorrow, but sometimes it's nicer when it's quiet.'

Aurora rose, and picked up Jojo's tatty black rucksack and walked as quickly and quietly as she could away from the campsite. Benners was talking – lecturing really – on the state of affairs in Pakistan. None of them seemed to notice her leaving.

The trees between her and the bank looked parched. Underfoot there were brown, crackling leaves. Beech, oak, ash, sycamore. Above, enough green to create shade, but scorched foliage, too. The never-ending summer was leaving its mark.

Dropping down towards the river, she found sunshine at last. An orange-yellow light that still heated her skin. The riverbank itself was steep, but there was a tiny, slightly muddy beach a little further up, and she weaved her way along to it before sliding down the bank.

She shielded her eyes and looked around. The far bank of the river was in shade. The shadows of the trees turned the water black and ominous. But close to her the shelf of sand shone yellow in the light, and the water above it was almost perfectly clear.

She let Jojo's rucksack fall on to the sand. Unzipping it, she found not a costume, but a tight Lycra vest and a small pair of shorts. A mismatch of turquoise and white.

Quickly, she pulled off her underwear and hid them inside the bag. She slid the shorts up under her skirt as she thought about what Jojo had said about the boys.

She realized there was no way of changing her top without nakedness, and decided to do it quickly, all in one. She emerged from the Lycra vest to see the wood and the river-bank still silent and empty.

She slid off her shoes last, and stuffed everything into the bag. She moved it a little further up the bank, trying to skip over the dusty sand and occasional spiky beechnuts. It was worse on the way back into the water when she trod on an embedded stone.

But under the water there was soft sand. As she waded in, the coolness over her feet and up to her shins felt delicious. She took a few steps, and then leaned forward into the water, submerging herself as far as her neck.

It was a lot colder than the air. Breathless, she swam to the edge of the sand and then along it. She began to relax into the cold as she went. Once she'd swum up and down a few times, she felt almost warm.

She lay back to look at the deep azure of the sky for a while, drifting, until trees appeared overhead once more and the water was suddenly much colder around her.

Aurora swung herself upright, realizing that she'd drifted downstream. Her shoes and clothes were out of sight.

She was on the verge of turning and kicking away when she heard voices on the bank. A lazy, flirty laugh she recognized well. A deeper voice answering, which made her freeze in place, her hands barely moving to keep her upright.

Please not him.

9

Jonah left Brett in whatever peace he could find for the evening. He'd requested his attendance at the police station at nine the following morning.

Jonah was in some ways distressed by the shadowed look of the man. He recognized someone seeing head-on the potential ruin of his reputation.

'We'll be informing everyone who was camping with Aurora that evening. We're expecting you to keep certain information to yourself, however.'

'I understand.' Brett was a little pathetic in his eagerness to please now. He had poured information at Jonah from the first. He'd told him how much he'd regretted trying a little of the Dexedrine.

'I don't know what I was thinking,' he had said, his eyes on the ice in his lemonade, a hollow look to them. 'Except that I was an eighteen-year-old idiot who wanted to be the coolest kid on the block. A stash of drugs? That's great, man. Seriously. I do drugs all the time, man. Even though I also watch every bite of food I eat and go to bed early so that I can train.' He sat back sharply, angrily. 'What the hell was I doing?'

Anna had slid her hand through his, and Brett had taken it without looking at her.

'Can you tell me where the drugs originated?' Jonah had asked quietly.

'Yes. Well, no. Not originated from.' And then he had

given Jonah an agonized look. DCI Sheens had seen many, many of those looks during his career. It was the expression of somebody choosing whether or not to throw someone to the dogs.

'My investigation is about Aurora,' Jonah told him. 'Whoever owned the drugs hasn't got anything to fear from me. It's thirty years ago, and I couldn't track down any buyers if I wanted to.'

It had been enough to tip him. It didn't usually take very much.

'Look,' he'd said, a pleading note to his voice after he'd spilled the truth. 'I know it looks like . . . I know there was a lot there, but Benners never meant to sell any of it. He's not like that. He was into his own fun, and helping his friends out. He didn't profit from it. And he only ended up with such a crazy amount because some acquaintance of his was in trouble with his dealer.'

'So all of you decided to keep quiet about it?'

'Yes,' Brett had said. 'We didn't know what else to do.'

Hanson was bright-eyed and half smiling as they climbed into the car.

'That's quite a motive for Daniel Benham committing a murder, isn't it? Being a drug dealer to his friends?'

'It is,' Jonah answered, a little more guardedly. 'It's one motive of numerous potentials.'

'But he'd have been looking at youth offenders' time,' Hanson persisted as she steered the car round a small, tidy circle of grass in the centre of the driveway and drove back towards the main gates. 'And if he wanted to go into politics then he would have known it was going to haunt him. That would have ruined him right at the start. Is he next on the list?'

'Yes,' Jonah said, his thoughts going to that small space in the ground and the drugs hidden within it. 'We need to talk to Benham. Brett said there was a lot of it, which I want to check with McCullough. But there's more than motive in that stash.'

'How so?'

'It's opportunity,' Jonah told her. 'How many people even knew that place existed? I count six.'

'Well, we don't know.' Hanson was hesitant. 'Other people may have stumbled on it.'

'You mean before the murder?' Jonah asked. 'If Brett was right, it had only been there three weeks. I'm pretty certain it was a well-guarded secret, that place. And that leaves us with a very short list of people who could have hidden the body there, and I make that Topaz Jackson, Brett Parker, Daniel Benham, Coralie Ribbans, Connor Dooley and Jojo Magos.'

Hanson nodded, and he could see her mind working. He let her follow her own train of thought. His mind went to Benners, the bleeding-heart liberal turned Conservative. He wondered, not for the first time, how the socialist schoolboy Benners had turned into Conservative MP for Meon Valley Daniel Benham. He couldn't see much remaining of the left-wing, humanitarian, anarchic and fiercely intelligent son of a tech-firm millionaire. Not in the news articles about the MP that Hanson had dug out. He wondered whether he would see something left of that boy when they spoke for the first time in years.

Jonah had visited Bishop's Waltham only a handful of times. Daniel Benham's house was an old rectory at the end of a lane full of postcard-pretty cottages. It was a surprisingly large distance from the church.

The gates were open, a growth of wisteria over one half suggesting they probably didn't actually close any more. There was more gravel here, but the lines were a little blurred between lawn, flower bed and driveway. There were wild flowers in tubs on the porch and pansies in window boxes. A real cottage-garden feel.

'Do you think this is paid for with drug money?' Hanson muttered. 'Another awfully nice pad.'

They parked alongside a gleaming black Range Rover, which made Jonah more envious than any huge pile in the country. Almost a hundred grand's worth of car, and it would never be within Jonah's reach.

At least Daniel Benham, when he opened the door, looked a little more middle-aged than Brett Parker. His long, thin frame had a slight hint of a paunch, and his hair was thin and greying. His clothes were a different kind of expensive. Hunter wellies over cream trousers. A pale-blue shirt. A tweed jacket.

Two chocolate Labradors came rolling out of the door with him, and Jonah tried not to grin at the way Hanson flinched. One of them responded by jumping up at her.

'Monty! Monty! Get down. For goodness' sake, Monty.' Daniel aimed a half-hearted shove at the dog, which moved aside and then jumped again. 'Get back in the house, you useless animal.'

He grabbed for each collar and bundled the two dogs inside, then pulled the door closed behind him.

'Sorry. Demented creatures. Ah, thought you were the advance party back from choir, but you're not, are you?' He gave Jonah a thoughtful look. 'Go on. Give me a clue.'

'DCI Sheens,' Jonah said. 'And DC Hanson. Are we all right to come in?'

'Oh. Well, yes. I was planning on a G and T and some *Countryfile*. But I suppose . . .'

There was no spark of recognition. At school, they'd chatted more than once over a cigarette, and even discussed Jonah's desire to join the police. But the MP had forgotten him at some point during the three decades since.

Benham opened the door a fraction and shouted through it. 'Polly! Polly, could you come and remove the dogs into the garden, please?'

'Why?' The answer from inside was a girl's voice rather than a woman's. A daughter, he supposed.

'Visitors! Come on, Polly. A little haste, please.'

There was movement within. Daniel stood shifting in his wellingtons, offering no conversation. Jonah was immune to the annoyance of a put-upon suspect. He stood equally looking at the flowers. It was twilight now, and their colours were luminous in the blue light.

Eventually, there was a call from the rear of the house, and Benham let them into the yellow-lit hall. He slid his jacket off and hung it on an overly full hook.

'I'm only just back from walking the dogs,' he said. 'I usually give them some ham. They'll be furious. But I suppose Polly can do it.'

He removed his feet from the wellies and inserted them into a pair of heelless sheepskin slippers, then led the way into a heavily furnished sitting room.

'Mary's at her mother's, so you can forget about talking to her.' He sat in a leather easy chair and gestured impatiently for the two of them to sit on a sofa. It was so deep in cushions that it was hard to find space to perch on the edge.

'That's quite all right, Mr Benham,' Jonah said, smiling.

'We don't need to speak with her at present, and we won't take up much of your time.'

'How good of you.' The look Benham gave them was all sarcasm. It cheered Jonah a little, seeing that innate dislike of authority still in him. Though the boy he half remembered from school was not the important thing, unless that boy had killed a fourteen-year-old girl and hidden her body amid mud and foil. 'So what is it?'

'Aurora Jackson,' Jonah said. 'Her remains have been found, not far from the campsite.'

Jonah had wondered if he might face disbelief and had anticipated a long silence. What he had not expected was for the silence to be broken by a heaving sob, and for the MP for Meon Valley to suddenly have tears running clear on to his face.

'Oh, god. The poor kid. Jesus, the poor kid.' He was rubbing at his face with the back of his hand, but the tears were finding ways down the lines in his skin.

Hanson produced a clean folded handkerchief from somewhere in her pinstripe jacket, and he took it without a word. He used it to dab at his face.

There were slightly heavy footsteps beyond the rear door to the room, and a brunette twenty-something with her hair in a braid and wearing a pale-blue polo shirt ducked into the room. Polly, Jonah assumed.

'All right if I take the car, Daddy?'

'Yes.' Benham's embarrassment increased visibly. He turned away from his daughter and lifted a hand in an effort to wave her away. 'Yes, no problem. You going to see Pippa?'

'Film with Greg.'

'Fine. Fine.'

Polly paused in the act of exiting the room. 'You all right, Daddy?'

'I'm absolutely fine, Polly. Have a nice evening.'

Polly stood for a moment. She looked worriedly at Jonah and DC Hanson.

Jonah tried to smile at her. Which seemed to be enough for now.

'OK,' Polly said. 'See you later.'

She left, and Jonah heard her stomping around in the hall for a few moments before the front door closed with a slam.

'I'm sorry to cause you distress, Mr Benham,' Jonah said, sitting forward and letting his wrists dangle. It was difficult to assume a professional pose while feeling like he was about to slip off the sofa. 'But we need to ask you a few questions.'

'I'm not . . . Yes. Fire away. I suppose the investigation's open again, then, is it?' He nodded, and folded his arms in front of him, but continued to look towards his feet. 'That'll please Tom, at least.'

'Mr Jackson?' Jonah asked. 'You've kept in contact with him?'

'A little. Not much latterly, to be honest. I lost my father two years ago, and now we have Mary's mother to look after. But before that, when I had more time and energy, I kept up with them. Tom was always angry about how it all went.' He gave a sigh. 'I suppose it's difficult not to be angry when you've lost your daughter. But he felt the police had let them down.'

Jonah remembered only too well. He'd been at Totton station on more than one occasion when Tom had stormed in, rage and sadness turning his face pink between the wild hair and the equally wild beard.

'We're looking at new lines of enquiry now,' Jonah said, with a glance at Hanson. 'The position of the remains has raised questions. She was buried beside the river along with a stash of Dexedrine. We have reason to believe that the cache of drugs belonged to you.'

Jonah had been watching Benham, and there was a void where there should have been a reaction. He was absolutely still, and for a good few seconds afterwards he moved nothing but his eyes.

The silence was broken by a single sound. 'Ah.'

Jonah watched the creases in his face, but kept his silence. 'Can you confirm for us that the drugs belonged to you?' he said finally.

Benham's expression became pained. 'I don't know if I . . . What's the relevance of the drugs? It's not part of the investigation, is it? I don't . . . it's Aurora that matters. That's what you want to know about. Aurora. Isn't it?'

Hanson glanced at Jonah, uncertain.

'The drugs are directly relevant to our investigation of her death,' Jonah said levelly. Which was exactly the reverse of what he had said to Brett within the last hour. He could feel Hanson watching him.

'I see.' Benham sat up a little and tucked his hands further round himself as if cold. 'Then I think I'd better wait until I have a solicitor present. Don't you think?'

He sounded peculiarly regretful. But unmoving.

'That's for you to decide,' Jonah said, rising. 'I am requesting your attendance tomorrow at Southampton Central police station at nine thirty a.m. You are not under arrest, but if you fail to attend, then a warrant will be issued for your arrest.'

Jonah felt tiredness descend in a rush as he sat in the passenger seat. He knew that he was getting to the stage of being sloppy now. He tried to weigh up the advantages of seeing them all tonight versus being effective.

'I'm going to get O'Malley to update the Jacksons over the

phone,' he said. 'There's no need for us to go there tonight. Connor and Topaz will know the score by now. O'Malley can tell the two of them to come into the station, and I can see them tomorrow.'

'OK,' Hanson said, and he could hear the relief in her voice. She was probably thinking of home and the sofa as fondly as he was. 'There wasn't any reply from Coralie's mobile when I tried her, and she's a hundred miles away. So it's just . . . Jojo Magos to see tonight.'

Jonah nodded, and before picking up his phone to call O'Malley said, 'And I want you to take the lead on this one. Start to finish. OK?'

Hanson smiled, a little flash of teeth in the dimness. 'OK. Thank you.'

10. Aurora

Friday, 22 July 1983, 8:00 p.m.

She moved silently through the water, imagining that she was a serpent. Perhaps an eel. She was in shadow, and hoped she was as invisible as she felt.

She could still hear his voice, and now could almost make out what he was saying.

'. . . to see you here.'

A sluggish bend let on to a stretch of open bank alongside a beech tree. The bank was bare except for two figures.

Aurora felt a squeeze in her stomach seeing him there with Topaz. He was no longer wearing a suit or sports kit. Instead he wore a pale-blue checked shirt that made him look all the more tanned. Jeans and hiking boots. Sunglasses perched in his hair. A midsized backpack over his shoulders. All of it outdoorsy and effortlessly handsome.

Topaz was smiling, her arms folded in front of her and a white beach bag slung on her shoulder. She had her weight on one hip, which let the other leg trail. There was something almost mocking about the pose.

Aurora grabbed on to an exposed root. She anchored herself on it against the tugging current, breathless and dizzy.

'We're camping. We do it a lot. Want to see my tent?'

'That's kind of you, Topaz. But I have my own tent.'

She wondered if she heard a light note of sarcasm in his voice, or if he was saying something more. Was it an

67

invitation? She couldn't see his face properly. She didn't dare to move any closer or to let go of her grip. She felt she might be washed away.

'Where are you camping? Close by?'

He gave a small shrug. 'A few miles further on. I've got a few places in mind.'

'It'll be dark soon,' Topaz said. 'You might get lost.'

Aurora was sure he smiled at her when he said, 'I know where I'm going. Don't worry.'

He moved towards her, past her, and Topaz only half moved out of the way.

'You should come for a beer later,' she said. 'Once you're all set up. We're only a little way from here.'

'I'll bear it in mind.'

'Bye, Mr Mackenzie!'

He raised a hand but didn't turn round. He kept moving, and ducked under the beech tree. Aurora realized at that point which tree it was. It looked different from the river, and the low-hanging branches masked the trunk and the hollowed-out store completely. She held her breath for a moment, expecting him to stop and say something. For the stash to be discovered. But he emerged at the far side, and kept walking along the bank and under another overhanging tree.

Topaz only moved once he was gone. She unfolded her arms and took a brief look into her bag. She hitched it up her shoulder, and began to walk slowly back towards the camp.

Aurora watched her go, and trod water for a full minute before she began to swim onwards, away from her clothes and the sandbar, towards the retreating figure in the checked shirt.

It was fully dark before they had followed the satnav the thirty-five miles from Bishop's Waltham to Jojo's small, brightly coloured cottage outside Fritham. Jonah recalled a much younger version of Jojo Magos and a nineteen-year-old version of himself in uniform.

He remembered a pair of figures caught in the headlights of his squad car. The half-sprayed hammer and sickle and the bold writing on the side wall of the Co-op. The way the two of them had looked round, startled, two short heads of hair illuminated and one hand flung up in front of a face.

His sergeant had pulled the car up sharply, and Jonah had been climbing out by the time the two of them had dropped everything and run.

'I'm after the big one!' his sergeant had shouted. Jonah had agreed with the choice. He relished the challenge of chasing down the nimbler, faster figure.

He had almost tripped on a discarded sweater as he started his pursuit. He faltered, recognizing the black-on-white Guevara silhouette. His sergeant was ahead of him as he ducked back to pick it up, and then fixed his eyes on that small figure and ran after it down the high street.

'Police!' the sergeant shouted. Woodman? Had that been his name? He was no longer quite sure. 'Stop where you are!'

Neither of them stopped. The bigger one turned down the Romsey Road. His sergeant almost overshot. He wasn't made for agility. Jonah carried on straight, following that swifter form. The figure ahead of him turned to glance at him.

About to make a turn, he thought, and smiled slightly as he watched her break suddenly right, down what he knew was a cul-de-sac.

Jonah turned after her, only twenty feet behind now. He wasn't naive enough to think that he'd have her cornered. She didn't disappoint. She flung herself at the garden fence at the end of the road, hands going up to grab and feet pushing off the wood until she was over.

He couldn't help being impressed by the ease of movement, by the speed with which the small form had vanished. He knew he would be slower, but jumped for it anyway. He had trained himself hard for pursuit, and rarely had a chance to use it. He couldn't help smiling to himself as he slung the sweater over his shoulder and heaved himself up. He got one foot over the fence and then jumped down into a small, leafy garden.

He heard running steps retreating beyond the house and followed them at a headlong sprint down a small passage beside the house. He was provided some illumination as he emerged into the front garden by a light being turned on.

She had emerged on to a side street, one he vaguely recognized but could not have named. He was certain it joined up to another road further up, though. He kept his pace up as he followed the retreating figure, which had opened up the lead a little.

They didn't stay on the road for long. Within a hundred yards, she was off again, vaulting a gate with apparent ease and finding a gap down the side of another house. He began to lose track of how many fences they had jumped and gardens they had run through, and was no longer certain where they were. He suspected they had looped back on themselves at some point.

He began to grow tired, the constant sprinting and climbing murder on his lungs. He was sweating profusely into his uniform, uncomfortable and hot. But he was also a hound on a scent, and he wasn't going to give it up.

The fleeing figure made a mistake in the end; she turned down the side of the renovated Stag Hotel and met a sheer wall with unforgiving brickwork to either side. He had to slow swiftly to avoid running into her.

He hadn't really needed to see her face as she turned round, rebellious and sheeny with sweat. He'd known it was her as soon as he'd seen the design on the abandoned pullover. It had been confirmed over and over by the way that she moved, and by her speed.

He pulled the sweater off his shoulder, and said, 'You could have made it a bit easier.'

He threw it to her, while she stood, bristling. It fell in front of her feet, and she glanced down at it and then back up, suspicious and tensed to run. He nodded to her and, still heaving for air, began to back away. 'Thanks for the exercise, Jojo,' he said. 'I'll see you soon.'

She didn't say anything until he'd turned away and started to jog back. A slightly mocking, 'You're not too slow for a rozzer, Copper Sheens!'

His sergeant had been waiting alone back by the car, twitchy with impatience.

'I lost him,' he said, as Jonah slowed to a walk. 'He ducked into one of those council houses and I couldn't tell you which.'

Jonah shook his head. 'Same here. Bloody maniac, that one. Over half the fences in the village and then vanished.'

His sergeant shook his head and opened the driver's door. 'At least there's no arrest report to file.'

'Yes,' Jonah said, and looked over the bold, red slogan on the wall.

FREEDOM KNOWS NO DIVISIONS
OF WEALTH OR

He supposed it would probably have said 'class'. It was almost a shame not to finish it, but it would be gone within a few days. Painted over.

Jonah had dozed off at some point on the way, lulled by Hanson's sedate driving and the gathering dark. He woke up dry-mouthed and disorientated when his DC said, 'Sir.'

'Sorry.' He remembered where they were now. On the way to Jojo's pale-blue house. They were driving down some unrecognizable stretch of curving road. He reached into the back to find his kitbag and rooted in it until he found the water bottle from his bike. He took a long draught from it. 'I didn't snore, did I?'

'No, you're OK,' Hanson said, smiling slightly. 'And if you dribbled, you did it out of the other side of your mouth.'

Jonah shook his head, but still rubbed at his mouth to be certain.

'So, Jojo Magos,' Hanson said, and for a disconcerting moment Jonah imagined that she knew about that night in Lyndhurst and the chase and the sweater. But of course she just wanted information, because he had asked her to take the lead.

'She was a core member of the group, unlike Brett Parker,' he said. 'Bit of a tomboy back then. Actually, still a bit of a tomboy as far as I can make out. Now a landscape gardener. Did you look her up?'

'Do we know what she did that night?' Hanson asked. 'I mean, I know we're waiting on O'Malley and Lightman going through the notes, but . . .'

'There was only a brief mention of her in the overview. She went to bed at a bit before one, the same as the others. Though when I say went to bed, she passed out sprawled on the ground with a sleeping bag half over her. Says she stayed that way until Connor shook her awake sometime after five. He asked her to help look for Aurora, so apparently she did.'

Hanson nodded. She had slowed the car down to a crawl, either lost in thought or wanting a few more minutes to mull. The satnav told them it was only a mile until their destination.

'Were you one of the officers who investigated back then?' she asked abruptly.

'Only in the most basic sense.' He glanced at her. 'I was recently off training, and I was a regular uniformed PC. I got sent knocking on doors like the rest of the local force, and I spent more hours than I can count searching through the woods. By two days after she'd gone, the area of woodland we were actively searching had been extended to cover twenty square miles. It was an extraordinary level of search. Like nothing I've seen since. I don't think most of us slept for the first couple of weeks. It seems incredible that we missed her.'

'I assume they did all this stuff we're doing? Interviewed the kids?'

'Endlessly,' Jonah agreed. 'For months. I got used to seeing one or other of them dragged in most weeks. Particularly Connor Dooley.'

'Why him?' She stopped the car altogether, and looked at him keenly. Her eyes looked a great deal harder than usual in the dim light.

73

'Because they thought he was white trash,' Jonah replied. 'And because he was Irish by descent. We were in the midst of the Troubles, and the suspicion towards anyone with an accent was enormous. Plus he was covered in tattoos, and known for getting into fights. He was the obvious choice.'

'But they didn't find anything?'

'No.' He glanced behind them, where a pair of headlights had swung into view. Hanson put the car into first and moved off again a little hurriedly. 'No, not as far as I know. Which doesn't mean that there wasn't anything to find, obviously. It also might mean they were looking in the wrong place.'

Jojo's house appeared out of the darkness ahead of them. Now, at night-time, it looked more white than powder blue, and the tumbling plants in the front garden that grew up and over half of the house seemed colourless instead of cheerful.

Jonah knew it fairly well from the road. An old school friend had pointed it out to him, and on many of the occasions he'd driven this way since, he had slowed slightly to take in all the colours. He had even seen her here on one occasion, working away in the front garden in a vest top with mud smudged across her face and a gleam of sweat over her. She hadn't looked up, and he had driven on feeling uncomfortably like some kind of voyeur.

'So they stopped investigating after a while?' Hanson asked, as she signalled and then turned slowly into the driveway.

'Things moved on,' Jonah replied. 'A group of IRA angries plotted to blow up Southampton City Hall early in eighty-four. There was a great deal of alarm at how close they'd come, and all of our focus was suddenly switched to finding them instead of a missing girl. Aurora's case stayed open, though, and occasionally there would be a resurgence of interest.'

He didn't add that he had volunteered to be part of the task force each time the enquiry had re-opened. That he had never really stopped looking for Aurora.

Hanson turned off the engine, her expression thoughtful. 'And it's further in the past now, too.' Then she added, 'But we have a body now. And a defined list of suspects, I suppose.'

'We'll see how much that counts for,' he said, climbing out of the car.

It was late for them to be calling. Gone ten o'clock. An anti-social time. He hoped she hadn't already gone to bed. They would have to retreat if so, and try again tomorrow. Though perhaps by then he would be less dazed, and struggle less to distinguish between the person he had been and the person he was now.

He edged past a tatty, dark-red Jeep Wrangler with its soft-top down and bamboo plants standing up in the back. Despite the dominant and almost wild-looking presence of plants all around the driveway, the paving was immaculate, with clean cement between cream tiles.

They ducked under a vigorously healthy clematis on a trellis to make their way to the door. It was already ajar. Behind it was a lean, tanned form in loose cotton wrap-around trousers and a vest top.

'Can I help?'

Everything about her spelled wariness. Jonah could see a hard ridge of muscle standing up along her forearm, and her fingers were pressed hard into the door, ready to close it in a moment. The pose was so profoundly like the cornered figure that night in Totton that it was disorientating.

'We're with the Southampton Police,' Hanson said. 'I'm DC Hanson, and this is DCI Sheens. Can we come in?'

Jonah was sure he wasn't imagining the reaction at his name. There was a slight relaxing of the body, followed by a slow half-smile. Jojo, unlike her friends, had recognized him.

'OK,' she said, and then a little archly, 'if you promise I'm not in trouble.'

Hanson smiled, and Jonah gave her a tiny shrug. Her smile faded a little, but she backed away from the door and let them in.

Hanson gestured for him to go first, and Jonah followed Jojo at a slight distance. She still walked like someone who spent most of her time moving. She had an easy, loping stride that covered ground.

The house was tidier than he'd expected, and the space was larger. It had looked like a doll's house, but the hallway opened on to a large kitchen that had been extended on one side into a conservatory, and on the other into a sitting room. The colours were cheerful, seaside-like. Blues and fresh yellows and bleached wood. One blue-and-white mug of tea was on a small oak coffee table and a book face down next to it. No sign of anyone else living there, which was as he'd expected. As far as Jonah knew from the local gossip chain, Jojo hadn't dated for years. Not since she'd lost her boyfriend to a climbing accident.

'Do you mind if we sit?' Hanson asked.

Jojo shook her head, and folded herself into an armchair opposite the sofa, watching them questioningly.

'So. What's going on?'

It was Hanson's turn to put into words the fact that a long-vanished girl was dead.

'Some remains have been uncovered in Brinken Wood. They're Aurora Jackson's.'

Jojo was quite still, and then she nodded slowly. She reached forward to grab her mug of tea with a hand that shook slightly.

'I suppose she had to be dead, didn't she?' she said, and took a large gulp. 'But it's not nice knowing it. What do you think happened? Was she murdered?'

'We're trying to establish what happened,' Hanson said, with the natural evasiveness of a good interviewing officer. 'We'd like to ask if you know anything about the location she was found in. It was a hollow underneath a tree.'

'What?'

It was whip-sharp, that word. Almost angry.

'The location of the remains was alongside the river. A hollowed-out area of earth under a beech tree. Do you know anything about it?'

Jojo gave a strange, harsh laugh. 'Of course I know about it. It was our secret stash. Our repository for more drugs than we could have used in a lifetime.' She looked over at Jonah, a slightly pleading look in her eyes. 'Do you need to know where it came from?'

Jonah leaned forward slightly, telling Hanson that he would answer this. 'We've been given that information by another witness, but it would be useful to hear what you've got to say about it.'

'It's so . . . so strange,' Jojo said, and Jonah could see her eyes moving left to right, right to left, recalling something. They focused on him again. 'Was she put there? Was it deliberate? Because that would mean . . . it was one of us.'

Jonah held her gaze, aware of the way her face had drained of colour. 'It's quite possible,' he said.

There was a pause, while Jojo's gaze felt like it was piercing him.

77

'We don't know what happened yet,' Hanson said in the end, across their eye contact. 'So we need you to tell us anything you can that might help.'

Jojo shifted in her chair. She looked at Hanson now, and nodded.

'It doesn't make me look great. A friend of my brother's had a problem. He'd purchased this big supply of Dexedrine for some rich prick in Southampton. And then said rich prick got picked up for cocaine possession right before the sale, and he was in real shit. I told Benners and asked if he'd like to buy it. I told him he could get it for nothing . . .' Jojo shrugged. 'I don't know if that counts as dealing or what. But it was me who set it up. I put them in touch. Benners' parents were loaded, and it seemed like a great opportunity. We thought we'd sit on it and just use it little by little. We were big into Dexedrine then. It was our pick-me-up on party nights, and Benners sometimes used it to help him with essay deadlines.'

'How much was there?' Jonah asked, remembering what Brett Parker had said.

'Fifteen kilos,' Jojo answered, her mouth a little twisted. 'An insane amount. It could have done us for years.'

Jonah kept his reaction to himself. He remembered the cluster of packets. There had been nowhere near fifteen kilos. Nowhere near a kilo, even.

'So how long before that night did the purchase happen?' Jonah continued. He could feel Hanson's tension beside him. He wasn't letting her take the lead like he'd suggested.

'A few weeks. Really not very long,' Jojo said. 'It was still a big, exciting treat.'

'So I suppose you'd used only a few hundred grams by then.'

'If that,' Jojo said. 'We really weren't heavy users, any of us.'

'And after she'd gone missing,' Jonah said, 'you decided to leave it there?'

Jojo gave him a hollow smile. She placed her mug down with an audible clunk. 'We had to kick off a search for her, and we knew the place was going to end up crawling with coppers. We were bricking it, and we agreed we'd have to leave it. Later, Aurora going like that left a . . . shadow, I guess. And none of us wanted anything to do with the stuff. At least, that's what I thought, when I did think about it. We didn't talk about the drugs afterwards.'

'None of you talked about them?' Hanson asked curiously. 'Not at all?'

Jojo hesitated.

'No, not . . . I think Benners was pretty keen on us staying away from there. He was the one who was going to be in the shit if they were found, after all.'

'Did he tell you to stay away?'

'Not in so many words.' Jojo gave a slight shrug. 'He just said we'd all have to act like that place didn't exist for a while.'

'He didn't say how long for?' Hanson persisted. 'He didn't say he was planning on going back a while later?'

'Like I said, I don't think he said that much. At least, I can't remember him saying anything. I assumed everyone felt the same way I did. It felt like they were tainted.' She took an unsteady breath. 'Jesus. She was there all the time. Waiting for one of us to go back there, and none of us ever did.'

Except one of you might have done, Jonah thought.

A brief silence ensued, and then Hanson asked gently, 'Did Aurora know about the drugs?'

'Oh, she knew about them,' Jojo said. 'We all did, even Brett. Topaz was showing off to him, and because she wanted to show him, Aurora had to see too.'

'So Topaz was interested in Brett Parker?'

Jojo gave a slight laugh. 'Yes. Connor didn't get a look in back then. Poor Connor. He had to watch her fawn all over Brett, who was just totally smug at that age. I guess that's what happens when everyone adores you. I think Aurora vanishing made him grow up a bit, you know.'

'Was Brett interested in Topaz, then?'

'No, not really. She probably found it frustrating. There weren't that many people who said no to her.'

Jonah stood as Hanson went on questioning her. He could feel Jojo's eyes on him as he wandered around the room, looking for clues to the last few decades.

'How close are the six of you now?' Hanson asked.

'Fairly close. We ended up having to lean on each other quite a lot back then. Brett was the first to move away, because he was in the year above and went to Loughborough, but as soon as he had the money he bought a place back here, and that gradually became the centre of everything.'

'Did you talk about Aurora?'

'Yes, of course. But we talked about a lot of other things, too. We were friends.'

Jonah's wandering had taken him to the point where the room met the new conservatory. He found a bookcase with six photo frames in it. He recognized Jojo's younger brother, Kenny, who still lived in Lyndhurst and worked at the outdoor shop.

'And now?' Hanson was asking.

'We drifted a bit when Topaz and Connor moved away,' Jojo replied. 'I mean, I still see Daniel and Brett individually.

Coralie's off in London now, and she's never been that bothered about seeing me. The lack of feeling is fairly mutual.'

Jonah was storing all of that as he looked at the other photos. There were two pictures of children: nieces and nephews who belonged to Jojo's older brother Anton, at a guess. One photo was of her father at a younger age, olive-skinned and grinning in his overalls as he repaired a roof.

Jonah picked up one of the last two pictures. It was of a slightly younger Jojo, perhaps aged thirty, soaking wet on a drizzly day, her face pressed close to a man's. He was all strong jaw and five o'clock shadow. Behind them was a rain-drenched view of the sea and cliffs, and both of them were grinning despite the abysmal weather.

He heard Jojo rising and coming to stand near his right shoulder. She was shifting her weight from foot to foot, agitated.

'That's Aleksy,' she said. 'He was my boyfriend.'

Jonah nodded. He'd recognized Aleksy Nowak, the New Forest's adopted, celebrated free climber, from the photo of him in the paper. There had been a tribute from Jojo, too.

'I heard that he'd died. I'm sorry.'

Jojo shook her head, and rubbed at her forearm. 'He didn't know Aurora. I didn't meet him until a lot later.'

'Sorry,' Jonah said, and placed the photo down. 'I shouldn't . . . I'm not here to pry into your life.'

'OK. That's OK.'

Hanson rose before they had a chance to sit back down. 'I think that's all for this evening,' she said with a questioning glance at Jonah.

He nodded, and told Jojo, 'We'll see you tomorrow, then. At eleven.'

'All right. I was supposed to climb but it looks like it'll be stormy anyway.'

Jonah found himself watching her, curious. 'You still climb?'

Jojo nodded. She gave a slightly defensive shrug. 'It was either that or lose something else I loved.'

She followed them to the door, and watched them as they returned to the car. She only shut the door once they had climbed in.

Jonah should have gone to pick up his bike from Godshill and cycled it the thirteen miles to his house in Ashurst. He hated leaving it locked up anywhere out of his sight, even in low-crime Godshill. But it was almost eleven now, and he still needed time to read the overview again in preparation for the press briefing tomorrow.

'Drop me at home,' he told Hanson. 'I'll sort my bike out tomorrow.'

'Sure,' she said, and then, after a pause, 'Where's home?'

He sighed. 'Sorry. I'm in Ashurst.'

'Can you . . .?'

She waved at the satnav, and he dutifully took it down and punched in his postcode.

'So the drugs . . .' Hanson began, once they'd pulled out on to the road.

'Are an interesting feature,' Jonah agreed.

'How much did they find there?'

'A fraction of that amount,' he answered.

'So it sounds like Daniel Benham went back there,' Hanson said. 'And if he saw her, and didn't report it, in all probability he killed her.'

'Somebody, at some point, removed a large quantity of Dexedrine from around the body of Aurora Jackson,' Jonah corrected her, 'and afterwards failed to report it. We don't know that it's one of them, never mind being certain that it was Daniel Benham.'

'But it's the likely answer, isn't it?' Hanson pressed.

'Likely isn't good enough,' he said.

He heard a small out breath from Hanson, but she said nothing. A silence grew as they drove, and Jonah inwardly went back over the interview with Jojo. He found himself circling around that conversation over the photograph, remembering what Jojo had said about her boyfriend. It took him a while to notice that Hanson was looking at him whenever she could get away with it.

'You were friends with her, weren't you?' she said. 'Jojo. That's why you wanted me to take the lead.'

'Only in the very loosest sense,' he answered. 'I was really friends with her older brother. I sometimes went to the house or hung out with both of them at the recreation ground. There was a lot of that in my childhood.'

'So you aren't worried about a conflict of interest? You're not close?'

'No, we were never close,' Jonah said, feeling slightly defensive again. He was beginning to recognize that Hanson didn't like letting things go. 'I've probably only bumped into her four or five times since, and never done more than say hello. None of those times has been recent. I stopped hanging out with her brother once I started training college, too. It was a conscious choice, in part. He had so many friends who broke the law as a matter of course, and I know he did it himself, too. Though I think he's cleaned his act up now.'

Hanson nodded thoughtfully. And then she volunteered, 'I've cut ties with a few of those myself.'

It surprised him to hear it. He'd read her CV, and thought

of her as straight-laced, from a very different background to his. Though he knew well enough that a CV didn't tell you everything.

'Well, anyway, that's good,' she added, with a smile. 'Knowing someone in a half-arsed way isn't going to complicate things.'

'No,' Jonah agreed. 'It isn't.'

And he tried not to think about all the things he wasn't telling her.

12. Aurora

Friday, 22 July 1983, 9:25 p.m.

She was shivering with cold as she picked her way back to the campsite. It was almost fully dark, and her hair was still dripping wet from the river. It had started soaking into her top the moment she'd pulled it on, turning it translucent in patches. She kept her eyes on the luminous red of the fire through the trees as she walked. She hoped it would be warm enough to dry her off.

Topaz, Benners and Brett were standing in a bunch in front of it. She could hear Topaz's voice, high-pitched and aggressive, before she had cleared the trees.

'Well, she shouldn't have told her to! For fuck's sake. She's probably got lost swimming down the river.'

Aurora could feel the desire to hide overcoming her again. She often retreated inside herself when her sister was angry.

But then, in a rare moment of rebellion, she wondered why Topaz felt she had the right. Topaz had gone off and left her with people she barely knew. She'd invited her and then acted like she shouldn't be there.

'Have you checked to see if she's left clothes on the bank?' Jojo called from where she was bent over beside Connor, pegging down one of the tents more thoroughly.

'No, I haven't,' Topaz said.

'We should try and find her,' Brett said, glancing towards the path to the river. 'She could have got into trouble in the water.'

Aurora didn't want to step forward, but she also didn't want them to come looking for her. 'It's all right. I'm here.' She moved into the clearing.

Topaz turned on her. In the firelight, she looked aglow with anger. 'Where the hell have you been?'

Aurora came close to the fire and crouched beside it, letting Jojo's swimming bag drop down beside her.

'Swimming,' she said, and had that strange sense of rebellion again. She didn't want to apologize this time. Didn't want to appease her sister. She felt no need to do anything but huddle close to the flames and stare into them.

'For an hour and a half?' Topaz asked. 'You've spent *an hour and a half* swimming?'

'Yes,' Aurora said. 'Just like you spent an hour and a half looking for firewood.'

There was a silence after that, broken only by the snap and rumble of the fire. It was searingly hot this close. Aurora revelled in it. She breathed in the heat and let her face become painfully warm.

Eventually, she heard Topaz mutter, 'Fucking ridiculous,' and stalk away. Aurora could just make her out over the top of the flames, sitting huffily next to Coralie. Coralie put her arms round her and started stroking her hair.

'You need some food,' Benners said, breaking through the silence. He went to the camping stoves, which were no longer lit. 'I'll warm something up for you.'

She could feel Brett hovering next to her, but her eyes were still on the fire; on a section of log that was just beginning to ignite.

'Did you get in some kind of trouble swimming?' he asked quietly.

'No, I was fine.' She realized her reply had been a little

terse, and gave him a quick smile. 'I just went a long way up the river and then had to swim back.'

'Good. I was – We were worried about you. So that's good.'

He dropped his hand to her shoulder and squeezed it, before going to stand next to Benners.

Aurora watched him, uncertain. She had always associated his effortless popularity with selfishness; with lack of care. She was surprised to find some concern for her, when she was fourteen and at the far end of the popularity spectrum.

When she looked away from him, she realized that Topaz was staring at her, her body rigid and her jaw set. Topaz was so often irritable with her, but this was more than irritation. There was a look of hatred on her face so fierce that it made Aurora feel cold again.

13

Jonah could have done with silence the rest of the way home, but Hanson was alert and talkative.

'How long have they been working for you, the other two?' she asked him, a few miles from Jojo's.

'Five years. Well, Ben has for five years. Domnall came the year after. He was a late recruit to the forces. Used to be in the military.'

Hanson gave him a delighted grin. 'Really? He doesn't . . . seem the military type.'

'No, I would agree. I've never met a man who hates being told how to do things as much as Domnall O'Malley.'

'Maybe that's why he left,' she said.

'Could be.'

He knew otherwise; knew about the drinking and the warnings and the eventual benders that had put Domnall out of action during active service. He knew also that Domnall had been through a great deal to take him to that point, and had put himself through a great deal to drag himself back. As far as Jonah was concerned, that was Domnall's story to tell their new DC, if he wanted to. Jonah wasn't going to be the one to break his confidence.

'What about Ben?' she asked. 'Where did he spring from?'

'The more standard graduate applicant,' Jonah replied. 'He was always set on being CID, and he did his degree in sociology because he felt it would help him. I hired him as soon as he became a DC, like I did you.'

'Where did he do his uniform time?'

'With the Met, interestingly enough.' Which was not a common path. Those who started in the Metropolitan Police usually chose to stay there.

'Wow. City boy.'

'Adopted city boy,' he said. 'He grew up in Morestead. Which is why he's back. Family. Siblings, nieces and nephews.'

'Wife?' Hanson asked.

Jonah tried not to smile. They always asked, the young women. Some of the young men, too. It didn't matter that Lightman was reserved, and polite rather than warm. The look of him was always enough to drive their interest.

'No, no wife. And no girlfriend, either, as far as I know. He's all about the job, is Ben.'

He could see her considering that. He wondered if she was interested. She didn't look as starry-eyed as they usually did. Either way, the interest would wane when she realized that the pretty sergeant's veneer of cool never rubbed off or broke down. When she realized that flirtation and lingering gazes and striking eye make-up did nothing.

A moment later, Hanson's phone buzzed where she'd stuffed it into a cupholder. He saw her eyes cut sideways to it and then back, and it didn't surprise him when she paused at the next junction and picked it up.

'Sorry,' she said, as she unlocked it and read.

'No problem,' he answered, wondering if he was keeping her from a boyfriend. Whoever it was, she didn't answer. She shoved the phone back into its place, and Jonah could see a tension in her that hadn't been there before.

He was up until two, eyes going in and out of focus as he went over the Intelligence report. He climbed into bed irritable at the thought of five hours' sleep, and dreamed off and on about searing hot weather, and a faceless girl being in danger.

His phone rang intrusively at just before seven. His sleep-fuzzy mind went to his ex. His eyes tricked him for a moment into reading Michelle's name, until he realized that it read Mum.

When was it going to stop, the instinctive assumption that everything was Michelle? When he threw himself into the next doomed relationship? Or would Michelle be the one he could never quite get over; the one he regretted for the rest of his life?

His voice was croaky as he answered. 'Everything all right?'

'There's someone – I recognize them.' Her voice was choked and incoherent, and he felt a familiar wave of depression. 'They've been outside all night. They're friends of his. They want me dead.'

'Mum,' he said, as patiently as he could. 'Nobody wants you dead. You need to take some breaths. It's a long time ago, Mum. They don't care about you, or us. Not any more.'

'Stop it! You always try to say . . .' She made a choked sound. 'Why aren't you here? You're supposed to protect me!'

A rush of rage in her that, as always, ended in an equally swift flood of tears.

'Where are you, Jonah?' she sobbed. 'I'm so lonely. It's been days. I've seen no one.'

'I'll be over this evening or tomorrow,' he said. He'd become pretty good at soothing her over the last few years. There were tears almost every time they spoke. 'You aren't on your own. You have Deborah popping in at lunchtime. You can talk to her.'

'No I can't.'

She sounded like a toddler. Petulant and tearful.

'But you like her.'

'She never stays any more. She just does my lunch and then she goes.'

Jonah started to argue, and then realized this might be true. The funding situation had changed, and that might well mean less time. He needed to call up the care company and find out.

'OK. Well, I'll be over later. And I'll arrange for Barb to visit, too. OK? She likes coming to see you. We'll invite her for lunch or something.'

He was always careful when he talked about Barb. He always tried hard to make it sound like she was a friend, and not someone he paid as a companion to keep up the facade that his mother still had friends and a normal life.

'She should have come yesterday. I wanted her to.'

Jonah felt tripped up for a moment. 'Did you ask her to? Did you call her up?'

'No. I thought you would.' She was sulky, self-pitying. It was difficult not to find it infuriating. 'It's just the two of us now. I need you to look after me.'

Jonah sighed. He'd been looking after her for decades. Ever since she'd fled from Tommy Sheens and started a new life in Lyndhurst.

Even at ten years old, his relief had been profound. Tommy had only occasionally been physically violent, which he supposed was what had made it so hard for his mother to leave. His abuse was verbal; emotional. He had controlled and manipulated until his mother had doubted her own thoughts. Until Jonah had possessed no shred of self-confidence, and begun to believe his father when he claimed that obeying his every whim was what a loving family should do.

'I was working all day yesterday, I'm afraid, Mum,' Jonah said lightly. 'But I'll call her.'

'Maybe you shouldn't bother. Maybe she doesn't like me any more.'

'Of course she does,' he said. 'I'll ring her in a bit. See you this evening, all right?'

He ended the call and stayed lying there for a moment, feeling frustration in all the muscles of his head and arms. He could gladly have thrown his phone across the room. But instead he rose, found Barb's number and sent her a message instead of calling. He wasn't willing to wake her up early, and he would forget if he left it till later.

He picked up a towel from the radiator and went to the bathroom. He stood for too long in the shower, thinking the same circular thoughts about his mother that he always did. That he somehow needed to save her from herself, but that he didn't know how. That it wasn't his fault that she was like this. That it had been Tommy Sheens who'd caused it all, from the moment she'd married him.

By the time Jonah had dressed in his charcoal suit and pale-blue tie, his standard media-facing outfit, he had shelved thoughts of his family. He had forty-five minutes to prepare himself to face the press.

He opened his front door on to a misty day full of drizzle, which seemed like an unfair let-down after the day before. He checked his phone before climbing into his Mondeo. No messages or emails from McCullough. He would be giving the briefing without the tox report. Which in some ways was better. He didn't have anything to hide. He just had to stand up there and tell them it was Aurora, and that they were pursuing new lines of investigation.

Hopefully, by the end of the day, they'd actually have a few lines of investigation to pursue.

*

Topaz hated being in her parents' house. She hated the clutter and the unchanging nature of it; the way it made her feel her life draining away while they sat in the tired kitchen and drank tea out of stained cups. More than that, she hated the fact that coming here made her a child again. It made her remember the person she had been.

And then there was Aurora's room, which was still so very much her younger sister's. It was dusty and tired-looking now, but it was still festooned with butterflies and flowers, from bedspread to ceiling.

Connor was already in his jogging kit, and seemed unfazed by the persistent rain and the increasing muddy puddles. He was drinking coffee in little gulps, and she found herself watching him while her mother clattered around making breakfast.

They'd barely talked about Aurora since they'd left Edinburgh. For most of the flight they'd made nothing but stilted, facile conversation about practicalities. About getting shopping in for her parents on the way from the airport, and about whether they'd decamp to a hotel for the next night.

They also hadn't mentioned Daniel or Brett, or Coralie or Jojo. Even though Topaz was burning with curiosity to know what the others were doing, and how they were holding up.

And she wanted to talk to them, too. To Daniel, maybe, who would be sympathetic. To Brett, who would just listen without judgement. Or even to Jojo, who would probably make them both laugh in spite of everything.

Connor finished the coffee, and nodded to her before heading out. He usually kissed her before leaving. But for some reason she wasn't sure she even wanted him to. She couldn't help thinking about Aurora, and her own fractured memories of that night.

It was almost a relief once Connor was gone, but the moment she was alone with her mother she regretted it. She found the pretence of caring about her mother's friend's new dog, or the shop parking, infuriating. There was such restless frustration in her that she felt raw.

Eventually, she excused herself from the kitchen for a short while on the pretext of making a work call, even though it was still early, and she'd told them she was taking time off. She climbed the poorly lit stairs and headed up on to the landing, and then she saw Aurora's bedroom door move slightly in the breeze from the open window.

She faltered, remembering in a vivid rush an early morning when she'd crept back in from a night out with Coralie and some of the sixth-formers. It had been dim and greyish, just like this, and Topaz had felt suddenly empty and worthless and used. She had been aware of shame-filled tears building somewhere in her as she climbed the stairs.

And then Aurora's door had opened, and Topaz had flinched. Her sister was standing there in her nightdress, a gauzy, floaty thing made out of purple lace that had become too short for her once she'd grown. But for a moment, in the half-light, she'd looked ethereal and beautiful, her eyes big and luminous in the light.

'Glad you're all right,' Aurora had whispered. 'I couldn't sleep. Do you want tea? I can do it in a pan on the hob. It won't wake anyone.'

Topaz had studied her sister's face, expecting to see some kind of judgement there. But there was none. There was just a patient offer.

The wholesomeness of her sister, and that offer of a homely, pure comfort, had the strangest effect on her. She felt like she could walk away from the shame, and be like Aurora somehow.

94

She'd never in her life wanted to be like her sister before.

'Thanks,' she'd said, trying not to let her voice crack with emotion. 'I'd love a tea.'

In the end, they'd sat at each side of the kitchen table and talked about some of their school teachers, and rolled their eyes about their parents.

Topaz wasn't sure if she'd ever thanked Aurora for that night. She thought not. By the time she got up again, the drive to be desirable had become too strong once more, and her younger sister had been returned to her place as an embarrassment in Topaz's life.

It was a strange time to really realize that her sister was gone. She'd known it for years. But seeing that landing now, empty of Aurora, and knowing that it wasn't her opening the door, drove the truth of it into her.

She walked slowly to Aurora's door and pushed it open. The butterflies and the flowers and the riotous colours no longer seemed claustrophobic. There was something glorious about them. She walked around the room, running her fingers across gauze wings and painted designs on the walls.

And then she climbed on to Aurora's bed, and curled up round the unchanged pillow.

The press had been unusually placid this morning. The most challenging question had been whether the case was being treated as a murder. He'd answered readily.

'We can't rule anything in or out at this stage,' he said calmly. 'Any other questions?'

There were none. They were too young, these journalists. They didn't know who Aurora had been. He stepped down from the small stage calmly, and could already see some of them with their smartphones out, googling Aurora Jackson. Working out how big this was.

Wilkinson was waiting at the back of the room, his small, stocky frame plain-clothed and unobtrusive. He gave a little jerk of his head that asked Jonah to follow.

He went after him dutifully enough. It was generally good to have the detective chief superintendent's input, even if he wasn't involved.

Wilkinson swiped his card at the door to CID and then waited, holding it open. 'How's the new constable getting on?' he asked, quietly.

'Good, I think,' Jonah replied. 'Waiting to see how she handles a murder.'

Wilkinson kept walking through the half-occupied office, nodding to a few of the officers who attempted a greeting. He occasionally offered a quiet, slightly sombre, 'Good morning.'

He paused outside his office, hand on the glass door, and gave Jonah a slightly sympathetic look. 'When have you got interviews starting?'

'Nine.'

Wilkinson lifted his wrist to look at his watch. He shrugged. 'Lightman and your new constable are here. They can hold the fort. Come and give me a run-down.'

Jonah let himself be herded in.

'It's somewhat unexpected, isn't it?' Wilkinson said. 'This all coming back to bite us thirty years later.'

'Yes,' Jonah said, wondering whether the past was having the same effect on the DCS. He'd been, what? An inspector back then? Jonah hadn't known him all that well. It had taken some time for the two of them to become direct colleagues and then friends. It had been an unlikely friendship, the traveller's son and the public schoolboy.

Wilkinson turned in his chair and cast his gaze over the retail-unit view beyond the window. 'So, a group of kids, and a stash of Dexedrine. Are we thinking they buried her together?'

Jonah had been through this thinking before. He had little to offer against it except gut feeling. The way they had each reacted. Perhaps one of them could have pretended to be shocked, but not all of them.

'I'll have to get back to you on that,' he said non-committally. 'I want the tox report back before I look at any one theory. I'd also like to see phone records for the group.'

'They stuck together pretty well, those kids,' Wilkinson went on, brooding. 'It was a united front. Which in itself might be quite damning.'

Jonah didn't argue, but he was thinking that there might be other things to hide than murder. Things that even thirty years on could come back to bite you. And the thought gave him another small twinge of anxiety.

He could almost hear the chief super thinking through the idea of accessing the phone records. It was his job to make sure that his department acted lawfully and justly, and stood up to external scrutiny. He would do everything he could to aid his investigators within that remit, but he would clamp down on anything that looked wrong to him.

'OK. I think phone records are justified. You won't get anything from the time, but if there's collusion going on now, you might see it.'

'Thank you,' Jonah said.

'Gut feeling so far?' the DCS asked.

'That it could take a while to untangle,' Jonah said with a half-smile. 'I can't be any more specific at present.'

'Sitting on the fence, of course,' Wilkinson said, and

added, 'You'd probably better shelve your work with Portsmouth International for now. Unless anything happens, this is going to be our priority for the foreseeable.'

'Yes, sir,' he replied, thinking of the weeks his team had put into the dockside investigation. But his heart was no longer in it, anyway. He'd been drawn back into the enigma that was Aurora. He let himself out into the increasing buzz of CID.

Topaz's phone rang while she was still lying on Aurora's bed. She saw that it was Coralie calling her, and considered ignoring it. But Coralie could be persistent. It was often easier just to get it over with.

She picked up the call, and said, 'Hi, lovely,' in as normal a voice as she could manage.

'I've booked a train to Southampton,' Coralie said, as if this were a greeting. Her voice was tauter than usual. She sounded unhappy.

'Oh, really?'

'I'm going to stay at the Regent. Daddy often uses the suite there.'

Of course she'd stay there. It was in Coralie's nature to choose the most of everything: the most expensive, the most extravagant, the greatest status. All of it enabled by her father, who was still Daddy even when he was eighty-five.

'What time do you get in? Connor and I can come and have a drink with you later, if you like,' she offered. At least she would be out of the house that way.

'Why didn't you tell me?' Coralie asked, ignoring the suggestion.

'What, lovely?'

'About Aurora being found.' There was a hint of hurt in Coralie's voice.

'I'm sorry,' Topaz answered. She couldn't seem to get any real emotion into her voice. 'I hadn't really stopped and thought yet . . .'

'But I could have come down last night,' Coralie said. 'I could have been there to support you.'

'Yes, I know. I wish you had been.' There was a slight pause. 'Have you talked to any of the others?'

'Yeah, I rang Benners.' Coralie let out a small sigh. 'He kept saying he couldn't talk about it. He sounded stressed out. I think the police are giving him a hard time.'

'God, not again,' Topaz said. 'I'm just waiting for them to tear into Connor.'

'He's the big professor now. They'll be nice to him.'

'But they'll be judging him on who he was, not who he is,' Topaz argued.

'Well, I guess he should have been less aggressive.'

'Coralie!' Topaz said sharply.

'You think I'm harsh with him,' she said, a little breath-lessly. 'But you know what he was like. You know. And he was obsessed with you.'

'No, he loved me,' Topaz said firmly.

'We all loved you!' Coralie countered. 'And the rest of us used to matter. Now it's all just him, always.'

'You all still matter,' Topaz replied. 'If you feel like I've let you down, then I'm sorry. But talking about it now is not a good idea.'

The numbness was going, to be replaced by anger. Why was Coralie choosing now to say this? It was as if she had an instinct for Topaz's most fragile time, and chose to attack.

'What is it he has over you?' Coralie asked, ignoring her

response. 'Why did it all change that night? Was there something that happened after we'd gone to sleep?'

'Fuck you, Coralie,' Topaz said, shaking with fury. 'How fucking dare you? You – No, you know what? I'm done.'

She ended the call, and then hurled her phone at the wall. It bounced, and landed on the pastel carpet, apparently unharmed.

'Fuck you!' she repeated. And then, as much out of fury as out of grief, she gave in to sobs that moved her whole body.

She heard someone walking up the stairs, and down the landing to her room. She hoped they'd leave her to it.

But then there were steps towards the door, and her father's voice outside it. 'Topaz? Are you in there?'

He must have known she was. The noise of her crying would have been pretty audible.

When she said nothing, the door opened slowly.

'Go away,' she said, and turned away from him.

'Sorry,' Tom said, but he didn't go straight away. He took a few steps, and put a hand briefly on her shoulder. 'I'm here if you . . . if you need to talk. OK?'

Topaz kept her face away, but she nodded.

Tom left a few moments later. She heard him close the door, and only then did she crumple back on to the bed and bury her head in the pillow again.

Her phone buzzed once a little while later. She knew it was Coralie messaging. Topaz had a violent wish to have been harsher to her former friend. To have hurt her more. Coralie was probably apologizing, which was how it worked with Coralie. Her moments of angst never lasted.

Topaz picked up the phone to read her message.

It wasn't an apology.

> I'm going to talk to the police once I arrive. I think there are a lot
> of things they'd be interested to know.

She wanted to fling the phone away again, but instead she typed a message back with shaking hands.

> You can say whatever you want. I don't give a shit. They won't
> believe your psycho stories.

They were brave words, and probably stupid ones. She wished they were actually true.

Lightman was at his elbow before he'd had a chance to close Wilkinson's door behind him. Jonah took in the notebook and pen. He wondered what time Lightman had arrived. He looked immaculate and refreshed, as always.

'Brett Parker is here already. I've put him in Room Four.'

'Thanks.'

'Before you go in, I have a few notes on the case reports. I've worked through the initial interviews in the first three days after the missing persons report went in. And there are a couple of interesting points in the transcripts, which haven't been flagged up by previous investigating officers.'

'Hit me.'

'Connor Dooley and Jojo Magos each made a reference to Aurora going off swimming for a while during the evening. Jojo's statement makes it sound like a fairly run-of-the-mill thing, but Connor, later in his statement, referenced Aurora's sister being "still angry with her for taking herself off swimming". None of the others specifically referenced it, but Daniel Benham mentioned them all worrying about her and trying to look after her. He stated "we got a bit edgy if she was even out of sight. I don't understand how we can have let this happen".'

Jonah smiled. This was classic Lightman work. Rigorous, careful cross-checking, stage by stage. A level of detailed analysis unmatched among his colleagues.

'So,' he summarized, making his way towards the interview suite, 'she took herself off for a while and worried them all. We don't know what she was up to, or if any of them had followed her. And not a lot was done to follow up on that back in eighty-three.'

'I think it's worth asking them about,' Lightman said.

'Anything else?'

'A couple of other related queries for now. Topaz Jackson and Coralie Ribbans left the campsite after an argument with Daniel Benham and Connor Dooley.'

'Left in what sense?'

'They took themselves off into the woods for a while.'

Jonah nodded. 'What was the argument about? Any details?'

'Yes. They both, independently, attributed it to Connor and Daniel not really wanting Brett there. But Daniel Benham, in his statement, downplayed it and said it had hardly been an argument. I'd want to know more about that disagreement. And also, Topaz Jackson ended up alone. Coralie came away from her to "let her have a little time to herself", according to her testimony. It looks like this coincided with Aurora swimming. I'd be interested to know if she, in fact, met and argued with her sister.'

Lightman stopped at his own desk, and Jonah stopped with him. He was mentally putting these statements together. He was wondering what could have happened to a fourteen-year-old girl out in the woods that might have precipitated her death.

Hanson's bag was looped over her chair, though the chair

itself was empty. O'Malley was sitting amid his scattered paperwork on the next desk along. He looked up to give Jonah a nod, and then returned to his reading, with the pre-occupation of a man who was building something.

'Thank you,' Jonah said to Lightman, taking a printout from him. 'Who's going to do a round of coffee?'

Lightman nodded and turned away, while O'Malley called out, 'I want sugar today. At least two.'

'You're not allowed sugar,' Lightman called back.

O'Malley shook his head. 'Thank you, Mummy.'

Hanson reappeared, her expression enthusiastic.

'Juliette,' Jonah said. 'I'm about to talk to Brett Parker. Domnall's coming in with me, and I'd like you to come and watch from outside. Observe, and see what you think.'

He couldn't help smiling at her eager expression.

'Yes, sir.'

Jonah hovered next to O'Malley for a moment. 'What are you in the middle of?'

O'Malley looked up at him. 'Ah, I'm not sure I've got anything yet. I can come and grill Brett Parker, sure.'

'OK. That's good. Ben, I'd like you in the observation room too.'

Hanson was back moments later, and Jonah led the three of them towards the interview suite. He was well aware that Wilkinson hated this kind of use of resources. Four police officers for one interview. But the chief superintendent's grumbles never meant much. When it came to it, Wilkinson wanted the right conclusion. He generally left Jonah to get on with it.

'Ready?' Jonah asked O'Malley, glancing in at where Brett Parker was waiting. He wore a pale-grey suit today, and a white shirt with no tie. He was tanned enough to look healthy even under the artificial lights. His expression was bland, but one heel tapped the floor rhythmically.

'Do you have something in mind for me to ask?' the sergeant said.

'Anything that occurs to you,' Jonah said. 'Though keep it light, for now.' He glanced at Hanson. 'Juliette, I'd like you to give it ten minutes, and then come and get me. Just say I'm needed.'

Hanson gave him a quizzical look. 'OK.' She nodded. 'Ten minutes.'

Jonah opened the door and let himself in, leaving O'Malley to follow.

Brett Parker seemed relieved to see him. He gave him a nod of greeting and a slight smile.

'We're all ready to go, Mr Parker,' Jonah said. 'Thank you for coming in.'

He seated himself in the chair closest to the door, and let O'Malley take the other one.

'It's all right. I'm happy to help.'

Jonah looked him over. He saw that there was a sheen of sweat on his forehead and that his eyes looked dry and tired.

'Do you have any objection to us recording this interview?' Jonah asked him.

'Of course not. Of course not.'

Jonah inserted a fresh tape and clicked the recorder on.

'This is DCI Jonah Sheens, interviewing Mr Brett Parker. Also present is DS Domnall O'Malley. Mr Parker. I want you to take us over a few details.'

'Of course.'

Brett leaned forward and rested his hands on the table.

'According to the original statements of Connor Dooley and Jojo Magos, Aurora did not remain at the campsite for the whole of the evening. She took herself for a swim while dinner was being set up and cooked.'

A distant look as Brett recalled. A thirty-year gap being traversed.

'Yes, I – I'm not sure when she went, but she did go swimming. We'd talked about it earlier and I think she got bored.'

'You didn't go as well?' he asked.

'No. No, I didn't see her go. She was alone.'

Jonah nodded. 'Do you recall how long she was gone for?'

A pause, and then Brett shook his head, slowly. 'I really don't . . . I might have remembered back then. Maybe look at my original statement?'

'Your original statement doesn't mention it.'

Jonah waited, his face fixed in a neutral expression, while Brett thought this over.

'Oh . . . I – I don't know why I didn't think to say. I can't remember. I'm sorry.'

'That's fine, thank you.' Jonah let his eyes wander around the room before coming back to Brett. 'Do you remember that some of the group were concerned about her? That there was some upset over her disappearance?'

'I . . . suppose I do. It's not the clearest thing in my mind from that night, but . . . yes. I think Topaz was a bit concerned. Yes, she was. Because she got a little angry with Aurora when she came back.'

'And you're certain that she'd been swimming?' O'Malley asked.

'Yes.'

'How, if you don't mind my asking?'

'Well, her hair was wet,' Brett replied. 'She was shivering.'

'Do you remember whether anyone went looking for her at that time?'

Brett shook his head. 'No. I don't think they did. I think we thought she'd be back any minute. And when you're a little drunk, it's . . . hard to keep track of time.'

'How drunk would you say you were?' Jonah asked.

'Christ,' Brett said with a short, nervous laugh. 'That's about one of the hardest questions . . . I don't think I was rolling. I was talking, and dancing, and laughing, and I didn't get anywhere near passing out.'

'What were you drinking?'

'Vodka, mostly.'

'Neat?'

'God no,' Brett said, pulling a face. 'With mixers. Tonic. A couple of orange juices.'

'Was that all?' Jonah asked, glancing at O'Malley's scribbled note-taking.

'I think so,' Brett said. 'Someone had some rum, I think, and I might have had one with some Coke. But it's unbelievably sweet. Not my thing.'

'And you're not a beer man?'

'No. I find it foul-tasting, and it's wasted calories,' Brett said. 'Which has always been awkward socially.'

O'Malley laughed. 'Jesus. If you'd grown up in Kilkenny, you'd have been burned at the stake.'

'The others were largely drinking beer, though?' Jonah continued.

'Yes, they were,' Brett agreed. 'Even Aurora, a little. Later on, though. She took some persuading.'

'Who persuaded her?' O'Malley asked.

'All of us to a certain extent,' Brett said, a little awkwardly. 'It's . . . For some reason, when you're kicking back and having fun, having one person in the group who isn't joining in is irritating. I think we peer-pressured her a little. We were teenagers. We thought she couldn't be enjoying herself without alcohol in her.'

'You'd say she enjoyed herself, then?'

'Yes, I'd say so,' Brett replied. 'She was a little quiet after she'd been swimming. I think she was probably cold more than anything, but the fire was going like crazy and she must have thawed out.'

'And then you all persuaded her to try a few beers,' O'Malley said. 'Which helped.'

'Yes, I think it did,' Brett replied. He frowned slightly. 'It can't have been that easy for her. Everyone else liked their drink, and the others liked their drugs.'

'Not you?' O'Malley asked.

'No, not me. I did . . . I did try a very little. I felt like I looked stupid. But a fraction of what they were having, and I didn't snort all of it up. I was too health-conscious. And if it had got out that I'd been taking drugs . . . my career would have been over before it had started.'

'So Aurora stood out,' Jonah went on.

'Yes. She'd clearly never drunk before. And she felt like an outsider, instinctively.'

'But you all put some effort into making her feel welcome?' O'Malley asked.

'Yes. Yes, I'd say so.' Brett nodded. 'Perhaps not Coralie, who was never much good at getting on with people. And Topaz found her sister a little infuriating. But all of us talked to Aurora. She wasn't left alone. It wasn't – She didn't wander off because we were ignoring her. There was nothing cruel or callous about that group. They're nice people.' His eyes were slightly bright, and Jonah nodded.

'We spoke before about the drugs, which we know from several sources belonged to Daniel Benham,' Jonah said, changing tack. 'Was there no discussion about going back for them? About retrieving them?'

'Well, they weren't ours,' Brett pointed out. 'Daniel said he'd take care of it, when the time came. But I suppose he never got round to it.' He gave a slight shrug.

At that point, a knock came at the door, and Hanson appeared round it, on cue. 'Sir?'

Jonah rose. 'If you'll excuse me for a minute.'

He left, and closed the door carefully behind him. Hanson was frowning at him, but Lightman's eyes were on the interview room.

'Are we agreeing with the statements so far?' Jonah asked.

'Some variations,' Lightman answered. 'Topaz, Benners and Coralie all insisted that Aurora didn't drink at all. Jojo also said, at one point in her statement, that Aurora went to bed before the rest of them because she felt lonely.'

'So we're getting a rose-tinted all-nice-people memory from Brett, and a different vision on the drink.' He glanced over at Hanson, who had watched the exchange with an expression of slight concern. 'Any thoughts, Juliette?'

'I wondered . . . Well, I don't think his answers about the swimming were that satisfactory. He remembers that she had wet hair and was shivering, but not how long she might have been gone for. His body language said otherwise, in my opinion. I think he did know how long that interval was. And he didn't confirm that he stayed at the campsite while she was away, even if he didn't go with her at the time. Was he definitely there with the group the whole time? Or had he followed her and had some kind of encounter with her?'

'Good questions, constable,' Jonah agreed. 'To be asked in good time.'

'You're not going after him now?' she asked, looking between him and Lightman.

'No,' Jonah said. 'We've got Daniel Benham to see in five minutes. I'm going to give Brett a little time to consider. He isn't going anywhere.'

Hanson nodded, and gave him a slight smile. 'OK.'

He ducked back inside the interview room. 'I'll have to be a short while, I'm afraid,' he said with regret. 'I'm sorry to leave you hanging around. Can we get you a coffee? A tea?'

'Yes,' Brett said with a slight smile. 'Yes, a tea would be enormously appreciated.'

'Sergeant, could you do the honours? And then I'll need a few minutes of your time.'

14. Aurora

Friday, 22 July 1983, 10:45 p.m.

Benners was already snorting a line by quarter to eleven. Topaz was leaning over him, one hand on his shoulder, to say, 'Go on. Cut me one.'

Aurora sat further away from Benners, next to a banked-up pile of leaves at the edge of the fire. She felt a surge of disappointment in him, though she'd known the drugs were his. This was what he'd come to do.

There was a sudden boom of sound from Connor's portable stereo. A fuzzy bassline Aurora didn't recognize. Over the top of it an electronic sound, and a cracked, hoarse melody.

And then there was a sudden sound next to her, a rustling in the pile of leaves, and Aurora gasped and scuttled backwards.

Jojo, squatting close to her with a beer bottle dangling from one hand, stood quickly. 'What is it?'

'There's . . .' Aurora pointed to the moving leaves, and Jojo moved forward instead of away. She picked up one of the sticks she'd been using to prod the fire, and lifted some of the leaves carefully. And then she grinned.

'It's a hedgehog,' she said. 'Look.'

The ungainly, backside-heavy shape was suddenly uncovered as it shuffled away from the campfire. Aurora watched it waddle off into the darkness, her heart pounding.

'You OK?' Jojo asked.

'Yes, sorry,' Aurora said, trying to laugh as she pulled herself slowly back to where she'd been sitting. She was overwhelmingly glad that the music and the drug-taking had covered up her embarrassing response. 'I was just being stupid.'

'You weren't. Fear is a natural reaction. You need it, sometimes. To tell you when something's really wrong and you should be afraid. Imagine if that had been an adder in there. If you hadn't moved quickly, it could have bitten you.' Jojo squatted back down. 'That's what fear is for.'

She'd stopped looking at Aurora. She seemed to be talking about something else entirely.

'Jojo!' Benners called. 'Come on!'

Jojo rose. She walked round the fire to Benners. She bent low over the top of the stove and inhaled through Benners' rolled-up cigarette paper. Brett was right behind her, laughing as he brushed powder from Topaz's nose.

Aurora felt a twinge of fear. They were all going to do it. They would be something other than themselves from now on. Not only drunk, but wired. High. Different.

The music changed, becoming faster. Upbeat and catchy.

Benners straightened up from the tin with a shout of 'Great track!'

He bounced on his heels and then held a hand out to Topaz. Aurora watched her sister shake her head, smiling slyly, and take Coralie's hand instead. The two of them pressed themselves up against each other, their bodies moving over each other in a well-practised routine. Topaz turned her back and shifted her hips from side to side. She bent her knees to lower herself with each swing, and then raised herself back up again in stages. It was as if she were hearing a different music. A slower and more sensual melody.

Aurora saw Brett's expression. She watched him watching them. She realized that Connor was frozen in place, too. The show wasn't aimed at him, but his reaction was the same. And then she grew tired of that same hungry look they all had, and went to find the marshmallows from the food bags.

15

Hanson was absent from the corridor when Jonah re-emerged.

'Has the constable got bored of my interviewing techniques already?' he asked.

'Topaz Jackson and Connor Dooley arrived,' Lightman answered. 'She's gone to talk to them. You might have a timing issue coming up. Topaz Jackson wants to know what's going on, according to the duty sergeant.'

Jonah glanced at his watch. Three minutes until the next interview was due to start.

'Is Daniel Benham here yet?'

'Not yet.'

Jonah hesitated momentarily before deciding to move on with the interviewees who were here.

'I'll see Topaz and Connor now,' he told Lightman. 'We might need to separate them out if they're giving us the outrage treatment, but I'm not giving them suspect status straight away. Can you meet Benham when he comes in? Make him coffee?'

'Sir.'

'And then come and loiter in the observation room again while I talk to Topaz and Connor. I'll put them in One if it's free.'

He felt more than a little curious as he emerged into CID and saw three figures through the glass wall of his office. He hadn't laid eyes on Topaz or Connor in fifteen or more years. He knew that Connor had become respectable, his scattered tattoos hidden from the world under shirts and academic gowns. He also knew that Topaz had surprised all of her frustrated teachers by becoming hugely focused and driven. She had ultimately gone into management, and excelled at it.

It occurred to him now that they had all of them gone on to be successful. Brett in the most obvious way, but the others as well. With the exception of Jojo all of them had jobs with inherent status: Olympian, executive, professor, politician . . . and what was it Coralie did now? Media? Something fashion-related, he thought.

He wasn't sure why he found their successes so surprising. Perhaps because loss was a sort of damage you carried for life, and yet Topaz and Benners had both gone from lazy students to driven ones; from anti-establishment to firmly pro. Which set Jonah to wondering whether a desire for status was really a sign of health, or was, in fact, the damage he had been looking for.

'What do you think of him?' O'Malley asked.

Hanson glanced in at Brett, who was fiddling with his phone.

'Hard to tell so far. I think he's not telling the truth, the whole truth, and nothing but the truth . . . but then, most people don't.'

O'Malley laughed. 'I meant what you thought of the chief, so.'

'Oh!' Hanson found herself blushing very slightly. 'He seems great. And smart, too. I hope I'm going down OK with him.'

'Ah, you're doing fine.' O'Malley gave her a nod. 'Just go on paying attention and you'll be grand.'

Hanson gave him an awkward smile, and headed back into

CID. She switched on the screen of her desktop PC with a sigh. None of them had given her anything in particular to do. Which meant she'd better start looking at paperwork.

It was hard to look away from Topaz. In part, it was a game of memory. Jonah traced in her only slight changes from that intoxicating fifteen-year-old who had dangled half the boys in their school. The long, dark, glossy hair was much the same. The huge, light-blue eyes barely touched by lines; the prominent lips. And her figure looked like a schoolgirl's, too. Her bare legs were still tanned and smooth, her stomach flat under her white figure-hugging dress. Only her expression had changed. She'd lost the openly flirtatious, knowing glance. She was more brittle and less certain now.

Connor was almost unrecognizable. His skinny frame had bulked out to become stocky. He had grown his buzz-cut hair into a side-parted mane, and the slight waves of it were almost all grey. He had added a short, clipped beard, and with his navy-blue jacket the whole appearance was of privilege and education. Not a trace of that volatile, angry kid whose dad was known to bash him about every so often.

Jonah settled himself in the larger interview room. O'Malley came in a moment later, and pulled up the other chair.

'I'm sorry that the eventual news of Aurora was so sad,' Jonah began. 'It wasn't the news any of us wanted.'

'Can we stop being sorry?' Topaz asked, her voice clipped. 'We've had fifteen minutes of sorry. I want to know what's happening. Have you found out how she died yet? Was it murder?'

Jonah shook his head gently. Tried to soothe. 'We don't know the answer to that yet. I hoped that the two of you might be able to help us.'

Topaz gave a slightly twisted smile. 'More than we did thirty years ago? When we were dragged in for interview after interview and nothing ever came of it?'

'We have more to go on now,' Jonah told her quietly. He glanced at the tape machine. 'Are you happy for me to record this interview?'

Topaz frowned. 'I'm not sure I like the implication.'

Connor leaned forward and put a hand on hers. 'It's OK by me,' Connor said. His voice was perhaps the greatest surprise. No trace of his family's Irish-by-way-of-Southampton. He sounded pure upper-class Edinburgh.

Topaz's mouth moved as she thought. She tucked her lip behind her upper teeth, and then gave a brief sigh. 'All right. You can record it.'

She sat rigidly while the tape was started, and through the introductions made for its benefit. And then she said quickly, 'Tell me what's going on.'

Jonah glanced down at his hands, and then nodded. He decided that shock might be their friend here.

'Aurora was found buried in a drug cache you all knew about. Cause of death is currently unconfirmed.'

There was a pause, and then Topaz said sharply, 'What was she doing in there? What happened to her?'

Jonah found his eyes travelling to Connor. He wondered about him, this changed man. Jonah had been wary of Connor at school thanks to his sudden fits of violence, but he'd also known him as a firm protector of the girls in his group. He was almost old-fashioned in his beliefs. All about virtue, and honour, and female frailty. Which were in some ways the same tenets Jonah's bastard of a father had held.

'We're trying to find out what happened to Aurora,' he said. 'We need your help with that. I want to know how

Aurora ended up with your friends. Was there anyone in particular who invited her? Was it you?'

Topaz did not answer for a moment. Jonah saw the swift cut of her eyes across to Connor, and the slight movement in her mouth, which she then stifled.

'It was all of us,' Connor said.

Topaz gave a slight sigh. 'It was the others really. I didn't want her to be there. I know it's . . . it's not nice. She was my sister. But at that point I found her embarrassing. I found my whole family embarrassing. A scruffy bunch of hippies who had no clue about the modern world.'

Jonah gave a nod. 'Not wanting your sister there isn't a crime.'

'No, I know,' Topaz said, her eyes on the table. 'But I didn't look after her, did I? I didn't make sure she was OK. I was too busy having fun . . .'

Jonah let a brief silence ensue, and then asked quietly, 'Do you remember who suggested it first? If anyone was particularly keen for her to come?'

Topaz shook her head. 'I think everyone felt sorry for her. School was lonely for her.'

Jonah let O'Malley make a note while he asked, 'You don't think any of the boys had a particular interest in her? That they had any designs on her? I'm sorry to ask you in front of your husband, but I am including him in that.'

Topaz's face was immediately full of revulsion. 'No, I don't. She was so . . . so goofy and childish. There's no way.'

He was aware that Connor was watching Topaz, and not him.

'But she was a beautiful girl, your sister,' Jonah pressed. 'Some might not have been put off by her naivety. It might, to be blunt, have excited some of them.'

'That's a horrible thing to say,' Topaz said. 'Just horrible.'

'Well, what about Daniel Benham?' he went on. 'He was only two years older.'

Topaz was shaking her head, and gave a harsh laugh. 'Look, you don't get it. She wasn't fanciable. She wasn't in the least bit sexual. She'd never had a boyfriend and never been asked out. She just drifted around in her own little world, looking at plants and flowers. Up until, I don't know, maybe earlier that year, when she stopped being so gawky and started looking pretty, she wasn't even on anyone's radar. Not even a little. And even then, once everything sorted itself out, she wasn't *sexy*. She was pretty and spacy and a classic hippy love child. She was my baby sister. She wasn't being preyed upon by anyone.'

Jonah didn't respond immediately. He lowered his eyes to his notes, feeling a strange desire to argue with her. To tell her no, the boys had been fascinated with Aurora, even if they weren't sure what to do about it.

The silence was all it took to show the cracks in Topaz's certainty. 'Did you find something?' she asked. 'Had . . . had she been . . .?'

Jonah made a slightly non-committal noise, his attention moving from Topaz to Connor, who had raised his hand to his hair in a jerky motion. Connor looked profoundly uncomfortable.

'We haven't confirmed anything yet. Data analysis for the site isn't back. More coffee?' Jonah asked, looking between the two of them.

'I think we're OK,' Connor said, his voice tight. Jonah nodded slowly, and left them to each other for a while. He could feel the two of them watching him all the way out of the room.

*

Benham looked stressed. More than any of them so far, Jonah thought. His face was pale, and his gaze darted from point to point around the room. He was sweaty, too. Sick-looking.

His solicitor, next to him, was calm. Her jaw was raised in slight belligerence. Forty-something and stocky in a tailored skirt suit, with a Pandora bracelet and a diamanté watch. He didn't know her. She was probably too expensive for most of the people Jonah interviewed.

The taped introductions done, Jonah let a silence elapse. The only sound was O'Malley's periodic rustling of paper as he looked through a printout.

'You wanted to know about the drugs,' Benham said eventually, and his solicitor cast him a sideways glance.

Disapproving, Jonah thought.

'Yes,' he said, 'among other things. We have reason to believe that they belonged to you. Witnesses have confirmed that you purchased them from a contact you had used previously.'

Benham was already opening his mouth to answer when his solicitor said, 'Is this relevant to the current murder investigation?'

'It may be,' Jonah said. 'After all, if the drugs were being sold, the owner stood to lose a great deal if they were discovered. Even as a minor, he'd have been looking at potential correctional time, and certainly his expulsion from school and a permanent blot on his record.'

Benham shook his head. 'That doesn't mean I'd do anything to hurt anyone.'

'Mr Benham is here voluntarily, in order to give information to you as a witness,' his solicitor said quickly and sharply. 'If you wish to question him as a suspect, then you will have to do so under a separate interview.'

Jonah gave her a small smile, then nodded, and carried on. 'I'm not attempting to assert, at this point, that you did anything to protect yourself. But I'm interested in those drugs. The threat of being caught was a motive for anyone in the group. With that in mind, I'd like you to confirm that they were yours, and to indicate where you bought them from, and why.'

His solicitor leaned over to murmur to him, and Benham nodded.

'They were mine, but I'm not going to make any comment beyond that,' he said, 'beyond affirming that they came from someone entirely unconnected with Aurora.'

'Did you intend to sell them?' Jonah persisted.

There was a pause, in which Benham's solicitor shook her head.

'I never had any intention of selling drugs. Any connected with me were for the sole – and free – use of the people around me.'

Jonah couldn't help smiling slightly. It was such a politician's answer.

'What happened to it all afterwards? The Dexedrine?'

'Nothing happened to it, as far as I'm aware,' Benham replied.

'So you left a hefty supply of drugs underground?' Jonah asked. 'You didn't think about the money it represented, or about the chance of it being found and you being in trouble?'

'Are we back to attempting to view my client as a suspect?' his solicitor cut in.

'Not at present,' Jonah said calmly, 'but I do want to know whether you tried to go back there.'

'I think that's connected –'

'It's all right,' Daniel said, holding his hand up to her. 'I'd rather . . . I meant to go back.' He looked up at Jonah. 'I told the others I'd wait till she was found. I thought it'd be quick. And then as time passed, I decided I'd better wait until things were quieter. But it went on, and the longer it went on . . . the more I felt like I couldn't. How could I be worrying about bloody party drugs when Aurora was gone? And there was a bit of me that blamed myself for her vanishing. I felt like I'd failed her. If I'd checked up on her, or slept nearer . . .'

Jonah let the silence extend, but Benham seemed to be done.

'So you never went back.'

'No.'

'And did the others know that?'

Benham pulled a face. 'No, I don't think so. I'd told them to leave it to me, and as time went by I didn't want to admit that I'd left it. So I never went back, and that meant I never found her. And isn't that a big irony? I was thinking about her all the time and she'd have been found years ago if I'd just got on with the job.'

Jonah nodded, slowly. At the front of his mind was the fact that the stash had been lifted, whatever Benham said. Either he had taken it, and thought they were unaware of the size of the original load, or he had no idea that it had gone.

Jonah decided to keep that little piece of information to himself for a while. He sat back, considering. 'Would you mind telling me about your friendship with Aurora? How well did you know her?'

'Not very well,' Benham said. 'Not as well as I knew her sister. And the group of us was really just me, and Topaz, and Connor and Coralie and Jojo. But I'd go round their house now and then, and Topaz and Aurora took the bus back to

Lyndhurst most days as well. I'd talked to her enough to think she was a nice girl.'

'Hmm. So you hadn't ever been involved with her?'

Benham gave him a mystified look. He glanced at his solicitor once again. 'No, I hadn't. I don't think she ever had a boyfriend. Though she didn't exactly tell me everything about herself.'

'Nothing happened between you?' Jonah asked. 'Even on that night? I mean, there was alcohol flowing and you were all taking drugs. Sometimes these things happen.'

'No, it really didn't,' Daniel said firmly. 'I never had that kind of interest in her. I liked her, but that's as far as it went.'

'You weren't worried about her finding out about that Dexedrine, were you?' O'Malley asked, pausing in writing his scrawled notes. 'It must have been a concern.'

'I wasn't worried about her at all.' Benham sat upright. He gave O'Malley a firm look. 'I was pretty uncertain about Brett, who loved to pretend to be more of a bad boy than he was. But not Aurora.'

O'Malley tilted his head. 'You had reason to believe that Aurora was good at keeping secrets, then?'

There was a long pause, in which his solicitor watched him, on the verge of interrupting. And then Benham said, 'Yes, I did. I had reason. She knew quite a bit about me. Not because I'd told her. She stumbled across . . . I'm not one hundred per cent . . . straight, you see.' There was a tension in his voice and in his expression. 'I've had the odd relationship with a boy here and there. One of them was a sixth-former. A drummer in the jazz band. Aurora . . . happened on us. While Topaz was doing dance classes and Aurora took herself for a wander. Waiting for their parents, you know. We were down in the old allotment that backs on to the school sports field. People don't generally go there, so . . .' He tailed off.

Jonah was genuinely surprised by this little confession. He had for some reason always thought of Benham as the guitar-strumming ladies' man. He'd definitely fooled around with a fair few women.

'Did you discuss it with her?'

'Yes. Well, not exactly discussed it.' He grimaced a little. 'She just nodded and left, and I didn't get to see her until the next morning on the bus. I don't think I slept at all. My . . . my father was against all of that. Disgusted by it. He told me once that if I ever came out, I'd be out of the house. That would be it. And of course my mum wouldn't have argued with him.'

He leaned forward to the glass of water on the table and drank a large gulp of it.

'But Aurora was supportive when you spoke to her?' O'Malley asked. 'Said she'd keep it quiet?'

'Yes,' Benham said with a nod. 'I went and sat next to her on the bus. She was usually on her own, so she was . . . She was so obviously delighted that I'd chosen to sit there. Which made me feel pretty terrible. I mean, I'm not giving myself airs, but I'd never really thought about how it felt not to be . . . popular. I tried to sit with her a few times after that. But any-way, when I asked her about it, she was surprised. Honestly, it had never occurred to her that she might tell anyone. Or that anyone might think of doing so. And she didn't breathe a word. Long after the drummer and I had broken up, nobody had ever got to hear about it. She was a kind person, Aurora.'

His eyes were leaking tears, and he picked up his water and finished it.

Jonah waited, watching until the witness's eyes had dried

a little. 'I'm sorry to bring up a lot of unpleasant memories. But it is important that we ask.'

'I understand.'

'Could you tell me whether you believe any of the other members of the group were interested in Aurora? Whether anyone might have become involved with her that night?'

'I . . .' Daniel shook his head. 'I didn't think so. There wasn't necessarily much opportunity. We were all together, and then peeled off to sleep. And Aurora went to bed pretty soon afterwards.'

He could feel the sudden tension in O'Malley.

'According to all six statements from the day after the disappearance,' the DS said, 'Aurora went to bed first. Before any of the rest of you.'

'Sorry, I suppose . . . Right. Right. Well, I'm . . . It wasn't so much that they went to bed. People sort of . . . paired off.'

Jonah gave him a steady look. 'So there was sexual activity occurring between members of the group before her disappearance.'

'I don't know about sexual,' he said hastily. 'You'd have to ask them. Just kissing, from what I saw. And then people drifted off towards the woods.'

'Can you clarify who we are talking about?' Jonah pressed.

'Well, the others. I mean, Topaz, Brett . . . and Connor and Jojo were cuddled up, though I don't think it was any more than that.'

So the media hadn't been far wrong, some of them. Drugs and alcohol and sex, and half the kids only fifteen. It gave Jonah an uncomfortable feeling to hear it, despite his own memories of being that age – parties where couples had disappeared and then re-emerged, clothing on all crooked and a dazed look to them.

'So to clarify,' Jonah said flatly, 'Topaz left the campfire with Brett Parker. And Jojo left with Connor.'

'Yes. Yes, I think so.'

'And you were left with Aurora and Coralie,' O'Malley said.

'No, Coralie . . . Coralie left to go to bed when Topaz did. She wasn't much interested in talking to the rest of us. And Aurora decided to go to bed, to sleep, when she realized that the others were getting up to things. It wasn't really her scene. And I suppose with her sister being involved . . .'

'So, in fact, you were on your own,' O'Malley stated. 'You were left alone, by the fireside, with Aurora. And nobody saw her after that.'

A pause, while Benham's forehead drew into lines. And then he said, 'But someone did, didn't they? Someone killed her and put her in that bloody hole in the ground.'

Lightman had found a comfortable position in the observation room, his weight back on his heels and his arms folded. He'd grown used to this pose, and he didn't resent being the DCI's eyes, ears and memory.

There had been a short silence in the interview room, while Topaz sat back in her chair and folded one leg over the other. Connor had stroked her shoulder at first, and then risen and stretched.

'What if she was raped?' Topaz said, breaking the silence abruptly. 'How are my parents going to deal with it?'

'Maybe they won't need to know,' Connor answered, his hands in his pockets, his head turned to look at her.

'They'll have to know,' Topaz said shortly. 'I don't . . . But she can't have been, can she?' she asked, turning to him. 'I don't see how it can have happened. The chances of some stranger coming along and somehow doing that . . . And . . . she was with us. And it was just us. And Benners and Brett would never have done it.'

Connor shook his head. 'I don't know. I don't think so.'

'Come on,' she said more forcefully. 'Benners wouldn't hurt a fly. And Brett was unconscious.'

Connor turned his head away from her sharply. One hand came up to his mouth.

'And it was Benners who put her to bed, wasn't it?' Topaz went on. 'You said so. And he wasn't gone long.'

'No,' Connor said shortly.

'And you just chatted with Jojo, after that?' she said. Her eyes were on him intently. 'That's what you said, isn't it? You didn't try to follow –'

'Topaz,' he said sharply. And then he glanced over towards the window, where Lightman was watching. It felt to Lightman as though he and Connor were making eye contact for a moment, though he knew Connor could only see himself in the glass. And then Connor turned away again, and started to take short, erratic steps around the room.

Topaz watched him for a while, and then looked instead at her hands, her fingers picking at each other.

'She was checking up on her husband,' Lightman said quietly, once Jonah had returned to the observation room. 'There's clearly doubt there. She's not entirely sure that nothing happened between Connor and Aurora, or that he didn't follow her away from the campfire.'

'I'm going to talk to them again. Come on in with me,' Jonah said.

'How do you want me to play it?'

'Cold.'

126

Connor, who was still pacing, swung round when they entered. Jonah found himself subjected to a piercing gaze, and knew that Connor was looking for signs that they'd been watched. Topaz simply stared at them, her gaze level.

Jonah sat down swiftly. 'Sorry for the wait,' he said, deliberately brisk. 'It's been a busy morning.'

'Do you have a suspect?' Topaz asked immediately.

'We have leads. That's all I can say right now.'

Jonah settled himself back and considered her for a moment. And then he said a little tersely, without turning his head, 'If you wouldn't mind sitting, Mr Dooley.'

Connor approached grudgingly. He made a big deal of adjusting his chair until he was comfortable.

'It seems that parts of both your original statements were less than true,' Jonah said the moment Connor was still. 'Both of you maintained that there were no occurrences of a sexual nature that evening. But we now have evidence that there were multiple instances.'

He saw Topaz's cheek twitch. Connor cut his eyes sideways to his wife and then stared straight back at Jonah. Neither of them spoke.

'It seems that you had some involvement with Brett Parker that night,' he said to Topaz, 'and left the campfire with him.'

Topaz's colour rose. Jonah was aware that she kept her gaze well away from Connor's.

'Yes. Does it matter?'

'At the very least,' Jonah said, not bothering to pull his punches, 'it tells us where you were, when, and with whom. Quite vital information in a missing persons investigation. Why did you lie about it, consistently, at the time?'

Topaz gave him a slightly disbelieving stare. 'We live in a small, gossip-manufacturing community. Do you think I wanted my parents knowing what I was doing? It's bad enough that I didn't look out for Aurora. How do you think they would have reacted to the fact that she went missing while I was having sex with the school jock?'

Jonah let his gaze slide over to Connor. 'And it seems you slept with Jojo Magos that night.'

Connor held up a hand. 'I didn't even come close. Jojo comforted me when I got drunk and emotional, and she cuddled up next to me to sleep because she's kind like that, but there was nothing sexual about it.'

'What did you get emotional about?' Jonah asked.

'Topaz,' Connor said shortly. 'And Brett.'

Jonah let a long pause elapse. Connor held Jonah's gaze, his chin slightly raised and his mouth hard.

'Ask Jojo,' Connor eventually said. 'She'll tell you exactly the same thing.'

Jonah gave a very slight lift of his shoulder, and shifted in his chair. 'So you didn't have any sexual interaction with anyone that night? Not with Coralie? Not with Aurora?'

'Of course not with Aurora!' Connor said aggressively. 'And Coralie and I pretty much hated each other.'

'Nothing's changed, has it?' Topaz broke in, in a high-pitched, bitter voice. 'We're right back where we were. The two of us being torn to shreds, and the police not looking anywhere else. Why didn't that happen to any of the adults in her life? Like that creepy English teacher of hers? I told dozens of you that he was the one you should be asking. He was right there!'

Jonah was momentarily thrown off balance. 'What do you mean by "right there"?'

'Seriously?' Topaz replied, lifting her hands. 'You've read up on our sex lives, and missed the only significant thing I

128

saw?' She leaned forward and spoke loudly, as if to an idiot. 'Mr Mackenzie. Her English teacher. The one who used to give her extra lessons. He was out camping in the woods too. I spoke to him on the riverbank, and he said he had to walk another couple of miles. And then took a path straight past our stash.'

Jonah had nothing to say to this immediately. He recognized the name, and thought he could remember the man, but that was all.

'Jesus,' Topaz said, sitting back. 'Have you even read what we said back then?'

'We're wading through it,' Jonah said with a wry smile.

'He could easily have seen where the drugs were. Easily.'

'That's useful,' Jonah said, rising. 'Thank you. You're both free to go for now.'

He paused outside the door to confer with Lightman. 'Was there much in the statements about her teacher?' Jonah asked over his shoulder. 'Mr Mackenzie? Her English teacher?'

'I think Topaz asked if they'd talked to him,' Lightman said. 'But nothing more concrete in the first few interviews.'

Jonah nodded, and now remembered what it was that rang a bell about Mackenzie. It had been Topaz, bursting into the old police station, almost hysterically.

'You've already asked me everything.' She was almost shouting at the DC who was showing her up to CID. 'You've asked me over and over and over. Why aren't you asking Mr Fucking Mackenzie, hey? He's been carrying on happily with his lessons. Why are the rest of us the ones suffering?'

He should have remembered this. He'd even gone and asked his patient DCI about it.

'Look, I'm not involved,' he'd told him. 'Anything I do

know is the shortest of updates from the super. Mackenzie is apparently a total non-starter. He had an alibi for the entire evening.'

And yet Topaz had been determined he should be a suspect. There had to be a reason, however flimsy. Unless she had latched on to him as an alternative suspect, to take the heat off her friends.

He let himself out into CID, and glanced around vaguely until he found Hanson, who was standing alongside the big black-and-white printer as it spewed out pages.

'Can you look into something for me, please?' he asked her.

'Sure,' she said, glancing down at the printer display and then back up with a smile.

'There was a school teacher of Aurora's. An Andrew Mackenzie. I want to know if anything was said about him in the original reports, and what lines of enquiry were pursued.'

Hanson nodded. 'I've got ten more pages to print, and then I'm on it.'

16. Aurora

It was somehow the loneliest she had ever felt, despite the music, and the laughter, and the occasional cajoling. They wanted her to dance, to drink, to enjoy herself. She knew why. She was a constant irritation. A nagging sense of non-fun. But the more they pressed, the more she could feel herself retreating inwards. The more she became rigid and isolated.

She'd rarely had anyone to talk to at school parties, either. Her closest friend, Becky, was never allowed to go to any of them. Her mother, who looked after her alone and generally seemed to confuse love with feeding up, wanted her home safely as soon as school was done, in spite of Becky's desperation to join in.

Earlier in the year, it had seemed like her loneliness had been solved. Kind, lovable Zofia had arrived like a ray of sunshine into Aurora's life. She'd come with Aurora whenever she was going to be dumped somewhere with Topaz, and she'd chattered away to her in her strange English and made her feel like she was liked.

And then Zofia had been snatched away again. All because of one stupid night.

The thought of all that was still too fresh and too painful. She closed her eyes against it briefly, and against finding herself alone again, and feeling like she was separated from these friends of Topaz's by hundreds of miles.

When she opened them again, it was all still the same. She was still here.

She found herself watching Jojo after that, reassured by the difference between her and the other girls. Jojo chose to dance on her own, and to lose herself in the rhythm without ever worrying how she looked. Once or twice, Aurora found herself envying her. She wondered if she could be like her if she tried: capable, and wild. Aurora thought Jojo was quite beautiful in her wildness.

Perhaps that was the only way to be, when she could never be like her sister and her hip-grinding sexuality.

Even Benners was dancing: head back, bouncing on his heels, one hand tucked into his chest so that he could hold his hip flask. He'd stopped looking like the Benners she knew.

But it was Benners who eventually tired of the movement and came to sit with her. He dropped down next to her heavily and then had to use a hand to steady himself. He laughed, and swigged from the hip flask.

Aurora could smell the alcohol on him. She wondered if she smelled of the lemonade she was making her way through.

'I've felt like that before,' he said with a grin.

'Like what?'

'Like I wasn't part of anything. Like I was totally alone and unnoticed, and the more I thought about it, the more alone I became. Actually, it happens to me quite often.' He nodded at her obvious surprise. 'Too much thinking. If you think and think and think, then it becomes like a barrier between you and everything else. You can't enjoy anything, and all you're focused on is how wrong it all feels. How much you wish you were somewhere else.'

'I suppose so.' Aurora nodded.

'But I'll tell you something,' Benners went on, leaning towards her to speak earnestly. Puffing fumes into her face. 'And it's important, Aurora. Because you're this smart person and you've got a lot to give. A lot more than most of these.'

He paused, waiting, and Aurora dutifully asked, 'What?'

'You should never wish you were somewhere else,' he said, picking up her hand and squeezing it for emphasis. 'Never. No matter what you're doing, embrace it. Being away in your world and your head is important sometimes, but so is living. You need to let real life in to your experiences. You need to feel all this and let yourself get caught up in it. And that's about making a decision. A decision to enjoy it.'

Aurora shook her head slightly. 'It's just not really my thing.'

'That's not what you should be saying,' he said, for a moment almost aggressive. 'You should never say that. You haven't tried it. How the fuck do you know if it's your thing? You need to tell yourself that everything is your thing. And if you want to get joy out of your life, you should launch yourself into everything that happens. Because once you've done that, and . . . committed to it, and embraced it, it *will* be your thing. There's nothing out there that isn't for you. You just need to give the world a chance.'

She studied his fierce expression. She had a strange sensation of being poised on the edge of something. She wondered whether he was right, and she had a choice. Whether she could be more things than she believed. Whether she was losing out on some part of herself.

Benners swigged again from his polished silver hip flask, and then paused. He looked at it, and then held it out towards her.

'It's your choice,' he said with a level gaze.

And then Aurora took a breath in and held out her disposable plastic cup. She let him fill up her cup with whatever it was he was drinking. It went into the lemonade like oil into water.

Benners smiled at her. A real, warm smile. He held up the hip flask. 'To giving everything a chance,' he said, and she drank as he did, almost appreciating the burning tang in her drink after so much sickly sweetness.

17

The phone records clearance had arrived from the chief super by the time Jonah was back at his desk, and he immediately sent it over to Intelligence for action. Which meant, generally, filing an online form request through each network provider.

It was actually laughably easy to request phone records. There were only a very few carrier companies that requested proper authorization. It was an issue that Jonah had always found disquieting. It should take more than a simple online form to grant access to every call and text message someone had made for some months.

Lightman had tapped on his door before he'd had a chance to catch up on the notes his team had logged on the system.

'Coralie Ribbans has arrived downstairs,' he said. 'She says she needs to talk to you.'

Jonah was both curious and a little exasperated. He'd left multiple messages for Coralie to call them, and here she was instead, in person, without warning. But the timing could be worse. Jojo Magos wasn't due for a while, and he could probably push her back a bit.

'If you can find her an interview room, and see Jojo Magos later this afternoon, I'll see Coralie Ribbans now,' he said, and pulled up the electronic versions of Coralie's statements from 1983. The few paragraphs he was able to read were along the same lines as the others' had been. She was adamant that there had been no excessive drinking, and that there had been no arguments, no sex, and no drugs. Which was to say, she'd lied as much as the others had.

But Coralie seemed to want to talk to them about something, and Jonah felt that she might be a useful resource. Her life had taken a different path to her friends', and she had not remained close to any of them. In fact, nobody had so far mentioned Coralie as a good friend, and Jojo had said they didn't get on.

So perhaps Coralie, the one Londoner of the group, had become an outsider. Perhaps she was no longer as loyal to her friends as she had once been.

After a few minutes, he caught sight of a blonde-haired woman making her way through the office outside with Lightman. It took Jonah no time at all to recognize her. He might have missed her in a crowd, but with her in front of him there was no question that this was Topaz's constant shadow.

Topaz still looked like she had as a teenager, but Coralie seemed to want to look like a kid's idea of a princess. Her jewellery was diamanté and sparkling; her hair in a braided bun. The short skirt she wore was flared and layered with netting between pieces of white fabric, and the top she wore was a tight-fitting, sleeveless pink.

He watched her until Lightman had shown her into the interview suite, and then glanced over at Hanson, who had returned to her desk.

He opened his door, and called, 'Would you like to sit in on an interview?'

Hanson looked up, and beamed at him. 'I'd love to,' she said, turning her computer screen off immediately.

Jonah could smell Coralie's sweet, candy-like perfume the moment he and Hanson were through the door. He felt slightly nauseated.

'Ms Ribbans,' he said, settling himself. 'I'm DCI Sheens, and this is Constable Hanson. Thanks for coming in.'

'Whatever I can do to help.'

He tried to remember whether the high-pitched, front-of-mouth lisp was new or had always been there. A strange thing in someone in her forties, whose face had laughter lines and furrows under the make-up.

He could tell she didn't recognize him. Jojo had been the only one to realize he'd been at school with them. He supposed he had been unimportant to the rest of them. Peripheral.

'We'd like to hear from you afresh what happened the night Aurora disappeared,' he said. 'We're re-opening the investigation, and that means starting again. I'm hoping you'll have some information that was missed the first time round.'

'Yes, I . . . I said a lot, but I think there are some small things. Things we didn't want everyone to know in case we got in trouble.'

The phrasing and her manner, which was of a sheepish child instead of a fully grown woman, was a little uncomfortable to hear.

'We've heard a few things along those lines,' Jonah said carefully. 'I'd like to take you through that evening and just clarify a few things.'

He brushed over the arrival at the camp, and got quickly on to the argument between Topaz and Benners.

'You went with Topaz, I think?' he asked her.

'Yes, I did. I calmed her down, and then she said she wanted to sit by the river alone for a while, so I headed back to the campsite.'

'Did you also see Andrew Mackenzie, an English teacher from your school, at the river?'

137

Her expression turned to confusion. 'Mr Mackenzie? The young guy? He wasn't there.'

'You mean he wasn't camping with you?'

'No, I mean he can't have been nearby. Or at least none of us saw him. We all talked about it a lot afterwards and nobody ever said anything about him being there.'

Jonah nodded, glancing through his notes as if moving on to the next point, while his mind was on Topaz. She had seen Mackenzie, and gone on to point the finger at him. But for some reason she'd decided not to tell her closest friend. And none of the others had mentioned Mackenzie, either. Which implied that Topaz hadn't told anyone except the police. It was a very interesting omission.

'Let's look at the later part of the evening now,' he said. 'Despite your original statements, we've learned that Topaz and Brett Parker paired off. They went to have sex together, is that right?'

Coralie's expression took on a strange sort of amusement. 'Is that what Topaz told you?'

'It's been commented on by more than one of your group,' Jonah replied.

'That's interesting. Because it wasn't Topaz and Brett who had sex. It was all three of us, which was how Topaz liked to play it.'

Hanson, next to him, drew in a slightly sharp breath. But when he glanced over at her there was no visible reaction. He approved.

'It was all about seducing Brett,' Coralie went on. She tucked her hair behind her ear and shifted with a glance at the reflective glass. Did she think she had a larger audience? 'Topaz was fixated on him. He was attractive and sporty, and pretty much everyone at school wanted him. Topaz was used to being the desirable one, so she decided to go and get him. Only Brett proved to be tricky. He'd been . . . interested in someone else.'

'One of the group?' Jonah asked, curious about how awkward she suddenly looked. Had there been something more between Coralie and Brett?

'No, no,' she said quickly. 'Someone at school. We'd all been at the same party, a week or two before, and Brett . . . kissed someone else. Even though Topaz was there, and looking gorgeous. He went after a blonde girl from the year below.'

'The year below him?'

'The year below us,' Coralie said in a quiet voice.

He watched her thoughtfully. 'So he was interested in someone who was, what? Fourteen at most?'

'Yes. She didn't look fourteen,' Coralie replied. 'She was really tall and skinny, and looked like an underwear model or something. Nowhere near as sexy as Topaz, but still.'

'So you think Brett didn't know the girl's age?' he asked.

'I guess not,' Coralie said. 'But next time Topaz talked to him, he didn't seem interested. I think he was still keen on the blonde.'

Jonah took a note of that, thinking that if eighteen-year-old Brett Parker had liked younger girls, then he might have pursued Aurora that night, in spite of what everyone said.

'So what happened that night?' he asked, moving the conversation on.

Coralie pursed her lips and chewed a fragment more off her nail. 'Topaz wanted Brett to want her. So we did our usual thing. She kissed me in front of him, and then let him join in when he got excited.'

Jonah wondered why Daniel Benham hadn't mentioned this. Perhaps he hadn't felt it was his secret to tell. Or perhaps

Coralie was nothing more than a fantasist. But he got the impression this was more about telling tales on her friends in reaction to some perceived slight.

'So Aurora knew?' he asked.

'She saw us going off together.' Coralie was nodding.

Jonah made another note. He wondered exactly how concerned Topaz might have been about her parents finding out. Concerned enough to kill her sister? That would have been a pretty extreme reaction.

'And Aurora wasn't involved at any point,' he said. 'She wasn't a fourth member.'

The instinctive curl of Coralie's lip was almost comical. 'Are you serious? Topaz would have run a mile. And Aurora wouldn't have gone near that whole scene. She looked like she wanted to throw up as it was. Bloody prude.'

Jonah had to work quite hard not to suppress a smile. It was refreshing to hear someone talking about an exotic sex life without shame. For some reason police interviews always made people want to underplay everything.

'Was Aurora still there when you returned?'

'We didn't come back to the camp,' Coralie said, shaking her head. 'We were all of us drunk and we passed out. We didn't see her after that.'

'So you were asleep from then until morning?'

Coralie's mouth tightened. After a momentary pause, she said, 'No. No, I wasn't. I got up.'

Jonah glanced down, as if checking the original statement. 'That contradicts what you said originally,' he said neutrally.

'I know it does,' she said. 'Everyone told me not to say anything. They thought . . . they thought the police would grab hold of it. Because he was already being grilled. And I suppose I felt sorry for him . . .'

He heard Hanson shift in her chair next to him, and was aware that she knew as well as he did who Coralie was talking about. For the sake of the tape, however, he needed Coralie to say it.

'Can you tell me who you're talking about?'

'Connor,' Coralie said, and there was a real intensity to the way she said his name. Jonah could feel her antipathy. 'Connor Dooley. He told the police he went to sleep next to Jojo and didn't get up again. But he did. He got up, and he was sitting by the fire on his own when I got up.'

'You saw him there?' Jonah asked her quietly.

'Yes. I needed to pee.' She fidgeted slightly and dropped her gaze, making him wonder whether that was really what she had been doing. Had she got up to take more drugs? To be sick?

'What time was this?'

'Oh . . . I'm not sure.' She lifted a shoulder in a shrug. 'It was later on. I'd been asleep for a while, and then woken up again.'

'Brett and Topaz were both still there when you woke up?'

'Yes,' she said firmly. 'I crept away from them both and went towards the campfire.'

'You didn't just find a nearby bush?' Jonah queried.

'I don't . . . I was a bit disorientated, I suppose. I can't really . . . The fire would have been bright, I guess, so I headed that way.'

'You think the fire was still visibly burning at that point?'

'Yes. I think so.'

'And as you approached, can you explain what you saw?'

'I saw Connor Dooley,' she said, more certainly. 'He was sitting by the fire, with a can of beer.'

'Did he see you?'

'No,' Coralie answered swiftly. 'I backed away. He looked . . . angry.'

Jonah watched her as she shifted in her seat, the nails of her right hand tapping the table gently.

'Why do you think he was angry?'

She gave him a direct look. 'Topaz had gone off with me and Brett, and Connor hated it. He was obsessed with her.'

'You think his attitude to Topaz was unhealthy?'

'Damn right I do,' Coralie said. 'She didn't want to know, and she'd made it very clear to him a lot of times. But he still chased boys away whenever he could, and watched her with this . . . possessiveness.'

'Yet they ended up married,' Jonah pointed out. 'So Topaz must have had some interest.'

'I never understood it,' Coralie said with sudden emotion. Jonah could see reflections in her eyes. She was struggling with tears, thirty years on. 'It all changed that night, and suddenly Topaz was all about Connor. She shut me out . . .'

'Do you have any thoughts on what that might have been?' he asked.

'I wish I knew,' Coralie said.

Jonah let a silence elapse, waiting for more, but Coralie seemed to have come to a stop. He left with an image of Connor, alone and angry, burned into his mind's eye.

18. Aurora

It was a switch that had tripped in her head. She didn't even need to try. She was drinking and chattering next to the dimming fire, first just to Benners, and then to Jojo and Connor as they came to take a break from their manic movement. Topaz and Coralie were standing with Topaz's arm slung round little Coralie's shoulders, the two of them talking quietly to Brett. She wasn't worried what Topaz thought any more. Let her sister do what she wanted, and Aurora would do the same.

'We should cycle somewhere next week,' Jojo said, and Aurora got the feeling she'd missed some of the earlier conversation.

Connor shook his head at her. 'We only just cycled here.'

'No, I mean somewhere proper. A long ride. And then camp, and then ride again. Actually get somewhere. You got a bike, Aurora?'

'Yeah,' she said, considering her tatty, pale-purple town bike with its basket. 'It's a bit crap, to be honest.'

'We don't have to go fast,' Jojo said, grinning. 'And Benners is useless on a bike, anyway.'

'Like, a few nights in a row?' Connor asked, frowning.

'Yeah. Like a holiday.'

Connor's expression suddenly seemed a little angry. 'I can't do a holiday, Jojo.'

'It won't cost anything,' she argued.

'Doesn't matter. My dad would go mental. He's going to expect me to be working.'

'But it'd just be a few days,' Benners said. 'I'm sure you can talk him into being away for a few days.'

'You don't have a fucking clue, do you?' Connor was suddenly savage. 'Not a fucking clue. Either of you. Half the time it's enough of an argument getting him to let me come to school, when there's actual work I could be doing. Making money for him out of car parts, which are usually fucking stolen, or hiding things for him because he's heard the rozzers are doing the rounds. And despite him being the one who's dragging me through all his shit, it's me who gets knocked over if something goes wrong. How exactly do either of you think I'm going to persuade him to let me go on a fucking holiday?'

'Hey, hey,' Jojo said. 'I'm sorry. My fault. It wasn't fair. We'll find other stuff to do.'

She rubbed his shoulder. Connor was shaking, full of that fury that verges on tearful.

'We'll find other stuff to do,' she repeated, and pressed the side of her head against his.

'I just want to leave,' he said. 'I want to move out, but then I'd have to get a job somewhere. I wouldn't be able to stay at school.'

'Don't be soft,' Benners said. 'If you think my family's going to stand by and let you get a job when you're the smartest person in the country, you're not using your brain. My dad likes you better than he likes me. You're not on your own.'

'I can't do that,' Connor said quietly. 'I can't take someone else's money.'

'You can if they want you to,' Benners said.

'And if you don't want to move into posh land,' Jojo said, 'my brother's room'll be free from September. You can stay there.'

She squeezed Connor's hand. Aurora could see their sympathy undermining Connor's anger. It was driving the tears closer to the surface.

'Come on. Do another line with me and think about fun things,' Jojo added.

Benners stood up unsteadily.

'I want to dance. You're up, Aurora. Time to embrace another part of life.'

She only hesitated for a moment before taking his hand. She let him pull her a little way from the red-orange fire. He spun her awkwardly under his arm. The music was a little bit angrier now. Another song she didn't know.

As she started to listen to it, she found herself smiling. It reminded her of Connor, suddenly bursting into vocal rage before quieting down. It didn't suit the way Benners was holding and spinning her, like some inept ballroom dancer. She started to laugh.

'What?' he asked, as he tried to swing her round and tripped over a stick. He was grinning. Laughing along with her.

'It's like your arms and legs aren't even attached to you,' she said.

'You have no appreciation of my art.'

She felt her self-consciousness leak away. She was careless and light.

He spun her round by both hands, fast enough that she was leaning backwards against the spin. Then she screeched, half laughing, as she came close to the fire. Benners bent his arms and she was pulled towards him. She almost fell into him, and was breathless with laughter.

'Sorry,' Benners said, still holding on to her left hand.

'Seriously, Benners.' Connor was behind her, speaking over her shoulder. 'You're a disgrace.'

She looked round at him. He had a slightly glassy-eyed look. She wondered if that was what the drugs did. Jojo was crouched down behind him, rubbing at her nose. How much had they had?

Connor took Aurora's free hand, and pulled her into a different sort of hold. One that was closer, and a lot stronger. She was surprised by how strong Connor was. She hadn't expected it.

Benners released the hand he was still holding, and she put it on Connor's shoulder. She wasn't sure if it was because she wanted to enter into the hold, or to keep him a little way away from her.

'Try some real dancing.'

He began to nod to the beat, the pulse of it running through him. As he moved, it moved her, and she was shifting with him.

The carelessness left her in a rush. She was suddenly very aware of each and every part of her body. And of how she must look to him. Of her straggly, badly dried hair and her cheap nylon skirt.

And of him. And how he looked. That he was close enough for her to smell cheap aftershave and sweat. That he was smiling at her warmly, the boy who had always wanted her sister.

Topaz was watching her, too, but for the first time Aurora didn't care. Let her look. Aurora was going to give this a chance, like Benners had said, and her sister would have to learn to live with it.

19

Connor looked quietly angry as Jonah and O'Malley got themselves set up opposite him.

'Have you been offered a tea?' Jonah asked, deciding to give it a few minutes before the hard-line questioning.

'I'm fine, thank you,' Connor said coolly.

Jonah almost smiled. He guessed that Professor Dooley was used to having an effect when he was angry. It slid off Jonah like melting ice.

'So,' Jonah said, once the tape was running. 'A few things have come up during our investigation that we would like your help with.'

'I'm sure,' Connor answered, his eyes hard behind his glasses.

'By your account,' Jonah said, 'you went to bed after Topaz left with Brett Parker. Although we've since been told that she left with Brett and Coralie, and not with Brett alone.'

There was a brief silence, and then Connor shrugged. 'I don't really remember all that clearly. I know she used Coralie to draw him in. What happened after that . . . didn't really interest me.'

'You didn't see them leave together?'

'I don't really remember,' Connor said quietly.

'OK. But moving on from there,' he said. 'You've told us already that you went to sleep alongside Jojo Magos, and that she comforted you about Topaz and Brett. You didn't mention getting back out of bed at any point.'

'That's because I didn't.' Connor's voice was flat.

'Unfortunately, we have reason to believe otherwise,' O'Malley said, from a very relaxed pose.

There was another silence, while Connor looked momentarily at a loss. 'I'm sure – I'm sure I didn't get up.'

'So how were you seen by the fire, alone, after everyone else was in bed?' Jonah asked.

Connor shook his head. And then he sat forward, becoming more definite. 'Look, that's not something anyone has ever said to me. Back in eighty-three, we did a lot of talking, trying to piece things together. Why would it suddenly come up now?'

'The witness said there was a lot of pressure not to inform the police.'

Connor's eyes were moving, either in an effort to remember, or in an effort to think of some defence.

'No,' he said. 'I really wasn't up. I may have been drunk but I wasn't that bloody drunk. I would have remembered getting up. The first I knew of Aurora being missing was the next morning, and it took a good while to put two and two together even then.'

'And nothing happened with Aurora earlier in the evening? Before you'd gone to bed? Perhaps before Jojo comforted you?' O'Malley asked.

'For god's sake,' Connor said, putting his head down and rubbing at his forehead. 'How many times do I have to say it? Nothing happened with Aurora. Not with me, and not with any of the others as far as I know.'

'Then why,' Jonah said coldly, 'was your wife worried that you'd followed Aurora after she left?'

Connor started, and looked up at Jonah with an expression that was suddenly uncertain.

'I don't – Topaz wasn't unsure . . .'

'She felt it necessary to check with you about what had happened,' Jonah said. 'Thirty years on, she still felt that she needed to ask you what had really happened. I'd say that's very unsure.'

Connor shook his head. 'You're . . . you're misunderstanding the conversation.'

'What other reading can you give to that? I would welcome your insight.'

Connor looked down at the table, and said nothing.

'So do you want to tell me what triggered Topaz's concern?' Jonah asked.

'All right,' Connor said. 'It's not a big deal, but it could be easily misinterpreted. I tried . . . to kiss her.'

'Aurora?'

'Yes, Aurora.'

Jonah raised his eyebrows. 'You tried to kiss this fourteen-year-old, apparently unfanciable girl?'

'Look, I didn't . . .' Connor sighed, and looked up again, with an appeal in his expression. 'It wasn't about fancying her. It was about making Topaz jealous. I thought if I danced with Aurora, it would piss her off. And it did, but unfortunately she responded by trying harder with Brett. And when that happened, and she kissed him . . . I just . . . I tried to kiss Aurora, too.'

'Aurora wasn't interested?'

'Who would be interested in someone clearly using them?' he asked, with a shake of his head. 'No, she wasn't. And she told me to get off, so I did. At which point, she left the camp-site, and I went and sobbed my heart out to Jojo.'

'Would you say you were angry about that?' Jonah asked, his voice deliberately harsh. 'It must have been a real blow to your pride.'

'It was humiliating,' Connor said flatly. 'I felt like a total idiot, and like a shit for upsetting Aurora. But the only person I was angry with was myself.'

'Not with Brett Parker?' Jonah asked. 'I mean, he was off shagging your future wife.'

'No.'

'And not with the second girl who had rejected you that night?' he pressed.

'Of course not,' Connor protested. 'It wasn't her fault.'

'Because I could see you being angry about that,' Jonah went on. 'I could see you waking up again, and stewing on it. Going to the campfire and brooding, and then deciding that Aurora was going to take it.'

'Jesus,' Connor said. 'I did nothing like that.'

'I mean, you'd tried to kiss her in front of everyone. Maybe you'd got a little excited while dancing with her,' Jonah said, as if he hadn't spoken. 'You were a very volatile person, and your pride meant a lot to you. You probably felt you were owed a bit of a ride after everything Topaz had put you through.'

'Stop it!' Connor said, and Jonah could see that he was shaking slightly. He took a deep breath, and said, 'Everything you are saying is horrible. I didn't touch the poor kid after that. I left her to sleep. And then in the morning she was gone.'

Jonah let a silence elapse before he turned off the tape and suggested a break in the interview. Connor was still shaking by the time he and O'Malley had reached the door.

Hanson forced herself to stop looking at Connor Dooley's files after a good half an hour of browsing. He'd been in the interview room a good ten minutes, and she couldn't shake the feeling that focusing on anything else was wasting time now.

But she needed to do her job, even if that meant filling time with pointless asides. She exited Connor's entries in their file manager, and decided to search for Andrew Mackenzie instead, as the DCI had asked her to do. He'd insisted, firmly, that while Connor was a clear priority, there was reason enough to look at other people, and at the teacher in particular.

Mackenzie's police record was pretty quick reading. There had been only one interview with him, in which he'd explained that he had been camping with his girlfriend a few miles away and hadn't left her side all night. The account hadn't, as far as she could see, been checked. Which went straight on to her list of bad original investigative work.

Having finished that, she decided to google him, although with a name like Andrew Mackenzie, it wasn't going to be all that easy. She decided to add in 'teacher Southampton', and found what she thought was the man. There were a few articles where he'd been interviewed about particularly successful students. The pictures showed a broad-faced, stocky man looking terribly posh in chinos and a shirt. There was also a page about a charity hike in Corsica, and he was the founder of a website dedicated to reading Yeats's poetry in dramatic locations, which made her snigger.

And then there was an article about the retirement party of a Roald Mackenzie, who had been a DCS at the Met. Curious, she clicked on it to find any reference to Andrew, and read a brief interview with 'Roald's nephew, school teacher Andrew Mackenzie'.

'Jesus,' she said under her breath. So Mackenzie had been well connected with the police. No wonder he'd been deliberately missed.

She found it difficult not to jump up and tell Lightman straight away. But she could see that he was focused on his screen, a small frown on his face. And it was Sheens she needed to be telling this to really.

So she sat and reread the article, her foot jiggling with impatience as she waited for the chief to reappear.

Jonah left the interview suite full of the uncomfortable buzzing that filled him when he'd brought out the harsh questions. It was like the feeling when he'd had too much coffee. A tetchy restlessness that started to look for another target.

It was at times like this – and only at times like this – that he thought be began to understand his father. He was filled with a sort of righteous fury at the lies suspects told, and with an urge to beat them down until they admitted the truth.

What he'd said to Connor had been mild. He could go a lot further, though he didn't like himself a lot when he did. And that was difficult when it was one of the things that made him really good at his job.

It almost helped that Connor couldn't quite seem to remember what he'd done. It was an uncomfortable echo from Jonah's own past. He wanted to attack Connor for it, perhaps because he was tired of attacking himself.

'I don't know whether I believe him,' O'Malley said, catching up with him at the door to CID. 'Part of me thinks that's how I'd react if someone said that to me. And part of me thinks it's how a guilty man would react.'

'It's a hard one to call,' Jonah agreed. 'I want to give him some time to worry. And we need time to find further evidence. That's got to be the priority now. If he got up, and he raped her, there must be some way of proving it beyond Coralie's testimony.'

He caught the swift movement of Hanson's head and her scramble to rise as he walked back into CID.

'What have you got?' he asked her.

'Andrew Mackenzie,' she said, with what was almost a smile. 'He was only interviewed once, during which he provided an alibi. He explained that he'd camped overnight with his girlfriend, and never left her side.'

'Did she agree?'

'They never checked with her,' Hanson said with a note of triumph. 'Which seemed breathtakingly bad investigative work, but, in fact, may be worse than that. Mackenzie's uncle was a DCS in the Met at the time.'

'You're serious?'

'I am.' Her expression broke through into a full smile. 'Good thing he gave an interview at the super's retirement do, or I might not have got the connection.'

He couldn't share her excitement. Aside from the anger that he was still struggling to pack away, he'd seen enough corruption investigations to last a lifetime. They'd damaged both individual officers and the reputation of the force. If it turned out that there was a huge apology to be made for a killer remaining free for thirty years, Jonah did not want to be in the middle of it.

But what he wanted didn't really feature. There was no question that they needed to interview Mackenzie.

'Did you find out where he is now?'

'Yeah, he's head of department at a private school in Bristol.'

'Call the school, and tell them we need to speak to him,' he said. 'Today.'

He glanced at his watch and saw that it was almost two. Lunchtime had vanished somewhere into the cycle of interviews.

'And can you please apologize to Jojo Magos, and ask if I can see her either this evening or tomorrow? Ben can come with me and talk to this teacher.'

Lightman raised his head and gave an impassive nod. 'Are we shelving the briefing, then?' The sergeant unplugged his iPad from his desktop machine and stood.

'Yup, I'm moving it till later. If we've got to get to Bristol, I want to go now. I'll update you on a few things from this morning and let the other two know later on. Oh, and we need to tell Connor Dooley he's free to go.'

'I'll do that,' O'Malley offered.

'Good.'

'What shall I do after I've talked to the school?' Hanson asked. He could sense her disappointment. She'd been eager to go and interview another suspect. But he generally found it better to pull rank at expensive schools. A DCI and a DS were a good combination.

'Follow up with McCullough on any new forensics, and update us while we're driving. I want evidence against Connor Dooley if it exists. We'll talk to Mackenzie and see if that one's a runner.'

She sat at her desk silently.

'That was good work connecting him to the detective chief super,' he said. It was a slightly clumsy attempt to console her.

She gave a small nod, and focused on her screen.

The rain was starting as they left the station, and it had become a real storm before they hit the M3, a wall of water battering the car roof. He'd grabbed a sandwich from the canteen to wolf on the way, but it was hard to control the car and eat, so he gave up and left it till later.

He thought about talking through the case so far with Lightman, but it seemed like a mess at the moment. There were so many inconsistencies between all the statements that he didn't know where to start.

All they could be certain they had was a group of drugged-up, drunk fifteen-to-eighteen-year-olds and an innocent fourteen-year-old, who had gone to sleep at some distance away. Plus one school teacher, a few miles off and camping with a girlfriend. And a huge stash of Dexedrine.

Aurora may or may not have been drunk. They all may or may not have been high. The drugs had been removed later, maybe by arrangement, and maybe not.

There were many apparently insignificant lies being told. The friends were trying to protect themselves. But they might well be masking the truth of what happened behind their lies. There might be more about Connor, for one. Coralie had waited thirty years to tell them about seeing him by the fire. It all needed breaking down, lie by lie.

At that point, he remembered how Topaz had hidden her meeting with Mackenzie. Together with a failure to investigate him, there were clearly grounds for looking at Mackenzie.

'What do you have on the teacher?' he asked Lightman.

'Constable Hanson sent through Topaz's original statement. She did mention seeing Andrew Mackenzie,' he said, referring to his iPad as he spoke. 'But it was quite briefly mentioned, and she stressed that it had been a lot earlier in the evening. She thought it might be worth checking up on him. She didn't mention him again during those first few days.'

Jonah tried to dredge up some of his own memories of Mackenzie. The English teacher had joined only a term before Jonah left. He'd been young; Jonah remembered that much. He'd looked barely older than a sixth-former, broad-faced and sporty, in a slightly stocky way. More of a sprinter than a long-distance runner.

Had it been Mackenzie that the girls in his year had been crazy for, he wondered, suddenly? Or had that been the sports teacher? It had been one of them. And if they had been crazy about him, maybe Aurora had been besotted with him, too.

The M4 junction suddenly loomed up on his left. Jonah realized that he had the audio switched off on the satnav and had almost missed it. He signalled left and started to pull into the inside lane. And then he slammed on the brakes and swerved as an Astra that had been behind him tore round on the inside and accelerated past.

'Jesus,' he said, braking hard, and then, 'Sorry.'

'No problem,' Lightman said, removing his hand from the dashboard where he'd braced himself. He hadn't looked up from the iPad.

'Doesn't that make you want to vomit?' Jonah asked curiously.

Lightman glanced up at him. 'What?'

'Reading a screen in the car. I can do it for about five minutes and then I feel awful.'

'No,' Lightman said thoughtfully. 'I've never had that.'

It was things like that, Jonah thought, that made people start to wonder whether Lightman was a man or a robot.

Harforth School was a walled-in series of grey stone buildings dating from some time before the dawn of the twentieth century. Despite its dark-green welcome sign with its beautiful fonts, the effect was inelegant and depressing. Perhaps it was the weather, and perhaps the square greyness.

They drove over a series of small but vicious speed bumps to reach the school reception. A sports pitch to the right was covered with thin, scorched-looking grass and a small cricket square.

'God, I'm glad I never went anywhere like this,' Jonah said, as they climbed the shallow steps towards a door labelled 'Visitors' Entrance'.

'They look better in the sun,' Lightman said evenly.

Jonah glanced at him. He remembered a St Paul's or something school on his CV. He wondered if Lightman was actually a boarding-school lad. It wasn't something that had occurred to him before.

There was a glassed-in area behind a desk in the very square entrance hall. A hard-faced woman in her thirties sat behind it with a tag that read 'Headmaster's Secretary' in huge print. Her name was so small beneath it that Jonah couldn't read it. Order of priority, he supposed.

'Can I help?'

Jonah didn't sense a great desire to help anyone.

'Yes, thank you. I'm DCI Jonah Sheens and this is DS Ben Lightman. I believe my DC phoned you earlier today. We need to interview Andrew Mackenzie.'

'I'm sorry, my understanding of the outcome of that conversation was that it would have to be at the weekend,' the secretary said.

Jonah did his best not to rise to the cold, pedantic way of speaking.

'I'm afraid this is a police investigation,' he said, with a smile as cold as the secretary's. 'It's time-critical. We'll issue an arrest warrant to speak to him if we have to, but I think that will look a lot worse for your school.'

*

Mackenzie found them an empty classroom not far from where he'd been teaching. The school was eerily quiet. The summer school clearly wasn't using all of its facilities.

Mackenzie had left his bored-looking class of American high-school students with a young woman who must have been another teacher. Mackenzie had seemed ready enough to come away.

Jonah found himself sizing Mackenzie up as he walked. He looked the public-school part, from his pale-cream trousers and polished brown shoes to his dark-brown waistcoat and blue shirt. He was verging on stout, his forearms wide under his rolled-up sleeves. But Jonah thought there was power there.

'So what do you need to ask me about?' he said eventually once the door had clattered shut. Everything here seemed a little aged, Jonah thought. Once expensive and now run-down.

Mackenzie perched on the desk, leaving Jonah and Lightman to draw up some of the slightly short chairs from the school desks. Jonah wondered whether Mackenzie's assumption of the teacher's position was habit, or a deliberate statement of authority. The way the teacher folded his arms and took a few breaths was anything but authoritative. It was anxious. Perhaps frightened.

'Do you mind if we record this?' Jonah asked, pulling out his portable tape recorder. 'It's a lot easier to check our facts if we have everything on tape.'

'No, that's fine,' Mackenzie said. 'Go for it.'

Jonah clicked it on. Introduced himself. And then launched in.

'It's about Aurora Jackson,' he said. 'Her remains were found yesterday morning not far from where she went missing.'

In Mackenzie, the reaction was as much in his body as his face. A downwards slump of his torso; the slipping of one of his arms away from the other before he made an effort to return it.

Jonah waited for him to speak, but Mackenzie said nothing but, 'Right. Aurora.' He breathed in more heavily, and exhaled several times, and then turned away from them to look out of the window.

'This is clearly something of a shock,' Jonah offered. 'But we need to ask you about Aurora herself, and about that evening. As much as you can recall.' He gave a shrug. 'Obviously she was one of many students, so I don't expect a detailed portrait.'

'She was nothing like my other students,' Mackenzie said, a roughness to his voice that took Jonah aback. He fixed that flat gaze on Jonah, and for the first time Jonah became aware of Mackenzie's age. Of the lines and the tiredness. 'She was nothing like them. And not just because she vanished, but because I thought I was looking at the next Marquez or Woolf or Faulkner. It was a god-awful waste. The worst possible waste.'

Jonah could sense Lightman beside him, his body absolutely still. He could tell that the intensity of Mackenzie's reaction had surprised him too.

'You've not felt that any of your other students since were a match for her?'

Mackenzie shook his head. And then shrugged with one shoulder. 'I've had bright sparks every other year. There have been lots I would have tipped to become successful, and most of them have. I've had only a few writers or essayists or journalists out of a lifetime of teaching. But none of them . . . I don't know. None of them was original like she was. Or seemed to catch on to an idea as quickly. But maybe I've got a skewed memory of her because of what happened . . .'

Lightman asked neutrally whether he'd known Aurora personally.

Mackenzie snorted. 'As much as you ever know any student personally. I was shit-scared of one of the girls mis-interpreting any encouragement. I'd only had two proper girlfriends and I didn't have a clue how to go about rebutting unwanted attention. I remember a sixth-former turning up at my classroom late on a Friday when I was marking, and I pretty much shouted her out of the place. Poor thing was probably only after some extra help, but I was paranoid about being on my own in a room with her.'

'So there was never anything at all beyond the usual student–teacher relationship?' Lightman continued.

'Of course there wasn't,' he said, and sounded more disappointed in Lightman than anything. 'You get excited about students. About their abilities, and where they'll go in life, and how you can help them. You might like or dislike them as people, but you try not to let that affect you. I've had smart kids who I've thought were absolute shits before, but it didn't mean I didn't bend over backwards to help them.'

'Thank you,' Jonah said. 'We also need to know about that night. When Aurora disappeared. We think you saw at least one of the group at the campsite. Were you aware that there were others?'

'I saw Topaz,' he said, nodding. 'Aurora's sister. I have to say that it never occurred to me that Aurora would be there. They didn't really spend time together at school. Topaz was a very different person. She was smart, too, but she was

160

obsessed with self-image. I assumed Topaz was with her usual crowd. Benners and . . . Jesus. I've . . . Connor, that was it. And Jojo. And Topaz's little shadow . . . What was she called?'

'Coralie? She wasn't with her at the time?' Jonah queried.

'No, it was just Topaz. Wandering along the riverbank. I'd joined the path there for a while and I think I scared her.'

'What was she doing?' This from Lightman.

Mackenzie gave him a blank look. He made a considering sound. 'Well, she had a bag. She'd been walking the other way. I suppose she might have been going for a swim.'

'You didn't see where she'd come from?' Jonah asked.

'No,' Mackenzie said, shaking his head and glancing between them. 'Look, I . . . I know Topaz could be a bit of a cow to her sister, but I don't think she had anything to do with her death. She was devastated after Aurora disappeared.'

'That's useful, thank you,' Jonah said. 'You didn't see anything later in the evening?'

Mackenzie shook his head. 'I was somewhere between two and three miles further on by the time I camped.'

'With your girlfriend?' Jonah asked. 'Is that right?'

'Yes. Ex-girlfriend,' he added. 'I mean, obviously, it was thirty years ago . . . I'm married, and not to her.'

'What time did you meet up with your girlfriend?' Jonah asked.

'Ahhh . . . To be honest, I can't remember. I probably gave a statement at the time.' He rubbed a thumb across his forehead, his skin puckered in a frown.

'I'm sure we can check, thank you,' Jonah said. 'And once you were there, at the campsite, you didn't leave at any point? And you didn't hear any sounds, or witness any other walkers?'

Mackenzie shook his head. 'We weren't that close to any of the roads,' he said. 'Which was a conscious choice. The official campsites can be heaving at that time of year, and the weather was perfect. Mind you, my choice pissed Di off. She wasn't a fan of hiking a mile and a half down a track in the dark to get there. I had to go and meet her.' He gave a half-smile. 'I should probably have taken that as a sign of ultimate incompatibility.'

'You had a few drinks that evening?' Jonah asked. 'I think there's a report that you'd both had wine.'

'Yes, I think we had a couple of glasses.'

'So it's possible you would have slept through some sounds,' Jonah said.

'Oh. Yes, I suppose it is. Not the world's lightest sleeper anyway.' He gave a slight shrug; a half-smile.

'Thank you. Could I just have your ex-girlfriend's name?'

'Oh. Diana . . . Diana Pitman.' He gave a short laugh. 'I had to work to remember that.'

'Is there anything else at all you can think of that might be useful? Anything that occurs to you?'

Mackenzie considered for a while. 'No. I don't think there is. I . . . I'm not sure how much I really remember at this stage. And how much I've misremembered by now. I've probably overwritten a lot of what really happened by trying furiously to remember things, and beating myself up over not camping closer by. Not hearing anything.'

Jonah nodded. 'This is my card. Please let me know if anything occurs to you. If you have anything useful, like diary entries or records of Aurora's work, that would be appreciated.'

Mackenzie took the card, peered at it, and nodded. Jonah felt a faint dampness in his fingers as the teacher took it. The teacher was sweating.

He watched them leave in silence.

20. Aurora

Everything had become fragmented. Confusing. She was dizzy with alcohol and spinning. Dizzy with contact. With the pervasive smell of Connor.

'I feel a bit . . . weird.'

She pulled back from him, her skin blooming into full sweat. She lost her footing slightly, and Connor steadied her.

'OK?'

'I don't know.'

She heard a peal of laughter, and Connor went rigid. He was looking past her, towards her sister. Of course it had been Topaz laughing.

She found herself turning to look too. Topaz was standing close to Brett, and whispering in his ear. Her hand was on his shoulder, and her long hair was brushing his forearm. It made Aurora feel profoundly uncomfortable.

Brett was smiling, but his gaze moved and fell on Aurora. She didn't have time to pretend she was happy that her sister was moving in on him.

His smile faded, and he pulled away from Topaz a little. 'Hey, we should dance!' he said. He bent to put his drink down and then moved a little closer to Connor and Aurora. 'Come on!'

He started nodding his head and swaying slightly.

Topaz didn't approach him. Instead, she walked over to

Coralie and took her hands. She drew her friend towards her and began to dance too, pressed against her, with her hands on Coralie's back.

Aurora jumped as Connor suddenly started to move again. He pushed at her to get her to go with him.

'Sorry. I don't really feel like dancing any more,' she said quietly.

'Don't be stupid,' Connor said, and he pressed closer to her.

She didn't want him to touch her any more. More than that, she didn't want him to force her to move with him. Her arms felt limp and her feet had turned into heavy, clumsy things.

She saw Topaz spin Coralie round, and then look from Brett to Connor, and back again. Both of the boys were watching her, and Aurora couldn't help watching too.

With a smile, Topaz half turned and drew Coralie towards her, tilting her head until their mouths met. Coralie did not resist. She responded by putting her arms round Topaz and pulling her further into the kiss.

Aurora couldn't help staring. She was as mesmerized as Connor and Brett, for very different reasons.

She tried to ask herself if Topaz was really into girls and not boys. If she had missed it somehow in Topaz's behaviour. But she remembered too many boyfriends; too many trysts outside the PE hall or behind the bus shelter. Too much flirting and touching.

Brett laughed. 'Whoa, girls.'

Topaz only paused for a moment. She looked away for long enough to give him a wicked grin and then took a bundle of Coralie's hair and drew her head backwards. Topaz lowered her mouth to her friend's throat and began to lick and kiss along the top of her collarbone.

Brett moved towards them slowly, one hand to the back of his own neck as he watched. And then he moved in closer, and Topaz opened the group to include him. She let him press his mouth down on hers. His hand moved to Coralie's back, and then slid down inside her skirt.

Aurora's nausea grew. She pulled away from Connor, but he was trying to hold on to her.

'I want to go,' she said, and wrenched herself free.

'Don't,' Connor said. It was a little bit desperate, the way he said it, but Aurora was done with all of them.

She turned and tripped away from the campsite, out into the darkness of the trees.

Jonah called through to O'Malley and Hanson via Bluetooth the moment they were moving again. Hanson answered immediately and with enthusiasm.

'Can you get Domnall on the line, too?' Jonah asked.

'I don't know where he is,' Hanson replied. 'I've not seen him since you left.'

Which wasn't that unusual. If the DS had a lead, he would generally pursue it in whatever direction it took him without taking the time to communicate with the team.

'All right. I'll call his mobile later. Give me your updates.'

'OK. I've got something from forensics. Linda McCullough wants you to call her. They've taken a proper look at a beer can that was in the stash with the body, and it's half full of Dexedrine.'

'Half full?' Jonah asked.

'Yes,' Hanson agreed. 'There's something really off about it, she says. There's only a little of it towards the bottom that's been dissolved, and the rest is still totally dry.'

Jonah processed this. 'So the powder went in there after the can had been drunk,' he said.

'That's what she thinks.'

There was something disconcerting in that. Jonah could see a few possibilities: that it had been a failed attempt at spiking someone's drink after the drink had been finished; that it had been a hurried disposal of the drugs; or that it had been planted there to mislead. He was inclined to rule out the second option. There were much easier ways of disposing of drugs than pouring them into a narrow opening in a beer can and then burying it. If a failed attempt at spiking, why had Aurora still ended up dead? Why had it been buried with her?

Jonah had an unsettling feeling that it was the third option, and that someone had planned for the eventuality that Aurora would be found. Could it have been Connor? Had he raped and killed her, and then tried to make it look like Daniel Benham by planting a can full of drugs?

He was aware of Hanson speaking to him.

'Sir?'

'Sorry, what was that?'

'Mackenzie. I've found the girlfriend who went camping with him. Diana Pitman.'

'That's good work,' Jonah said, remembering that he'd only just got hold of the name himself. 'Where is she?'

'She's teaching in a school in York now. Do you want me to contact her?'

Jonah sighed at the thought of a long drive. 'Yes. See what you can talk her into. If we have to go to York, we will.'

'OK. I'll call her. I've also had a pretty clean report back about Andrew Mackenzie so far. Google doesn't find much, either. But I've submitted a request to Intelligence for more.'

'You may as well go ahead and call up all the schools he's taught at to check his record with them,' Jonah said. 'If his CV's on LinkedIn, use that as a starting point, but check all the dates. The easiest way of hiding career problems is to pretend you never worked somewhere.'

'OK.'

'But leave it until you've looked at Connor,' he added. 'There's no reason yet to see Mackenzie as our main suspect.'

'All right.'

He could tell that Hanson was less than pleased about this. She'd clearly been excited about Mackenzie being a missed suspect, and wanted to pursue that line. Half of being a good copper was instinct, he knew. And the other half was knowing when to do the grunt work.

'Anything from Jojo Magos?' he asked.

'Yes. She said she'll be at Southampton Climbing Wall the rest of the day. She'll be back on her mobile at about eight.'

Jonah glanced at the dashboard clock, which read 16:52. Even allowing for traffic, they would be back well before then.

'Should I try and get hold of her?' Hanson asked.

'No,' Jonah said. It might be more productive to speak to her at the wall. 'I'll sort it out. If you contact the ex-girlfriend, and keep digging at Mackenzie, we'll look at the others.'

He rang off, thinking about Hanson and how she could fit into his team. The way they worked together had always mattered a lot. Everyone brought their own abilities, and he used them when they were needed.

Juliette Hanson was very different from the arrogant, impulsive constable he'd recently got rid of. He couldn't see her pursuing aggressive, bad-cop lines of enquiry. Which also meant he couldn't see her wrecking entire cases.

But Jonah was trying to work out exactly where she did fit. She was proactive, certainly, like O'Malley. More intuitive than logical, unlike Lightman. Jonah also saw in Hanson a need for praise and recognition that could be either useful or difficult to manage, depending on how it panned out.

He shelved the thought for now, deciding that he'd better think through that interview with Mackenzie while it was fresh in his mind. The teacher's reaction to the news, and his ferocious pride in Aurora, had been a warning note. Jonah wasn't quite sure he believed that it was all regret at not being there for her. He'd only taught her a few times a week.

There was a sustained pause while the slightly lessened rain continued to sweep down the windscreen in streams. The traffic was building now, becoming a maze of starred red tail-lights.

'Once we've got the ex-girlfriend tracked down, we should see what Mackenzie's colleagues have to say about him,' he said after a while.

'You're looking for inappropriate relationships with students?' Lightman asked.

'I'm looking for anything,' Jonah said. 'But if he's got a problem with young girls, that's indicative.'

'Want me to look into it?'

'No, I'm happy for Hanson to do that,' Jonah replied. 'Let her feel industrious and useful. She'll be hooked before she realizes how bloody boring the job really is.'

Hanson caught sight of Lightman letting himself into CID, and glanced up at him. His warm smile was a little embarrassing somehow, and she ducked her head back down to look at her screen.

She still wasn't sure whether she trusted him. But, frustratingly, she also found herself trying to make Lightman like her. It was as if the teenage Hanson was still in there somewhere, wanting the popular boys to chat her up.

Lightman made his way towards her, and folded his coat over his own chair. Trying to ignore him was made harder by the fact that his desk was opposite hers. There were only a couple of slimline screens between them.

'How's it going?' he asked.

'It's OK,' she said. 'Two of the schools have talked to me about Mackenzie, and I'm waiting for a call-back from the head of his second school in Bournemouth.'

'Anything strange?' He was still standing, an expression of interest on his face.

'Nothing significant.' Hanson shrugged. 'At his previous school, he went to an anti-war protest during school hours. A student who should have been in school saw him there. The parents reported him, but the school did very little about it. His students were doing well, and he was popular. They concluded that it was none of the school's business as long as he didn't miss any lessons.'

'Fairly irrelevant, then,' Lightman commented.

Hanson glanced over at the door, realizing that the DCI hadn't appeared through it after Lightman.

'Is the chief on his way?'

'No, he's off to interview Jojo Magos.'

Hanson made direct eye contact for a moment. 'At the climbing wall?'

'Yes.'

'Isn't that a tough place to conduct an interview?'

'There are pros and cons of going to where the suspect is,' Lightman said with a small smile. 'And generally, I find the DCI is pretty good at knowing when to control a situation.'

He sat carefully at his desk, and she busied herself with the second page of Google results on Andrew Mackenzie. She dutifully clicked on the dull links, most of them about other Andrew Mackenzies, and kept on going to the later pages.

Her extension rang at six. She was hoping it was the school rather than the chief. She wanted to have something else to report to Sheens.

'DC Hanson.'

'Oh, hello. I'm calling from Bournemouth East.' A young woman's voice. Gentle, and a little northern, Hanson thought. 'I'm one of the deputy heads. You wanted some information on Andrew Mackenzie. Sorry it's taken so long. I had to talk to a few different people.'

'That's not a problem at all,' Hanson replied. 'I really appreciate you calling.'

'That's all right. He had a good record here, but there was one thing I thought you'd appreciate knowing. He began a relationship with one of our sixth-formers after she'd left the school. It wasn't legally problematic, as she was over-age and no longer a pupil. But given that he met her here, as her teacher initially, it wasn't entirely popular with the parents.'

'That could be interesting, thank you,' Hanson said, pulling a cap off her pen and beginning to take notes on an A4 pad. 'Do you think the relationship really did start after she left? It wasn't happening covertly while the girl was at school?'

'The staff generally think not,' the deputy head said. 'But it's difficult to be certain. They did their best to find out at the time, and to look for any grooming. It seemed to be above board. The girl herself was quite certain that it was only a few months after she left, when they'd bumped into each other at a pub, that it even occurred to either of them. I think the school did everything it should have done, under the circumstances.'

'Yes, thank you,' Hanson said. 'Do you have the girl's name?'

'I assume this isn't going to be announced publicly?' the teacher said, suddenly a little guarded.

'No, no,' Hanson said. 'This is purely for investigative reasons. It might well be unimportant.'

'All right. According to our solicitor, it won't violate any confidentiality if I pass on the information, given that she was no longer a pupil. Her name was Pria Anand.'

'Great,' Hanson said. 'Is it all right if we talk to you again if we need to?'

'Yes, that would be fine,' the deputy head said, 'though I'm off on holiday next week. I'll give you my mobile in case you need it.'

Hanson took it down and rang off. She could see Lightman's curious expression.

'Inappropriate relationship?' he asked.

'Maybe,' Hanson answered. 'Apparently it only started after the girl left. But we're talking a few months after she left. I'd say that's fairly suspicious.'

O'Malley announced his return at that point by slamming the door to CID. He came over to them both with a slightly distant expression.

'Successful afternoon?' Hanson asked.

'Possibly,' O'Malley replied. 'I'll update you once we're at the pub.'

Jonah walked the mile to Southampton Climbing Wall in less time than it would have taken to sit in late-afternoon traffic. His suit trousers were heavy with water by the time he arrived, but the outdoor jacket had kept the rest of him dry. He couldn't help feeling that the rain should be warmer; that this summer storm should be a hot and tropical thing instead of a miserable, chilly grey invasion.

The front desk at the centre was overshadowed by a protruding piece of climbing wall; a dark-blue bulge covered in dayglo-bright holds. He showed the skinny young man on the desk his ID.

'Oh . . . Do you need to see the manager?'

173

'I just need to ask a member a few questions,' he said. 'She's agreed to see me.'

There was a slight hesitation, and the guy looked around for someone to ask advice from, before shrugging.

'OK. But . . . don't disturb people too much when they're climbing. And don't stand underneath anyone when they're on the wall, OK?'

Jonah gave him a small smile. 'I'll try not to.'

It took him almost fifteen minutes of searching to find Jojo. The place was more complex than he'd imagined, with room after room opening off each other, each with a different challenge. Some very high climbs with ropes; some overhangs; some high and low walls; and some where there were a series of footholds only.

In every room, a few climbers were working away. They were as varied as the rooms. Some of them moved like spiders across the wall and others strained to stay on. The air was dry with chalk from dozens of pairs of hands, but there was something nice about the smell of it.

Jojo was in one of the double-storey roped rooms, in a group of four. She was almost at the top of the wall when he walked in, roped up but with her short hair uncovered. He watched her traverse sideways, moving constantly but carefully, her wiry arms and legs working. It was graceful, and a touch hypnotic, her hands and feet always finding tiny purple holds and not touching any of the others.

There was a pause for a short while, as she hung off one hand and dipped the other into her chalk bag.

'I think you're going to have to dyno it,' one of the men at the foot of the wall called. 'Your arms aren't long enough.'

Jonah thought he could see why she'd stopped. There was a final purple hold, way off to her left and higher up.

'Fucking dyno it,' Jojo called, shaking her head. 'Do you ever have any less-shit advice?'

Instead she leaned gradually to her left, balanced on what looked like a single toe, her weight shifting over her knee. Then she lifted her right foot and tucked her toe into a hold that must have been at her waist height, her left hand still loose and all of her weight poised between that right arm and that left foot until the toe was lodged in place. Her body set, she shifted, somehow removing her weight from the left leg and reaching upwards, pushing herself steadily off that right arm and leg.

Her left hand closed on the hold, which he had thought must be too high for her. She swung off it, letting go with her right hand, and then called, 'Coming down.'

The rope tightened and her belaying partner – Jonah remembered enough about his climbing to get some of the terms right at least – lowered her down.

'Not bad,' the belayer said. He was more the build Jonah would have expected of a climber: tall and rangy, with shoulders wide enough to make him look triangular. He had slim legs beneath, with muscles so defined that Jonah could see them when the guy was just standing there at rest.

'Better than dynoing, anyway,' Jojo said, with a grin, and began to unhitch herself from the rope.

Jonah moved forward, and she glanced up at him. Her face did a funny little twist as she recognized him. It was somewhere between a smile and a grimace.

'When I said I was going climbing,' she called, 'I meant I was busy.'

Jonah gave her a shrug and a small smile. 'It seemed like a much better idea than sitting in a room with no windows. Can I just have a few minutes?'

He could feel the other three watching him. The wait for an explanation.

Jojo gave him a slow look, but she was smiling slightly as she did it. 'All right. A few minutes. Come on.'

She led him back through three of the rooms, and then through a dusty archway into a harshly lit seating area with a series of vending machines around it. There was nobody else there.

Jojo walked to a table in the corner and pulled up one of the hard plastic chairs, and settled herself on to it with one foot up on the edge.

'There's crap coffee in the machines if you want it,' she said.

'That's OK. I have all the crap coffee in the world back at the station.'

He sat opposite her, aware that she was watching him.

'What do you want to know?'

'A few things,' Jonah answered slowly. 'To start with, I thought there was something that was bothering you. Not just Aurora's death, but perhaps connected with it.'

He watched Jojo's gaze fall to her hands, and how she started fiddling with some tape she had round her middle fingers. She said nothing.

'Was there anything you wanted to say? Something that's difficult to talk about?'

He knew that he had been right. He could read the urge to talk battling with a fear of consequences in her expression.

'I just . . .' And then she breathed in, an unsteady inhalation. 'I told you that we all left the stash alone. But it wasn't that simple. When we realized she'd gone, and that we'd have to call the police, we panicked.'

Jonah nodded at her. 'There were fifteen kilos of illegal substances a third of a mile from the camp. I'm pretty sure I'd have panicked too.'

Jojo's cheeks lifted in a small grin, but she looked at the hand tape, not at him.

'So we . . . discussed it, and somewhere in the panic we realized we had to hide the Dexedrine. So Brett and I went down there and caved in the entrance. We didn't look inside . . . we just wanted it hidden. We kicked at the bank above it until you couldn't see anything.' She looked up at him now, finally. And he saw tiredness; horror; a strange sort of fear. 'We buried her in there, and we didn't even know.'

'You and Brett Parker?' Jonah asked quietly.

'Yes.' Jojo nodded. 'Brett Parker.'

There was a pause, while Jonah imagined the two of them scrambling to hide the drugs. He tried to imagine the rush, and the decision to do it without looking inside.

'When will you know how she died?' Jojo asked, in a slightly hoarse voice.

'I honestly don't know,' Jonah said.

'I keep wondering if she was just asleep in there or . . . or injured and . . . What if we killed her without knowing?'

'All I can tell you is that we'll do our best to find out what happened to her,' he answered. He leaned forward slightly, and was suddenly close enough to inhale a little warm chalky, slightly sweaty scent off her. 'It's unlikely that someone would have put her into that hole alive.'

'No,' Jojo said. 'I suppose not.' She went on picking at the tape, pulling it until it had all rolled in on itself into a thin, sticky string.

'I need you to come and give a statement about hiding the

entrance,' Jonah said, after she'd given up pulling at the tape. 'Obviously it's hard to say it, but if you didn't know she was there, there's nothing criminal about your actions.'

'There's something stupid about them, though,' Jojo said. 'And cowardly. We should have faced up to what we were doing. We could all have taken the blame.' And then she gave a sigh and stretched her neck to one side. Rubbed at it.

'But it was everyone's decision?'

Jojo nodded.

'And nobody disagreed?'

'I think we were all equally afraid. Imagine what our parents would have thought . . . and the school.'

Jonah nodded, and allowed a brief silence to elapse.

'How long will you stay?' he asked, tilting his head towards the room outside, where a pair of climbers were working at a route not far from the door.

'A couple of hours,' she said. 'Until the shaking gets too bad to make it worthwhile.'

'How many times a week do you come?'

'Four or five, though sometimes we meet at someone's house. A lot of people have a wall in their shed.'

'Jesus . . .' He shook his head. 'And you have an active job. You make me feel lazy.'

Jojo smiled slightly. 'That's nothing to how much Aleksy used to do. Two sessions a day, minimum. One day off every fourteen.'

Jonah nodded, considering. And then he said, 'Was it a big fall? The one that killed him?'

Jojo's arms suddenly became tense, and she looked away from him.

'Sorry,' Jonah said quickly. 'I'm not very good at –'

'It's fine,' she said briefly. 'It was a climb he'd done before a lot of times. Just a warm-up before a harder one. It should have been fine, but that's the trouble with free climbing. You only need a momentary slip in concentration.' She paused for a moment, and then said, low and intensely, 'Such a bloody idiot.'

'I'm sorry,' Jonah said quietly.

Jojo rubbed at her neck again and he was wondering if she'd pulled a muscle on that climb.

'There was something else I wanted to mention when you came to the house. It wasn't . . .' She paused. 'The trouble is, it's such a long time ago, I'm really not sure if it's real. It's a half-memory, and I was drunk and . . . and high. I remember not being quite sure at the time whether it had happened.'

'It's probably worth saying,' Jonah said. 'Even if you aren't sure. I'd rather have a dozen false leads than miss a real one because someone wasn't sure.'

'OK, well, I'm not even sure it's a lead . . .' Jojo gave a half-smile. 'I've probably overplayed it. It's just that I think I might have got back up at some point. Because I have this memory of Aurora being by the fire, and talking to someone. Only I couldn't see who she was talking to because they were outside the firelight. And you know how you're not sure if you've convinced yourself of something? Well, when she went missing, I never said so, because I really, really didn't know.'

'Interesting,' Jonah said. 'You don't remember what she was saying?'

'The only thing I thought I remembered was her saying she was thirsty, and really,' Jojo said with a shake of her head, 'I could easily have made that up.'

'Well, it's worth knowing anyway,' Jonah said, thinking of

what Coralie had said about Connor. If he really had been up later on, then perhaps Aurora had got up and had some kind of altercation with him.

'Do you need me to come to the station now?' Jojo asked. 'To give my statement?'

'God no,' Jonah said. He gave her a half-smile. 'I want to go home. Tomorrow will do fine.'

She gave him a look that was at once wary and slightly humorous. Then she pulled one shoulder up in a shrug, and smiled.

'Whatever you say, Copper Sheens.'

'Nine o'clock?'

He saw her hesitate.

'Is that a difficult time?' he asked.

'I'm pretty grumpy before ten,' she said, with a small grin.

'Well, ten is probably all right,' Jonah said. 'Anything for a quiet life . . .'

'Great. I'll see you then.'

He reached into his pocket and pulled out one of his cards. It was slightly bent, but she took it with a momentary, sober nod.

'In case you need to talk to me about anything before then. Enjoy your climb.'

Despite being lost in thought as he let himself back on to the street, he still recognized the neck-crawling feeling of being watched, and turned quickly to look over to his right. He had only a glimpse of a figure in a large coat and hat before it disappeared round the edge of the building.

He jogged the length of the building and turned the corner, but whoever had been there was now out of sight. The road was glistening wet and empty.

*

O'Malley insisted on what he called a 'proper' pub, instead of the refurbished, brightly lit bar opposite the station.

'If there isn't dim lighting and cloth-covered stools, it's not a real watering hole,' he told them both.

So they ended up walking half a mile to an unpromising-looking place called the Boathouse, which had a grubby black sign and a freestanding blackboard on the pavement with a badly spelled quote about drinking.

Inside, it was better, Hanson decided. The furniture looked comfortable rather than ragged, and it was warmly lit. Given the rain that had soaked into her suit, she was glad of the unseasonal fire, too. She made her way towards the table in front of it and hung her bag over the back of a chair.

'I'll get this round,' she said.

'Ah, no, you're all right,' O'Malley replied. 'My idea, my shout. What'll you have?'

'Umm . . . Staropramen. But I've got to drive, so it's going to have to be just the one.'

'Pale ale for me,' Lightman said. 'I don't really mind what kind.'

As O'Malley made for the bar, Hanson asked, more for something to say than anything, 'What was Mackenzie like, then? Did he say anything interesting?'

'The chief thought he was a little odd,' Lightman replied. 'He seemed quite emotional about it all.'

'Mackenzie, or the chief?' Hanson asked with a small smile.

Lightman laughed. 'Mackenzie. DCI Sheens isn't known for breaking down in interviews.'

'What about you?' she asked, because she was curious. 'Do you find cases get to you?'

There was a brief silence, and then Lightman said, 'I try very hard not to let them. I don't think it helps. And I don't play the emotional card in interviews. I'm not much good at getting people to warm to me.' He paused again. 'But that doesn't mean I don't feel anything. Particularly with murder investigations. Some of them . . . I mean, when you're interviewing a mother about the partner who's just killed her daughter in a fit of rage, it's hard not to feel for them.'

Hanson gave a slow nod. She remembered, vividly, going to investigate a house where a baby had been screaming for hours and the neighbours had reported it. She'd been a constable back then. She remembered her sergeant questioning the exhausted, tearful mother; his gentle fiddling with items of baby gear on the counter. And then how eventually he'd picked the kid up and looked in his mouth, and then told the mother quietly that they were going to have to go to the station. The mum had been putting boiling water into her tiny son's bottles, and his mouth had been full of blisters.

Hanson hadn't been able to sleep properly for a week after that. She would find herself thinking about the defenceless child, or about the slow nod of the mother who knew she had been caught, and how she'd asked if it meant someone else would look after the boy now. She'd been so hopeful. It had made Hanson afraid that you couldn't trust anyone when they were pushed too hard. It had also made her realize that the ways people could find to hurt were endlessly imaginative.

She decided to change the subject before she got caught in a lot of very dark thoughts. 'So. Give me a cheat sheet. How do I impress the chief?'

'It's basically to do with playing to your abilities,' Lightman said. 'He's all about the psychology of teams, and he wants the team to be self-supporting. He knows where his weaknesses are, and he uses us to make up for them.'

'So . . . you're more thorough than he is?'

'I've got a better memory,' Lightman corrected her, 'and I'm more accurate. But he's a lot smarter.' He gave a small smile.

'What about Domnall?' she asked quietly.

'He's good at easing information out of suspects, and he's quick-thinking, and intuitive. He can do leaps of intellect and act quickly, which the DCI finds difficult until he's built up to it. The chief takes what I'd call a holistic approach, which slows him down.'

That made Hanson wonder what she could bring to the table. She was smart, and keen-eyed. Those had always been features her colleagues had picked up on. Even the inspector she'd worked for previously, who'd generally filled her reviews with comments on her 'good communication' and 'support of the team', and thought she'd like them.

'Here,' O'Malley said, stepping up to her and handing her two pint glasses and returning to the bar.

He came back with a tall glass full of clear sparkling liquid and a slice of lime. So he'd ignored the beer, and gone for gin and tonic. Which she knew was a good way of hiding a love of liquor. Everyone else could drink pints while he sank triples.

'So,' she said, as O'Malley settled himself on to a stool that made his big frame look a little comical. 'What have you been doing with yourself?'

'I've been talking to a few dealers. Trying to find out if anyone offloaded a lot of Dexedrine after Aurora's death. I mean, I hardly think they'd dig it up and hang on to it, would they?'

'Any luck?'

'There's potentially something interesting. I mean, it's not like they keep records, so it's hard to check, but one of them said that the market got flooded a year or so later, and it drove the price down, but unfortunately he didn't buy, so he doesn't know where the hell it came from.'

'Would fifteen kilos be enough to flood the market?' Hanson asked.

'Yeah, if someone offloaded a lot at once to other small-time dealers.'

'Were there any other sales they remember?' she asked.

'Not a lot. One of them remembers a small deal with a girl he'd never met before, but we're talking five or ten grams, and he's not sure if it was earlier. Another one reckoned he had a few deals with some guy he'd only met a few times, but much, much smaller amounts again. He didn't think they'd have added up to that much.' He drank his drink off in one solid go, and then said, 'Jesus, I'm dry. Too much talking. Anyone need a top-up?'

Hanson was acutely aware that she'd barely started her lager, and shook her head. She drank a quick couple of mouthfuls.

'Let me get it,' she said, but he was already on his feet.

'No, you're all right.'

'Is he going to think I'm useless if I can't keep up?' she asked Lightman quietly, as O'Malley returned to the bar.

'Domnall?' Lightman replied, and shook his head. 'You don't have to worry about impressing him. He doesn't drink. It's tonic water.'

'Do we have any early wagers on the killer?' O'Malley called from the bar. It made Hanson wince slightly, but the bartender didn't seem to care.

'I might want to spread my bet,' Lightman replied. 'I'd go evenly between the four males.'

'That's no way to gamble,' O'Malley said. 'Have some balls and back your instincts.'

He paid up, and returned to the table with his drink.

'What about you, Juliette?' asked O'Malley.

'Ah, I don't know. I'd want to know more.'

Her phone buzzed, and she pulled it out to check it. She felt an unpleasant twist as she saw that it was from Damian again.

She hated the effect it had on her, his name on a message. Every time she thought she'd closed things down, another message arrived.

She could see the first line of the message in the preview on her home screen. It began with, 'I'm sorry . . .' but she'd had messages like that before. She'd also had a lot that raged at her. That told her she was a fucking idiot, and that she'd been wrong about everything. That she'd left based on a stupid assumption. That she should have helped him through a difficult time and not walked out.

And then there had been the other kind, where he'd accused her of cheating on him, and tried to pretend that was why she'd left. Which was the kind of warped logic that he seemed to function on.

She felt the same draining away of energy that she did every time he messaged. The same drop of her positivity, and the same anxiety in her chest.

'All OK?' O'Malley asked, and she glanced up at him, and then at Lightman, who was watching her with another unreadable expression.

'Yes,' she said, looking down at the phone and then putting the screen to sleep. 'All fine. Just a pain-in-the-arse ex-boyfriend.'

She no longer felt like staying with them and talking. She finished up the rest of her lager, and rose.

'I'd better get going,' she said. 'I've got a few calls to make . . .'

'I'll walk back with you,' Lightman said, and stood to drain his pint.

'Good thing I don't mind drinking alone,' O'Malley said wryly.

'Oh. Sorry.' Hanson felt a stab of real guilt. She hadn't bothered to think about O'Malley, and the fact that he might need company. 'I'm sure I can . . .'

'I'm fine, I'm fine,' he said, with a laugh. 'I ought to get back to work, anyway. People to see. Drug dealers to find. I'll head back to the station soon.'

Lightman held the door open for her as she left, and then, instead of trying to talk, walked along next to her in equable silence. Her thoughts went quite quickly back to Damian and the girl whose two passionate messages she'd found on his phone.

Hanson hadn't even known her. The girl had turned out to be in a relationship with one of Damian's colleagues. It hadn't been the first time she'd suspected him, but he had so often attacked her, and made her feel guilty for so much as smiling at a man, that the focus had never been on him. She'd always been on the back foot.

She'd come to realize that he'd been hiding an awful lot behind his jealous attacks on her. She had no idea how long that particular thing had gone on for, and he had denied and denied that there had been anything besides the girl being unhappy in her relationship, until she'd found a picture of them together on his computer from weeks before.

There was part of her that still wanted to interrogate him to the point where he admitted the truth. But she had had to accept that she wasn't going to get the truth, and that the only thing to do was to walk away.

'We should do the pub thing again,' Lightman said suddenly, 'when we're not in the frantic stages of a case, and when there aren't other distractions.'

She expected him to smile at her, but his expression was quite serious.

'Yeah,' she said, not really meaning it. 'We should.'

Lightman gave a half-smile. 'All right, so you probably have better things to do. But Domnall and I don't. So as long as you humour us once in a while . . .'

For some reason, she found herself trying to make him feel better.

'No, I really don't,' she said. 'It's nice to see you two outside work. Sorry I'm being miserable and useless. I'm not normally. I promise. Sarge.'

'You're all right,' Lightman said, and then, after a pause, added, 'Comparatively.'

It made her smile in spite of herself.

Jonah began the walk back to the station slowly in spite of the rain. He tried to bring his mind back to the case, and not to let the unsettling memory of the figure watching him from the shadows take over.

If he had to attach himself to a theory, he thought it most likely that Aurora had been persuaded to go down to the stash with someone, and then murdered there. Whether that had been by strangling, or by overdose – or by some other method – wasn't yet clear. If Coralie and Jojo were both right in what they'd said, then Aurora and Connor had both been back up. A suspicious couple of events.

He thought about everything else Jojo had said, and found

himself running over his memories of her as a girl. She'd had that same taunting, competitive, wild expression. He was trying to work out the limits to that wildness, and to her willingness to try anything.

The thoughts became circular, though. There were so many things to think about; he couldn't afford to get stuck on anything. So he did what he always did, and put the thoughts aside, somewhere in the background, ready for later.

Hanson was still at her desk when Jonah arrived. He shook his head at her, and then came and sat in a neighbouring chair.

'I'm pretty sure I told you lot to sod off. Didn't you get the memo?'

'Sorry, sir,' Hanson said, with the ghost of a smile. 'Ben started it. And I felt like I should compete, and then, by the time he was ready to go, I'd got a little bit stuck in . . .'

'What are you looking at?'

'A few things,' she said. And then she added, 'There's something that is really bothering me. Actually, there are two things, but one more than the other.'

Jonah was absolutely ready to go home. He was wet and tired and feeling grumpy. But he'd been where Hanson was. Working on a first homicide case with feverish enthusiasm. Finding heart-racing excitement in discrepancies. 'Let's hear it.'

'The search started with people on foot,' she said. 'None of them saw the stash, which makes sense if it was behind an offshoot of the beech tree. The most anyone would do would be duck under the tree and move on, yes?'

'Yes,' Jonah said. 'I'm happy with that.'

'But at five p.m., they brought in dogs from Southampton,' she said, handing him an old report from the investigating officer at Lyndhurst. 'They were primed for Aurora's scent, and they'd all been trained on suspicious substances. So how did all of them fail to find a place that we know she had visited before, and which must have reeked of Dexedrine?'

Jonah frowned. He took the report and read over it. He had a hazy memory of the dogs arriving at the scene. But on that first day, he'd been moved to the door-to-door search with his sergeant. They'd spent the evening knocking and questioning.

'You're right. I don't . . .'

He thought of Jojo's confession. Of how they had caved the entrance in.

'Jojo Magos is coming in tomorrow,' he said slowly. 'She wants to make a statement to the effect that she and Brett Parker caved in the entrance to the stash. Caving it in would make it a lot harder for the dogs to pick up the scent, but if Aurora had been in there beforehand, there should have been a trail leading right to it.'

Hanson nodded, her cheeks gaining a slight flush of excitement.

'If they covered it up, that makes sense of some of the weird statements from the following day. They were trying to cover up two of them hiding it . . . Yeah, look.'

She had stuck tiny, fluorescent tabs to some of the pages in a stack of statements, and she pulled one open to show him.

'Topaz said Brett went towards the main road to search, and Jojo stayed at the camp. But Connor said Brett had gone to wade in the river and that Jojo had gone looking towards the road. Brett agreed that he'd been wading, but the one slightly canny bit of interviewing involved him being asked why he hadn't been at all wet when the police arrived. He's on tape as saying he removed his trousers before going in, but they've indicated a pause in the transcript. Here.'

Jonah couldn't help smiling at the thoroughness. It was a refreshing feature in a new recruit. It was usually just Lightman who went for the meticulous approach.

He glanced over the statements. Nodded. 'Good work, Juliette.'

'So do we think that's all they were hiding?' she asked. 'Was it just that they'd gone to hide the drugs, or was there something else? Were some of them deliberately laying a false trail for the dogs, either to hide the drugs, or because they knew she was there? And if so, how did they know how to do it? The talk we had from the guy at Vice said it's really hard to do.'

'You're right,' Jonah said thoughtfully. 'I had that talk too. That stuff about how they smell in the same way we see. Not just one thing at a time.'

'So whoever did it probably had a good working knowledge of narcotics,' Hanson agreed.

'Yup. Benners.'

'Or Jojo Magos, through her brother.'

Jonah nodded. He found himself thinking again of Jojo hiding the stash.

'You should definitely go home now, Juliette,' he said. 'I'm heading off in the next thirty seconds. And thank you. That's significant information.' He started to walk away, and then turned back. 'How did everything else go? Anything specific on Connor?'

'Oh, no,' Hanson said, slightly flustered. 'I was looking into Connor when I realized about the dogs . . .'

Jonah nodded. 'In the morning, please. And if you get stuck, Facebook and LinkedIn are a good bet.'

Hanson nodded. 'Sure.' Her face was a little pink, her nodding a little over-eager.

Jonah felt sorry for her. He was genuinely pleased with her work. But he also knew that the little things could be as crucial to an investigation as the inspired leads and analysis. And he needed orders followed as well as instincts. He'd learned the hard way how much devastation could be caused by officers who didn't listen.

22. Aurora

Saturday, 23 July 1983, 12:50 a.m.

The images in her head were as confused as the trees whipping past her. Topaz kissing Coralie. Connor's iron grip on her. Brett so caught up in them that it was like watching someone hypnotized.

And threading through all that, sharper and more painful, the memory of twilight, and the ice that had gone through her after she'd followed Mr Mackenzie. After she'd crept, dripping, through the trees and seen him – her Mr Mackenzie, Andrew – put his arms round a little brunette woman and kiss her.

She had so many questions that she wanted to fire at him. So many things she badly wanted an answer to. How he could do that to her. How he could hide it from her. How he could turn his back on everything they had.

And there was a creeping voice inside her that said, *Maybe he didn't think you really had anything. Maybe he's never really cared about you. Maybe it was all in your head.*

There was nowhere for her thoughts to go that didn't wrench at her insides, and she felt sick as it was. Sick and hot and dizzy.

The nausea stepped up in a rush, and she bent down and retched. Liquid poured out of her mouth and her nose, and kept coming. She couldn't keep her balance, and was afraid of falling in it, so she moved sideways and thudded on to her hip, her legs pressing into twigs and stones.

She had never felt more alone.

23

Jonah did not sleep well. He spent too long reading the case files, time passing him by without being noticed until his phone buzzed at 12:52 and startled him.

It was a one-line message from a number he didn't recognize.

> We're going to the wall again on Thursday. You should get some shoes and come along.

After a second or two, he found himself laughing. He sent a reply.

> That's a kind offer. You know I didn't actually give you my card for sporting invitations, though, right?

He closed down his machine, and another message arrived shortly afterwards.

> Doesn't mean it isn't a good idea, though, Copper Sheens. Night.

He decided not to reply, though it was tempting to get involved in some banter when he was feeling weighed down with the past. But if his phone records ended up in court one day, he wanted no record to suggest that he hadn't done his job properly.

Once he'd finally got into bed and dozed off, he had a series of disconcerting dreams about going camping with Jojo and Benners and Topaz and Connor, sometimes with the others there and sometimes not. In every dream, he suddenly became aware that Aurora was missing, and that something terrible had happened to her. But in each dream, he couldn't get the others to worry. They kept on drinking and dancing and laughing while he ran between the trees desperate to find her. At some confused point it was a baby he was looking for, and Michelle was there, too. It was a wakeful night.

During his time awake he found himself rehearsing a conversation with Wilkinson about Andrew Mackenzie. He wasn't relishing telling his chief super about potential police corruption.

He showered at six thirty and drove to the station. The roads were clear, but it was still raining, and the surface was slippery under the Mondeo's wheels.

He expected to be the first one in, but Lightman's mop of hair was visible over the top of his screen as he let himself into CID.

Jonah made his way towards his office, thinking he would leave Lightman to whatever was occupying him. But as he drew closer, he could hear something like the sounds of a football match coming out of the speakers of the desktop, and realized that Lightman was watching Brett Parker in action.

'Barcelona Olympics in ninety-two,' Lightman commented. 'The four hundred metres.'

The commentator's voice rose in pitch, and Jonah watched Brett's long, powerful stride pick up in pace. He moved past the leader in a matter of three steps, and crossed the line a few moments later.

'I hadn't realized quite what sporting royalty he was,' Lightman admitted, as the video finished.

'Royalty is probably fair,' Jonah agreed. 'He was pretty unstoppable for a few years.'

'There isn't much around after the late nineties,' Lightman commented, scrolling through the suggested videos. 'Even though some helpful fans have uploaded a lot of stuff to YouTube.'

'He switched to triathlon,' Jonah replied. 'At the point when he stopped being able to take medals at sprinting.'

'Think he's still in any clubs?' Lightman asked. 'They'd probably know him quite well.'

'It's worth finding out,' Jonah agreed.

'Other obvious lines of enquiry are school friends of his and Aurora's,' Lightman went on. 'Particularly of Aurora's. I can ask the Jacksons for their help.'

Jonah experienced a slight dropping sensation in his stomach. It had been an inevitable part of the investigation, but he'd still been hoping that it wouldn't happen.

'I'll do it,' he said. 'I've got to give them an update as soon as it's a human hour. See if you can find any of Brett's school friends without asking him about it.'

'OK. I'll see what I can do.'

'Let me know when everyone's in,' Jonah said, as he made his way to his office. 'We'll have a proper sitrep.'

He wasn't quite sure what he was doing, taking over talking to the Jacksons. The idea of one of the team doing it panicked him, but if they came up with one of the names he thought they would, there was nothing he could do about it. He couldn't hide a potential witness from the team.

He sat at his desk and then rose again, too restless for sitting still. He put a call through to Wilkinson's office on the off-chance that the chief super was there, but wasn't surprised that it went unanswered.

He started trying to get his head round the team briefing, but struggled to focus on that, too. And then, at a little after seven forty, McCullough rang, despite the forensics lab technically not being open for another hour and twenty minutes.

'Digital analysis is back,' she said without any greeting. 'We've got a fracture to two metacarpals, and another to the sacral side of the left sacroiliac joint. It's a pelvic joint, and it's difficult to fracture. Taken together, they are strongly indicative of rape. Though sacral fractures are unusual.'

Jonah had a strange, cold sensation around his heart. The reality was that McCullough's findings weren't unexpected. Aurora had been fourteen and beautiful, and a probable murder victim. But he could still remember her as a gawky twelve-year-old, her hair falling over the pages of a book and her feet kicking at the stone wall outside the school while she waited for her sister to come to the bus with her.

'What does that suggest?'

'That one leg was leaned on and placed under a lot of pressure while the attack took place, by someone a lot stronger than she was,' McCullough said. 'The fractures to her hands are likely to have occurred while attempting to protect herself.'

'Likelihood of any DNA retrieval?'

'Extremely slim,' McCullough said. 'I'll swab what tissue we have and start going through soil and fabric in detail, but there's going to be a lot of data loss over thirty years.'

'OK. Thank you. Are you able to rule out animal interference in the removal of drugs? It looks like that stash of Dexedrine used to be a lot bigger.'

'How much bigger?'

'Fifteen kilos.'

'There's no way animals removed fifteen kilos of Dexedrine from underground,' McCullough said definitively. 'That has to be human action. I'll see if we can find any shovel marks or other signs of interference. The site's still covered.'

'Thanks. Anything on toxicology . . .?'

McCullough sighed. 'To clarify my earlier comments, we've got no hair or nails or eyeballs, meaning no testing there.'

Jonah could hear the lack of finality in her voice.

'But . . .?'

'There isn't really a but. I've been as thorough as I can, and sent soil samples from directly around the body for column and gas chromatography, and if we're really, really lucky, we might manage to separate out non-metabolized Dexedrine from other compounds in the soil and confirm presence in sufficiently high quantities to indicate ingestion by the victim. But if there have been sufficiently high temperatures in that dug-out, there is zero chance, and it was a hot summer.'

'Well, naturally,' Jonah said. 'Common problem . . .'

'Piss off, Sheens,' McCullough said.

'Thank you,' Jonah answered on a laugh. 'Genuinely. I know you're busy at the moment.'

'I'm always busy,' McCullough said. 'I'm going to start saying no more often, and go home at five, and all of you lot can complain to my answerphone instead.'

'But what would you do with all the spare time?' Jonah asked.

'Have a life? Maybe?'

'Yeah. I hear they're overrated . . .'

He ended the call, and sat thinking about a violent attack in as unemotional a frame of mind as he could manage. From an investigative point of view, it clarified things quite a lot.

In essence, it was unlikely that any of the girls had killed her. It was extremely improbable that she had been attacked violently by a male attacker and then murdered by a separate female.

But that didn't mean that one of the girls hadn't been peripherally involved, or that none of them knew anything. If one of them had covered up for one of the boys, it wouldn't be the first time. Not by a long way.

The other thing it meant was a difficult conversation with the Jackson family at some point. As a feeling human being, he wanted to make the revelation as easy as possible. But as the man tasked with finding out who had killed Aurora, he had an opportunity to use that information to shock.

O'Malley woke up five minutes before his alarm. He felt vaguely optimistic about today. He'd done some good work yesterday on the drug supplier that might well help them. He'd gone to see Jojo Magos's older brother, Anton, straight after the pub.

Anton hadn't been exactly nonplussed when he'd opened the door. It was a rare man who liked having his evening interrupted by a detective, and Anton had the grudging, wary look of someone who thought coppers were the bad guys. O'Malley guessed, as Anton sized him up, that the elder Magos brother hadn't been automatically treated with respect by the force. His greying hair was dreadlocked and tied back, and he wore a wiry wool cardigan that smelled faintly of animals.

But O'Malley was good at coming across like a human being instead of a copper, and his accent generally helped him. Most people saw it as unthreatening. So Anton had let him in, and in the end had admitted that he'd been the one who had set up the deal where Daniel Benham had bought fifteen kilos of Dexedrine. His contact had been a man called Matt Stavely, for whom he provided an address on the Thornhill estate.

O'Malley had sighed inwardly at that. The Thornhill estate after dark was not his idea of fun. But at least he didn't have a flash car or a uniform to worry about.

He'd climbed into his Fiesta and made his way there, which was at least a quick journey at this time of night. He found Spring Terrace, which was about as unspring-like as it was possible to be. There was a series of desperate-looking low-rise flat blocks and then one towering high-rise at the end with a recreation ground in its shadow.

Stavely lived in the last of the small blocks. It had a small car park outside it with no attempts at trees or flower beds anywhere.

O'Malley parked up underneath a street lamp without any real hope of that dissuading anyone from damaging the car. Thornhill was increasingly gang-run and lawless. Though after having to come and talk to numerous residents over a number of years, O'Malley at least had a reasonable relationship with some of them, and understood that the root of gang culture was fear rather than aggression.

He took the flat block's external stairs two at a time, determined to make this quick. Stavely was in number 36, up on the second floor. The door had no number on it, but it had two faded patches where a three and a six had once sat, and four screw holes.

He could hear a TV from somewhere, playing something that involved shooting and yelling. A moment or two after he knocked loudly, the sound shut off. He thought he caught footsteps approaching. There was a pause, which he would have expected. You didn't open your door without checking on this estate.

And then there was a click as the door was opened a fraction, the security chain still on. A thin, bearded face appeared in the gap.

'Matt?' he asked, as unthreateningly as possible. 'I need a little help from you. Can I come in for a minute?'

'What help?'

O'Malley glanced up and down the empty hallway, and then drew out his wallet. He flexed it open, showing a few tens and twenties inside.

Stavely gave him a hard look, and then the door closed as the chain came off. He opened the door fully, and O'Malley got a full view of him. A loose grey hooded cardigan on a thin frame. A black beanie over hair that was almost all grey, and skin that looked like it didn't get enough light.

'Here,' Stavely said, walking ahead of him down a very short, very bare corridor that had only two doors opening off it. They passed a bedroom that was in darkness. Little except a mattress and a cupboard were visible. The whole place smelled of stale smoke, though it was cleaner than O'Malley had been expecting. There was no mouldering food odour, and Stavely himself was well washed.

Stavely led him to an open-plan kitchen and sitting room, which was dominated by a large screen and a PlayStation. The screen was a frozen image of a fierce gun battle. It looked like Russia from the buildings and weaponry, and it was uncomfortably real-looking to O'Malley.

Stavely sat near the remotes, where a can of beer was waiting for him.

'What are you looking for?' he asked in a very neutral tone.

'Nothing for my mood,' O'Malley replied, leaning against

the kitchen counter. 'It's actually information. And it's not the kind of information that's going to get you into any trouble.'

Stavely went very still. He looked at O'Malley, and then reached for a cigarette from a packet stuffed between the cushion and the arm of the sofa. He shifted his hips in order to reach into a pocket and pull out a lighter, and then lit up without speaking.

'It's information thirty years old,' O'Malley went on, 'so it's pretty stale. It's about a large sale of Dexedrine you made to a boy called Daniel Benham.'

O'Malley caught a strange twist to Stavely's mouth, but he still said nothing.

'You probably remember the missing girl, Aurora Jackson.' He waited for a reaction, and in the end Stavely nodded. 'We've found her remains. The trouble for us is that she'd been buried next to a very large quantity of Dexedrine, and we need to rule those drugs out of any involvement. We're not, and I need to be firm about this, interested in pursuing any dealing or distribution crimes against anyone.'

There was another silence.

'How does tracing them help you?'

'If they came from a fairly normal source, we can show that it wasn't connected to Aurora being murdered. Which is what happened to her.'

He waited again while Stavely thought this over. He was a careful man, O'Malley thought, and possibly not stupid. O'Malley had low expectations when it came to small-time dealers.

'So you want to show that the Dexedrine wasn't dangerous to know about,' Stavely said.

O'Malley nodded. 'I don't believe her death had anything

to do with them. But I have a DCI who is thorough as hell, and is going to be relentless about pursuing the drug connection until we can close it down. I want to close it down.'

Stavely took a long drag on the cigarette and then tapped it into an ashtray. 'I don't know, man,' he said slowly. 'It sounds like trouble.'

Stavely was closed off, in the way that people who survived by keeping things secret often were.

'You're going to have to help at some point,' O'Malley said, in a low voice. 'The chief is not going to let this go. If you knew the man, you'd realize that. Your best bet, as god is my witness, is to be helpful now, while it's still your choice, and make him want to overlook you.'

Stavely balanced the cigarette on the edge of the ashtray, and watched it for a while. 'What do you want me to do?'

'Just answer a few questions for me. About the drugs, and Daniel Benham.'

Stavely let out a large sigh, and shook his head. 'I asked you in for a sale.'

'Think of it,' O'Malley said, drawing out his wallet again, 'as a different sort of sale.'

He held out two twenties, and Stavely's attention was immediately on the money. It was a noticeable shift.

'Here,' O'Malley said, and put the two notes down on the table in front of the dealer. Stavely watched them, his hands moving slowly over each other. O'Malley decided that was enough for him to continue. 'You ended up with the Dexedrine after a deal fell through. Is that right?'

There was a pause, but to his relief Stavely said, 'It was a guy I'd sold to before. Upmarket guy. He wanted it to sell on. So I got it from my supplier.'

'But the buyer backed out?'

Stavely shook his head. 'He got busted. He'd been selling at expensive parties and some girl died. Her boyfriend pointed the finger at him.'

'And you couldn't return it to your supplier?'

Stavely looked up at him, momentarily incredulous. 'You can't. You can never do that. Never. And if you tried it, they'd never supply you again. It's not a fucking department store.'

'But you still needed to pay them, all right, so,' O'Malley said, soothing him.

'Yeah. And I was generally sweating it. But . . . I got put on to Daniel Benham.'

'By Anton Magos?'

There was a silence, and then Stavely lifted his shoulder in a shrug.

'Doesn't matter,' O'Malley said, quickly. 'Tell us about Daniel Benham. He wanted to buy it.'

'Yeah. Well . . . He seemed like he wasn't sure.'

'He wasn't all that keen?'

Stavely shook his head. 'No, he . . . He asked why I had the stuff, and I explained. And he asked what would happen if I couldn't pay, and I said – Well, I said they'd cut my fucking legs off. Which wasn't really a joke.'

There was a pause, while Stavely fiddled with the cigarette.

'And did he ask anything else?'

Stavely shook his head. 'No. He made his mind up then. And you know, I don't want him getting . . . I know he's a crappy politician now, but, you know, he did me a favour, all right? And actually I think he bought the stuff because he wanted to help me.'

O'Malley nodded, but he wondered if Stavely was right about that, or whether Benham had had his eye on a very drugged-up party or two.

'Has he bought anything from you since?'

Stavely hesitated, which piqued O'Malley's interest.

'We're just keen to know more about him,' O'Malley said. 'As a person, like.'

'I can't remember,' Stavely said, a stubborn look on his face.

'OK. So did you know the others that well?' he asked, acknowledging that Stavely wasn't going to say any more. 'Connor Dooley, Topaz Jackson . . .'

Stavely shook his head and picked up his cigarette again to take a drag. 'I knew Jojo some, because I hung out with Anton sometimes. She was usually around the park when we were. I didn't know the others.'

O'Malley let a silence descend, and then nodded. 'Thank you. That's all fine. I might need you to come in and say a bit of that on record sometime.'

'Fuck's sake,' Stavely said quietly.

'It'll be worth it for you,' O'Malley said with a fixed look. Stavely held the look, and then gave a shrug.

Stavely didn't get up as O'Malley let himself out. With the door closed behind him, O'Malley moved sideways slightly, out of sight of the peephole. He waited for the sound of the computer game to start up again, but instead, after a pause, he heard Stavely's voice.

There was no other voice in reply, and then, after a pause, Stavely spoke again, though none of the words reached him. A phone call, then. And given that no phone had rung, one Stavely had made off the back of O'Malley's visit. Which was more than a little interesting.

At ten past eight in the morning, Jonah arrived at the Jacksons' house. He had toyed with calling the family to save himself the trip, but he knew that news of this kind was better handled in person.

It was Tom who answered his knock this time. He was rubbing at his mouth, presumably having been in the middle of breakfast.

'Good morning, Mr Jackson,' Jonah said. 'Sorry for the early call, but I just wanted to catch you up with what we're doing.'

'As I've said many times to various police over the years,' Tom said, a little patronisingly, 'I'd much rather be updated than not, at whatever hour of the morning.'

He stood aside, and Jonah squeezed into the small space along the corridor. It actually looked a little tidier than it had on his last visit. There were orderly piles, and even a few gaps in the detritus. Perhaps Topaz and Connor had been busy.

They were all in the kitchen. Joy, sitting at one end of the table, gave him an owlish glance, her eyes wide and wary. Topaz was leaning out from her position in the corner to look at him. Only Connor kept eating, working his way slowly through a bowl of porridge with his head down, until Jonah spoke.

'I'm sorry,' he said again. 'I'm interrupting breakfast.'

'It's fine,' Topaz said swiftly. 'What's going on?'

'We have some news,' Jonah said, and Joy suddenly rose and moved a chair round the table so that he could sit facing them. Tom returned to his place in front of a plate of eggs and crossed one long leg over the other. 'We've had digital analysis back, and various signs point to some form of sexual assault on Aurora before she died.'

Topaz flinched, visibly. Connor finally stopped eating. He rested his spoon carefully on the edge of his bowl, but didn't make any move to comfort his wife. From Joy and Tom there was nothing. It was as if they were frozen in place.

'It's clearly a distressing finding,' Jonah went on, 'but it does help us to be clearer on who we're looking for.'

'Who are you looking for, then?' Tom said, his voice a little thick.

'A male, and potentially one of the group she was camping with,' he said carefully. 'We're looking into whether anyone else knew about the place where Aurora was found. We can't be conclusive about that yet, but we do know that the kids who were camping were familiar with it. We're also investigating possible drug use at the party.'

Jonah felt instinctively guilty at having to give him so much disturbing news at once. But it was better for them to know now, he knew. Delaying it only made it harder if further evidence was found.

He saw Topaz's face colour, and she put a hand out to a glass of water and drank from it with a hand that shook slightly. Tom glanced at her, and Jonah thought that there might be a difficult conversation coming up.

'Do you think it was connected?' Tom asked eventually.

'It's possible,' Jonah said. 'But I'm not assuming anything just yet.' He took a momentary breath. 'I wondered if we could ask for something from you.'

'What's that?'

'We want to talk to Aurora's other friends,' Jonah said. 'Anyone she was close to or might have confided in.'

'Well, I can't . . . Topaz and Joy can help, I suppose,' he said, nodding to his wife. 'I've never been much good with names.'

'No, he hasn't,' Joy agreed a little breathlessly. 'Terrible memory, haven't you, Tom?'

'That's fine,' Jonah reassured him. 'The three of you can talk it through and let me know later today. You can give the names to one of my team if I'm not available.'

'Your team,' Tom said, considering. 'How many are there on your team?'

'Three, apart from me,' he said. 'Constable Hanson you've already met. I also have sergeants O'Malley and Lightman, and support from the DCS, the forensics team, and other teams as needed.'

'Four of you directly working on the case, then,' Mr Jackson said. He nodded his approval, though his voice still sounded unsteady. 'That's good to know.'

Jonah rose and left, regretting that he couldn't be there to hear Tom and Topaz discuss those drugs. It would have made for interesting listening.

O'Malley was the last one to arrive, at 09:20. An early enough morning, but it seemed halfway through the day to Jonah.

Jonah asked them into a briefing room to tell them about Hanson's thoughts on the dogs being fooled, and about the confirmation that Aurora had been raped.

They all nodded grimly when he was finished.

'So our key question,' Jonah said, 'has to be whether Connor Dooley was the one to rape her. What do we have on him since yesterday?'

'Not a lot,' Lightman said. 'Coralie was the only one to see him up and about, and we've yet to hear more about him attempting to kiss Aurora.'

'That's something to press our other campers on,' Jonah replied.

'I've checked his account of the following morning, when he realized she was gone, and there aren't any holes. He gives a good account of himself, with a few details that drop in and out as you'd expect from someone trying to remember what happened. And he seemed eager to find her.'

'Or at least, pretended to be eager,' Hanson chipped in.

'He was up first,' Jonah pointed out. 'He could have gone and made sure he'd covered his tracks before he woke anyone. I'd like to check those statements in detail for anything about the next morning. Any traces they might have seen that were later forgotten.'

Hanson and Lightman both nodded, and O'Malley raised a hand.

'I tracked down the dealer who supplied Daniel Benham with those drugs,' the sergeant said. 'I went and had a little chat with him, and he could potentially be persuaded to come in and give a statement.'

Jonah blinked, slightly knocked back by the speed of that development.

'When did you do that?'

'Yesterday evening,' O'Malley said, with the ghost of a grin. 'He's an interesting one. He confirmed how the sale had worked, via Jojo and her brother. He felt Daniel Benham largely did it to help him out, but denied any further involvement with any of them. I'll type up a report.'

'Thank you, Domnall. That's . . . excellent work. Anything else?'

'Mackenzie's girlfriend will be here by twelve thirty,' Hanson volunteered.

'That's great. All right. Off we go.'

Coralie checked her phone again, but there were no messages. Not from any of them. And she felt a sick surge of loneliness that wasn't helped by the isolation of a hotel restaurant at breakfast.

She hadn't really expected Topaz or Connor to be in touch, though they might have wanted to rage at her for betraying their secrets. She'd almost been looking forward to it, despite the guilt that twisted her stomach. Jojo wasn't going to message, obviously. She'd never bothered to contact Coralie in all the years they'd known each other.

But from Brett and Daniel that behaviour hurt. She'd messaged each of them twice last night. She could see that all her messages had been read, and yet neither of them had replied.

After everything between them all, it was hurtful. It made her feel excluded, and afraid. Were they talking to the police about her now? Had they turned on her?

She'd suddenly had enough of waiting. She snatched up her phone and the key-card for her room, and left her breakfast half eaten.

She was already calling Brett's number by the time she'd reached the corridor.

The DCS arrived at Jonah's office shortly after the briefing. Which, in his experience, could mean there was trouble brewing. Jonah gave him a nod, and let him into the office, thinking that there might be more trouble once the DCS knew about Mackenzie.

'I don't know if you've been reading the news,' the superintendent said, closing the door behind him, 'but there's a lot of *Secret History*-type speculation going on about a group of kids getting up to warped practices. I'd like you to be able to issue an update today, to calm the theorizing.'

'It's only the third day of the case,' Jonah protested.

'But you've had some developments?'

'We have, but there's nothing I'd be happy giving to the press.'

Wilkinson let out a huff of air. 'Fair enough.'

Jonah could tell that he was disappointed, but he'd known Jonah long enough to trust him. 'I do have a few things to pass on, though.'

'Tell me,' Wilkinson said, and pulled up the chair opposite Jonah's desk.

So Jonah summarized for him the poor investigative work into Mackenzie, and the teacher's strange attitude towards Aurora. And then he went on to tell him about Connor, and the fact that he was now the most likely suspect in Jonah's eyes.

'I want to look hard at everything related to him,' Jonah finished. 'I'd particularly like to know whether he was brought in so many times because something just didn't quite ring true, or whether it was pure bigotry.'

Wilkinson was pulling at his lip thoughtfully. 'I can see the need to look into him. But we need to make Mackenzie our prime suspect.'

'Don't you think there's a lot more pointing at Connor Dooley?' Jonah protested.

'That isn't clear yet,' the DCS said. 'Mackenzie has gone almost uninvestigated.'

'He seems to have no knowledge of the place her body was hidden.'

'How do we know that for certain until we look into the man's movements?' Wilkinson countered. 'I know, I know. We don't want to ignore a potential lead towards Connor Dooley. So have one of the team keep looking at him. The rest can focus on Mackenzie. We've got to do it right this time,' he added more quietly. 'If corruption occurred thirty years ago, we need to be absolutely squeaky clean now.'

Jonah felt a dull sense of resignation settle over him. He knew the chief was right, however much it seemed like the wrong course of action.

'All right,' he said. 'As you say.'

Wilkinson rose, and then offered, as a form of amelioration, 'I'll give your apologies at the Community Cohesion meeting.'

'Thank you, sir,' Jonah said, trying to pretend he hadn't forgotten all about it.

24. Aurora

She couldn't think about anything except the vomit. Everything had been reduced to the heaving of her stomach and the opening of her throat as it poured out of her.

She was sitting with her head and body turned sideways, one hand instinctively pulling her hair out of the way.

Part of her was afraid of the sickness. Of having damaged herself somehow by drinking.

'Hey.'

There was suddenly an arm round her. A gentle rub at her arm. But she was unable to look up and see who it was. Her body was fully involved in being twisted and bent double, retching and retching what looked increasingly like water.

'Let me get you some orange juice.'

It was Benners, she realized. She didn't want him to leave her, even to go and get something that might help. She was too afraid. Too miserable.

But the retching eased up a little, and she was able to nod. She didn't want him thinking she was pathetic, either.

She finally felt like she was ready to stop just before he came back. She looked up and saw a warped version of him through eyes that didn't seem to want to stay focused. She could still read the sympathetic smile as he settled himself next to her and tore open the carton.

'Here you go.'

It was difficult to drink it from the ragged spout. It ran out of her mouth and down her chin in a tepid rush.

She stopped drinking to wipe her chin. 'God. I must look awful.'

Benners laughed. 'Nobody looks great like that. But it's all right. I'm not judging you.' He lifted the carton again. Her hand followed it, slack and uncoordinated. 'Come on. Have some more. You need to get something else into your system.'

She tried again, and got a thin stream into her mouth. A mouthful. Another.

And then the nausea rose back up, and she turned to the side again and released the juice in a rush.

Benners let her puke, rubbing her shoulder again and making soothing noises. Some of her hair swung forward and he caught it for her.

'It's miserable, isn't it?' he said. 'But you're doing fine. I still end up like this every few months. I think I'm on top of it, and then I have a few and I get cocky. Alcohol does that. It's like its method of reproduction. Once it gets you, it whispers in your ear and tells you to keep on going.'

Once she was done, he lifted the carton again. 'It'll stay down soon. And you need the water and the sugar.'

She didn't want to drink, but she took it to please him. She drank a lot more this time and immediately felt better for it.

'I shouldn't have drunk anything,' she said, after she was certain it was staying down.

'That's not true,' Benners argued. 'You can't go around avoiding doing everything in case this kind of thing happens. This is a moment or two of life. A few minutes of misery, and then usually a pretty rancid hangover the next day. But this – this suffering, right now – is what makes the liberation and the joy you felt earlier sweet. How can you enjoy pure bliss without suffering for it?'

She still couldn't see his face properly. He seemed to be sliding sideways.

'But how can you call it bliss when you know this is coming?' she asked him. 'When you have a moment of joy, and then this lands on you?'

'Because that's what makes it bliss,' he said. He leaned close to her, making his point so earnestly that it was hard to disagree. 'If it wasn't temporary, then it would just be normal, wouldn't it? Normality. And then it would become immediately boring. Disappointing. Nothing.'

She was suddenly afraid that she smelled of vomit. She leaned away from him.

'Sorry. I'm browbeating you.' He grinned at her.

'No,' she said. 'You're right. I just . . . I saw Zofia like this a few times, and I decided I was never going to do that.'

'Zofia . . . The blonde one? Who used to get the bus sometimes?'

Aurora nodded. 'Her parents took her away. She'd got friendly with some of the sixth-form girls who were really into drink, and ended up in hospital after a party. They decided the school was bad for her.'

Benners nodded, and then shrugged. 'But we're not going to let you get like that,' he said. 'You can have fun without it ending badly.'

'I suppose so.' She gave him a slight smile. 'I'd rather not puke again, though.'

'We can have some harmless, non-drinking fun for the rest of the night,' Benners said, and started to clamber to his feet. 'Come on. It's still warm by the fire and I left Jojo and Connor arguing about synthetic music.'

She needed his help to stand, and then to balance. He let her lean on him the whole way, his feet sometimes stepping sideways to avoid hers. She still trod on him twice.

'I don't fit in,' she said, halting suddenly. 'I'm not one of you. Or one of anyone.'

'No, you're not one of anyone,' Benners said. From close by, he looked taller. Fiercer. 'You're one of you. Just one of you. And that's worth more than anything.'

And then she lost his attention, as his head turned sharply. They were close to the fire. There was illumination limning every tree trunk. It reminded her of Bonfire Night, and then, suddenly, of a horror movie where the gates of hell had opened.

Benners took her hand and tugged her forward. Her balance was no better and she went crashing into one of the trees, her shoulder scraping it.

He paused for a moment, but then pressed on, until they were at the edge of the clearing, the fire turning everything a rich, sensual orange.

Someone there gave a cry of what sounded like pain, and she pushed past him to see, her heart pounding behind her ribs. Her breath short.

There were two forms by the fire, huddled up beside it, one of them making strange sounds. She kept walking until she was closer, not able to make them out.

And then her double vision slid into one for a moment and she realized that Connor was crying. His whole body was heaving as he sobbed, and Jojo was curled round him, shushing him.

'It's OK,' she said. 'It's OK.'

'I hate him,' Connor said. 'I hate him.'

It was almost as bad as finding them naked together. She

felt her cheeks burning as Connor glanced up and saw her. He looked like he hated her, too, just then.

'Sorry,' she said quietly.

She and Benners were close to the tent; the sleeping bags; the supplies. Aurora pulled herself free of Benners and ducked down. She had to put a hand down three times to steady herself while she pulled a sleeping mat out from the pile and picked up one of the tightly packed sleeping bags to go with it.

Benners gave her a strange look when she stood up again. One that was between embarrassed and disappointed.

He followed her as she walked back into the darkness, away from Connor and Jojo and that intimate moment of grief, and away from Topaz and Coralie and Brett. She stopped only once she couldn't hear anything any more. On what looked like a smooth enough patch of ground, she threw the mat down.

'Are you going to be all right this far out?' Benners asked.

'Yes,' she said. 'Thank you.'

There was a pause while she made a mess of unpacking the sleeping bag, and then couldn't lay it straight. She could feel him hovering behind her.

'Do you want me to stick around and talk for a bit?'

Aurora shook her head. 'I want to go to sleep.'

She waited for him to argue, or to agree. But Benners said nothing while she unzipped the sleeping bag and climbed in laboriously. In the end, it was only his quiet footsteps on the fallen leaves and twigs that let her know he had gone.

25

Jojo was solemn as she repeated, for the benefit of the tape, everything she'd told Jonah at the climbing wall. She detailed how she had worked to cave in the entrance from above while Brett had stood below, and how much she regretted not looking inside first.

'To the best of your knowledge,' Jonah asked, once she was done, 'was there anyone outside that group who knew about that hideout? Before or after?'

Jojo's eyes moved to his face, and then away again. 'I don't think so.'

'You didn't see anyone else close to the camp that night? Nobody mentioned spotting someone who could have seen the group coming and going from there?'

Jojo shook her head again. He found himself looking at the definition of the muscles in her arms.

'Did you climb back then?' he asked her, and he could see that she was disconcerted by the way she looked up at him. Lightman, sitting beside him, gave no reaction, which was one of the best things about the sergeant.

'I – Yes. I've climbed since I was eight. My older brother, Anton, got me into it when he worked weekends at the outdoor centre near Ashurst. Well, he let me try it properly. I basically lived up trees by then anyway.'

'So you've always been outdoorsy? Strong?'

'I guess so,' she said hesitantly.

He was thinking about that broken bone in Aurora's hand.

Wondering about whether there had been someone to hold her and someone to attack her. And he thought further about Connor and Jojo cuddled up together that night.

But he felt instinctively that he would get more out of Jojo if she felt that he was on her side, as she had at the climbing wall. That they were almost friends.

He smiled at her. 'I was thinking how strange it is that you ended up friends with someone like Coralie. She's not exactly . . . a strong, active type.'

'Oh,' Jojo said, with a wry smile. 'Well, Coralie and I were never that close. It was all about Topaz for her. I always thought it was more than friendship for Coralie, and I know she's had girlfriends as well as boyfriends since, so it probably was. She liked Benners a lot too, actually. He was quite protective of her even if he found her a little vacuous. I guess we were just thrown together.'

'How did that play out later?' Jonah asked. 'The friendships?'

'Aurora vanishing definitely made us closer for a while,' Jojo said. 'I think . . . I think it was hard for us to talk to anyone else. They hadn't been through that loss. And everyone else was always gruesomely interested . . . and Brett became a core part of the group after that, too. And having thought he was a bit of a twat, I ended up liking him.'

'But then Topaz and Connor moved away.'

'Yes, that was . . . what, seven years ago, though? Not so very long. They still come back every now and then. They're just a little more out of reach.'

'Did you miss them?' he asked.

Jojo seemed a little startled by the question. 'I suppose so,' she said, in the end. 'At that point . . . I suppose I was trying not to feel too much about anything. It was only a year after I'd lost Aleksy.'

Jonah nodded. 'And how did he fit in?'

'Pretty easily,' she said, with a slight smile. 'Aleksy may have looked chiselled and hard, but he was a bit of a goofball underneath it all. He liked to joke around and prank people, and our group needed a bit of that. He left a big gap.'

'Was he particularly close to any of them?'

He saw the momentary tightening of her mouth, as if she was thinking of refusing to answer. He expected her to tell him it had nothing to do with him. But then she seemed to change her mind.

'Daniel, Brett . . . and Topaz really. Connor and he were never quite as close. I think because Connor's so bloody serious. And Coralie was a little bit mystified by him, though she wasn't averse to being teased.'

'Have you been talking among yourselves since?'

He saw a very slight flush appear on Jojo's cheeks.

'Well . . . I know you said not to, but . . . I felt like I needed to talk it all through. What had happened. Over again. I wasn't . . . I just had a chat to Daniel and Brett. Separately. Just over the phone.'

'Not Topaz?' he asked, interested. 'I would have thought, given that it was her sister . . .'

'No,' Jojo said, a little awkwardly. 'No, I didn't feel it was as easy to talk to her.'

'But you've always been close to Connor?' he asked.

'Yes . . . I suppose so.' She nodded. 'We've always understood each other.'

'Did that understanding ever cross any lines?'

Her mouth twisted humorously. 'I told you how obsessed he was with Topaz.'

'So nothing . . . physical happened between you that night?'

She was definitely awkward now.

'Oh, well . . . to be honest, I'm not sure. We hugged. And I . . . I sort of woke up thinking that we might have kissed, and feeling unbelievably embarrassed about it. I mean, we were friends. There wasn't anything else except a bit of mutual support and a lot of alcohol between us.'

'You didn't talk about it?'

'It didn't even matter,' she said, in a voice that was suddenly harsh. 'Once we'd woken up that morning, and not found her . . . Who gave a shit whether we'd snogged?'

Jojo sat back, and folded her arms across each other.

'And you don't remember Connor getting up in the night?' he asked. 'You don't remember being awake, and him not being there . . .?'

'I was asked about that at the time,' she said, with a small sigh. 'I didn't think so. I have no memory of him moving, or coming or going, but if it was hazy back then when I was hungover, it's a lot more so now.'

'Could you just reiterate for me the half-memory you mentioned in our last talk?' he said. 'And that will be all.'

Jojo did so, sounding even more hesitant than she had. She finished up with an impatient sigh. Jonah reached forward to turn off the tape. He gave her a smile.

'Thank you for doing that. It was an important thing to get on tape.'

Jojo nodded, and then gave him a slightly quizzical smile. 'Any time, Copper Sheens.'

Lightman asked him, once they'd seen Jojo out, about the questions over her late boyfriend.

'Is he of interest?' he asked.

'Yes and no,' Jonah replied. 'There's no particular reason

to think so, but he was part of the group for a while, and his is the second unexpected death to happen among them. I think it would be an omission not to ask questions.'

Lightman nodded. 'I'll look into the police reports on it.'

'Good man.'

Jonah found himself thinking about the past again as he sat at his desk. About that beauty of Aurora's, and what she could have achieved in her life. How she might have been seduced, perhaps before that night.

Aside from that, he was bracing himself for Tom's call. For the name he hoped not to hear. Whenever he thought about it, it was like standing on the edge of a steep drop. He couldn't afford to be drawn into memories that threatened to undo him.

He gave a sigh, and decided that it was time to go over his team's notes on the original interviews. It was immediately absorbing, not least because of the gross difference in the number of interviews. Coralie had been brought in only twice, with Jojo interviewed four times, Brett five, and Topaz seven.

And then there had been a big jump to the number of transcripts for Daniel Benham, who had come second to Connor Dooley in the number of interviews he'd been given only by three.

Daniel had been brought in fourteen times to have things checked and double-checked. They wanted to know why he'd been the one to go for help. Why he hadn't looked for her. What time he had last seen her, because his account wasn't quite like everyone else's. Though, in fact, everyone else's account had proven to be false, too, and none of them was quite like anyone else's.

And yet they'd kept on at him, the bright young son of a well-known and wealthy local businessman. The kind of boy who usually got away with whatever he wanted. The kind of privileged male who breezed through life.

Jonah could find no reasoning behind this apparent distrust. There was nothing stated in any of the interviews or notes to point the finger at Benham above any of the other kids. So had it been his attitude that had been wrong? Something that never made it into those clinical transcripts? Or had it been the way he liked to argue every point and was known to be a pot-smoking anarchist?

He tried re-imagining Daniel Benham's life. He thought about how it might have been shaped by murder.

At fifteen he had been a vocal socialist. He had been champing at the bit to be old enough to vote, and to join the Labour Party. He was going to stand up against the prime minister he thought was killing the vulnerable by removing support. He had been a humanitarian on a grand scale, and if his socialism had been of the champagne kind, it had been heartfelt. It had driven him to attend rallies and to found a socialist group at the school.

But his principles had fizzled out somewhere. His socialism had changed to a centrism that, with age, had slowly turned to downright Toryism. Had his own actions as a killer changed him? Or was it a reaction to the disappearance of the girl he had liked?

He found it difficult to place Benham in the role of killer, somehow. But that was true of all of them, he thought.

At a little before twelve, Tom Jackson called him back with the list of Aurora's friends.

'There are two of them,' Tom said. That fact alone gave Jonah both a twinge of fear and a twinge of sadness.

'Topaz says the only person she really talked to much was Becky Morris,' Aurora's father said. 'She came round here a couple of times. Very quiet girl.'

'Did Topaz know where we might find her?'

'Yes, she said she's found her on Facebook and she's accepted her friend request. She says if you give her an email, she'll send you a link to her profile.'

'That would be very useful, thank you.' He read out his email address, and Tom read it out in turn, presumably to Topaz.

'And then there was Zofia Wierzbowski.' Tom spelled the name out carefully, and Jonah could feel sweat breaking out across his skin. 'They did drama together after school and sometimes waited for the bus together, Topaz says. I think she was supposed to come round, but she never did. Topaz has no idea if she's even in the country any more. Her parents took her out of school some while before . . . before Aurora. She'd got in with a bad crowd, and I remember Aurora distancing herself from her.'

He wondered if Tom could tell that his heart was in his throat as he said a slightly strangled, 'Thank you', and hung up.

He stood looking at that name. An intense urge to screw the paper up hit him. If he wrote a new note, with just the other friend's name on, nobody might ever know that Zofia had been mentioned. Tom Jackson wouldn't be checking up with the rest of the group, would he?

But what about Topaz? What if she decided to contact the girls themselves? What if the case came to court, and a decision to hide his own actions undid everything?

He could contact her himself, to try to limit the damage. But that would be the worst possible thing. She would recognize his name, and doubtless react. And then he'd have to offer up her messages as evidence.

His one chance would be to let the team talk to her, and hope that his name never came up. That she wouldn't think him relevant to any of their questions. Or better still, that she would have forgotten.

He felt light-headed as he left his office. Lightman and Hanson were both on their desktops, so immersed that neither looked up until he spoke.

'The Jacksons have given me the names of two of Aurora's friends,' he said, as lightly as possible, and Lightman reached out to take the note. It took him a fraction of a second longer to let go of it than he'd intended, but Lightman didn't seem to notice. 'I know you've both got things to be getting on with, but I need the second one tracking down. Topaz is sending me Facebook details for Becky, so I'll get in touch.'

'OK. I'll take a look,' Lightman said. 'Mackenzie's ex-girlfriend called back. She's going to let us know what time she can come in once she's worked out childcare.'

'Good. Anything through from Intelligence on Mackenzie himself yet?'

Lightman gave a very short laugh. 'Apparently asking for anything back today is optimistic. Amir says they're snowed under at the moment.'

Jonah sighed. Intelligence was always snowed under. It was a perpetual state. Or at least they liked to say so. 'I feel for them. But tell them it's the DCS's priority, and they'd better look sharp about it.'

'Will do.'

'Anything to report?' he asked Hanson.

'Not much,' she said. 'I'd quite like some of the files O'Malley's been looking at . . .'

She looked at the chaos of O'Malley's desk with a grimace, and Jonah managed to laugh. 'I'd wait till he gets back.'

He retreated into his office again, and logged into his laptop. His heart was still pounding, but he told himself to breathe. He had to put thoughts of Zofia aside, and not sit waiting for his team to find something.

Topaz's email had come through, and the link to Becky Morris's profile. Her photo was from some kind of professional shoot, with vivid make-up and a coy pose. She looked uncomfortable, her round face uncertain.

A quick look at her profile showed him that Becky was now a jewellery maker. She ran her own online store called Bells and Whistles, which also had a small shop only a mile away. It was open now.

Jonah grabbed his jacket, and called to his team breezily, 'I'm heading out to see Aurora's friend Becky. I should be less than an hour. Call me if anything urgent comes up.'

It was a huge relief to walk out of the station, away from where they were searching for a Polish woman he had once known. He was so steeped in the feeling that he forgot his own advice to be careful until, halfway down the steps, the sound of a revving engine startled him.

He spun, and saw the departing tail of what looked like an old Fiesta on the far side of the road. But with two lanes of traffic in between, he could see little else.

His heart was back to its accelerated rhythm as he walked more watchfully down to ground level and round to the front car park where his Mondeo was waiting. He paused before using his remote to unlock it, and then, feeling slightly ridiculous, ducked underneath to check for any strange devices.

There was nothing there, but the feeling of danger remained with him all the way to Becky's shop.

*

Hanson was struggling to get on with her work, and wasn't entirely sure why. Her thoughts kept returning to the DCI, and Jojo, and the tension she noticed in him sometimes when discussing Aurora or her friends. He had been jittery as hell before he left, and she wondered if he knew this Becky Morris he was off to see.

Lightman, sitting opposite her, was absorbed in files on his screen. She was half desperate to talk to him about it, and half afraid of saying anything. In the end, she leaned round her screen, and said, 'Ben, what do you think of the chief working on a case where he knew the victim? You don't think it's a bit . . . awkward?'

Lightman focused on her, and then nodded slowly. 'If he'd known her well, I'd say it was a bad idea. But being at the same school, and having done nothing more than catch sight of her a few times . . . I don't think there's any harm.'

'You think that's all he knew of her?' she pressed. 'I mean, surely he'd talked to her a few times.'

'Not that I know of.'

'And Jojo?' she asked, with that anxiety in her stomach. 'He definitely knew her quite well.'

Lightman pulled a considering face. 'I don't think it's going to get in the way. Like I said, he's not exactly emotional.'

Hanson nodded, trying to align herself with his trust. Perhaps she just needed to get to know the chief better. But she still felt, at some level, that something was up with Jonah Sheens. And she wanted very much to know what.

Bells and Whistles had the small ground floor in what should have been an attractive nineteenth-century building. But the chip shop and betting shop on either side were both run-down and shabby, and their signs dominated the building.

The shop had a lot of pink and a lot of glitter. The sort of place that small girls would be drawn to like magpies. It was empty of customers at the moment, however. He could see only someone reading a magazine behind the counter.

He was immediately certain on entering that it was Becky sitting behind the counter, despite the lack of make-up and frizzy hair. She had the same round face, and the air of uncertainty.

'Can I help?' she asked, standing as he approached. Her accent was pure working-class Southampton, with a slight trace of a wheeze to it.

'I'm DCI Sheens,' he said, as lightly as possible. 'I'm looking to have a quick chat with Becky Morris. Is that you?'

'Yeah,' she said, looking a little hunted. 'Sorry, you're . . . from the police?'

'Yes. It's nothing to worry you. I'm the officer in charge of investigating Aurora Jackson's death, and I wanted to ask you a few questions.'

'Aurora?' she asked. 'Yeah, OK. I mean . . . I don't think I can help much.'

'That's fine,' Jonah said. 'I just thought you might know a few more things about her that could help us.'

'Right. I haven't got anyone who can cover today. We'll have to talk here. Do you . . . do you need a seat?'

'No, that's all right,' he said with a smile.

Becky perched herself back on the high chair behind the counter. 'OK. What did you want to know?' she asked.

'I'd like to know if Aurora seemed happy to you in the days before she vanished.'

'I think so. I mean . . . As happy as she generally was.'

'She wasn't all that happy a person?'

'Not . . . not really. Not unhappy. Just not, you know, really cheerful. School was tough for both of us.'

It was strange watching her. She visibly shrank as she spoke, as if weighed down by memories of that time.

'Were either of you bullied?' he asked.

'Yeah. A bit.' She was a mixture of resentful and embarrassed, which was something he'd heard in a lot of bullying victims. Even grown men and women like Becky who by rights should have moved on and forgotten about it. But that kind of thing left a mark on people.

'That's sad to hear. Was there anyone in particular?' he asked.

'Mostly a couple of girls in the sixth form,' Becky said. 'Lisa and Emma. They were twins, and they were pretty crap to everyone.'

'Would you say Aurora had been driven to despair?'

'What do you mean?'

'You don't think she was on the verge of doing something stupid?'

'No, it was nothing like that.' Becky gave a half-laugh. 'Actually, it'd got a bit better. Topaz'd had words with them.'

Jonah was taken aback. He couldn't remember Topaz ever sticking up for her sister.

'What did Topaz say to them?' he asked.

'She saw them pushing Aurora and me around in the middle of the schoolyard, and she stormed over,' Becky said, and he could hear a little note of worship in her voice even after thirty years. 'She said to get their fucking hands off us, and if they touched us again, Connor would beat the life out of them.'

Jonah found himself smiling. That was a little typical of Topaz, to use her hanger-on to her advantage. But she'd gone to her sister's aid when she needed it, despite her embarrassment at her spacy sister. He wondered whether she would still have done that when drunk or high, and if the person threatening her sister had been someone she was interested in.

'Sorry, I don't think this is very . . . I probably don't know anything that helpful,' Becky said uncertainly, smoothing her hands down over her skirt.

'It's helping me understand Aurora better,' Jonah reassured her. 'What about boyfriends?'

'Who? Aurora?'

'Yes.'

'No. Neither of us was . . . She didn't have anyone.'

He caught something in her expression. For the first time, someone wasn't laughing at the idea of Aurora dating.

'Had she had someone before?'

'Not . . . not exactly.' There was a momentary pause, and then she said, 'Sorry. I need my inhaler.'

She scrabbled under the counter and came up with a blue Ventolin inhaler.

'Asthma?' Jonah asked. 'That's a pain.'

She took a puff, held her breath, and then nodded. 'Always had it,' she said, once she'd breathed it out. There was a slight breathlessness to her voice. Jonah knew to be patient, even when he was itching for her to continue.

'So was there some kind of complicated situation? Someone who pursued Aurora, maybe?'

'It . . . it wasn't . . . it was someone she liked.'

Jonah waited, beginning to suspect that he knew what she was going to say.

'She was totally in love with our English teacher, Mr Mackenzie. I mean, we all were a bit. But Aurora could hardly talk about anything else. And she was always going to see him about stuff, having extra lessons with him . . .'

'He gave her extra lessons?' Jonah asked. 'Outside school?'

'Yeah. He was helping her with a competition she was entering, and she'd written a book, and she wanted him to read it.'

'So would you say . . . that he might have encouraged her a bit?'

There was a very brief silence. 'I don't know. Maybe. She was always telling me how he looked at her, and there was this thing between them. I guess part of me believed her and part of me thought it was all in her head.'

'She didn't mention him touching her? Kissing her?'

'No.' Becky seemed positive about that. 'I think she would have told me. If she was all excited about a nice comment on her work, she would have told me if something had actually happened, wouldn't she?'

Jonah made a non-committal noise of agreement, thinking that that might not be true, if the teacher in question had warned her not to tell anyone.

'What about the week before she went missing?' he went on. 'You can't think of anything between them then?'

'No,' Becky said hesitantly. 'No, but I was angry with him in a weird way. She only agreed to go camping because she thought it'd impress him. It was the kind of thing he always talked about doing. Big long walks, and camping in the wild . . . It wasn't Aurora's thing at all. She liked her room and her books.'

Jonah felt a flicker of unease. 'Did she tell him she was going?'

There was another brief pause. 'Yeah. Yeah, I think so. I remember she was terrified of the summer holidays coming up and not seeing him for six weeks. And she was a bit obvious about stuff like that . . . Yeah, I think she said it in front of the whole class, actually.'

Jonah was very aware of his heartbeat as he wound down the conversation, and thanked Becky for her help. She apologized for not having more to tell him. As far as Jonah was concerned, she'd told him plenty.

He found all three of his team at their desks when he returned. O'Malley looked up, and immediately said, 'Ooh, look who's got something to say . . .'

Jonah couldn't help grinning, in spite of the slightly sick feeling that had been with him all day.

'We're bringing Mackenzie in,' he said.

'Come on, chief. Dish the dirt,' O'Malley said, swinging his chair round and stretching his legs out. Hanson's gaze was locked on him, too. 'You look like you're about to burst.'

'Aurora's closest friend has been telling me that Aurora had a crush on her English teacher,' he said. 'She says Aurora's decision to go camping was about impressing him, and she's fairly certain that Aurora told him and her whole English class that they were going.'

Hanson's expression turned into a half-smile. 'So he knew she was there.'

'That's interesting,' Lightman said, as neutrally as ever. 'Taken alongside the relationship he had with a former pupil.'

'Oh, well there's more on that,' O'Malley said. 'It turns out that the pupil and he are now married. They've got three kids. So her name is Pria Mackenzie these days.'

Jonah wasn't immediately sure what to make of that.

'Wow, OK. She might be someone to talk to later. But for

231

now, we bring Mackenzie in. Mackenzie, and Topaz, who I'm sure will have more to say about him.'

Topaz arrived quickly, having been in town shopping. Once Jonah was inside the room, she didn't wait for any questions. She attacked first. 'Have you started looking at Mr Mackenzie yet?'

'I can't give any details, but yes,' Jonah replied. 'It's one of our main lines of enquiry.'

'Along with me, I take it?' she asked.

'Along with all six of you who were there when she vanished,' Jonah replied. 'You're all in a position to give us information about what happened. I'd like you to help us as much as you can.'

'I'm already doing that,' she said.

'Your help with Aurora's friends is appreciated,' he said, nodding. 'But we have more questions. About Mackenzie, first of all.'

'Fire away,' she said, lifting her chin.

'When you met him on the riverbank, you were close to the stash, weren't you?'

'Yes. I told you.'

'But you didn't tell any of your friends,' he said. 'Which seems strange when you spent some while going over everything with them.'

There was a slight hint of a blush to Topaz's cheeks, but she merely shrugged.

'Had you arranged to meet him?'

'No!' she said sharply. 'Of course I hadn't. I had no clue he'd be there, and I had no interest in him.'

'You weren't selling him drugs?'

'What? Don't be stupid,' Topaz said, but the blush grew across her cheeks. He was either right, or very close to it.

'You know that we aren't interested in any drug-selling,' Jonah said gently. 'Just in Aurora.'

'I know, and I wasn't doing that.' She shook her head, sharply. 'Me being there was a coincidence. The important thing is that *he* was there, and after he walked on he could have seen the stash.'

'All right,' Jonah said, making a mental note to press Mackenzie on this subject, too.

'What sort of a sick fucker would rape her?' Topaz asked suddenly. 'She was just a kid.'

'Do you mind me asking if you were sexually active at that age?' Jonah asked.

Topaz lifted her head, with eyes that were shining and angry. 'That was different! I was a different person. I knew what I was doing. I understood, and I . . . I wasn't a child like her.'

'But someone found her sexually attractive,' Jonah pressed. 'You wanted us to look at Andrew Mackenzie, but I think it's your husband that you're not quite sure about, isn't it? Did he tell you we'd questioned him about Aurora?'

She folded her arms, in what he took as a defensive pose, but then she took a deep breath, and said, 'Yes, he did. He explained to you about trying to kiss her. But it was pure jealousy. I know it was. He wanted to prove to me that other people could like him too. But she told him no, and left.'

'Did he try . . . to force her to?'

'I don't think so,' Topaz said. 'I mean . . . I think he was a bit pissed off that she made him look bad, but that's all.'

'And he didn't try to follow her?'

'Not as far as I saw,' Topaz said quietly. 'I left with Brett. By that point, he was pretty into the whole thing and it was exciting. He was the one everyone wanted, so I guess . . . I guess I just went with it.' She gave a sudden, exasperated sigh. 'Why does the focus have to be on the teenagers, instead of on her teacher?'

'We will be questioning him,' Jonah reassured her. 'I know that you feel strongly about him.'

'You would, too, if you'd seen the way he looked at her,' she said, with a twist to her mouth. 'She only had to open her mouth, and he was already smiling and telling her how wonderful she was. It was all wrong. It was always all wrong.'

Jonah spent a few moments synching up with Lightman and Hanson, edgy with tiredness and the feeling of his thoughts being overloaded. He needed them to keep him on task, and make sure that nothing got forgotten.

What he wasn't so much in need of was Hanson's cheerful 'I've found Zofia Wierzbowski. She's on Facebook, and calls herself Zofia Wier. I'm sure it's her. She has Southampton College listed on her education.'

'Right,' Jonah said, trying not to show a reaction. 'Is she local?'

'No, she's in Wroclaw, or however the hell you say it. But I've sent her a message, and if I don't get a reply, I'll see if I can find a phone number.'

'Great,' he said, feeling anything but. 'Anything else for me?'

'Not yet,' Lightman said, and Hanson shook her head.

'I might need you in the interview room shortly, Hanson.'

He headed back to his office and then diverted to make himself more coffee. He'd had too much already, but he was hoping it would somehow break through the boiling fog in his head.

Mackenzie's ex-girlfriend arrived before Mackenzie did. Jonah watched her being escorted past his doorway. Soft cardigan. Baggy tunic top. Round figure. Short, slightly wavy grey-brown hair. And when she turned to Hanson, who was ushering her in, a warm smile. An aura of overwhelming motherliness.

An inevitable feeling of guilt towards his own mother, who had never been anything like that, surfaced. It was compounded by the guilt of not having seen her the night before, and not having managed to reach her yet today. He'd have to try again. He picked up a board marker and scrawled 'Mum' on to the notepad on his desk, before walking after Hanson and the ex-girlfriend.

He realized on the way that he'd forgotten her name somewhere along the line. He thought about asking Hanson when she paused outside the door with a questioning look, but he was pretty sure that the woman was going to hear through the open door.

'Sit in on this one,' he said to the constable, and they went in.

Jonah thanked the woman for coming, and spent a short while writing a date and time on his notebook, but by the time he'd finished, her name still wasn't there.

He wrote another note and leaned it towards Hanson.

Can't remember her name. Kick things off, please?

Hanson shook her head slightly, a small smile on her mouth.

'We'd like to record this interview, if that's OK, Diana?'

'Of course,' she said, that warm smile in place once again and her eyes creasing up behind her thick glasses.

Hanson held her hand out towards the tape recorder, hesitantly, and Jonah waved a hand. 'Be my guest, constable.'

'This is DC Hanson and DCI Jonah Sheens, interviewing Diana Pitman-Wells.'

Jonah wrote the name down, and then sat back to listen while Hanson started in with a few questions.

Diana talked easily, and was happy to take them through the night of Aurora's disappearance. What she told them synched up with what Mackenzie had said – that they had camped together and slept from before midnight until seven a.m.

Satisfied for the present, Jonah asked her to explain the history of her relationship with Andrew Mackenzie – a month and a half before that night – and then, from there, to expand on what had happened between them afterwards.

It was in the gradual break-up of their relationship that Jonah found the greatest interest.

'It basically started going wrong after that night,' she said. 'His student had gone missing. I understood that. We found out together when we got back to his house on the Sunday evening. We put the TV on to watch something. I'm not even sure what now. Probably a drama. He did like his dramas. And before it started, the news came on . . . I don't think he was ever really my boyfriend after that.'

'How so?'

She took a breath, and swallowed. 'Sorry. This is ridiculous. I'm a happily married woman and it's thirty years ago, but talking about it is still . . . I suppose that's wounded pride, for you, isn't it?' She gave a small, slightly bright-eyed smile. 'Lasts a lifetime. I still remember how . . . We were sitting there, half on top of each other on the sofa, both of us tired and a bit hungover. And then he was bolt upright and flinging me off. He was just staring at the TV. And he wouldn't tell me what it was, so I had to work it out from the report, which said she was a pupil at his school.'

'He seemed upset?' Hanson asked.

'More than upset,' she said. 'He was shaking. And then he rang the headmaster at home, and wanted to know what the school knew, what they were doing. He ended up by asking what he should do, and I don't think he got a very clear answer. I asked what the headmaster had said once he'd hung up and he just stared into space. He didn't seem to hear me at all. And then he suddenly started walking out of the house.'

Jonah waited a moment for more, but she seemed to have reached a sticking point.

'He left the house?'

'Yes.' She seemed to find some momentum again. 'He didn't explain . . . until I followed him out to the car. It was like talking to someone on drugs. I asked him three times where he was going and eventually he seemed to hear. He said he was going to join the search, and said I could come if I wanted. But I don't think he cared what I did, to be honest.'

'That's a pretty strange way to react, wouldn't you say?' Hanson asked.

'I thought so,' she agreed. 'But I suppose . . . I realized it would upset any of us. One of our students going missing. And he'd hardly been teaching any time. He probably felt responsible for her somehow.'

'Had you heard about Aurora from him before?' Jonah asked.

'Umm . . . Not that I can remember.' Diana gave a small shrug. 'We didn't talk about specific pupils all that often. Perhaps because we were too busy complaining about the management, or paperwork. But . . . he talked about almost nothing else afterwards.'

'To the point where it struck you as unhealthy?' Hanson asked.

Jonah made a mental note to talk to Hanson about leading questions. It wasn't the worst he'd heard, but they couldn't afford to do anything wrong here. If Mackenzie had had anything to do with Aurora's death, then the police and their practices were going to be under a lot of scrutiny.

'I don't know,' Diana said, clearly very discomfited.

'Would you mind describing how his behaviour continued?' Jonah said.

Diana's face had lost its motherly charm. She looked pained. Hurt.

'I remember that he . . . stopped doing anything else,' she said. 'For the next few weeks, if he wasn't out searching for her, he was reading news articles or sticking posters up. He had a map that he stuck up in the kitchen, with pins in. One of them was the campsite. And one of them was where we slept. I remember that. We were reduced to a pin, and he never even referred to us when he talked about it. Just about how much he regretted not having heard anything. Not having stopped walking sooner and been closer to her.'

'Was it your impression that he wanted to find her?' Jonah asked quietly.

'Yes,' she said. 'He was desperate to be the one who found her. He even made friends with the chief inspector who was put in charge of it. He would call up and suggest angles, and he took it upon himself to talk to her school friends.'

'I suppose all this took a toll on your relationship,' Jonah said.

'It ended our relationship,' she corrected him. 'After three months of being essentially invisible to him, when spending time with him meant listening to his mutterings about where she might be, I was done. It didn't matter how much I sympathized with him, or how sad I felt for that girl. You can't be invisible to the man you love.'

Jonah gave a nod. Her account was interesting. He had known killers spearhead search attempts before. He had known boyfriends, fathers, wives and even a daughter who had been the face of the public appeal before their house of cards had fallen down. But in those cases that kind of behaviour had been reserved for public appearances. For moments when they felt visible as a poor, bereft family member. The hunt had not been the driving force behind every waking minute. Which had been part of what had tripped them up.

And a small internal voice added to this. It told him that Mackenzie's obsession with finding Aurora reminded him of his own. Had it gradually lessened for Mackenzie, too, but never quite died out?

'The camping trip,' he said, thinking back to Becky Morris's statements in the shop. 'Can you remember how long in advance it was planned?'

'Oh. Yes, I think . . . He'd spent a few weeks talking me into it. So quite a long while ahead of time.'

'And had you picked a place to go?'

Diana's face creased into a frown. 'I think we discussed that for a while. He wanted a really long walk, and I wanted something shorter, which left me some time to see my sister during the day. So I'm not sure. Maybe we pinned it down a few days before.'

Jonah nodded. 'Do you remember if you or he suggested the approximate area?'

'I'm sorry, I don't,' Diana replied, 'but I would have been keen on it being close by.'

Jonah nodded again, thinking about the possibility of some kind of premeditation. Could Mackenzie really have intended to get his girlfriend drunk, and then to slip away? And had he really organized his whole weekend around seeing Aurora? He knew she would be with friends, and not alone.

Or had he and Aurora arranged it somehow? Had her comment to him been a coded message that the rest of the class hadn't understood?

'Can I just ask a final question?' he continued, aware that a silence had arisen.

'Of course.'

'In your honest opinion, as one who knew him well,' he said, 'would you describe Andrew Mackenzie's behaviour as suspicious? Did you start to wonder if there had been anything . . . improper between him and his pupil?'

He saw her face tighten. 'I didn't ever think so. I thought he was a good man. I still think he is, but I suppose . . . it's been so long . . .' She shook her head. 'It's so hard to be sure! I wonder if I remember him as he really was, or whether it's gradually changed.'

'Nothing more definite?'

'What can I say?' Diana asked, looking wretched. 'I don't want to believe that he was involved, and I never thought he was. But that's all I've got.'

'Thank you,' he said. 'You've been very helpful.'

He stopped the tape, and rose, letting Hanson show Diana out while he retreated towards his office.

He was almost at his sanctuary when he saw the door to CID opening. O'Malley was standing aside to let Andrew Mackenzie in.

Hanson was only yards away with Diana. The ex-girlfriend stopped without warning. She put a hand up to her mouth.

Mackenzie saw her a moment later. The look he gave her was sick with fear.

26. Aurora

Saturday, 23 July 1983, 2:50 a.m.

It was the cold that woke her up. Or the shivering. Her whole body was convulsed by it, a teeth-chattering shaking that ran through her.

Her mouth was so dry it made breathing uncomfortable. She didn't want to get up from the warmth of her sleeping bag. Didn't want to move. But the thirst was too much, and after she had tried to curl up and ignore it for a time, she unzipped the bag and scrambled out of it.

She was disorientated for a moment when she realized that she was in deep darkness. The bright beacon of the fire behind the trees was gone, and the sky was moonless.

Still racked by shaking, she stood with her arms folded and tried to see which way to go. She tried to remember.

She'd set her sleeping bag up with her head away from them all. She'd done that on purpose. So she needed to walk towards her feet to find them again.

She took small, hesitant steps. She couldn't see what her feet were doing. Why had they let the fire go out?

Between the trunks, she eventually started to see a deep red light. Low-down, like footlights.

She emerged into the clearing to find it empty, the fire nothing but pale white ash and orange-red embers. There were no sobbing people. No music. No conversation. Nothing but the susurrating wind between ash leaves, punctuations to a profound quiet.

And she was cold still. Really cold.

Aurora approached the fire and ducked down next to it. She tried blowing on it to stir it, and then hunted around for more firewood. She found a bundle of sticks tied not far from the remaining beer cans.

She decided to open a can. She drank three mouthfuls of it, but felt no less parched than before.

The shaking was still running through her as she put it aside. Her fingers were heavy and useless on the string that tied the firewood. They slipped three times. Four. And she lost patience. She yanked at a long, thick branch until it came free. And then she did the same again and again until she had six of them ready to be fed to the orange embers.

If the shivering hadn't been so bad, she might have left the fire as it was. Left its luminous whiteness untouched so that she could watch it. It was beautiful.

But she felt cold to her centre. She threw the wood on to it jerkily. The last piece she snatched back, remembering that she would need to stir the flames up, too.

She was leaning over it, using the long stick to turn it all over, when there was a sound. A crunching sound like a footstep on the dry ground.

She looked behind her sharply, her heart a wild thing in her chest.

She scanned the trees frantically, her vision overlaid by bright-blue blotches where the fire had left its mark. She couldn't make anything out. She wondered if it had been her imagination, until she caught movement. There was somebody there.

27

Jonah didn't approach the teacher as someone to be broken down. Mackenzie looked broken already, and he responded to pressure with despair, rather than anger or panic.

His young, rather cold solicitor had arrived shortly after Mackenzie had. Jonah found him difficult, largely because his polished glasses reflected light every time he turned his head, and he did it a lot. The glare put him on edge from the start.

He'd decided to bring up Becky Morris's comments straight off, reasoning that Mackenzie wasn't going to be lulled into any kind of security in the shell-shocked state he was in.

'One of Aurora's friends has suggested that Aurora told you she was going camping that night, and where,' he said. 'She's told us that Aurora actually told the whole of her class, but that it was clearly directed at you.'

Mackenzie looked bewildered. 'I don't remember that at all,' he said. 'Not at all. And Diana and I had arranged that trip weeks before.'

'But you hadn't established what the route was, had you?'

'We – I think we had.' He glanced between Hanson and Jonah. 'Did Diana say we hadn't? I don't . . . I don't think I would have left it till the last minute. It was complicated. We had to meet up somewhere, and make sure she was walking as far as she wanted, and I was walking much further.' He shook his head. 'I'm sure I would have planned.'

'You can't confirm that?'

'My client has already told you as much as he can remember,' the solicitor interjected.

'Well, then,' Jonah said, with a slight smile at Mackenzie. 'Take me through your relationship with Aurora.' He took a more settled pose in his chair. He was signalling that he was here to stay.

'I was her teacher,' Mackenzie said, a little hopelessly. 'I told you yesterday how much I admired her intelligence.'

'How do you think she regarded you?'

Mackenzie gave a small, awkward shrug. 'She probably liked that I liked her work. And she was lonely. I think . . . I think I was one of the few people who would talk literature with her.'

'What kind of literature?'

'A lot of classics, and the modern American greats,' he said immediately.

'You seem to remember very clearly . . .'

'Because that was what mattered to me,' Mackenzie said, leaning forward and spitting slightly with the earnestness of his speech. 'I was her teacher, and I loved to teach. I still love it.'

His momentary energy seemed to leave him, and he slid back into his chair again.

'You do have some history of blurred boundaries with a pupil,' Jonah said, after a moment. 'There was a complaint made against you by a concerned parent later in your career. You began a relationship with a pupil, who later became your wife.'

'She wasn't my pupil,' Mackenzie said immediately. 'Nothing happened until after she'd left. And I promise you, I didn't even think about it until I bumped into her in a pub that October. There was nothing wrong with any of it, and that particular parent reported it in reaction to her son being suspended.'

'So she was, what?' Jonah asked. 'Eighteen when you met again? Nineteen?'

'Eighteen. Nineteen shortly afterwards.'

'How old were you?'

'Twenty-six.'

Jonah nodded slowly. 'And when you bumped into her, you were immediately interested?'

'No, I wasn't,' Mackenzie replied. 'I was happy to hear what she was doing. Pri was out with uni friends, and I'd always expected her to do well. She'd gone to Oxford, and that was where I saw her. We talked about work, and what she was and wasn't enjoying. And eventually arranged to meet up on another occasion.'

'And you hadn't had a sense of interest from her before?' Jonah asked. 'You hadn't felt that she'd been infatuated with you as a pupil?'

Mackenzie's mouth opened, and then he hesitated. His expression was more than pained. Jonah could hear Hanson shifting next to him in the pause.

'Maybe,' Mackenzie said. 'I was a young male teacher at a school. I was probably idolized more than I should have been.'

'Do you think that was the case for Aurora, too?'

Mackenzie's mouth twisted. 'I don't know. Probably.'

'Probably?'

Mackenzie brought a finger down to jab at the table. 'You don't understand what it's like. You're the only young man most of them know, at a time when romance is everything. The first year I taught, I got eight valentine's roses. I mean, for fuck's sake. They were surrounded by thoughtless boys, and I was a fraction older and not a total moron emotionally. Add in that they were supposed to focus on me for an hour at a time, and of course they all thought they were in love with me.'

Jonah glanced at Hanson, who was looking very thoughtful. 'Do you think Aurora's sister shared that interest in you?' she asked.

Mackenzie gave a wry grin. 'Topaz was a very different sort of girl. She just wanted to make me interested in her. She wanted everyone, man, boy – even her little shadow, Coralie – to want her.'

Hanson was frowning. 'You think her relationship with Coralie was more than friendship?'

'Not in any real sense,' Mackenzie replied. 'I don't think they were ever an item or anything. But I'm positive that Coralie's interest in Topaz was sexual. The staff were all fairly certain she was bisexual.'

Jonah thought that decidedly interesting. If Coralie had wanted Topaz for herself, it would have been ample reason for her to hate Connor. Enough, perhaps, to point the finger at him to the police.

'So when you saw Topaz that night, at the river,' Jonah said, moving the conversation on, 'nothing went on between you?'

Mackenzie snorted. 'Of course not. I may have been young, but even at that age I knew girls like that were pure trouble.'

'It wasn't a planned meeting?'

'No!' Mackenzie said. 'Like I said, I had no idea they'd be there, and I wasn't all that pleased about it.'

'You didn't meet her to purchase drugs?'

Mackenzie looked genuinely stumped. There was a brief pause. 'Why would I be doing that? I don't use, and Topaz wasn't a drug dealer.' There was another pause, and Mackenzie said, with what looked like genuine curiosity, '*Was* she?'

'Well, let's put it another way,' Jonah said. 'Topaz saw you at the riverbank, and never breathed a word to any of her friends, even when they went over the events of that night over and over among themselves. Which tells me there was something not quite right about that meeting. Don't you think?'

The teacher looked at him and gave a very slight half-laugh. Not, Jonah thought, out of amusement, but out of a sense of absurdity.

'It's not . . .' Mackenzie shook his head. 'There was nothing odd about it, and no planning.'

'So she didn't show you any places of interest while you were there?'

'What places of interest? It was a campsite.'

Mackenzie looked genuinely mystified, and Jonah decided to leave it there for now, largely to give himself time to think.

Jonah didn't like the look of O'Malley's expression. The sergeant started to stride towards him as soon as Jonah entered the floor of CID, his phone in his hand. He had the aura of a messenger with bad tidings.

'The shit has hit the Twitter fan,' O'Malley announced, and Jonah took the iPhone off him with a feeling of immediate stress.

It was the BBC News Twitter account. BREAKING: Aurora Jackson's teacher brought in for questioning. The image link took him to a cross-street but sharp photo of Andrew Mackenzie being escorted into the station.

'Fuck.'

'That's what I said,' O'Malley answered.

'That's a press photo,' he said.

'Not guilty, sir. But I'm happy to go and ask the constable who came to pick him up if he's been a colossal prick and would like to explain himself.'

'Do that,' Jonah said with depression rather than anger. Publicity like this meant pressure, and he was profoundly uncertain about Mackenzie. He was willing neither to charge him nor to release him at this point. He'd warned the teacher to expect an overnight stay. He had forty-eight hours to keep him for questioning before he had to charge him or let him go, and it looked like he would need to make full use of the time.

He braced himself for a conversation with the chief super. Wilkinson was probably going to be pissed off about this.

Wilkinson had already heard about the social media storm. He was clearly displeased, but didn't believe any of Jonah's team to be responsible. Jonah was relieved, as it would have been easy for Hanson to take the flak as the new, unknown one.

'On the plus side, switchboard says we've had one girl call in and tell us that she thinks Mackenzie sexually assaulted her,' Wilkinson went on. 'And another girl's mother has accused him on her behalf. The benefits of social media,' he added drily.

'Right. We'll look into their statements,' Jonah replied.

'Do. And keep doing it all properly. More resources on Mackenzie, if anything.'

'Yes, sir.'

Jonah left Wilkinson's office, and approached his team

thoughtfully. All three of them were sitting at their desks, and looked up at him expectantly.

'We're under a little media attention now,' he said, 'as you'll have seen. That, and the fact that we have only forty-eight hours to question him without charge, means keeping the focus on Mackenzie, even when there's still good reason to look at Connor fairly hard. Ben, I'd like you to arrange for him to be housed overnight, and then get in touch with his wife and arrange an interview. Ring up all his former schools again, as well. Push and see if they've been covering their backs.'

'Sure.'

'I had a thought on the whole Topaz-selling-Mackenzie-drugs thing, you know,' O'Malley said. 'In my look into the Dexedrine being sold, one of the guys mentioned a brunette who he'd never seen before who sold a small amount. My guess is, she'd lifted some Dexedrine from the stash and that's why she didn't want to admit to her friends that she'd seen Mackenzie.'

Jonah processed that. 'So she was the brunette,' he said.

'She was the brunette,' O'Malley agreed.

'That's a bloody good thought. Give her a call and see if you can talk her into admitting it.'

O'Malley grinned. 'Sure. Pretty sure I'll find a way.'

'What about me, sir?' Hanson asked.

'In the short term, I want you to call the Jacksons and update them about the as-yet-unnamed schoolteacher who we are questioning and no more. Explain that there were reasons for bringing him in for questioning, but as yet we're not at a stage to be certain of anything, we haven't arrested him, et cetera, et cetera. I'm sure you know the score.'

'Yes, sir.'

'Once you're done, let's get you looking at Connor again.'

'Yes, sir.' And then there was a brief pause, before Hanson asked, 'Will you want me to interview Mackenzie again with you tomorrow?'

'It'll probably depend on what Ben finds out,' Jonah replied, as Lightman rose, presumably to organize Mackenzie's accommodation. Jonah glanced at Hanson's slightly troubled expression. 'Did you feel there was more we should have asked him?'

'I just think he's the most likely candidate. He was there, nearby, knew she was there, and clearly has a predilection for young girls, or he wouldn't have hooked up with an eighteen-year-old.'

Jonah took a half-seat against the edge of the desk opposite hers. 'It's hard to say that definitively, though,' he said slowly. 'I could tell you several different stories about that. One is about a twenty-six-year-old teacher who is aware that many of his sixth-formers like him, but who likes one girl in return. He does nothing about it, because he knows he can't. Later, they meet at the pub, by chance, and he realizes that they both feel the same. That it's possible now. And having always known that they were right for each other, life proves that to be true. They marry, and have children.'

'OK,' Hanson said.

'And then there's another twenty-six-year-old teacher, who really shouldn't like his pupil but is a little weak about it. They flirt, though he knows it's wrong. Maybe they even kiss once, while alone, though she promises to say that nothing happened, and she's not allowed to say that they're together until months later.'

'Hmm. OK.'

'And then . . . then, there's a teacher who has convinced a

series of young girls that they love him, and that he loves them. He has groomed all of them, and persuaded them to be silent. Because he's picked his victims well, it's worked. And then one of them grows up and is still interested in him, and he thinks he may as well marry her. Because who would suspect a man happily married to a beautiful young wife?'

There was a brief silence, and Hanson nodded.

'So we need to find out which is the true representation, don't we?'

'Yes,' Jonah agreed. 'But bear in mind that one person is really a lot of different people. Back then, Mackenzie might have been both the man who wanted a family and a good career in teaching, and the lustful twenty-something who couldn't quite resist getting together with a student. It would depend on the situation, and the difficulty is working out which version of Mackenzie was there that night. Which version of all of them,' he went on. 'Was the Connor Dooley who was there the self-contained academic, or the angry teenager who regularly got into fights, and was taking abuse from his dad? Was Brett Parker the conscientious athlete, or the libidinous jock who had form with young girls?'

Hanson put a hand up to fiddle with her lip as she thought. 'Any of them could have been anyone, in some ways,' she said. 'But I don't see how we can find out what happened if we don't push them.'

'Maybe so,' Jonah said. 'But there's a right time for that. OK. I'd better go and get my bike and then do the dutiful son thing. Don't stay too late or you'll make me feel bad.'

28. Connor

Saturday, 23 July 1983, 5:20 a.m.

He could feel the hangover before he fully woke up. It was a full-on head-crusher. He felt like he might vomit if he moved, and his body was on fire.

He lay there for a while, feeling like he was really dying this time, but the need to urinate grew too strong to ignore. He opened his eyes and turned his head away from the light.

It was early, probably not long past dawn. Jojo was lying next to him. She was on her side with one strong arm stretched out above her, the other bent so that her wrist covered her face.

He had a momentary worry that something had happened between them. He had cried, he thought. And she had comforted him. He had ranted and raged to her about Topaz.

It made him feel wretched. Humiliation fought with nausea. He tried not to think about it. He just needed to pee, and to drink something that wasn't beer.

He watched the ground as he walked clumsily in the opposite direction from the campfire. He stepped carefully over an empty sleeping bag when it appeared in his vision. One of the others had to be up, then.

Relieving himself took a long time, and standing made him feel hotter and sicker. He was close to vomiting as he made his way back to the fire and his backpack. He dug in it, pulling out a lighter, a pack of mints, a compass – a selection of the useless shit he'd got in there. Where was the aspirin?

He found it in a side pocket in the end. He remembered that he'd put it there for easy access. He took a half-drunk bottle of water and went to sit on a log near the fire. And then he sat there, staring at a single point of sunlight on the ground while he waited for the painkillers to kick in.

He remembered Topaz and Brett all of a sudden, and felt a rush of dread low down in his guts. They would probably still be asleep together, with Coralie. The three of them wrapped round each other.

Sickness and anger drove him to his feet. He was leaving. He didn't want to be anywhere near any of them.

Part of the way to the car park, he saw Benners sprawled on his back on a patch of dry-looking grass. His sleeping bag was half over him, his mouth gaping open.

Connor was almost to the bikes when he remembered his sleeping bag, which was still next to Jojo. He thought about going back for it, but it seemed too difficult. Everything except treading onwards was too hard. He focused on the ground and kept moving.

And then the memory of that other sleeping bag came to him and he paused.

Aurora's. It must have been Aurora's. Benners had his own, and Jojo's was still in its bag next to her stuff. He didn't know what Topaz and Brett and Coralie had got to cover them, but they wouldn't have left a single sleeping bag at the far side of the camp.

He went on uncertainly, thinking that she might have got cold, and gone to sleep in the car. He made it to the car park and peered into the car through the slightly dusty windows. There was nobody there.

It seemed like a very long way back to the camp, and further still to where he'd seen that sleeping bag, but he turned round anyway. He had a silent monologue of rage the whole way back, telling himself she'd probably be back in the sleeping bag by now.

But when he reached the far side of the camp he saw that nothing had changed. The sleeping bag lay as it had, open and empty.

He stopped and crouched down. He thought he might actually be sick this time. He needed to eat something. But he needed to make sure she was OK first.

He put a hand into the sleeping bag. It was icy cold. He began to feel a sense of something wrong.

He thought about the river. She'd gone for a swim before. But once he'd made his tortuous way to the river, he found the tiny beach empty; the water clean and glittering and unmoving.

He could feel anxiety rising in him, part alcohol and part worry. As he hiked back up the bank, he thought about the one last place he needed to check. He felt like he'd rather die than follow the path Topaz had taken through the trees with Brett and Coralie. But he went anyway.

The first thing he saw was a mound of bodies, with bare, pale skin visible even at a distance. He hadn't thought it was possible to feel any closer to vomiting, but he did. Yet it all stayed down somehow as he drew closer.

The skin was Coralie's. Her short skirt had been pulled up to expose her backside. She wore no underwear and she was topless. He looked away from her, with the single-mindedness that came with a hangover.

Brett was not far behind her, lying on his face on a sleeping mat. He was clothed, which was a small mercy.

Topaz was beyond Coralie, and Connor trod towards her, trying not to look at any of them. Topaz was dressed, too, and even tucked into a sleeping bag. She looked untouched and uninvolved, and only the fact that he'd heard her gasping from his seat by the campfire told him she had been part of the fun.

There was no Aurora. Of course there wasn't. Topaz wouldn't have let her sister close to this.

Connor crouched down over Topaz, watching the frowning face; the spray of hair; the bronzed skin. He knew she would be angry if he woke her. But he knew, too, that she had to be woken.

'Topaz,' he said quietly. And then he pushed gently at her shoulder. 'Topaz,' he said. 'I can't find Aurora.'

29

Jojo pulled her feet up on to the sofa and leaned her head against a cushion, grateful that in all Brett's meticulous interior decoration, he'd managed to include a room that was genuinely comfortable.

It had taken her a long time to feel at ease here. The scale of the house, with its high ceilings and distant walls, had seemed all wrong. She'd been far more comfortable in Benners' slightly tatty pile, which had been where they'd gathered for years with the full blessing of his father.

Not that she and the others hadn't been impressed with the place. But it hadn't felt homely to any of them. When they'd first gathered here at one of Brett's parties, surrounded by his newly created stark aesthetic, they had clustered together and spoken in quiet voices.

Then, little by little, they'd grown used to it. It was partly that Brett had been there, cajoling and smiling and trying so hard to make them comfortable. And partly that Anna was such a wonderful hostess, refilling glasses with a quiet grace before they'd even noticed they needed another one and producing exquisite food.

Jojo had also been here five days a week for six months the following year, turning the main gardens into the perfect creation they were. Well, a kind of perfect. Brett's kindness in giving her the job had been matched by a very polite disagreement with her over what the garden should look like. And so they'd compromised, with Jojo accepting that he wanted manicured lawns and straight edges, but insisting on colour and greenery and life. In the end, they had both admitted to each other that the place was spectacular.

And somehow, during that time, Brett's house had morphed from somewhere that felt cold and unwelcoming to a form of refuge. Even after the garden had been completed, Jojo would come to see Brett and Anna, sinking into the sofa while the two of them chattered away so that she didn't have to. She wasn't sure she'd have managed the months after Aleksy died without this place, and without those two.

Tonight, feeling as though she might never stop reliving the caving in of the stash, she had instinctively sought this place out. Brett had let her in with an expression of understanding, and she could see the same shadow to his eyes that she'd seen in her own in the mirror.

'Come and drink tea,' he'd said quietly. He'd put an arm round her briefly and squeezed her shoulders, and then walked ahead of her to the sitting room without speaking. She was as grateful for his silence as she had been for the brief gesture of sympathy.

'You can have your usual spot,' he said. 'Anna's already making coffee and cookies.' He gave her a briefly worried look. 'Will you be OK if Daniel comes, too? He called earlier.'

Jojo grinned at him, and curled into the corner of the sofa. 'I'll be fine. But I can't promise we won't gang up on you,' she said.

'I'd miss it if you didn't,' Brett said wryly. 'I'll get you a cuppa.'

Jojo watched him leave, feeling a sudden stab of uncertainty. For the first time, it really struck her that nothing was going to be the same after this. How could they all trust each other, when it was overwhelmingly likely that one of them had killed Aurora Jackson?

Her customary spot on the sofa was just as comfortable as it had always been, but she couldn't feel the implicit safety any more. It had gone, and she doubted that it could come back.

Brett rubbed the back of Anna's shoulder once he'd returned to the kitchen. She was poised, a little nervously, in front of the oven, watching a timer.

'How are we doing?'

'Almost done, I think.'

Brett moved her gently out of the way, and pulled the door of the oven open, peering in at the slightly browned cookies.

'They need to come out now,' he said, and pulled the tea towel off the handle on the oven door.

'Sorry,' Anna said. 'I was waiting for the timer to beep.'

'You have to look at how brown they are,' he said. 'Nobody likes an overdone cookie.'

He slid the tray out, using the tea towel to keep the heat off his hands, and deposited it on the stovetop. They smelled right – chocolatey and wholesome – twelve of them in perfect circles.

'I should have done two batches,' he muttered to himself. 'The others might turn up, and Connor will probably have four . . .'

'We've got biscuits if we run out,' Anna said, moving back over to the coffee pot and giving him a reassuring smile over her shoulder.

Brett wasn't in the mood to be reassured. He felt like he had to get this exactly right, or it meant some kind of disaster was on the horizon. It wasn't an uncommon thought process for him. That not being able to control a small thing meant that everything would slip.

259

It was a side he tried to hide from his friends. Only Anna really knew the anxiety that went into every social event, and that it had invariably been Brett doing all the shopping and fussing around making food beforehand.

It was more than control, though. It was how the group functioned now. Somehow, as Benners had morphed into Benham, and had become both a parent and a more solemn individual, Brett had become the glue that held them all together. He wasn't convinced that the others really saw it, but he was conscious of the pressure on him, as much as he enjoyed it. He felt instinctively that without his willingness to soothe, to listen, and to persuade, the group would fracture.

He took a spatula and slid the cookies one by one on to a large plate, and thought they at least looked good. He wondered whether he ought to feed Jojo one or two now, or wait until Benners arrived. And whether he should have asked the other three, too.

Although neither Jojo nor Daniel had been invited, it somehow felt a little like complicity in something. The thought made his stomach knot up. He hated the idea that Aurora being found was going to finally, thirty years later, set them all against each other.

There was a clatter from behind him, and he turned with his heart thumping to see that Anna had knocked the jug of milk over before it had made it to the steamer.

'For fuck's sake,' he said immediately. And then equally immediately regretted it.

'Oh, god,' Anna said, grabbing for the dishcloth. 'I'm so sorry.'

'Just an accident,' he said, quickly and apologetically. 'It doesn't matter.'

He moved over behind her and slid one arm around her

waist. With the other he took the dishcloth. 'I'll do it,' he said quietly. He kept his arm round her as he mopped up the spillage. 'See? All fine.'

He kissed her on the side of the neck, and she put a hand up to his cheek, and leaned into him.

'I'm a grumpy bastard today, aren't I?' he murmured.

Anna laughed a little tensely. 'I think you have good reason.'

'Never a good enough reason to be sharp with you,' he disagreed. 'You look gorgeous in that dress,' he added. And then, with another kiss, he extricated himself. 'I promised Jojo tea.'

'It's brewing,' Anna said, tilting her head at the pot.

'You're wonderful.'

He grabbed the big, straight-sided blue mug that Jojo liked and put a slug of milk into it, and then poured in the tea. He worried that it was slightly too strong, but he decided to leave it. Anna had been trying to help.

He felt his phone buzz in his pocket as he carried the tea back through to Jojo. And then it buzzed again, a call instead of a text.

He knew, somehow, that it was Coralie, without having to check. He felt a slight sinking in his stomach. He should have told her that Benners was coming. She was wound up tightly at the moment, and somewhere between angry and devastated over Topaz rejecting her.

He pulled the phone out, and saw her name, plus the beginning of a message about needing to talk. With a slight sigh he put the mug of tea in front of Jojo, who had a brooding look about her.

'Coralie. I won't be long.'

*

Connor was sick of the car journey long before they arrived. Or, in fact, sick of the silence. Being in a car next to his wife simply amplified it. It was a sharp contrast to their usual openness, and to the way they both liked to think everything through by talking.

A large part of him wanted to comfort Topaz. But he felt resentful towards her, too. Was this really what they had come to after more than thirty years? This level of distrust and doubt?

It even told in the way she was driving. Although she was generally happy to fling the car around, tonight, Topaz was restrained. She accelerated slowly, stopped at every junction, and kept well within speed limits. Their progress was infuriatingly slow, and he wondered if she was doing it to annoy him.

'What do we do if he's not there?' Connor eventually asked, set on getting some kind of response out of her.

Topaz gave a tiny lift of her left shoulder. 'Go home,' she replied.

Connor couldn't remember ever before feeling like he wanted to shake his wife.

Luckily, they didn't have to deal with the possibility of going back home. Brett answered the buzzer with a voice that sounded more downbeat than usual.

'Hi Brett,' Topaz said a little uncertainly. 'It's me and Connor. I'm sorry for not ringing . . .'

'It's OK,' Brett said. 'You know you're always welcome. Come on in.'

Topaz kept up her moderate pace as she drove up the driveway. Connor was slightly disconcerted to see that Jojo's Mitsubishi was already pulled up to the right of the house.

'Looks like we're not the only ones,' he muttered.

Topaz, not unexpectedly, said nothing, but he saw a deeper furrow develop in her forehead.

He wasn't quite sure why it bothered him that Jojo was already there. Perhaps because it was no longer all of them against the police. Not now they knew what had happened to Aurora.

But there was another feeling of unease. He'd always felt close to Jojo. Aside from Benners, she'd been his closest friend for most of his life. He felt jealous, somehow, at the thought that she might be closer to Brett now. But that was what happened when you married and moved away, he guessed. People forgot you.

The feeling didn't improve when Brett ushered them into the sitting room and he saw that Jojo was at her ease on the sofa, a mug of tea in her hands and a distant expression on her face. It took a long moment for her to break into a grin, and rise to greet them.

'It's so good to see you,' she said in a husky voice. She directed it somewhere between him and Topaz as they hugged her in turn. Her hug felt reassuringly strong and warm, though.

Brett hovered behind them, and said a little apologetically, 'We're going to have a full house. Daniel should be here any minute, and Coralie's on her way now, too.'

'Oh,' Topaz said, rubbing at her arm. 'You'd better tell her we're here. I don't think she's very pleased with me right now.'

Jojo gave her a lopsided grin. 'I don't think she's ever that pleased with me.'

'Tell me about it,' Connor said.

For some reason that seemed to upset Topaz. She gave him a quick, angry look, and stalked past him to sit on the other end of the sofa.

'It's probably better if we're all here, anyway,' Jojo said, with a slight sigh. 'Nobody should end up feeling like they're being kept out of things.'

Connor wasn't sure if he agreed with that. There were a number of things that he never wanted to talk about again.

There were looping phrases running through Coralie's head as she drove. Some of them she'd heard, and others read, but she could hear them as if they'd all been spoken aloud.

From Daniel, guardedly, *Not tonight. I want to just sit at home and think things over . . .*

Brett's slightly guilty *You should come over. Everyone's here . . . No, don't be silly, sweetheart. Nobody's ganging up on you. If I'd had any warning, I'd have told you to come.*

And over and over, Topaz's words, spoken with venom: *Fuck you, Coralie.*

These people who were supposed to be her friends. The people she'd spent her whole life trying to please. The people who were supposed to be there for her.

Only it didn't feel like they were any more. Not since Topaz had chosen Connor over her.

It was a hurt that had never healed. She almost thought she could have stood it if it had been someone else. If it had been anyone but him.

Choosing him had poisoned their friendship. She had seen it within the first few months. And even if it had brought the others closer for a while, in the end it had leached into everything.

She felt sick and dizzy with fear as she climbed out of the car. What had they been saying about her? Had they decided to unite against her? How could they?

Her heart was thumping and her palms were sweaty as she

rang the bell. She might have just let herself in, once. But she felt like an outsider tonight.

It was Brett who opened the door, and there was a hint of balm in the warm smile he gave her.

'I'm glad you came,' he said quietly, and gave her a brief, firm hug. 'Come and bring a little sanity to the proceedings,' he added, as he released her.

The panic lessened a little further, though she wished that he'd put an arm round her or something as they walked in. It felt like a hostile environment the moment she was through the sitting-room door. They were absolutely silent in that way that suggested she'd been the topic of conversation.

Daniel smiled at her, but then looked away quickly, and she wondered if he'd been the one doing the talking. Brett perched on a sofa arm, distancing himself a little, she thought.

'Hi, Coralie,' Jojo said, and then unfolded herself from the sofa. 'Sorry. Too comfortable.'

Jojo loped over and hugged her, but Coralie found herself unable to relax as she felt her lean arms round her. Hugging wasn't something she and Jojo generally did.

The silence returned as soon as Jojo had sat down. Topaz and Connor wouldn't even look at her. Topaz had her eyes on the floor and one arm folded over the other, everything about her angry.

Coralie felt the panic returning. They didn't want her here. She should leave.

But then there were footsteps from behind her, and Anna appeared with a tray full of coffee cups and a plate of cookies.

'Coralie, my darling!' she said, and put the tray down quickly on the small glass coffee table before straightening up and giving her a real, warm hug. 'Oh, we've missed you!'

Although slight, Anna somehow managed to engulf her

in the hug, and it was profoundly comforting. Coralie felt her eyes water. She'd sometimes been uncharitable to mousy, uninteresting Anna in the past. And yet she made her feel genuinely welcome. Loved, even.

'I'm sorry,' she said, as Anna released her. 'London has this bad habit of ensnaring you in all the rubbish.'

'Brett's just as bad,' Anna said, with a small smile at her husband. 'Once he's there, he barely remembers to message me.'

Brett gave a low laugh. 'I remember – I just choose not to. Glad to finally get a little peace and quiet . . .'

'You gobshite!' Jojo exclaimed. 'You talk enough for four people!'

It suddenly felt like it used to feel, despite Topaz's silence. They were bantering together again, and Benners was sitting back with a grin and watching them all, presumably biding his time before launching into some diatribe about economics.

'Come and sit,' Anna said, and drew Coralie to the smaller sofa with her. 'Oh, coffee.'

She sprang up again, and started handing out cups. She'd made Coralie a cappuccino, remembering her preference. She started passing cookies around, though only Jojo and Connor actually took one.

'Look,' Topaz said suddenly, over the general chatter of serving. 'I know we turned up unannounced, and maybe you don't all want to talk, but . . . I'm going mad with all this and I . . . I want to know what's happening.'

There was a brief silence, and then Daniel said gently, 'You mean what the police are doing?'

'Yes,' Topaz said. 'They've brought Mr Mackenzie in for questioning. Her English teacher. I told them to look at him thirty years ago. I hope that means it isn't too late, and they've got something . . . So what have they asked all of you? And what did you say?'

'Oh. I'm not sure . . . that they want us doing that,' Brett said apologetically. 'I was specifically told –'

'Screw that,' Jojo said, and put her mug down on to the table with a sharp bang. 'The thing that's become really obvious is that we've all been hiding small things from each other. For three bloody decades. We've been keeping tiny things and . . . and that has to stop. It's too important now. I feel like we've managed to hide a murderer in all the bollocks, whether it's a teacher or not, and it's time to stop it.'

'We didn't know,' Daniel said quietly.

'No, we didn't,' Jojo countered, 'but we were thinking of ourselves. Me as much as anyone. In the end, who gave a shit if we got in trouble for drugs? We would have found Aurora, and she might even have been alive.'

They were very quiet. And then Connor said, 'Are you sure you can remember everything clearly? Because I'm not. There are things I've gone over so many times I've probably changed them out of all recognition.'

'That doesn't mean you shouldn't say them,' Jojo said. 'It'll all come out in the wash somehow.'

'I want to hear all of it,' Topaz said shortly. She fixed her husband with an unflinching gaze. 'I don't care if it's half remembered. I want to know what happened, and how he – how someone ended up raping and killing my sister when we were all right there.'

Coralie felt a strange twist in her stomach. It was impossible not to feel for Topaz.

She saw Daniel lean forward out of the armchair as if to get up, and then stop in the act. She wondered if he'd been going to comfort Topaz, or if it was something else.

'Are you sure? That she was . . .' Brett said, into the silence.

'The police are sure,' Topaz answered flatly.

Brett gave a long sigh, his eyes somewhere in the distance. Coralie felt as though she were waiting for him to think this out, and solve it all somehow. But it was Daniel who spoke next.

'I feel like most of their questions to me have been all about us,' he said. 'They haven't been pressing me about other people who might have been interested in Aurora, or who might have known we'd be there.'

'It's because of where she was found,' Jojo said, sounding weary. 'Who else knew about the stash in order to dump her body there? I can't think of anyone. And they did ask me.'

'There's a chance we were being watched,' Brett said. 'By Mackenzie, or by someone else entirely.'

'Did you see anyone?' Topaz asked swiftly.

Brett shook his head, with a slightly wry smile. 'I wish I had. I don't want to believe it was Mr Mackenzie, who I barely knew. Never mind one of us.'

'Of course it wasn't one of us,' Connor said. His voice was irritable. 'We know it wasn't. None of us is a bloody rapist.'

'None of you had fucking better be,' Topaz said, low and intensely.

Coralie could see Connor opening his mouth to say something angry, but Brett cut in, quickly.

'It's clearly bloody awful for you, Topaz. Worse for you than for anyone by a long way. She was your sister and you loved her. But we need to be on one side. We almost got torn apart thirty years ago, and I'm buggered if I'll let them do it to us now. Personally, I trust all of you. And I think we can solve this thing. We must know something that tells us who did it. We must. So if anyone told a friend where we were going, or bragged about the drugs, or anything – we all need to know. There's no blame. Nobody could know it was going to end up with her being killed. So anything you think you might have said to someone, or anyone you think might have known . . .'

There was a long silence.

'Fuck it,' Jojo said. 'I don't think I know. I could tell you about that night, or the morning after. The bits when I wasn't too drunk, but . . .' She shook her head.

'Can we at least try to think about it?' Brett said quietly. 'Because I don't want to lose a friend to prison because they don't have anywhere else to look.'

'Of course we will,' Coralie said, as positively as she could.

But Jojo was looking a little rebelliously at Brett. 'Yes, we will. But as far as I'm concerned, that's not the only thing I'm going to think about. It's time for the truth, the whole truth, and nothing but the fucking truth.'

Coralie found herself watching Connor. He took a small step away from the sofa, and then nodded.

'You're probably right,' Connor said.

Coralie looked away from him, feeling a little sick again.

30. Topaz

Saturday, 23 July 1983, 6:15 a.m.

'So you didn't think to check on her?' Brett asked, the fury in his voice biting. He had been striding through the woods for almost an hour, shouting for her with increasing desperation. He'd only returned to them now, when the lack of answer had finally started to mean something. 'After you let her sleep miles from anyone on her own in a bloody wood?'

Topaz couldn't keep still. She was taking pointless small steps, her whole body drenched in fear.

'I didn't think of it,' Benners said. When she could bring herself to look at him, she thought he looked all wrong, so white and frightened that he wasn't recognizable.

'Well, you should have done!' Brett said.

'Don't fucking stand there and criticize us,' Connor retorted, his voice low and vicious. He was crouched with his back against a tree, picking at the bark behind him with one hand. 'You were too busy shagging to care.'

Brett shook his head, and then said, 'I know, I know. I . . . I should have . . . I'm sorry. Blaming each other won't help. Look, one of us needs to go for help. And I don't think it can be me because I can't drive like this.'

'I'll go,' Benners said. 'I'm OK to cycle, and you all need to keep looking for her.'

'Fuck,' Topaz said, suddenly unable to keep it in. 'What do we do? What if someone . . .'

'We'll find her,' Brett said quietly. 'She'll be OK.'

'I'll get going,' Benners said.

And then, before he could go anywhere, Connor asked quietly, 'What are we going to do about the drugs?'

Topaz came to a stop for the first time in an hour. 'Oh, god. We're going to be in so much shit, aren't we?'

'No, we aren't,' Jojo said. 'We just need to hide them. We can cover them up.'

'The stash isn't obvious,' Brett said thoughtfully. 'OK. Let's do it. And then keep looking.'

Benners, who had simply looked between them, said, 'I guess it's me who should be doing it.'

'Don't be silly,' Jojo said. 'Nobody's getting in shit for something we all had some of. We'll deal with it. Go.'

Benners hesitated, and then started to lope off down the path towards the car park and his bike.

'Let's go,' Jojo said to Brett. As she made her way across the campsite towards the river, she called back over her shoulder, 'You'd better clear the campsite up a bit, too. There's a half-used packet of Dexedrine somewhere around.'

Connor got slowly to his feet, and Topaz found her gaze locked on his.

'What will happen?' she asked him.

'I don't know,' he said, 'but we're not going to leave her out there somewhere.'

Once on the road, Jonah wondered if he was driving out to Godshill at a crazily late hour for nothing. There was every chance that his Cannondale would have gone by now. It was such a sleek, expensive-looking machine that even a casual thief with no knowledge of bikes would be likely to covet it.

He did his best to park that worry as he drove, letting his mind wander to Andrew Mackenzie. He agreed with what Hanson had said, in spite of how he had cautioned her. Mackenzie was the most likely candidate. And yet the teacher had seemed to be genuinely unaware of the hollow where Aurora's body had been hidden.

Jonah's instinct was still to look at Connor and Daniel and Brett, who had all been there with Aurora that night, and had known about the place she had been hidden.

As he passed through Brook and saw signposts to Fritham, his thoughts went to Jojo Magos's cottage. And from there he began thinking again of the morning after Aurora's disappearance. To Jojo and Brett, panicking as they sealed off the hole in the ground that held Aurora. He needed to go over that in detail with Brett. Part of him still found it a strangely cold reaction, and that troubled him.

He drew level with the junction of Furzley Lane, the road that led past Jojo's cottage, and glanced down it. And then he slowed the car, and looked again at the orange-red halo against the navy blue of the sky. It looked almost like the sodium glow of street lamps. Only there were no street lamps along the road, and the light was coming from somewhere near Jojo's.

There was an icy feeling in his chest as he slewed the car to a stop, and then yanked it round in a U-turn. It was lucky there had been nobody behind him. He hadn't even checked.

The traction control came on as he took the corner into Furzley Lane. He ignored it and kept the acceleration up. He whipped past two driveways, his eyes going constantly to the glow that was now on his right. He could see smoke now. A pillar of dirty black blotting out the rich glow.

It was coming from Jojo's house.

Hanson switched her desktop off at eight, feeling vaguely dissatisfied. She didn't really know what she was looking for in all the notes, and hadn't seen anything today that looked like a strong inconsistency or lie.

Lightman was still working. He gave her a distracted smile when she said goodbye to him.

She had only driven a hundred yards from the station when a call cut through the radio. A moment later, Damian's name flashed up on the screen on the dashboard.

She had a falling sensation in her stomach. She thought about ending the call, but knew he would just ring again. So she turned the volume right down and let it ring out. Nine rings, and then the noise ended and the radio cut back in.

A few moments later, the radio was interrupted again by the sound of a text arriving. She kept driving, and willed herself to ignore it. But she was caught by a red light on Midway Road, and after a second or two of resisting she turned the engine off and reached to fish her phone out of her bag.

She had time to unlock her phone and see Damian's message pop up as a banner at the top of the screen.

I need to see you. I'm at your house.

The falling feeling stepped up into a wave of anxiety. What the hell was he doing in Southampton? She thought she'd finally left him behind when she'd moved away from Birmingham.

The lights changed. She shoved the phone on to the passenger seat, started the engine hurriedly and began to drive. She was only two miles from home, and the traffic was light. She would be there within minutes.

She felt disconnected from her body as she continued to drive, her mind going in circles. What did he want to talk about? Was he angry? Was he going to plead with her?

At the next lights, she picked the phone up again and typed back, **I'm not there. Working late. I'll call you tomorrow, maybe.**

His reply came less than a minute later, and she glanced down to read it on the screen.

I'm not going anywhere. When will you be home?

She could feel her heart picking up its pace. Home was getting ever closer. She imagined him waiting next to his car. Maybe smiling. Maybe tight-faced with fury.

There was another buzz as a new message arrived, but this time, she saw it was from her boss. She hesitated for a moment, but decided not to read it. It was too late for work, she thought, and if it had been urgent, she was sure Sheens would have called. Which was really just a justification for not being able to deal with anything else right now.

Half a mile further on, she made a sudden left turn towards the ring road. She picked up the pace, and roared out on to the M27, listening for the sound of the phone ringing again.

It stayed quiet for the ten minutes it took her to get to the Holiday Inn.

Her legs were unsteady as she climbed out of the car. She thought about leaving the phone, but somehow not knowing what he was saying was worse.

She reached in to pick it up, and grabbed the small over-night bag from the back of the car. She'd thought about taking it out once she'd broken up with him, as it had really been there for times she decided to stay over without planning to. But she hadn't quite got round to it.

Midway across the car park, the phone buzzed again. She didn't want to read his messages.

She found herself opening it anyway.

Are you not coming home, then? Are you staying with a man?

She thought about ignoring him. But she decided it wouldn't help.

No. I'm working. Sorry.

He was already typing again by the time she'd sent it.

So if I turned up at the station, you'd be there? That's what I should do, then.

She typed back quickly. You know that's not appropriate.

There was almost no pause at all before he replied.

Haha! You're a fucking liar. You're with a man, aren't you? I knew you'd left me for someone else. You were cheating on me, weren't you? You fucking slut.

Hanson felt as though she half stumbled, half floated into the Holiday Inn. There was no queue, which was lucky as she wasn't convinced that she'd be able to stand for long without falling. She booked a room for the night and didn't even hear how much it was going to cost her. And then she carried the phone carefully upstairs, and laid it on the bedside table next to her to wait for the series of messages she knew was going to come.

Jonah hammered on the front door, and then, barely pausing, tried the handle. The door swung open on the unlit hallway. There was a thin haze of smoke, and through the conservatory at the back of the house a bright, wavering glow.

It was an outbuilding that was on fire, he realized. But it was dangerously close to the house, and he doubted they had long before the cottage itself went up.

He took a few steps inside. None of the downstairs lights were on, which meant she had probably gone to bed.

'Jojo!' he called, and started to climb the bare wooden stairs two at a time. He didn't have time to worry about intruding. The slightly acrid smoke was only going to increase as the blaze got worse, and if she was sleeping, she was in real danger.

He rounded the corner in the stairs, and took the last few steps on to the landing. He saw three open doors, one of them a bathroom. He called out to her again, and ducked into the door to his left.

It was a spartan double room with cushions piled on the bed, and he moved back out immediately. A guest room, he was certain.

There was still no sound of movement as he pushed the door open fully on to the other room. It was a large, airy room with wooden boards on the floor and skylights in the roof. It was in darkness, but he could make out the duvet and pillows on the bed. They were carefully made, and the bed was empty.

That empty bed sent a surge of unease through Jonah, coupled with the lights being off and her car being parked outside. She had to be here somewhere. Unless she was where the fire was . . .

He moved back out as quickly as he could, feeling the slight bite of smoke in his throat.

'Jojo!' he yelled again, and ran down the stairs and along the hallway until he was in the large space of the sitting room and conservatory at the back of the cottage. And suddenly he could see the fire through the glass. It was tearing through the outbuildings that adjoined the house, a ferocious, hungry blaze. Silhouetted in front of it was a short-haired figure.

He moved towards the garden door, slightly light-headed with relief. Jojo turned as he opened it, her eyes wide and her arms folded across her, almost as if she was cold in spite of the heat coming off the blaze.

He had a moment to take in the scene: that she was fully dressed, and unmoving, and that there was a plastic petrol can next to her. And then he heard the sound of oncoming sirens.

32. Jojo

She wasn't exactly quick that morning. It was an obvious idea to solve a very big problem. But at least she'd got there.

'Where are you going?' Brett was calling after her. 'It's this way.'

'You can start hiding the stash, but making sure it's not visible isn't going to be enough,' Jojo called back. She paced forward, scanning the ground. It had been somewhere here.

She smelled it before she saw it. A pungent, sweet-sour reek. Even this early in the morning it was humming.

She followed the stench off the path and tried not to retch. Closer to, the stoat's remains were almost unbearably foul.

She put her left shoulder across her nose and mouth and crouched down to grab at its hind legs, which were relatively whole. She got quickly to her feet, keeping it as far away from her body as she could.

She half jogged towards the river. Brett was waiting for her outside the shade of the tree, clearly not having taken the initiative to start without her.

'What the fuck are you doing?' he asked, as she drew closer.

The smell must have hit him hard. He'd turned an awful colour. He moved away from her, down the bank, but Jojo jumped down too until she was right next to the water. She lowered the stoat until its bloated head and half-rotted back

278

were on the ground, and then she dragged it, swiftly, towards the tree with the stash in it.

Behind her, Brett made a gagging sound, and then full-on vomited into the river. It was a revolting sound, though she had to admit that she felt for him. The stoat reeked.

She kept moving until she had ducked under the tree and gone just past it, and then she let go of the stoat, her lips and nose curling up involuntarily. Brett stopped being sick, and came towards her, wiping the back of his hand across his mouth. His eyes were bloodshot and watery.

'Why the hell . . .?'

'It's for the dogs,' she said. 'Because if they don't find her, there are going to be dogs, and we need a reason for them to be interested in this area, and something for them to fixate on that isn't the stash.'

Brett pulled his T-shirt up to cover his nose.

'You could have waited till we'd hidden the fucking stuff,' he said. 'If I vomit into the hole, it's not going to make anyone look good.'

Jojo ignored him, and climbed up one of the roots until she was crouched above the hole, with banked-up loose earth below her. The entrance to the cache was invisible from up here. All she could see was the top of the sapling that had grown up out of the beech's roots. Soon, she thought, it was going to be invisible from everywhere.

She kicked at the earth below her. It was dry, and it started to crumble and then to fall in layers.

Brett was below her, near the entrance, still trying to cover his face from the stench.

'Come on,' Jojo said. 'You need to kick it over the hole or they're going to see it.'

He was still protesting as he moved the sapling aside. He

pulled some of the earth down with his hands, and then shuffled his feet and stamped earth down below her.

'That was in my fucking face!'

'Is that enough?' she asked. 'Is it covered?'

'Yeah,' he said, stepping back and letting the sapling move back into place. 'I don't think anyone's going to see it.'

Jojo jumped down, and peered critically at where the entrance had once been. They were lucky that it had been hidden well to begin with, behind the sapling. And lucky, too, that the hole was low down and easy to press earth over.

Looking hard at it, she could tell that the soil had been recently moved, even through the leaves of the sapling. Parts of it were darker, less dry. But it was already hot, and the rest of it would have time to dry out before anyone else arrived.

'OK,' she said. 'That's going to have to do.'

Brett nodded, and finally pulled his T-shirt back down from his mouth. He still looked green. Jojo might have felt like mocking him in other circumstances. He'd been pretty confident he could drink more than she could.

'Thanks for . . . for sorting it,' he said after a minute. 'I'm no good to anyone today, and I know I probably stand to lose the most.'

Jojo gave him a long look. 'That's OK,' she said eventually, in a low voice. 'I'm used to covering things up for these guys. And you're one of us now.'

33

Hanson gave up on sleep at five. She'd woken pretty much every half hour, and on two occasions had been so drenched in sweat that the sheets were wet through.

She felt angry with herself. She wasn't really sure what she was afraid of. What was Damian actually going to do to harm her? If she'd gone home, what would he have done, other than repeat some of the awful things he'd said to her?

She was equally angry with herself for reading all of his messages until they had eventually stopped after midnight, and for checking her phone every time she woke up from then on. She should ignore him, but couldn't.

She washed, put on the clean shirt and underwear from her overnight bag, and made herself a coffee using the kettle in her room. It was too early for breakfast, but she couldn't face eating anyway, with her stomach squeezing with anxiety every few seconds. She drank some of the coffee while she checked out, and then took the rest out to the car.

The roads were clear and sunlit. It took no time at all to reach the station and park up. She was at her desk and finishing the second-rate coffee before quarter to six. There was nobody else in yet, and she found the quiet soothing somehow.

She switched on the desktop, and spent a while looking at the records of the suspects, starting with Brett Parker. She scrolled through the various interviews in 1983 but found nothing else. She tried Connor Dooley next, and found his name mentioned in relation to a complaint in 1982.

When she opened it up, she read with a feeling of unease that it was actually Connor's father who had been the subject of the complaint. Connor's neighbours had reported him to the police for hitting his son. A couple of uniforms had visited the next day, and remarked that Connor had bruising to his forearms. But the dad had denied everything, and Connor had insisted mulishly that he'd hurt himself climbing a tree. He'd kept it up when he'd been interviewed on his own, too. The officers had asked him to call them if anything happened in future, and left it.

There was nothing else about it, and the remaining entries were all notes on interviews about Aurora's disappearance. Nothing since. She wondered whether Connor's father had continued to abuse him, and how profoundly that had affected him. Enough, maybe, to make him treat others with the same level of violence?

She wrote a note about it, and then searched for Jojo Magos.

There was nothing recent, but eight years ago there had been a fire at her property. Hanson found herself reading with increasing interest. Aside from the fire, there had been a great deal of vandalism, which implied that Jojo had really pissed someone off. But the insurance company, she read, had been unwilling to pay up, because the fire had been started using Jojo's own mower petrol, and she had no proof that anyone else had been on the property.

She scribbled herself a series of notes, and then, as she was exiting, saw a whole new file pop up. She opened it, and suffered a momentary disappointment as she assumed it was a duplicate. And then she saw DCI Sheens' name appear, and the date, and her disappointment turned into a strange sort of anxiety.

What the hell had he been doing at Jojo Magos's house late last night?

In spite of the anxiety that had gripped him the night before, Jonah struggled to surface in the morning. He hadn't got to bed until past three, by which time the firefighters had got the blaze fully under control. In the few minutes it had taken the crew to arrive and get set up, the blaze had spread to Jojo's cottage.

Before their hoses had been ready, Jojo dashed past him and into the house. Jonah had yelled after her, and gone towards the door before being told to back away by one of the fire crew.

'One of the lads can go in once they're suited,' he said.

But then Jojo had appeared again, clutching a box and a stack of photographs. She'd gone back, he realized, to rescue what she still had of Aleksy's belongings.

Jonah had put a call through to the uniformed police in Southampton, and then dropped his team a message telling them that their killer appeared to be attempting to threaten witnesses, and that they ought to take particular care. He decided to leave other explanations until the morning.

The uniforms, when they arrived, asked Jojo a few questions and took photographs while the firefighters soaked the place. It became clear that the blaze had been started in a pile of Jojo's tools and supplies, all of them piled up inside the outbuilding and doused in petrol. The police had taken a further look around, too, and called Jonah to look over the greenhouses, which had been methodically smashed.

Jojo had walked down there after them wordlessly, expressing no surprise at what she saw. Jonah had focused half of his attention on the damage, and half of it on her. He was trying to read something into this dazed acceptance, but was failing.

The night had felt both endless and strangely brief. He'd found himself largely unable to look away from the initial spreading of the blaze, and then at its slow decline into almost nothing.

He and the other officers had eventually suggested that Jojo find a hotel. She'd nodded, that same glazed look to her, and started searching on her phone. Before she left, Jonah looked down at the box of Aleksy's possessions she had picked up to carry with her. 'Do you still have Aleksy's phone?' he said.

Jojo gave him a confused look. 'Why . . .?'

'Your house has been set on fire, and your partner died suddenly. Those might be unconnected, but it would be madness to conduct a murder investigation without looking at those things too. I think we need to spend some time talking about Aleksy, and what happened to him, just to make sure we've covered everything.'

Jojo's eyes fell on the box. 'Will you look after it?'

'Of course,' Jonah said quietly.

She hefted the box awkwardly, half opening the lid. It was a shoebox, he saw, that had once held hiking boots.

Jojo rooted until she came up with an old Motorola, and handed it to him. And then, wordlessly, she had closed the box and walked over to her Mitsubishi.

Once she had driven off, Jonah conferred with the uniforms and agreed with them that he would be the one to speak to her about the blaze in the morning. He had finally driven home without his bike.

Despite his tiredness, sleep had been a long time coming. It had been almost impossible to shake a sense of threat, even after he'd left Jojo's, and he had become tense every time he'd seen headlights on the road behind him. His tired brain had protested that this wasn't how cold cases went. That investigating old crimes never felt present and urgent like this.

He had intended to be in the office by seven, before anyone else arrived, to give himself the space to think. But that had gone out of the window when he'd snoozed his alarm from six onwards.

He eventually dragged himself out of bed at seven forty, and went to make coffee. For some unknown reason he pulled two mugs out of the cupboard instead of one. The moment of realizing that he had been alone for months now was not a pleasant one. He put both cups away and poured the coffee into a thermos instead.

Jonah dropped Aleksy's phone with the tech team and asked for a run-down of all the messages and calls on it, and then made his way up to CID slowly, and let himself in. Hanson swung round in her chair as soon as he was inside. She looked well settled behind her desk, a nearly empty disposable coffee cup next to her and her jacket slung over the back of her chair. It was only eight fifteen. There were a couple of other DCs and DSs in, but no sign of Lightman or O'Malley yet.

'Sir,' she said. 'I saw a crime report for Jojo Magos on the system.'

Jonah gave a half-smile. 'Good news travels fast.'

Hanson shifted in her chair, clearly ill at ease. 'You were on scene, it said . . .'

'Yes,' he said. 'Which was a stroke of luck. I went to get my bike from Godshill, and I could see the blaze from the road. It was quite some fire.'

'Right,' Hanson said, nodding. 'Right. Well . . . that wasn't the only report I found.'

He gave her a small smile. 'Tell all.'

'It's not the first time it's happened,' she said significantly. 'She had a major fire in one of the outbuildings at her house just over eight years ago. It spread to the garden and she lost a large number of tools, including some pretty pricey things like mowers and generators. It also took a swipe out of the kitchen.'

Jonah stared at her, trying to process the description. It was all but identical to what had happened last night.

'That doesn't sound accidental,' he said slowly.

Hanson shook her head. 'The insurance company suspected foul play and put an investigator on it. It looked like she'd done it herself. There was a can of petrol for the mower, which was sitting open, and it had clearly been used on the fire. They found a set of Jojo's overalls bundled behind one of the greenhouses, and they stank of petrol. There was a long wrangle, but they eventually paid out. Her solicitor did a good job, I think.'

'That's interesting,' he said with a nod. 'Well done.'

He felt a little disconnected as he remembered the can of petrol, and Jojo beside it. Jojo, fully dressed, her bed not slept in, doing nothing to stop the spread of the blaze.

'It seems more than convenient that it's happened again just as Jojo is being investigated for murder,' she added. 'She gets to play the victim when we're looking for a killer. And I'd want to have a good look at what was being burned, too.'

'Agreed,' he said, trying to smile. 'We should take a good look. As long as you're prepared to accept that it might just turn out to be a peculiar coincidence, of course.'

In his office, he slowly lowered himself into his chair. He

thought further: from Jojo's lack of reaction to it all, to her love for her garden. He wondered whether she could bring herself to damage it in order to distract them, or whether she'd angered somebody enough to do this. And that creeping sense of threat resurfaced. He had to restrain himself from going back out to warn Hanson to be careful. She wasn't going to come to any harm in CID. But, he decided, the team had better know that their thirty-year-old case had reared its head into very modern-day activity.

Hanson felt uneasy. It was profoundly unlikely to be a coincidence that Jojo had suffered vandalism twice, and the petrol threw a very suspicious light on the current damage to her property. But the DCI didn't seem to be excited about that. Which could have been caution, or could have been something else.

DCI Jonah Sheens was on scene . . .

She couldn't help thinking about the way he had interacted with Jojo, and about the trip to the climbing wall to interview her alone. She wanted to feel enthusiastic about solving this case, and instead she felt a weight of worry descend.

She could tell that the slight ache in her head was going to step up into a full-on throb soon. She pulled up the various reports into the arson, and pressed the print button, and then sat and kneaded her temples for a while.

She was still in the same pose when she heard a cheerful 'All right, constable?' from beyond her shoulder, and realized that O'Malley had arrived.

She looked up, slightly disorientated, and tried to smile at him. 'Fine. But painkillers definitely needed. Have you got any?'

'Oho! Rough night, was it?' He beamed at her, bent to open one of his desk drawers and threw a packet of Panadol at her. 'Knock yourself out.'

'Tempting,' she said, and rose to find water.

She met Lightman leaving the kitchen with two mugs, and felt a rush of embarrassment as she realized that he'd probably come into the office while she'd had her head in her hands.

'I got you one,' he said, holding up one of the cups.

'Oh . . . thanks.' She took it with a vague smile.

'You look like you've been in a while.'

'Yeah. I woke up early, and I figured I might as well.' And then she added, on impulse, 'I'll send you some stuff about Jojo shortly. It's interesting. A previous arson, probably deliberate.'

Lightman, at least, might think it was exciting.

'Thanks,' he said, 'send away.'

Jonah realized it was almost time to brief his team, and he'd done very little to work out what they were focusing on. He tried to snap himself out of his unsettled daze by pulling his notes out. He'd been reading for only a couple of minutes when O'Malley knocked on the door.

'Matt Stavely has just called,' he said. 'He wants to know if he can come in and talk to us further. He says he's got more to say.'

'Interesting,' Jonah said. 'And the answer is definitely yes.'

'OK. I'll see when he can make it.' O'Malley returned a minute later. 'He says he has a Jobseeker's meeting, but he could come in at three.'

'OK,' Jonah said. 'That's fine. Let's do our briefing.'

O'Malley nodded, and called to the other two.

Lightman picked up his notes and rose, but Hanson didn't react at first. She had a five-mile-stare that was focused somewhere on the desk next to hers. She looked about as zoned as he felt.

'All OK?' he asked, taking a few steps towards her.

She gave him a startled look. 'Yes. Sorry. Just . . . processing.' She picked up her coffee mug and iPad and followed him inside.

'So, a quick sitrep,' he said, as Hanson closed the door behind them. 'We have Andrew Mackenzie in custody for questioning until tomorrow at latest. I'd like to talk to his wife at the earliest possible, and then will probably want to interview him again. Ben, can you call her and book her in?'

'Sure,' the sergeant replied, making a note.

'In terms of where we're at, we know that Aurora was raped, and that she had a crush on Mackenzie. Mackenzie knew that she was going camping. So we're pretty interested in him, but we've also had some developments with Jojo Magos. A fire on her property, which seems to be the exact duplicate of one that happened eight years ago. It's unclear, as yet, whether someone else set the fire or whether Jojo did it herself for some reason, but I'm making talking to her a priority. She may not have raped Aurora, but that doesn't mean she didn't help someone else to.'

He could see O'Malley nodding, while Hanson was simply watching him thoughtfully.

'And, related to that fire, I'd like you all to be careful when out of the station. It looks like someone is angry, and willing to act,' he said. 'Sorry for the slightly cryptic text messages last night, but I don't want any of you putting yourselves in danger if someone's feeling threatened. All right?'

The three of them nodded, and he told them to carry on

with the case and then went to grab his coffee mug, which was full of the last half-drunk cup. Hanson was in the small kitchen already when he arrived, pouring herself a hefty slug from the pot.

'Did you sleep badly too?' he asked, emptying his mug down the sink. 'There are a lot of unpleasant things to think about. After, what? Twenty-eight years as a detective, I still end up going over and over things when I should be sleeping.'

Hanson gave him a vague smile, and took a large gulp out of the cup. 'You must have seen worse things.'

'Yes,' Jonah said, nodding. He finished up the pot and ignored the printed sign that told him to make a new pot if he'd had the last bit and putting it back empty on the hotplate. Nobody ever refilled it unless they were after a cup. 'But I'd seen Aurora in the flesh. That definitely makes it harder.'

There was a brief silence, and when he looked up at her Hanson was giving him a very searching look.

'Do you remember the last time you spoke to her?' she asked.

'Aurora?' he asked. He gave her a small half-smile. 'I never spoke to her. I'd just seen her around. She was a lot younger.'

He could feel his heart somewhere in his throat. It was the first time he'd ever had to lie to one of his team. He felt like the lie was all over him, and he turned away from Hanson and went back to his office with the back of his neck tingling. He could feel her watching him the whole way.

Back at his desk, he pulled out the reports on the blaze at Jojo's house eight years before, and tried to concentrate on them, even while his mind was full of dim lighting, and the spin of a disco ball glinting off blonde hair.

None of that mattered right now, he told himself harshly. The only thing that mattered was finding Aurora's killer.

So, Aleksy, he thought. There was something wrong about Aleksy, and that fire.

When he had asked Jojo for Aleksy's phone, it had been about due care. But there was now a much stronger reason to look at her former partner's death. Aleksy had died – what? – a mere week and a half after the first blaze?

That apparent coincidence meant that he needed to start thinking about Aleksy's death as a possible murder. It was quite possible that someone had been warning Jojo and Aleksy off by setting a fire and trashing Jojo's garden the first time, and that Aleksy hadn't taken the hint.

If it had indeed been murder, it had been a much more recent murder than Aurora's. Which was a plus. Where investigating Aurora's death was plagued by problems of data loss, poor memory and incomplete initial investigations, this one looked a great deal easier to get to grips with. They now had Aleksy's phone, for one thing, which was by far the best way to recover messages and call data. Standard phone checks only gave the traffic to and from a number, and not the actual message contents.

Working on a murder from eight years ago also meant fresher memories that hadn't been rewritten over time by repeated interviewing. And there was the added advantage that it was an unexpected line of enquiry. If Aleksy had found something out, and died for it, then Jonah could potentially follow the trail left by one murder to solve another.

He mentally ran over everything he could remember the group saying about Aleksy. There hadn't been a great deal. He felt that there were a lot of questions to ask them on that score.

He turned to his desktop PC and searched the database for Aleksy Nowak's name. There was a single entry: a coroner's report. It wasn't long.

The county coroner had concluded that Aleksy had died falling from a climb. He had not landed directly on his head, but on his back. The damage to his spine and the secondary impact on his skull indicated that he had fallen at a speed of between twelve and seventeen metres per second, which meant a fall of at least nine metres. Death had been instantaneous. The coroner noted that a landing mat was usual when climbing without ropes, but that the deceased had not been in the habit of using one, and that from that height serious injury would have been likely regardless.

The report went on to describe how Aleksy had been found, which had not happened until the following day. Jojo had alerted the police late on 14 July, when Aleksy had failed to return home. She had explained that he had been climbing, and tried to suggest where that might have been, though the choices were fairly wide as Aleksy had been willing to travel all day for a few hours on the rock.

It had therefore been a climber who initially found Aleksy at the heath in East Sussex. She had alerted the police. The climber had made a statement about finding him at the foot of a climb called Mechanical Vert.

Jonah googled Mechanical Vert, and found a climbing site that gave details. It was a pinchy 6a, the guide explained. One that involved using fingers and toes a lot.

The guide went on to detail the various moves. It assumed that it would be climbed roped, he noted. It was eleven metres, above rocky ground. The site described numerous challenging moves early on, but said there were no challenges after the four-metre mark. It advised climbers to push on through to the easier moves towards the top.

He spent a while looking up more about Aleksy after that. There were dozens of YouTube videos of him on impossibly high climbs, with the kind of drops that made Jonah feel like he was about to fall himself. He had been an extraordinary climber, it became clear, in quote after quote and film after film. He skipped through them, and confirmed Aleksy's skill to himself.

And yet, Jonah thought, he had fallen from a comparatively easy climb, once he'd got past all the challenging moves. He was more and more convinced that there had been foul play.

Hanson felt badly in need of something certain. Her personal life, with Damian's messages, felt like an unmitigated disaster and a source of profound anxiety. And now her work life had become a huge worry, because she was certain that her boss had lied to her.

What was the protocol for this? And what was it she suspected him of? Vested interest? Some kind of former interest in Jojo? Or in Aurora . . .?

Which was ridiculous. She obviously didn't think he was the killer when there had been six teenagers and one of Aurora's teachers there on the night. But he was lying to her, and she assumed to all of the team. He was pretending that he hadn't known any of those kids well.

She sat staring at her screen with nothing but nervous dread in her stomach.

And then Chrome flashed up an alert about a Facebook message, and she saw that it was from Zofia Wier. All she could see on the brief alert was the beginning of the message:

Hello, yes. I was Aurora's friend. I would

Almost automatically, she clicked on the alert, and waited while Chrome loaded a tab with the Facebook messenger app on it. She hadn't looked at her messages in a while. There were several unread ones, which she ignored in order to click on Zofia's. The full message read:

Hello, yes. I was Aurora's friend. I would be happy to talking, but I did not see her for time before she died. The last time was a party. The next day, my mother took me away from the school and I was sent to Poland to my grandparents.

Hanson started typing a reply, hoping that she was making sense but partly not quite caring.

Hi Zofia. Thank you so much for contacting us. We have some other questions about Aurora that you might be able to help with, as well as the party. Would you be happy to have a phone call with me and DCI Sheens, who is in charge of the investigation?

She saw a tick and a 'Seen' pop up next to her message. Zofia was online.

An icon appeared to show that Zofia was typing, and then vanished. She was presumably considering her response.

The typing started again, and then her message appeared.

I can but is that the police officer Jonah Sheens?

Hanson felt a strange little twist in her stomach.

Yes, it is. Do you know him? she typed back.

Another pause, and another typing symbol.

Yes but you can ask him about the party. He was there too.

Hanson spent a good minute looking at that message before she managed to type a light reply saying that she would set up a call if Zofia gave her a phone number or Skype ID. And then she stood a little unsteadily and walked towards the DCI's office.

34

Hanson's tap on the door was so quiet that he barely heard it. He nodded her in, feeling unaccountably nervous.

She closed the door behind her, and then said in a tight voice, 'I'm worried about a few things. You told me that you didn't know Aurora. But one of Aurora's close friends knows you. Beyond that, she says that you were at a party with both of them the week before Aurora went missing.'

Jonah felt more panicked than he could remember feeling. It wasn't just that he felt like his career was about to drop down a precipice and never recover. He also felt shame in front of his newest recruit. The idea of telling her everything made him want to run a mile.

But he was beginning to notice that Hanson didn't let things go. In the end he said, 'I was,' wondering how he could push her interest aside. How he could distract her.

'And you didn't talk to Aurora at all there? Even though her close friend seems to think you know all about what happened to Aurora that night?'

'It's not about Aurora,' he said, and then he felt as though he'd reached a tipping point. There was only one thing he could do. 'Come and sit,' he said hoarsely.

He saw Hanson hesitate, and then draw up the chair on the far side of the desk.

'I was hoping you wouldn't find Zofia, because of that party. It . . . I didn't want to talk about it. It had gone wrong before I even got there.' His throat was dry, and he had to swallow before he could continue. 'My family were . . . my dad was a traveller, and my mum married into the community. She was totally besotted with him, like a lot of people who fall for narcissists. She was pregnant by the time she started to see him for what he was: an abusive, manipulative bully who couldn't stand anyone going against his control.'

He found himself telling her everything, even the really humiliating parts of it. He told her about the erosion of his self-esteem along with hers, and the way he, Jonah, had been used as a tool to hurt his mother.

He told her how his mother had finally seen what was happening to her son, and had walked away. How over the next nine years, his father had tried repeatedly to force her to come back. Tommy Sheens had made the fifty-mile trip to their home in Lyndhurst on numerous occasions, and when his mother had stopped opening the door to him, he'd started targeting his son.

'He was furious with me that day,' Jonah told her. 'He'd found out I'd become a copper. It had taken him pretty much a year to catch on, and he was incensed. There was no group he hated and feared as much as the police.'

He could see Hanson growing impatient, and he skipped onwards to how Tommy Sheens had turned up with an old friend of Jonah's named Duke, and tried to force him into the car. How Jonah had ended up fighting both of them. He'd knocked Duke out, and kept walking to the party.

He could see Hanson's expression. She was unimpressed. And he almost found himself laughing, thinking that she hadn't heard anything yet.

'It only hit me that I'd done a really stupid thing when I got to Martin's. I was covered in blood, and my eye was swollen, and there was every chance that my dad would report me. Which would probably have been the end of my career in the police. So I did what a lot of people would have done and got blind drunk.'

'And Aurora was at this party,' Hanson said flatly. 'So, let me guess. You were drunk, and something you regret happened.'

'Maybe,' Jonah said. 'But not with Aurora.'

He'd wandered over to talk to Aurora at what must have been nine or ten p.m., once the punch and the whiskey had gone down. She'd been standing awkwardly at the edge of the room, alone.

'She was surprised I remembered her,' he said, with a slight smile. He didn't need to tell Hanson more, but he did. 'And I said she was clever and funny. And really beautiful. Which I then decided was an asshole thing to say.'

'Yes,' Hanson said coldly. 'It was. To a fourteen-year-old girl.'

'And then her friend Zofia returned from getting drinks,' Jonah pressed on, ignoring that dig. 'I'd never met her before. She looked sixteen but explained she'd joined Aurora's year after Christmas. Zofia saw the blood on me, and the swollen eye and lip, and she started clucking over me. She went to get me ice, and then got me to sit on the sofa with her and stroked my hair while she put the ice on my head. And it was such a nice thing, being looked after like that.'

He stopped short of telling her more. About his mother, and how he'd turned into the one looking after her instead of the other way round. About the absence of touch and care in his life. It would have sounded like an excuse. Though maybe it was just that.

'You slept with her?' Hanson asked.

'In god's honest truth, I don't know,' he said, and found

his mouth suddenly absolutely dry. He reached out for the dregs of his coffee, and drank the remainder, even though it was utterly cold. 'Someone got the tequila out, and a whole load of us started doing shots. I didn't know half of them, but we were cheering each other on anyway. And then Zofia suddenly said she felt sick, and rushed outside. So I went to look after her, and then I found Aurora and asked how she was getting home.'

'How Aurora was getting home?'

'Zofia,' he corrected. 'Aurora was really upset about it. She said Zofia was supposed to stay with her, but she couldn't let her parents see her being sick as they'd be bound to tell her mum. So I said I'd sort it, and I talked Martin into letting her sleep in his absent parents' room.'

Jonah paused, his mouth dry again. There was no coffee left to help him through it. 'I remember taking her upstairs, and sitting on the edge of the bed with her, and feeling like shit when the tequila suddenly hit hard. I think I lay down. And that's all I have. There's a vast gap between that point, and finding myself halfway home at midnight, without my jacket and with blood still all over me. By Monday, Zofia had been removed from school and sent back to Poland. I tried to get hold of her through Topaz, and found out that the chance was gone. And then Aurora, who might have found out the truth for me, vanished, and there's never been an answer for me.'

There was total silence after he'd finished speaking. Hanson's gaze burned into him, and he lowered his eyes to his hands, which were shaking badly.

'Jesus,' Hanson said. 'Do you have any idea how many men have tried to use that excuse? The "I don't remember" trope? And this is all aside from the stuff with Jojo. I assume you were at her house late last night because you were sleeping with her? With a suspect?'

'No, I wasn't,' Jonah said, his voice firm this time. 'I've never been involved with a suspect. I'm trying to solve a case, Juliette. Everything else is secondary. Everything. I gave you Zofia's name because I'm determined to solve it, even when that meant letting you find out about something I've been ashamed of for most of my life.'

Hanson shook her head, and said in a slightly unsteady voice, 'You're supposed to be –' And then she turned round without finishing the thought, and left.

She didn't need to finish what she'd started saying. He knew what she meant.

He felt, profoundly, that he had failed her. Her next step must be to report him. And there wasn't anything he could do to stop her.

Fear ended up taking over Jonah's afternoon. Every time Hanson moved or said anything outside, he found himself moving to watch her, wondering what she was telling the other two. The combination of anxiety and lack of sleep was deadly and his focus was anywhere but on the case. Where it needed to be. It bloody needed to be.

O'Malley tapped on his door at quarter to one, and Jonah found his pulse picking up again at the thought that his sergeant was about to weigh in about Zofia. But O'Malley's expression was neutral.

'You'll probably be interested to know that the first phone records are just through,' the sergeant said. 'I've got Topaz, Brett and Daniel for this year. Looks like Connor and Coralie are with O2, so that's going to be a manual permission.'

Jonah nodded. He'd been through this process a lot of

times. Aside from the online portals used by many of the major phone companies, there were still those who only gave out records when permission had been sought and given manually. Requests would go to staff members, who would make a decision and then send the information back. Those could be handled quickly, or could take several days to process, and there was no way of knowing which it would be.

He found a flicker of interest breaking through his tiredness and fear. There could be some interesting interactions between the three they already had. A lot of calls back and forth could be indicative.

It was frustrating that they didn't have the messages themselves at this point. Unless there was an overwhelming reason to ask for the content of messages, and approval had been given by a secretary of state, what the police had access to was simply who had called or messaged whom, at what time. Location information could also be gathered, but accuracy was in no way guaranteed, as recent cases had proved. Calls were routed through the nearest available mobile phone mast, which might not be close to where the call had actually been placed. For more precise information you needed a smartphone with GPS, and permission to access it.

The other problem faced in investigating older cases was records being deleted. The good news was that, thanks to various anti-terrorism laws, carriers now had to store records for a full year. But it was up to them whether they kept the information for longer, and it was hit or miss whether they would have data going back further. In terms of actual message content, only a few providers stored this at all, so even with the full weight of the law behind them, investigators often came up with nothing.

'OK,' he said to O'Malley, telling himself it was time to

pull himself together. 'Can you start with the last few days? Look at which of those three messaged each other, or any of the rest of the group?'

'Yup, will do.'

Jonah was rereading the reports on the two fires when Jojo's tousled blonde head appeared through the door to CID. He hadn't come to many conclusions. His gut instinct told him that the first fire had been to warn Aleksy off. But it could have been more than that. Aleksy had been in the house, while Jojo had been out drinking with a group of climbers, it seemed. Which meant it might have been a first attempt to kill Aleksy.

There was a lot to ask Jojo. He let himself out into CID, and said to Hanson as normally as he could, 'Juliette, can you take over from the PCSO?'

Hanson nodded, not making eye contact, and went to field Jojo from the door. Jonah could hear her reminding Jojo that she'd met her before. He couldn't catch any reply.

He continued to watch as they walked towards the interview suite. Jojo had seen him, but she gave him only a short nod before looking ahead again. She seemed, if anything, a little nervous. He wondered whether she was afraid of being asked more about Aleksy, or about the fire, or whether she'd been talking to one of the others.

'Chief,' O'Malley said, waving a hand at him. 'The messages from Aleksy Nowak's phone are through.'

Jonah stopped watching Jojo, and drew up a vacant chair with keen interest.

'I want to look before I talk to his girlfriend,' he said. 'Can you bring up any texts from the day of his death? The fourteenth?'

O'Malley opened up the database file, and searched for a

date range including only that day. There were a number of messages both to and from Aleksy's number.

'Start with the last one,' he told the sergeant.

O'Malley opened up the last text Aleksy had sent. It was brief, but immediately made Jonah's stomach tighten.

Sorry, I'm afraid I'm at the heath. Maybe another time.

'Looks like he told someone where he was going,' Jonah said. 'Can you bring up the whole conversation between these numbers?'

O'Malley copied and pasted the number into the search bar. It brought up only two messages, the first sent at ten thirteen on the morning of Aleksy's death. Aleksy had received a message from the unknown number that read:

I should have messaged before. I'm sorry about shouting at you. I really am. I was being a total dick and taking a lot of stress out on you. I know you weren't meaning anything bad, and that you actually care a lot. I'd really like the chance to explain, and salvage what I can of the two of us. Can you forgive and forget enough to at least go for a drink later?

Aleksy had sent his last message at just after twelve, clearly after a long gap.

O'Malley gave a huff of air at around the same time that Jonah had finished reading.

'That's pretty interesting,' he said. 'Particularly given those two messages had been deleted from the phone.'

O'Malley pointed to the tag 'RECOVERED' next to each message.

'Can you check that number? Is it any of the group's?' Jonah asked.

O'Malley dutifully opened up the main database on his

second screen, and typed the number in. It didn't suggest any matches as he was typing, and came up with no saved results once he'd submitted the search.

'So it's not the main mobile of Jojo, Brett, Topaz, or Daniel Benham,' Jonah said.

'Or Coralie or Connor, either,' O'Malley added. 'They're saved on the system, too, even if we don't have their records. So we're looking at a second phone, or someone else entirely.'

Jonah looked again at some of the phrases in those messages.

I'd really like the chance to explain, and salvage what I can of the two of us . . .

There was an implication to the message. It sounded like things someone would say to a partner. And the message had a jokiness that could easily have been Jojo's.

Aleksy's reply, too, sounded like the deliberate shut-down of a partner. It was slightly sulky in tone.

Had there been a row between Jojo and Aleksy? Was the reference to interference because Jojo had waded in on a conversation? Or was this someone else? Perhaps a lover of Aleksy's?

Though Jonah was inclined to think that the tone of the messages was wrong for an affair. There were no declarations of missing each other, no sexual undertones . . . none of the usual features of messages between illicit lovers.

Could they be between friends? In a close-knit group, references to the importance of the relationship between two of them were possible.

'What do we think?' O'Malley asked. 'Did the girlfriend do him in?'

'Hard to be sure,' Jonah replied, rising, 'but it's unquestionably time to give Jojo a bit of a grilling.'

35

Hanson took a few sideways looks at Jojo Magos as she showed her silently into Room One. She was wearing a tank top again, this one with a narrow racer back that left her shoulders exposed. It let Hanson see the amount of muscle that the woman carried.

She looked a lot younger than she was, despite her hours in the sun. She had a healthy, outdoorsy, left-field look to her that was appealing, even to Hanson. And acknowledging that only made her feel angrier at the DCI. Was all his apparent logic a huge sham? Did he just follow his libido around the place?

Sheens didn't take long to follow them. He said nothing as he inserted a fresh tape into the machine. Jojo watched him do it with her elbows propped on the table. Hanson thought she looked anxious, and she wondered whether the DCI had primed her for this somehow.

Jonah ran the tape, and made all the necessary introductions. And then he thanked Jojo for coming in to speak with them.

'So we've asked you here to ask a few questions about the vandalism and arson at your property,' Jonah said, in what was a surprisingly cold tone as far as Hanson was concerned. 'We've looked into a previous fire on your property. There was a strong suggestion that it was not, in fact, accidental.'

'Yes,' Jojo said a little hoarsely. 'I don't think either of them were accidental.'

'The insurance investigations suggested that it had been started intentionally, using an accelerant,' Jonah said, rotating a piece of paper to show it to Jojo. 'Your own petrol was used, and a petrol-splashed set of your overalls were found hidden. And here we have another blaze, this time clearly deliberate.'

Jojo's lips parted slightly, and for a moment she just stared at Sheens. 'I don't . . . What are you talking about?'

'Why were you outside when I arrived at the scene of the fire?' the DCI asked.

Jojo focused on him slowly. 'Because I saw the fire.'

'And yet you weren't doing anything about it?'

'I didn't . . . I was so shocked. I'd just woken up.'

The DCI raised an eyebrow. 'When I first arrived, I believed that you must be unconscious in the house. Receiving no response from you, I went to your room. The bed had not been slept in, and you were still wearing clothes.'

Jojo looked startled. 'That's because I hadn't gone to bed. I'd passed out on the sofa. Everything's been . . . exhausting. I went to the sofa to read and I passed out. And I woke up, and saw a fire, and a person. I was sure I saw someone out there. And the first thing I tried to do was find them, but they weren't there. Just this petrol can. And by the time you arrived, I was just looking at the fire thinking that everything was going to go.'

'The petrol can was next to you,' the DCI pointed out.

'I know,' she said, frustration sounding in her voice. 'I went over to it when I saw it. I knew it was deliberate. And I thought about before . . .'

'I believe Aleksy was alone at the house last time there was a fire,' Sheens said.

'Yes,' Jojo said. 'He was bloody lucky not to get caught up

in it. I was late back from a pub night with the climbers, and he was asleep.'

'And can the climbers confirm what time you left?' the DCI asked her. 'That you didn't, in fact, arrive home, smash up the greenhouses and start the fire?'

Jojo shook her head, looking between Sheens and Hanson as if this might just be some kind of a wind-up.

'Why the hell would I want to burn what I care about most? My garden, my tools, my house . . . Aleksy . . .'

'Perhaps because your boyfriend had found out something he shouldn't have about your involvement in Aurora's murder.'

Jojo looked as if she had been struck. Hanson felt a strange surge of sympathy for her. Sheens' harshness was raising a reaction even in her.

'That's bullshit,' Jojo said finally. 'I had nothing to do with Aurora, and I would never have hurt Aleksy. Not in a million years. And you can fuck off if you're going to pretend I would.'

The DCI shrugged, as if this wasn't a problem. 'Have you changed your phone number in the last few years?' he asked, and Hanson could see that Jojo was wrong-footed again.

'What? No. No, I've always ported my number. It's been the same . . . I don't know. For fifteen years. Maybe more.'

'Do you have a second phone?' he asked.

'No.'

'Not for work?'

'It's enough of an arse remembering where I've put one phone, never mind two,' Jojo replied with an attempt at humour. 'Why do you want to know?'

'On the day he died, Aleksy received messages asking him to meet someone, and establishing where he would be climbing that day. Messages that were subsequently deleted.'

There was a profound silence. Hanson was as stunned by this as Jojo clearly was, but Jojo seemed more than stunned. Her whole face seemed to drain of colour. She looked ill.

'What the fuck,' she said, and she put a hand up to her head and leaned sideways in a gesture that Hanson knew well.

'I'll get you a glass of water,' she said in a low voice to Jojo, and rose.

The DCI looked up at her with apparent surprise, and then nodded.

Hanson went out into the corridor and grabbed one of the plastic cups from the fountain. She filled it two-thirds full, and made her way back in. The two of them were still sitting in silence, and Jojo looked like she might be sick.

It was a shock reaction, and Hanson knew exactly how it felt. It had happened to her at the age of twelve when she'd seen one of the sixth-formers from her school hit by a speeding lorry outside the school. She'd seen it in a lot of people since, some of them guilty and many of them not. But whatever the reason, it wasn't going to help them if Jojo vomited or passed out.

Jojo took a few sips of water when Hanson handed it to her.

'Can't you trace whose phone it was?' she said unsteadily, after a moment. 'If someone killed him . . .'

'We're looking into it,' Jonah replied in a more neutral voice. 'But I thought you might know something about it.'

'The only thing I know,' she said, 'is that those messages weren't on Aleksy's phone when they found him. If they had been, I would have told the police eight years ago.' She gave a slow sideways shake of her head. 'If someone killed him, there was a lot of time to delete them. He wasn't found until the next day.'

'So you'd looked at his messages? Why?' Jonah asked.

'Why the hell do you think?' Jojo said, with sudden anger. 'I'd just lost him. I wanted every part of him I could lay my hands on. And . . . and I was looking for answers to whether . . . him dying was my fault.'

There was a moment of silence, and Hanson could see her DCI considering. She leaned forward, hoping she wasn't about to ride roughshod over his interview.

'Why would it be your fault?' she asked in a tone that was as gentle as possible.

Jojo shook her head again, and then said without looking at either of them, 'Something had gone wrong between us. I couldn't understand what it was. Aleksy messaged me that morning and said he was going climbing. He asked if I'd be around later, because he needed to have a serious talk with me.'

She saw Sheens sit up slightly, but he said nothing.

'Do you know what it was about?' Hanson continued.

'I didn't have a clue,' Jojo said. 'I mean, I made an immediate assumption. I assumed he was going to break up with me. I went ballistic at him. I texted him asking what the fuck that was supposed to mean. I said he could talk to me right now, and he didn't answer. So I rang him. I rang him a lot of times, but he never answered. I was so convinced he was about to walk out on me. And I was so hurt and so angry.'

'Did you have any reason to expect a break-up?'

'No, I don't . . . It wasn't like he was off with me,' she said. 'But I could tell something was wrong, and he was trying to hide it. He was always so upbeat, and suddenly he was . . . brooding, I suppose. Whenever he thought I wasn't looking. I guess I put two and two together.'

The DCI nodded, and interjected, 'Can you recall whether Aleksy met up with anyone the day before he died?'

Jojo's eyes became a little distant. 'I don't . . . I don't remember him doing.'

'He didn't mention meeting up with anyone?' he asked. 'That day, or on the day of his death?'

Jojo shook her head. 'Not that I can remember.' Her eyes were slightly over-reflective in the harsh light. 'If I'd had any hint that he was meeting someone else, I probably would have tried to turn up.'

'So you can't think of anything that might have triggered the brooding?'

Jojo shook her head, and then gave a slight frown. 'Maybe . . . There was a row with Brett when we were at his house. But Aleksy laughed it off. I'm actually not sure if that was just before, or . . . it could have been earlier.' She made an exasperated sound. 'It's so hard to remember. But there wasn't anything in his text messages after he'd died. Though . . . I suppose if some were deleted . . . Was there anything else I didn't see?'

'We're looking at the phone,' he said, and didn't add that he was curious about that, too. He moved the conversation on to ask, 'Could you confirm where you were earlier yesterday evening?'

'Yes, I was at Brett's,' she said. 'We all were.'

'The six of you?' Jojo nodded and Jonah went on, 'Did anything happen there that might have triggered the fire? Did any of them seem angry with you?'

'No,' Jojo said. And then she paused. 'None of them seemed angry, but I suppose . . . I was saying that we needed to tell the truth, even things we weren't sure about. I said it was time to tell everything, because Aurora's killer was getting away with it.'

Jonah nodded, and Jojo gave him a thoughtful look.

'I wasn't thinking that it was one of us really. I mean, I know logically . . . I just wanted us to find the killer, and for it to be someone else. That's all.' And then Jojo's eyes became distant again, and troubled, too. 'I've spent eight years think-ing I drove Aleksy to fall off the rock face with my calls and texts,' she said eventually, her voice unsteady. 'But he might have died because . . . because he'd worked something out about Aurora?'

'There's a strong possibility,' Jonah said. 'So if anything occurs to you at all about Aleksy and any strange conversa-tions, it would be good for us to know.'

Jojo nodded, her eyes fixed on a point on the wall. He wondered what she was remembering, but she said nothing.

'Tell me something,' he said, eventually breaking the silence. 'When you hid that stash, did you do anything else that might have kept sniffer dogs away?'

'Oh,' Jojo said, and Hanson saw a flush creep across her face. 'Yes. I'd . . . I dragged a dead stoat along past the tree and then left it a short distance away. I figured anyone search-ing would think the dogs had just found that, and would drag them away. It reeked, so . . .'

'You did that alone? Not with Brett?'

Jojo nodded, looking uncomfortable. 'I told him to get on with hiding the stash, but he was hungover, and a bit useless. So I got the stoat, and laid a scent, and he was still hanging about looking ill when I got back. And then after that we both went to cave the stash in.'

The DCI looked at her thoughtfully. 'It was definitely your idea?'

'Yes,' Jojo said. 'I wasn't . . . I was only trying to stop them finding the drugs. I never meant to stop them finding Aurora.'

The DCI let a silence elapse, and then said, 'Thank you

for all of that. If you think of anything else, please just let us know.'

He turned off the tape, and Jojo rose with obvious relief.

'I'll show you out,' he said, and gave Hanson a brief nod.

They were halfway across CID when Jojo looked sideways at Jonah. 'I'm glad you're back to being nice again. I didn't like my experience of Sheens the policeman back there.'

It was an uncomfortable feeling, being reminded that he was essentially a bully at times. Tommy Sheens had taught him well.

He gave her a slightly tired smile. 'I'm always Sheens the policeman,' he answered. 'But that doesn't mean I'm an arse-hole all the time.'

Jojo's smile widened slightly. 'Oh, I don't know about that...'

Jonah couldn't help a small laugh.

'Do you remember chasing me down?' she asked abruptly. They'd reached the door, but she paused in front of it, and he stopped, too. 'You probably don't. Life of a copper. But I do.'

'Yes, I do,' he said. He gave a small smile. 'Most irritating person I've ever tried to catch up with.'

He saw her mouth lift slightly at the corner. 'You should have given up.'

'I wasn't going to leave you without your sweater.' He looked away for a moment. 'And besides. I don't give up. Not unless I absolutely have to.'

He saw her nod from the corner of his eye.

She shifted as if she might leave, and then said, 'I heard about your dad. I know it was a long time ago, but I wanted to say I was sorry.'

Jonah shook his head. 'I wouldn't be sorry. Best thing that could have happened for my mum.'

Even if it had been horrific, the way he'd gone. Even if the idea of it sometimes woke him in the night, clawing to get out of his bedclothes and imagining that there were flames all around him.

'Everyone says he had a temper.'

Jonah nodded. 'He had. And even when he wasn't particularly angry, he was a nasty piece of work.'

'It was brave of your mother, leaving him like that. And leaving the travelling community. It must have been tough for her.'

Jonah struggled to imagine his mother as tough these days. It was hard to get beyond the fragile, paranoid alcoholic she had become. But Jojo was right. It was strange to be talking about it, after such a long time, to someone who seemed to understand it. Strange, and cathartic.

'It was hard for her for a long time. Divorces don't happen among travellers. Leaving doesn't happen. That's what they told her. We left when I was seven and they were still coming round when I was fourteen, fifteen. Still threatening or cajoling. He came round sometimes too, but it grew rarer after she called the police.' There was a beat, and he said, 'She left him for my sake. She didn't care much about herself, but she cared about me a lot.'

'I hope my mum would've been the same,' Jojo said. And then she put a hand out to the door, and Jonah pressed the green button to let her out.

'It'd be good if you could stay by your phone,' he said, before she could vanish. 'I may well have questions.'

Jojo sighed. 'I was going to go and get chalk and then try the Dagger-Edge climb again. And who knows? Maybe being grilled by you will give me the rage needed to make the final move.'

'Is it far away?' he asked.

'Maybe half an hour?' Jojo replied. 'It's near Burley. I'll probably be a good hour getting into town and back to replace my climbing shoes, and I won't stay that long as the climbs don't get the evening sun.'

'OK,' Jonah said, with his own sigh. 'That's fine. Good luck.'

She cast him a last, sidelong look before she left, almost back to being the Jojo he had half known for more than thirty years.

He tried to hide from her the fact that, in spite of their conversation, he was still thinking of her as a suspect and still willing to assume that she was lying.

The interview with Jojo hadn't helped Hanson's anger. She left it with a deeply unsettling feeling that it had been entirely for her benefit, though she was positive by the end of it that Jojo hadn't expected a grilling.

But then she worried that she was being ridiculous. They were in the middle of a case. Sheens was doing what a good officer did, and pushing a suspect hard.

She needed to talk to Zofia. Until she had some feeling of certainty about that incident, everything else felt like it was left hanging. It was impossible to think of working with a man who had committed a sexual assault.

She checked her Facebook account for what was probably the fiftieth time, but her message suggesting a time to Skype was still sitting there, unread. She felt like putting her fist through the monitor, but instead she rose, and told Lightman she was going to get some air.

Everything seemed to be getting muddier and more complex instead of clearer, and Jonah wasn't sure what to make of Jojo's reactions, or Aleksy's apparent coldness towards her.

He didn't believe that Matt Stavely's arrival, announced shortly afterwards by Lightman, was going to help clear anything up. But he took a look at Stavely as O'Malley walked with him to the interview suite.

He looked wired and jittery. His eyes moved all over the station, and he pulled off his beanie to reveal his greying, uncombed hair. It was clumpy with sweat.

Jonah picked up O'Malley's notes on his interview with Stavely and walked back into CID. He looked around momentarily for Hanson, expecting to find her watching him, but she wasn't at her desk. He was shamefully relieved.

O'Malley was hovering outside Room One and messing around with his phone when Jonah got there.

'All ready?' Jonah asked him.

'Yup. Witness looks like he might burst if we don't get on with it.'

Jonah had to agree. Matt Stavely was shifting his position every few seconds and jiggling his leg up and down between times. He pulled a cigarette out as Jonah watched, rolling it between his fingers.

He jumped when they walked in, and shoved the cigarette back into the pocket of his hoodie. He was barely able to keep still as they went through the introductions for the tape, and he looked anywhere but at Jonah.

'So, Matt,' he said, to kick things off. 'You have something you want to talk to us about.'

'Yeah,' Stavely said immediately. 'I was . . . I was thinking after the sergeant came to see me yesterday. There's some stuff that I think might be relevant.'

Jonah gave him a small smile as he glanced up. 'To do with your work?'

'Yeah,' Stavely said. 'There's a guy I got set up with in

315

eighty-nine. It was through another dealer, because he wanted . . . well, he wanted stuff that dealer didn't offer. Flunitrazepam.'

'Rohypnol,' Jonah said, with a small twist to his stomach. He had worked through the nineties, when the prescription drug had hit the recreational scene. He'd heard about men acting weirdly in bars who'd had packets of it on them, and there had been the much-publicized cases of date rape.

What the media hadn't commented on so extensively were the many cases where victims had been drugged and then robbed, with no sexual assault having taken place. The amnesiac effects made it as much a winner for thieves as it had been for rapists.

And more common still had been the addicts, forging prescriptions to keep the oblivion going. Some of those had ended up as suicides.

Rohypnol had been made a controlled substance in the late nineties, for all of those reasons, and Jonah and his colleagues had seen its use in crime drop off. But it still surfaced now and then as an aid to assault and robbery. Rape was actually, surprisingly, much rarer.

'Yeah,' Stavely said. 'Rohypnol. With coke on the side. Interesting combination.'

Jonah nodded slowly. A flunitrazepam addict was unlikely to be a coke user. They were very dissimilar drugs, one inducing a state of deeply somnolent oblivion, and the other creating an energetic high. Cocaine was a party drug, and if someone who liked to party liked to use Rohypnol as well, then there was an implication that it was for somebody else. A victim.

'Do you have a name for this buyer?' Jonah asked.

'No,' Stavely answered. 'It was all set up so he'd text me, and leave me payment. I'd take the payment and leave the drugs. The other dealer said that was how he worked with him, too. He didn't want anyone knowing anything about him. Which is always a bit fucking annoying. It's not like anyone dealing is going to go and talk about it.' He gave a big sniff, shifted on his chair.

'How much did you supply him with?'

'It was usually a strip of twenty-eight two milligram tablets.'

Jonah could only remember a few of the specifics of Rohypnol use. How many tablets would someone give a victim?

'As far as I know, you'd want three or four tablets to do the job,' Stavely said, as if he could tell that Jonah didn't know. 'Plus alcohol. And I want to say here and now, I supplied the stuff, but I've never used it on anyone. And I always kind of hoped the guy was just sedating himself after bad nights or something.'

'How often did you supply him?'

'It was generally every month or six weeks. Sometimes he'd just ask for coke, so I don't reckon all of the Rohypnol was getting used that quickly.'

'Where did you leave it?'

'It was originally under a bench in Southampton, and then from the mid-nineties it changed to a salt box outside the town hall in Waterlooville. Which was an arse to get to, but it was worth it. He paid twice the market value for the trouble.'

Jonah nodded. He'd been hoping for somewhere that pointed to one of his suspects, but it sounded like this buyer was a careful man.

'It stopped a little while ago,' Stavely added. 'Which was a shame. It was good, steady income.'

'So when did it stop?'

'Couple of years ago,' he said with a shrug.

'No more than that?'

'Definitely not more than three,' Stavely said.

It had been a long-running arrangement, then. Right through from 1989. That made him curious about why it had stopped in the end.

'There wasn't any reason for it stopping, as far as you knew?' he asked.

'No, other than he said he didn't need it now. I guessed he moved or something.'

That didn't tie in with any of his suspects, he thought. Connor and Topaz had moved seven years ago, and Coralie just afterwards.

'And you have no other information on him?' Jonah asked. 'You never saw him?'

Stavely shook his head. 'I wasn't curious enough to risk the deal by hanging around.'

'Do you still have the phone number?'

Stavely shook his head. 'It was just texts that I deleted.'

There was a pause, while Stavely's fidgeting increased. 'That's all. Can I go now?' he said in the end.

'Of course,' Jonah replied.

He stood to let Stavely out, and watched his slightly jerky movements thoughtfully.

'Was he that agitated when you saw him yesterday?' he asked O'Malley.

'No,' he said. 'I guess you'd say he was wary, but calm. Did you see in my notes that he called someone after?'

'You think the call has changed things?'

'Could have done,' O'Malley said. 'Or could be that police stations put the fear of god in him.'

'I'd like you to see if any of our suspects are connected with that place,' Jonah said. 'Or have been in the past. He might have been put up to it, or he might not. My suspicion is that there's more he's not telling us. A reason why he thinks it's linked. Maybe the buyer said something that suggested he'd committed a crime against a young girl. Or maybe he knows who it is.'

'I'll look into it, all right, so.'

Jonah smiled at the very Irish turn of phrase. 'Thanks.'

Hanson made it back to her desk ten minutes before the time she had suggested to Skype Zofia Wierzbowski, and saw immediately that there was a message waiting for her.

Zofia was happy with her suggestion, and had sent her Skype ID. Hanson loaded up Skype on her phone and added Zofia as a contact, and then went to find a free meeting room where she could still get WiFi.

It took a lot longer than she'd expected. For a modern station, Southampton Central was frustratingly low on signal. She ended up calling three minutes late, but Zofia didn't seem worried.

'Thank you for agreeing to speak to me,' Hanson said, speaking into the phone that she'd placed on the meeting-room table. 'I'm not recording this for now, but would you be happy to go on tape if needed?'

'Yes,' Zofia said, her accent rich. 'That is fine.'

'I need to ask you, first, about the party that you went to,' Hanson said, and wondered why she was quite so nervous. Perhaps because she hoped, like Jonah himself, that the DCI hadn't done anything. 'Can you tell me about how you got there?'

'Yes, no problem. I go to the party with Aurora,' she began, and proceeded to tell, in what was very awkward English, the same story that Jonah had told her. 'I should not have drunk,' she said. 'It was not right. I make myself sick, and he – Jonah Sheens – he had looked after me. He put me in a bed.'

319

Hanson took a breath. 'Could you tell me if anything happened between you that night?' she asked.

'Between me and Jonah?' she asked, and then she paused. 'I-I haven't told anyone this before. I should have . . . I was attacked that night.'

Daniel Benham looked pensive as Jonah and Lightman entered the interview room. His solicitor, on the other hand, looked steely.

'Thanks for coming in again,' Jonah began.

'That's all right,' Benham said.

'There are quite a few things I need to ask you, but I'll try to make it quick.'

Benham didn't react and neither did his solicitor, so Jonah carried on.

'To begin with, having identified and spoken to the dealer who supplied you with the Dexedrine, we need to know whether you showed him where the drugs were hidden, or mentioned them to him.'

'God, no,' Benham said in a low but intense voice. 'I might have wanted to help him out, but I wouldn't trust him as far as I could throw him. You don't tell a drug dealer where you're hiding their product if you don't want it stolen back again from under your nose. It's not like you'd have legal recourse if they took it back, and you'd be on dangerous ground threatening them.'

'He didn't ask any questions about what you were going to do with it?' Jonah persisted.

'No, he didn't. And I wouldn't have told him,' Daniel said firmly.

'OK. And to go back to the topic of any drugs purchases since,' Jonah said, 'the dealer has suggested that he did carry on supplying one of you. We're looking into it, but it would be a lot better for you to be open about that now if it involved you.'

'I'm not sure of the relevance,' the solicitor said.

Benham gave a short laugh. 'I've had nothing to do with Matt Stavely since that deal. Not just because I wanted nothing more to do with him or drugs after Aurora went. I became a politician, for Christ's sake, and Mary would have killed me.'

'Perhaps a reason to be covert about it,' Jonah said.

Benham shook his head. 'It wasn't worth the risk, and the whole idea seemed . . . revolting, after that summer.'

'OK,' Jonah said, nodding. 'There are also a few things that have come up connected to the death of Aleksy Nowak.'

Benham gave him a slightly blank look. 'Aleksy? He didn't even know Aurora.'

'No,' Jonah agreed. 'But he did know the rest of you, and possibly ended up knowing a little too much.'

Benham gave him a sceptical look. 'What could he know? He didn't get together with Jojo till . . . till twenty years later.'

'Given that we're busy investigating thirty years after Aurora's death, and information is still coming to light,' Jonah said evenly, 'Aleksy may well have found something out.'

There was a brief whispered comment from his solicitor, and Benham shrugged. 'All right. All right. Go on.'

'I'd like you to think back to the weeks before Aleksy's death, if you can.'

Benham gave a look halfway between worried and exasperated. 'That's not the easiest thing to do.'

'I know,' Jonah said, choosing to soothe. 'But some things might have stood out. Did he argue with anyone, for example?'

'Aleksy?' Benham asked, and shook his head. 'He didn't do arguments. He was too . . . I don't know. Too ridiculous about things. I mean, he sometimes drove people mad with pranking them or teasing them . . . but it was impossible to argue with him.'

'No arguments at all?' Jonah persisted. 'Even with Jojo?'

'Really, no,' Benham said, shaking his head. 'Those two were . . . they were one of those annoyingly compatible couples. You must know the kind. You and your wife are busy falling out over stupid things, and they're joking around and then smooching in a corner when they think nobody's looking.'

But then there was a momentary slip in Benham's expression.

'I . . . actually, there was . . . God, I'd forgotten about that. There was a falling-out of a kind. I suppose . . . I suppose I thought it was drink-related. And nothing much seemed to come of it.'

'I'd like to know, even if it seems unimportant.'

'Well . . .' Benham cleared his throat slightly. 'We'd got into the habit of having parties at Brett's after Mary and I had kids and stopped hosting so much. It was just a normal party at his. But there was some . . . thing. Some row. Which I think was because Brett had been cracking on to Jojo and Aleksy didn't like it.'

'Did you see him doing it?' Jonah asked.

'Yes,' Benham said, with a grimace. 'Quite a number of times. I think he admired her athleticism and strength. And Jojo is a lot of fun. I suppose sometimes Brett just felt like she was something Anna wasn't. Which isn't to say that he doesn't love Anna,' he added quickly. 'He clearly does. And I don't think he'd ever cheat on her.'

'So Brett liked to flirt,' he said slowly. 'Did Jojo respond?'

'No,' Benham said, shaking his head. 'Jojo might have been a little flattered by the attention, but she had boundaries, and if he looked like he was crossing them, she moved away.'

Jonah nodded, wondering whether Jojo might not have kept to those boundaries in private. The public routine may have been protecting a private affair.

'Look, I don't know if I've got that right,' Benham said quickly. 'About the argument. You'd have to ask them really.'

'Do you remember when this was?' Jonah asked.

'Oh . . . not really. I mean . . . it was after Topaz and Connor got married. So . . . that must have been . . . nine years ago. Or more recently. Though I suppose Aleksy's been dead for . . . eight years?'

'So we can't pin it down any more than that it happened in the year before Aleksy died,' Jonah summed up.

'I don't think so . . . And like I said, I don't think anything came of it.'

A brief pause was broken by Lightman. 'What about Aleksy?' he asked. 'Did he show any interest in anyone else?'

Benham shook his head. 'No, he really didn't. He teased Coralie and Topaz, and Mary and Anna, too, sometimes. But he teased the rest of us just as much.'

'He didn't meet up with any of them alone?'

'Not as far as I know.'

'OK, thank you.'

Jonah left the room, and found himself mulling on that argument between Aleksy and Brett and Jojo. Perhaps he ought to be talking to some of the partners of his suspects.

It was something that should always be done during an investigation in his opinion. Talking to people alone was like examining them in a vacuum. There was a lot more to all of those six than that one night in the forest, and how they accounted for their movements. He wanted to have as full a picture as he could, of all of them. Whatever complex series of events had occurred to lead to Aurora's death, it had been based on the kids who had gathered there; perhaps on their teacher's presence; on the baggage each of them had brought with them that night.

He checked the time on his phone. It was just gone five, and he realized he had forgotten lunch again. He checked for any spare food in his desk, but came up with nothing.

He headed out into CID again, where all three of his team were at their desks. He avoided making eye contact with Hanson, though he could feel her level gaze on him.

'OK. I'm going to see Anna Parker, and probably Mary Benham after that. Ben, you're with me. Domnall, I'd like you to release Stavely and then get on with the phone records. Hanson, I'd like you to stake out Stavely and find out if he visits anyone. And please be careful,' he added, thinking back to the fire, and the feeling of being watched. However worried he was about his own future, that threat was still there. 'Take a uniform.'

'OK,' Hanson said. 'And could I . . . have a quick word, before you go?'

'Sure,' Jonah said, keeping it light.

He let Hanson into his office, and perched on the desk instead of sitting. He felt like he was waiting for a verdict.

'I had a call with Zofia, and I thought you'd like to know what she had to say,' she said.

'I would,' Jonah said, not quite sure that was true.

'Nothing happened between you,' Hanson said in a tight tone. 'Zofia says that she was trying to talk you into it, and kept trying to get undressed, but you stopped her, and tucked her into the bed, and then left.'

'Jesus,' Jonah said.

He felt suddenly weak, and very much aware of the perspiration that was all over his face. It was all OK. It was all OK.

Hanson was still standing stiffly in front of him, not entering into his relief at all.

'There is a little more to it, though,' she went on, with a trace of censure still in her voice. 'It may well have no bearing on our case, but someone else did attack Zofia. She woke to find herself face down with someone on top of her. She never got to see who it was.' Hanson looked away from him, and folded her arms across herself. She looked as awkward as he felt. 'I did ask if she was sure it wasn't you, and she was very clear on it. She says she remembers it all in absolute detail. She remembers that his arms were covered by a shirt, and you'd been in a T-shirt. She'd had to clean blood off it earlier in the evening. He'd hissed in her ear that if she tried to move, he'd kill her, and once he was done, he left. She didn't dare look round for a long time.'

Jonah's relief turned into a cold feeling. The same cold feeling he'd had about Aurora having been raped.

'Did she report it?'

Hanson shook her head. 'Her mother wouldn't believe that she hadn't been willing. And then she sent her away.'

'Fuck,' Jonah said. 'So the big question is, do we now start investigating a thirty-year-old rape at a party, too?'

'I'll have to leave that to you, sir,' Hanson said.

Jonah could see that she was still angry. The fact that he could easily have done it himself was still with her. He understood the anger more than he wanted to.

'I'm glad you spoke to her.'

'Let's hope I don't have to do anything like that again, shall we?' the constable said acidly.

She was turning to go as Jonah said to her quietly, 'Thank you, Juliette.'

'For what?'

'For waiting to find out the truth before you reported it,' he said. 'And for finding it out.'

She nodded, but there was still that anger running through her.

He hoped the anger would go in time. In the midst of his own fear, it was still clear to him that she was a huge asset to his team. And despite the likely awkwardness between them going forward, he really hoped that she would stay.

36

He put a call through to Brett's business number on the way
to the house, and got Anna, as he'd hoped.

'Do you mind if we come and ask you a few questions?' he
asked, as if they weren't already on their way. 'It seems like
you know the group fairly well and might be able to help us.'

'Oh.' She sounded uncertain. 'Yes, I'm sure that's fine.
Would you . . . do you need Brett to be here? He's out on a
bike ride at the moment.'

'No, that's fine,' Jonah said, feeling that this was a piece of
good luck. It would be a lot easier asking for candour without Brett there to overhear. 'Perhaps we'll catch him before
we leave, but it's not vital. He's been very helpful so far.'

'Oh, good,' Anna said, clearly cheered by this.

He rang Daniel Benham's home as well, but this time was
not quite so lucky. He got Polly, who said that her parents were
both out. Daniel was probably still on his way home from the
station, Jonah thought, but he decided not to mention that.

'I'll try them later,' he said, in a relaxed tone. 'Nothing
urgent.'

The traffic on the way was good, and the roads had dried
up after the rain. Once they were off the bypass, it was almost
enjoyable to drive the rural lanes towards Brett and Anna's
home, eating crisps one-handed as he went. But his thoughts
descended quickly into cyclical attempts to make sense of
everything. Lightman knew him well enough to let him stew
in silence at least.

Anna treated them like guests when they arrived, just as she had the last time, and her warmth and her careful movements as she made coffee and tea and put homemade truffles on to a saucer were strangely soothing.

'I've got cream as well as milk, if you prefer,' she said to Lightman, who had asked for coffee. 'It would have to be cold, though. I can't do the foam thing with cream.'

'Whichever's easiest,' Lightman replied, and so she set about steaming some milk and pouring it over a shot of espresso.

'Come through to the sitting room,' she said, piling everything on to a tray. 'The breakfast bar isn't very comfortable.'

Jonah didn't think that anywhere in the sleek house looked that comfortable, but was pleasantly surprised to find a deep sofa to sink into.

'You're a great hostess,' Jonah said to her warmly. 'I hear you two generally have any gatherings of the group here.'

'Most of them,' she answered, with a slightly embarrassed smile. 'I'm not that great. Brett is the real expert. He's an amazing chef, and he likes everything to be just right.'

Jonah grinned. 'Are you less of a perfectionist? More a creative type?'

'I suppose so,' she said, with a slight laugh. 'If you want to put it nicely. I'm definitely a lot clumsier.'

He didn't think this was deliberate self-deprecation. Anna struck him as genuinely hard on herself.

'Well, you've done a great job today,' Jonah said, taking a truffle and demolishing it. He could have done with something more substantial, but they were pretty incredible, he had to admit. 'Can I ask about one of your parties?' he went on. 'There was one a while back that came to our attention.'

'Oh,' Anna said. 'Yes, if I can . . . if I can help.'

'It was a long time ago,' Jonah warned her. 'Eight years or so. When Aleksy was still alive.' He left a momentary pause, and when she nodded he went on. 'There was a row, which was apparently unusual within the group. It was between Aleksy, Brett and Jojo, I think. We're told that you intervened to smooth things over.'

'Oh.' Anna looked uncomfortable. 'Right. Yes.'

'You remember it, then?'

'Yes, I do. But it wasn't important.'

'I'm sure it wasn't,' Jonah said gently, 'but the thing I've learned in investigating crime is that the small things can often point towards the bigger things. Or hide them.'

'Well . . . yes, I suppose they must,' Anna said, her blue eyes a little troubled. 'But I don't think it had anything to do with Aurora . . .' She paused. 'If it was something . . . something else, that was a little bit wrong, would it get people in trouble?'

Jonah put his cup down, and said firmly, 'We're not interested in pursuing anyone for any crimes unrelated to Aurora's death. That's not the aim here. And if there is a small misdemeanour that we can write out of our investigations, it would be much better if we knew now.'

Anna nodded slowly. 'OK. Well . . . Aleksy had decided to snoop around. It was my fault, I think. I'd told him how Brett wouldn't let me in his study. I don't really know why I told him. It was sort of a joke about him, because he hates disorder and – you know, he's a little bit OCD really.' She gave a slight smile. 'It's quite endearing, and I've learned to fit around it. I shouldn't have told Aleksy about the study, though. It was a mistake. He decided there must be something to hide, and when he got a bit drunk and went off to use the bathroom, he decided to go and take a look.'

Jonah watched her, finding himself intrigued by this.

329

'And when I found them they were arguing. I sort of guessed what it might be about because they were in Brett's study, and I knew his business was doing so well at the time.' Anna sighed. 'I got a full explanation afterwards. He was so humiliated, and I think that was why he flew off the handle at Aleksy. He'd been filing false accounts. Not wildly so, but . . . not declaring things for tax.'

'Aleksy was very angry with him?'

'Yes,' Anna said. 'But I think I calmed things down. I reminded them that nothing was more important than their friendship and I reminded them they were both drunk.'

'Did anything more come of it?' Lightman asked, interjecting for the first time.

'No. Well, I texted Aleksy, apologizing after Brett and I had spoken. I said, look, I know about it all, and it's not ideal but I'm OK with it and I don't think it's going to continue. I asked him to please not mention it to anyone.'

'And what did he say?' Jonah asked.

'He said it was up to me,' she said, nodding. 'But that he worried about me and if it were him, he'd be disentangling himself right away.'

'Because you're heavily involved in the business?' Jonah said. 'So he decided to back off as a favour to you?'

'Yes, I think so,' Anna said, going slightly pink. 'I know that means I'm colluding in hiding a crime. But I'm positive it was never on any large scale, and he's been fine for a long time now. There's been no need for tricks.'

'Thank you,' Jonah said. 'I know it's a difficult subject.'

'That's all right,' Anna said. 'You don't . . . you don't think there'll be any need to pursue it?'

'I shouldn't think so,' Jonah said. 'It's fairly straightforward, and nothing to do with Aurora.'

The reality was that he could assume no such thing just now. But reassuring her seemed the right thing to do.

'Good,' she said, with clear relief. 'That's good to hear.'

There were sounds of movement out in the main hall, and Anna became silent and a little tense.

'I'm back!' Brett called from the hall.

'Just in the sitting room,' Anna called. 'The police came for a quick chat.'

There were padding steps, and then Brett appeared in cycling shorts, a tech top and fingerless gloves. His hair was all spiked up with sweat, and there were patches of it on the tight top.

For a moment, witnessing Jonah and Lightman, he looked thoroughly pissed off. But then he made an effort to smile. It amused Jonah. It seemed to be part of a middle-class upbringing that you should be polite and respectful to the police. It was something that Jojo had definitely side-stepped, and Topaz seemed more than happy to ignore.

'I'm a bit . . . odorous,' Brett said, walking towards them. His voice and movements were both weary. 'Sorry.'

'That's OK,' Jonah said. 'We're definitely intruding. The last thing anyone wants after a long ride is the bloody cops in their house.'

The friendly tone seemed to soothe Brett. Jonah felt he was partly soothing him to make sure that Anna didn't get in trouble. Reading between the lines of the chat, Brett could be quite critical when he wanted, and he didn't think Anna was likely to stand up for herself.

It was an interesting dynamic to note. He had interviewed numerous lawbreakers who were somewhat abusive towards their partners. Many of them were, like Brett, slightly controlling, and unkind when their partners didn't live up to their standards. But being a bit of a domestic bully didn't make Brett a murderer, any more than being a troubled boy with a temper made Connor one.

'Oh, can I ask one quick question?' Jonah asked Brett, as they headed for the door.

'Sure.'

'In one of your original interviews you said that you'd been wading in the river, trying to find Aurora. But you were queried on your trousers being dry when the police arrived.'

'Oh, god,' Brett said, putting a hand up to his head. 'I remember that. It was – I'd puked on my trousers. I was hungover and running around searching and it all hit me. There was a dead animal, and we had to go past it to get to the tree. When we . . . when we hid the stash. Jojo told you, didn't she? It smelled so bad, and I was so bloody hungover that I puked. And I didn't want anyone thinking I was drunk, so I changed into clean trousers. And then when I was asked . . .'

Jonah gave him a smile. 'You said you'd taken your trousers off? Understood. Thank you, Mr Parker.'

They let themselves out, and Jonah mentally added everything Anna had told him into the mix. The row had been about fraud, then. The business hadn't even been started back when Aurora had died, and he could see no link between tax evasion and the murder of a young girl years before.

The phone rang as he was turning out of Brett's driveway, and O'Malley's voice was loud over the Bluetooth.

'We've had Coralie Ribbans on the phone,' he said. 'She says she's got something important to tell us. She can be in for five thirty.'

'OK. That works. Tell her to come.'

'And in other news, I've found a link to that place in Waterlooville that Matt Stavely was delivering to. Andrew

Mackenzie ran a scout group there every Thursday evening for some years. I'm checking the dates.'

'Bingo,' Jonah said with a grin. 'Well done, Domnall.'

'You can thank Google. Well, me and Google. Say you owe us both a pint and we're square.'

Jonah rang off, trying to absorb that new piece of information. So there was a chance that Mackenzie had a history of rape. He wondered if he could be wrong about Aleksy. Could the first fire at Jojo's have been pure random vandalism? Could his death have been accidental?

The feeling of confusion and fogginess was descending again. It didn't help that he felt like his stomach had been hollowed out.

'Can you open the carrot and hummus thing?' he asked Lightman. 'And root around in the back and see if I've got any other food, before I kill and eat someone?'

Jonah went straight to O'Malley's desk once they were back, and pulled up a chair once again.

'Right,' he said. 'Phone records and Aleksy Nowak's phone. What do we have?'

'A few things,' O'Malley said. 'Messages between Aleksy and Jojo.'

'Great,' Jonah said. 'Can you start with the day of his death?'

O'Malley brought up a conversation between Jojo and her boyfriend from the fourteenth. Only it wasn't much of a conversation. It had been one message from Aleksy at 11 a.m. saying that they needed to talk once he was back, and then a frightened, angry reply from Jojo.

She'd sent him eight messages after that, asking him to answer his bloody phone. She'd phoned him twelve times, too.

Jonah felt a little uncomfortable reading that. It had the look of someone who'd flipped out. Could that have been enough to drive Jojo to hunt him down? Could she have wanted to kill him because he was about to reject her? Or because she thought he was?

But looking at the times of the calls, she'd still been ringing him after he must have been dead. Right into the evening.

'Can you bring up some other messages Jojo sent to Aleksy?' he asked. 'I'd like a comparison with our unknown sender who knew where he was going to be climbing.'

O'Malley nodded. 'She's had the same number for seventeen years, so it's easy enough.'

So Jojo was telling the truth about that, then, Jonah thought.

O'Malley scrolled back a few pages, to earlier that month. He opened up a message Jojo had sent on 2 July.

Jonah felt a little bit of a voyeur as he read.

Hey, hotness! Was it a good session? What time are you back? Any energy left for me . . .? Missing you xxx

Jonah nodded. 'Try a few others.'

O'Malley exited and clicked on another one, from a few days later.

She's now decided she doesn't like the concept and wants me to take the alpine bed back out. Considering planting thistles and giant hogweed and leaving . . . If you have time to get wine on the way home, I'm going to need it. A LOT of wine. Love you, even if I am savage right now xxx

The sergeant exited it again, and clicked on the very last one, which Jonah saw was from the September. He only had a moment to wonder why she was texting Aleksy after he had been dead for two months before the message was open.

Hey, hotness. I'm at Font. I made that 7a. Bloody finally! I really could have done with your advice on this one, but I got there in the end. I missed you a lot today. I wanted you there to celebrate with me. Actually, I just wanted you there to wrap my arms round, and kiss and hold. There still hasn't been a day when I haven't wanted that. Did I tell you I had a dream where I found you lying there, and I kissed you, and it revived you? I've never wished for a fairy tale to be true before. I miss you. I love you. I love you. Xxx

'Poor bloody thing,' O'Malley said.

37

By early evening, Hanson was feeling like a failure. She had followed Stavely home to his flat. He hadn't diverged, or stopped to meet anyone, and hadn't reappeared out of the entranceway, either.

In her tiredness and distraction, she hadn't done as the chief had asked and brought a uniformed officer along. Which turned out to be a good thing when her phone buzzed, and she made the mistake of reading the next message from Damian.

Did you sleep well? Was his bed nice and comfy?

She took two deep, steadying breaths before replying.

I didn't get much sleep. I was working, like I told you. I didn't stay with anyone.

She could feel her heart pounding uncomfortably in her chest again. She didn't start up the car. She knew she'd have another message in a minute.

Sure enough, her phone buzzed again.

Hahaha! Do you think I'm stupid? You didn't come home. I was there. I was waiting up for you to try and make things right and you were off screwing some guy. You're a pathetic slag.

It was like her body lost all its strength in a rush. She found herself sitting with her head on the steering wheel, as minute after minute passed.

She knew she needed to move. She needed to work. She had to throw herself into something and forget him. She had to succeed, too, and prove herself.

Despite feeling like she was no longer on the same planet as the run-down block of flats in front of her, or the investigation, or even as her car.

There was a little more in the recent phone records to interest Jonah. Daniel Benham had called Brett Parker the morning before. Coralie had then called Brett a few times after her arrival in Southampton.

Just last night, Daniel had messaged Coralie, but she hadn't replied. There was little else sent via text message, which was no real surprise. If Jonah had been under investigation for murder, he wouldn't have sent anything in writing, either, even though they actually had no access to that information.

And then there was a little flurry of communications, from Jojo to Brett, and Brett to Coralie, from the evening before.

'Them arranging to meet at Brett's,' Jonah said, with a nod.

Jonah thought about Coralie again. For some reason, she was the easiest of the group to forget. She didn't seem to be central to anything. Everyone saw her as Topaz's shadow rather than as a core member of the group of friends. And, in general, the others seemed to like her rather less than Topaz did.

She didn't come across as intelligent or dominant. Her career hadn't been academic or impressive. But he couldn't rule out the possibility that she was a hell of a lot smarter than she seemed, or that she had been persuaded by one of the others to help cover something up if not.

He pulled a brief set of notes O'Malley had made on her off the system, and read through them. There was nothing particularly illuminating except for a relationship with her father that seemed a little overly close. Much of her life had been shaped by him. He had got her into university, and got her each and every job. She spent a great deal of her time with him, even now, O'Malley noted, which was evident from her social media feeds.

Contrastingly, despite liking to tag herself in lots of locations and with numerous friends, there were very few references to the friendship group from school. Jonah brooded on that, on her role as an outsider. It made her the most likely person to be truthful, but also meant there were things that were probably hidden from her.

Lightman appeared at ten to six, having finished his interview with a woman who thought she might have been assaulted by Mackenzie.

'I'm pretty sure it's not a goer,' he said. 'She's almost certainly been assaulted, by a perpetrator who was slightly similar in look to Mackenzie, but given the location, which is somewhere Mackenzie is not known to have been, I think it's likely to be someone else. I want to pass it to DCI Matthews's team for a proper investigation.'

Jonah nodded, thinking again of Zofia and a sexual assault that had gone unreported for thirty years. He needed to decide what to do about it.

At that point, he saw Coralie finally arriving beyond Lightman's shoulder. She was in sports kit, and Jonah sighed. He didn't think being late for a police interview because of being at the gym was enough of an excuse.

He took in her pink-and-grey running shoes, which had the exact same colours as her pink top and grey leggings. Over the top, she had a thin, grey-blue hoodie. Her blonde hair was tied back in a high ponytail. It was an overwhelmingly young look once again. If it hadn't been for the slight looseness of the skin on her arms, and the lines on her face, she could have been still at school. And there was a nervousness to her movements, too, that made her all the more girlish.

'Come and sit in on this with me, will you?' he asked Lightman.

As he entered the room and sat in front of her, Jonah remembered decades-old gossip about the parties held at Coralie's house whenever her father had been overseas, which had been fairly often. He didn't remember ever having been to one, but he'd heard about the drink, the joints and the borderline sexual games that had gone on. And he remembered Topaz discussing one of the bigger parties, and who would and wouldn't be invited. Topaz had been making all the decisions, as if the house and the party had been hers and not her friend's.

'There was something you wanted to tell us, I believe, Miss Ribbans,' Jonah said for the benefit of the tape.

'Yes,' Coralie said, nodding. 'It was . . . You asked me about Mr Mackenzie before. And whether or not . . . whether I'd seen him. I wasn't expecting the question, so I wasn't really ready to think.'

'So you've had time to think now?' Jonah asked.

'Yes. Yes, I have. I mean, not about that night. I still – I never saw him. He could have been there. I just didn't see him. It's about before that.'

There was a sudden loud buzz. Coralie jumped slightly, and scrabbled in her shoulder bag. She pulled her pink iPhone out, which was continuing to buzz, and then, to Jonah's surprise, she answered it.

'Hi,' she said a little breathlessly. 'Can I talk later? I'm just at the police station. Helping . . . helping them.'

There was a pause, and then a male voice sounded faintly.

'Yes. Yes, OK. Speak later. Bye.'

Coralie hung up, looking somehow more nervous than she had.

'Just Daddy,' she said, as she put the phone away.

'That's fine,' Jonah said, despite wondering quite seriously about the relationship between Coralie and her father. 'Please go on when you're ready.'

'Yes,' Coralie said, and she pulled her bag back on to her shoulder jerkily. 'A few months before Aurora – before that night – I saw something at the school. I'd been late writing an essay, and Mr Mackenzie had told me to drop it in after school. I had to miss a dance lesson to do it, and I went up to his office at five thirty. The lights were on, so I went in, and I saw . . . I saw Mr Mackenzie and Aurora.'

Jonah waited for a moment, and then asked, 'What were they doing?'

'He was right up close to her,' she said. 'He was handing her a book, and smiling at her, but then he put his hand up to her face.'

And he knew she was camping that night, Jonah thought. *He knew she was there.*

'What was Aurora's reaction?' Jonah asked.

'She looked . . . uncomfortable,' she said. 'Maybe a bit scared.'

'Did they see you?'

'Yes,' Coralie said. 'Mr Mackenzie suddenly caught sight of me. And he was all smiling and asking me to come in, and saying he'd just been recommending a book to Aurora, as if nothing was wrong, and I started . . . to doubt what I'd seen.'

Jonah nodded slowly. He had heard that exact series of events before on numerous occasions, either from the victim of sexual abuse, or from observers like Coralie.

And yet he felt doubt coursing through him. He needed to think about this piece of evidence against Mackenzie, which fought with everything that was gradually building in his head.

'I'm sorry,' he said suddenly. 'I didn't offer you a hot drink. Let me get you something. I'll need a few more details from you.'

'OK,' she said, still with that tension in her. 'Coffee would be good. Thank you.'

Stavely had been looking out of his sitting-room window every few minutes, squinting down into the car park. The waiting around was killing him. He'd tried playing some *Doom* to distract himself, but he was too wound up. Four cigarettes smoked one after the other hadn't even put a dent in the edgy anxiety.

On what was probably the fifteenth check, he saw a car pulling up. He waited there, absolutely still, to make sure he'd got this right. And then he went to pick up his phone.

He sent a one-word message to the number that he had memorized, and then sat and waited. His leg was jiggling uncontrollably.

His phone buzzed thirty seconds later, and he felt a slight crawling sensation up his spine as he read Daniel Benham's name.

It was time to go.

He stood, shoving his cigarettes and his wallet into his pocket. He checked for his keys, and then let himself out on to the landing.

The anxiety was still there, but there was a large part of him that was really looking forward to this.

Hanson was still sitting outside the sixties monstrosity that Stavely lived in. It was within what she knew was gang territory, and she found her heart racing as a group of boys made their way from the nearby parkland across the car park and past her. There was no need for her to be here. The chief had only told her to follow him, not to sit on stake-out. But she felt frozen in place. Or weighted down, maybe.

Damian had texted her eight times since she had stopped replying. She'd been trying to gather herself together for the last half hour. She just needed to drive away, back to the station, but with every new message, the feeling of a wall between her and the world only deepened.

She half saw a figure leave the flat block by the stairs ahead of her, and she had watched him for quite a while before she realized that it was Stavely, his beanie pulled low over his brow and a hunch to his shoulders.

He was heading towards town, and in a sudden, flustered rush, she started the Fiat and began following him. His zig-zagging route took him to a graffiti-covered payphone on Merton Road. She carried on driving, and saw him speaking into the mouthpiece. He looked around him as he did it, and she wondered whether he was afraid of attack, or of being watched. She was glad that his eyes drifted over her without apparent recognition through the side window, and snapped her focus back to the road.

There was a three-car parking bay outside a chippie and chemist's further up, and she pulled in there. She could just see Stavely in the rear-view mirror, and she made a point of looking in her bag beside her in case anyone else was paying attention.

The phone call didn't last long. Stavely hung up, and then immediately began moving down the road towards her. He didn't glance her way as he strode past, head down. She was getting ready to start the car when he stopped at the bus stop twenty yards further up.

He propped himself against the seats, pulling out a cigarette. She let her hand drop from the ignition, pulled out her phone and made a show of fiddling with it. She wondered if she was being stupid. Was Stavely likely to be going anywhere in particular right now? He'd been home several hours after being released, and hadn't immediately gone to talk to anyone.

The phone call was the bit that piqued her interest, though. Why a phone booth? He had a mobile, surely. Who the hell used phone booths now? Or was that the standard MO when you dealt drugs, so nobody could ever trace you? But then, how did your clients ever get in touch with you?

A bus trundled past her and pulled in alongside the stop, and Stavely climbed on.

'You'd better not be going to bloody Tesco's,' she muttered as she pulled out after it.

Jonah had drifted back to his office without noticing he was doing it, and found himself standing in front of his desk, staring at nothing. He needed to understand all this. To understand what was going on behind the scenes.

There had been signs of guilt that pointed vaguely towards all of them in the beginning. Daniel Benham, who had bought the drugs and possibly removed them. Connor, who had been back up at the campfire. Brett, who had a possible predilection for young girls.

And two of those pieces of information, he realized, had come from Coralie.

And now, suddenly, two pieces of information that pointed towards Andrew Mackenzie had emerged. A two-step, devastating blow to his reputation. One from Stavely, and one from Coralie again.

What would you do, he wondered suddenly, if you wanted to hide a rape and murder, but wanted to protect your friends, too? What if you were smart enough to realize that you could cloud everything, point evidence towards multiple people, meaning that there could never be a clear case against one?

To convict, they needed to prove murder beyond reasonable doubt. But that was impossible when there were vague implications that others could have done it.

Had that been the intention from the beginning? Had the body been recovered decades earlier, would there have been fingerprints on that beer can, from Brett or Connor? And then the drug removal to point to Daniel Benham? Perhaps there had been a third indication of guilt to point to the remaining boy.

But then up had popped Mackenzie. He had been snapped going into the police station, and he'd hit the news. There was suddenly a new person to target, who was entirely outside the group, and meant nothing to the killer. And ever since evidence had appeared that made him look guilty. First from Stavely, and then from Coralie.

Someone was manipulating all of this. Planting evidence, and using Coralie and Stavely. And possibly ringing to check that Coralie was doing what she was supposed to.

He found himself thinking again of that can full of Dexedrine, and what it had been supposed to tell them.

It was supposed to imply an overdose.

But – the big but – that would only work if the killer knew

344

Aurora had died from an overdose. Otherwise, a can full of drugs at the crime scene would have meant nothing.

His hand felt a little disconnected from the rest of him as he put a call through to McCullough.

'Hi, Linda,' he said, at her wary answer. 'The original crime scene, from 1983. The campsite. There was a lot of peripheral stuff collected from there, wasn't there?'

'Yes, though it's nothing I've been looking at.'

'But you've got access to it?' he asked.

'If I go and dig around in the archives,' she said, sounding less than enthusiastic. 'Why am I thinking this is going to mean another late night?'

'The beer can,' he said briefly. 'We both agree that it was most likely planted. You might have been able to get finger-prints and saliva off that can if she'd been found, say, a year after her death, right?'

'Well, I was at school at the time,' McCullough said sar-donically, 'but someone here might have.'

'Assuming that had happened, we'd still have been able to tell whether or not she'd overdosed by then, wouldn't we? The soft tissue would have been there in part.'

'Well . . . yes, I suppose so.'

'So why leave it there, when it pointed towards her mode of death, unless it pointed the finger at someone else?'

There was a pause.

'So you're using this as, what? Evidence that she over-dosed?'

'I'm using it as a reason to look elsewhere,' he said. 'We don't have prints, but maybe we were supposed to have them. And because that beer can was there, nobody was supposed to look elsewhere for the source of the overdose. There were other containers found around the campsite. Lots of empty

345

cans and bottles and cartons, and a few cups. The case notes show that they were collected, but never tested, as back in eighty-three they weren't looking for traces of an overdose. And why would they? But now I'd like to know if any of them had traces of Dexedrine in.'

'Jesus,' McCullough said. 'That could be a lot of work . . .'

'But I think it needs doing,' said Jonah. 'If we had that, we'd have definite cause of death.'

Linda sighed. 'You're right. And I guess I'm finished with my normal day's work, and was fondly thinking of going home on time . . .'

'You're wonderful,' Jonah said, and hung up before she could argue.

Keeping track of Stavely at bus stops was difficult. At the first three, there was traffic coming the other way, so she'd had an excuse to tuck in behind the bus and watch who climbed off. At the fourth, there had been nobody coming the other way and she'd had to make her way round it, and then pull in a quarter of a mile further down the road.

She'd overtaken the bus and then let it past several times, until they were in the city centre proper. She was beginning to worry that they would reach a bus-only area and she would be stumped, but he had climbed off on Commercial Road just before it turned the corner on to Above Bar Street, and she was able to crawl along ahead of him and pull into the Frog and Parrot car park just round the corner.

She strolled towards the car park entrance, and saw him walk past along the street. It was easy enough to turn the corner and fall into step behind him. But then she almost walked into him when he turned suddenly to enter the big John Lewis.

It wasn't a good move from the perspective of someone tailing. Department stores with multiple exits were hell. She'd tried to follow a fake suspect through one during her training and had lost them within minutes.

She pushed open the first set of doors and stopped just inside it, trying to find him again. The displays weren't tall, and as she scanned them, she saw him bending over the top of one of them.

He was in the kitchenware section, which struck her as bizarre. She couldn't imagine Stavely browsing crockery on his weekends.

She ambled in his direction, trying to walk round behind him to keep out of his sight. She followed the aisle, and walked round in front of the tills until she was standing over his shoulder.

She was entirely unprepared for him swinging round and facing her. His eyes met hers, and she felt the animal sense of fear that usually only hit her when she was facing up to a violent offender.

There was what felt like an endless moment while he stood like that, and then he muttered, 'Excuse me.' His eyes cut away, and he stepped round her, making his way towards the tills.

She turned to watch him, not quite able to believe that he hadn't recognized her. That he wasn't about to do a runner or try to attack her. But then, she realized, he'd never actually met her. She was just a random woman to him, and not an officer who had peered at him through the one-way glass.

He was focused on the counter, and stepped forward quickly to one of the free check-out assistants. He was holding out a thin plastic packet with a protruding handle, and she was slow to realize that it was a large kitchen knife.

And it was only at that point that she realized she'd left her phone sitting on the passenger seat of her car and couldn't call this in.

Jonah only just remembered to make the promised coffee before he barged back in on Coralie. He put it down carefully enough in front of her, but that was the last of the care he was happy to show her.

'I don't think you've been telling us the truth, Coralie,' he said, and then he sat, not bothering to pull his notes out again.

'What do you mean?' she asked in a small voice.

'You've come in here with a sudden and convenient story about Andrew Mackenzie, a man who produced zero reaction in you before,' he said. 'You've previously arrived to point the finger at Connor Dooley, and suggested doubts about Brett Parker. Are you attempting to misdirect us alone, or are you being used by another member of the group?'

Coralie's cheeks flushed a hot red. 'I'm not. All I'm trying to do is tell . . . is tell the truth when nobody . . . nobody else will.'

'That doesn't quite wash,' Jonah argued, and then immediately he added, 'What were your movements two nights ago?'

There was suddenly an agonized expression on Coralie's face. 'What do you mean?'

'You visited a member of the group, didn't you? Covertly?'

'We all visited him,' she said, and he found himself momentarily wrong-footed. 'I was the last one there and I only went because the others did.'

Jonah's brain worked back over the messages between each of them. 'To Brett Parker's house?'

Coralie nodded.

'And where did you go afterwards?'

'Back to my hotel,' she said in a tight voice.

Jonah could see the lie in her expression.

'Where did you go?'

'I did!' Coralie protested. 'I did go back to my hotel. Really.'

Jonah gave her a level gaze. 'But not alone?'

'I don't . . .' She was absolutely silent, and then she said in a quiet voice, 'I want to go now.'

'I need you to help us, Coralie,' he said urgently. 'You're being used, and I think it's the killer who's using you. If they're a friend of yours, or a lover, it doesn't matter. They raped and murdered a young girl, and there is no guarantee that they haven't done worse since.'

'None of us did anything!' she said, fiercely. 'It was that . . . that teacher! We all went through hell because of him! I'm not going to help you hurt my friends when you've got the murderer sitting here.'

'How long have you believed that for?' Jonah asked. 'You didn't even know he was there until yesterday.'

'I wish I'd known,' she said fiercely. 'I would have helped Topaz have him arrested, and we could have . . . we could have got on with our lives and been happy instead of having to pretend to be people we're not, and I wouldn't . . . I wouldn't have been . . . alone.'

Something broke in Coralie, and she was suddenly sobbing, tears squeezing out of her eyes and childlike sounds of misery coming from her mouth.

Hanson was running now. Other pedestrians were giving her odd looks as she pelted down the pavement, but she wasn't worried. Stavely was already in a cab and driving north, and she desperately needed to get to her phone and her car.

On the plus side, she thought wryly, she'd managed to be away from the phone a good fifteen minutes without compulsively checking for messages from Damian.

Jonah left the interview room in a bit of a daze. He'd had nothing more out of Coralie, who had continued to shake her head and cry until he'd suggested a break.

He picked up his phone to make a call, and saw that Hanson had tried to call him. He had a moment of worry as he called her back, and was relieved to hear her pick up.

'Slight situation, sir,' she said breathlessly. 'Stavely's just been on the phone to someone, and has now bought himself a large kitchen knife and has got into a taxi. I have the reg number. I'm trying to follow but I've had to get all the way back to my car.'

'And you're on your own . . . ?'

'Sorry, sir. I know you said – I forgot to take someone.'

She read out the licence plate, and he recited it to O'Malley, who had followed him from the interview room and still had his pen and notebook handy.

'When I saw him, he was driving north along Above Bar Street. Vehicle is a black Passat,' Hanson added.

'Well done. Get after the taxi if you can, but warily. Any idea of a destination?'

'No, sir. Afraid not.'

'OK. We'll be on the road soon and we're calling it in. And be careful, constable. Get your stab vest on if you can and keep well back if he stops and gets out.'

He hung up, and called through to the switchboard staff up on the fifth floor. 'I've got a vehicle travelling north along

Above Bar Street. Black Passat. Licensed cab. I need a squad car on it.'

He was hurrying through CID as he spoke, and he checked in his pocket for his keys before he got to the door. O'Malley was right behind him.

The operator came back on and confirmed that a squad car had been dispatched and that the licence plate had been flagged. He hung up just before reaching the door of CID, and said to O'Malley, 'Where the fuck is Stavely going with a kitchen knife?'

38

Jojo climbed out of the car and stretched, grateful for the fresh air and the freedom. What would she have done if she'd had to stay in that bloody cage of an interview room? And what if she had to go back?

She tried to bury the thought under her appreciation of the beauty of the place. It was glorious out here. She used her phone to take a picture of the rolling wooded hills that led to the Dagger-Edge climb, and then posted it on the climbing forum to show everyone what they were missing out on. She hadn't had any takers for her earlier suggestion to come here. That was the trouble with people who had proper jobs.

She went round to the back of the jeep and picked up her backpack. She tucked the bottle into the side pocket, slung it all on to her back, and started to tramp down the forest path.

Jonah's phone rang through the Bluetooth moments after he'd started up the car.

'Linda,' he said. 'Any news?'

'Yes. It didn't take that long,' McCullough said. 'I cut open a few cartons and cans, and struck gold. There's an orange-juice carton with the remnants of a pile of Dexedrine in it. It's been dissolved at some point.'

'Enough for an overdose?'

'Easily,' McCullough said. 'There's probably half a gram

of it in the dregs, and a lot of it around the edges of the carton. I'll weigh it up, but if a whole bag went in there, then
that's four or five times the amount you'd need to kill
someone.'

'That's great work,' Jonah said.

'Can I go home now?' she asked. 'Or do you need all the
results tonight?'

'Tomorrow will be fine.'

He rang off, and stopped to think. He'd always assumed
that Aurora's death had been murder, and that it had been a
deliberate act. But what if that hadn't been the case at all?
What if the killer had only realized what they had done the
morning after?

It would have been a horrifying discovery.

He began going over, in his mind, every account from the
morning after. From Connor stumbling around trying to
find her, to Benham's shell-shocked guilt and Brett's hungover attempts to cover up the drugs.

It suddenly seemed blindingly obvious, as if he should
have worked it out a long time ago. There was only one of
them who could have been criminally stupid enough to
empty a whole bag of Dexedrine into an orange-juice carton
as a method of rape. Only one of them who could have gone
back to sleep and left Aurora to crawl away and overdose
alone in a hole in the ground.

And in a strange rush of memory that made him feel that
he wasn't quite in his own body, he remembered the party
thirty years ago, and the boy who had encouraged Zofia to
drink. Who had kept on and on refilling her shot glass. And
who had asked Jonah where he was taking her, as if out of
solicitousness.

He knew then. He knew for certain. That same person was

353

the only one of them who could have realized that she was dead the morning after, because he had seen her there.

There had been a frustrating mile where Hanson had seen nothing of the Passat. She'd turned left on to Commercial Road, hoping the cab had done the same. She knew there was a chance the taxi had continued north, along the bus route through the park. She was beginning to think it must have done, and trying to work out where she should go, when she caught sight of it again with a flood of relief. The taxi was turning left on to the dual carriageway of Havelock Road.

It was the route she took to head back out of town. It led to the flyover, and on from there towards the New Forest. Stavely had picked the busiest time to travel across town by taxi. It was all stop-start, which made it easier for her to keep him in sight, but must be costing him a fortune. Which only added to her impression that Stavely was being paid to do whatever it was he was doing.

They crawled until they reached the flyover, but things started moving a little more quickly from there. She accelerated to keep the black Passat in sight, and checked the rear-view mirror, half hoping to see the squad car. She was torn between fear of that knife he was carrying, and a desire to be first on scene.

Once she'd reached a section of road with no exits, she took one hand off the wheel, and rooted around behind her until she found her stab vest. Putting it on while driving was not her idea of attending to the road, but if it was that or faffing around with it while Stavely attacked someone, she'd choose the slightly hairy driving any day.

Her phone rang while she had one arm in and one out. She glanced at the dash, expecting to see Sheens' number, but instead saw the word 'Damian'. There was no sinking feeling this time. She felt one hundred per cent pissed off with him.

He'd already tried calling again by the time she had the stab vest pulled on and fastened. Checking that Stavely's cab was still ahead, she picked up her phone one-handed, and swiped on the missed call from Damian so it brought up his contact details.

With only a slight surge of adrenalin she pressed the 'block' button.

Jonah's adrenalin was running pretty high, too, as he tore out of the station in the Mondeo. He would not have chosen the newest member of the team to be in pursuit of an armed suspect, however smart and generally sensible she seemed to be. Knives were absolutely not good fun to deal with. There had been one member of his year of recruits killed by one three months into the job.

He doubted, given the levels of traffic at this time, that he and O'Malley would be able to catch up with Stavely and Hanson. But that didn't mean he wasn't going to try. He'd switched on the blue lights and siren, and most of the cars ahead cleared well out of the way. But he still had to stop sharply at a pedestrian crossing for a middle-aged couple who had walked out without looking. He watched in disbelief as they continued to walk slowly across, despite all the noise.

'Do you ever hate people Domnall?' he asked O'Malley.

'Oh, Jesus, yes. All the time,' the sergeant replied.

The route was beginning to feel familiar to Hanson, but she couldn't tell why. She guessed it must be on the way to one of the suspects' houses, but she couldn't be sure which after only one visit. She called through to Sheens to tell him roughly where they were, and then waited for him to call back.

It didn't take him long.

'I've just had a call from the operator. The squad car's on the flyover, and for now has its lights and siren on,' he said. Hanson felt a surge of relief. 'They reckon they'll be up with you in ten minutes, assuming they have to turn the lights off once they're closer.'

Hanson's relief wavered slightly. They could easily be at Stavely's destination before then. They were well out of Southampton, off the dual carriageway and heading towards Lyndhurst.

She scrolled on her phone briefly, working out which suspects were where. He could be going to Jojo Magos's house, the Jacksons' or Brett Parker's. There was a vague chance that he was going a long route towards Bishop's Waltham and Daniel Benham's house, in which case they might have long enough.

'If he's going to Brett's or Jojo's, the squad car will be too late,' she said. 'We're only a few minutes away, I think? And the Jacksons' . . . probably still under ten minutes, if not by much.'

'If he stops before the squad car gets there, then block the taxi from leaving,' Sheens told her. 'And then tell Stavely calmly that the squad car is two minutes behind you. Give us a heads-up, and they can turn the sirens back on.'

'Right,' Hanson said. 'I'll let you know.'

She hung up, and mentally began to prepare herself for a confrontation. She'd at least been on the periphery of incidents like this in the past. It was all about calm, and an impression of authority. She knew that.

And not getting close enough to get stabbed. That too.

*

'Did your phone records run up to today?' Jonah asked O'Malley as he pushed his way towards the flyover.

'Yesterday, I think,' O'Malley answered. 'Why?'

'Once we've stopped Stavely doing whatever he's doing, I want to know for certain who called Coralie during our interview, because I'm pretty damn sure it wasn't her father.'

'It sounds like you know already,' O'Malley said, with a sideways glance at him that Jonah caught.

'I have a pretty good idea,' Jonah said.

It was Brett Parker's house. They were on the road that led past the end of his driveway, and there were no other vehicles in sight. Hanson had to drop back a little, and wondered what she would do about the gate. For that matter, she wondered what Stavely was going to do about it. They were hardly going to let him in if he announced that he was there to stab Brett. Would Brett or Anna even recognize his name?

She didn't have a lot of time to wonder why he was there, but part of her felt certain it had to do with threat. Brett represented, somehow, more of a threat to the killer than he was able to tolerate. Enough of a threat that he was prepared to risk sending Stavely there.

As she turned a bend in the road, she saw a vehicle coming towards her, and pulled over to let them past, instinctively. And then she realized that it was the taxi, and was cursing herself as it drew level with her, remembering that she had been told to block it in.

But with a flood of relief, she saw that the back seat was empty. Stavely had got out.

By the time she'd come to a stop, she was right outside the grounds of Brett's house. The high, grey-stone walls were next to her and the gates just ahead.

She pulled the car up just outside the gates, and shut the engine off. She wasn't sure what to do. There was no sign of Stavely this side of the gates, and the taxi hadn't had time to drive up to the door and back.

Had he climbed over the wall? she wondered. Or been allowed in on foot?

She climbed out of the car, checking that she had her baton ready in its slot on her vest, and moved slowly towards the gates. A quick glance through showed her a long stretch of driveway, and no sign of a figure anywhere on it.

Moving quickly to the side of the wall with the buzzer on it, and putting her back to it, Hanson pressed the button.

There was a slight pause, and then Anna answered.

'Can I help?'

'It's the police. It's Constable Hanson,' she said quickly. 'There's an armed man approaching your house. I need you to buzz me through the gates and leave them open, and then get somewhere safe with your husband. Lock yourselves in somewhere.'

There was a tiny pause, and then Anna said, 'Brett's not here. Are you sure . . .? I haven't let anyone in!'

'I followed him here,' Hanson said. 'He must be near the house by now. Can you buzz me in? There's a squad car on the way, too.'

'Oh, god,' she heard Anna say. 'I don't . . . I can only lock myself in the bathroom.'

'Do it,' she said. 'And keep quiet.'

There was a buzz as the gate swung open. Hanson slid through, and started to run down the long driveway, pulling out her mobile as she went.

*

Jonah's phone rang just after they'd joined the flyover. He was ready to ram half the cars around him. Despite the sirens, he'd still had cars trying to slide in front of him to avoid losing their place in the queue.

Hanson's name flashed up on the dashboard display, and he picked up the call quickly.

'It's Brett Parker's,' she said, sounding like she was running. 'Stavely's headed down on foot. The gate's open for the squad car. I'm . . . a little way behind him.'

Jonah glanced at the clock. 'They should be six minutes away. I'd keep my distance,' he said warningly.

'Anna's in there alone,' Hanson replied. 'I've told her to lock herself in the bathroom.'

'That should hold him off for long enough,' Jonah said. 'Stay outside.'

'The door's open,' Hanson said. 'Shit.'

'Stay outside, constable,' Jonah said, but she'd rung off.

Hanson ducked her head inside the door, half expecting to feel a knife across her throat. But nothing happened. The hall was entirely empty.

Out of the silence there was suddenly a loud bang that made her flinch. And then another, and another. She knew, without any question, that it was the sound of someone trying to break a door down. It was coming from the floor above.

Anna had locked herself in a bathroom up there. He must know where she was.

'Police!' she shouted, pulling her baton out. There was a pause, and then the banging continued.

She started to walk towards the stairs, her baton held in front of her in a hand that was undeniably shaking. The sweeping stairs were softly carpeted, and she made no sound as she hurried up them.

'Matt! There is a squad car behind me and we know you're armed!' she shouted again. 'Drop the knife and come out into the hallway.'

There was a final cracking, splintering sound that must have been a door being kicked in, and then there was a sudden, complete silence.

She stepped up on to the landing, seeing several closed doors ahead. And then, right at the end on the right, one that was open.

She didn't feel connected to her feet as she walked down the hallway. She breathed in through her nose and out through her mouth every two steps, trying to calm herself.

She slowed down as she approached the door. It had been kicked in. Splintered wood from the lock littered the carpet and there was a big dent in the panel near the bottom.

She moved round until she could see through the gap. There was a section of off-white wall visible, and as she approached, her view gradually increased. She saw a small painting, a chair.

It wasn't a bathroom, she realized. But it had been a room with a lock. Anna could have chosen to shut herself in there. But why hadn't there been any cries for help?

Into the silence came the distant wail of a siren. The cavalry on its audible way.

But he was already inside the room. Anna might need her help.

She pushed the door open very slowly, her heart thundering madly in her chest. She could see a desk now, with a slimline computer on top of it.

There was sudden movement ahead of her, and she froze.

It took her a panicked second to realize it was a curtain she was seeing. It had moved because the double doors beyond it were open on to the evening air.

She had a sudden fear that Stavely had harmed Anna and then fled. She kept moving until she could see all of the room. But there was nobody there. No Anna, no blood, and no hiding place.

'Anna?' she asked in a low voice.

There was no reply. The sirens were louder now. The car must be coming down the drive.

So Anna wasn't here. She must have locked herself up somewhere else.

Hanson looked around the room blankly. What had Stavely been doing? Why had he come here, and then run?

She approached the French doors as silently as she could, and peered out. There was a small balcony that served just this room. Below it was the big trellised canopy that ran over the terrace. There was no sign of Stavely, but it wouldn't have been hard for him to climb down the wooden struts.

She pulled out her mobile and called Sheens, who sounded angry. She ignored him as he asked what the hell she was doing, and said, 'Stavely's climbed out of a window and scarpered. For some reason, he kicked a door in and then left.'

'Was it the door to Brett Parker's study?'

'What? Yes, I guess so,' Hanson said, looking again at the desk.

'He didn't touch anything?'

'No,' Hanson answered, and then glanced at the computer. The screen was on, and glowing. It was waiting for a password. 'Well, I think he might have turned the computer on.'

'You'd better inform the uniforms that this is a crime

scene,' Jonah said, 'and then get them to seize the computer and any other technology they find.'

'What was Stavely doing?' Hanson asked, and then, as a few things fell into place, she said, 'Was that what he wanted? To make it a crime scene? Was he leading us to Brett Parker?'

'I'd guess so,' Jonah said. 'Before he died, Aleksy Nowak went into Brett's study and found something that caused a flaming row. Anna thought it was about finances, but I think he found a phone, and that it was full of messages from girls. Young girls. I think Brett has been a sexual predator for a very long time, and that he killed Aleksy to hide it. We'll have to see whether I'm right when we look at that computer, and if we find any phones.'

'Fucking hell,' Hanson said, then said, 'Sorry, sir. So . . . what do I tell Anna?'

'Just that some things have been disturbed by the intruder,' the DCI said. 'And that we'll need her at the station for a statement.'

'OK,' Hanson said, and hoped her deadpan would be good enough to hide from Anna Parker that her husband might just be a serial rapist and a killer.

39. Aurora

Saturday, 23 July 1983, 3:05 a.m.

'Sorry,' he said, emerging out of the darkness. He was unsteady; bleary. Drunk, she thought. And probably only just awake. 'Didn't realize you were here.'

Brett stopped a little way behind her, barely lit and swaying slightly. She had to crane her neck to look at him. Her heart was still pounding from the fright.

'What are you doing up?' he asked. 'Thought you went to bed.'

'I was thirsty,' she said.

He nodded. He turned to look around him a little vaguely. 'I'll find you a beer.'

She wanted to argue; to tell him that wasn't what she'd meant. But she didn't want to disappoint him again. She wanted him to look at her like he'd looked at Topaz.

Her stomach gave another squeeze as she remembered how he'd been all over her sister. She didn't want to think about what else they'd done. It made her feel colder. Sicker.

Brett spent a while scrabbling around in the food bags, and then brought her a beer. He opened it for her with a hiss before handing it over. And then he half sat, half fell down beside her. He knocked into her, and she shifted, but he moved over. Put an arm round her back.

She felt herself becoming rigid. She remembered how recently he had had his hands up her sister's skirt.

'Sorry,' Brett said, leaning back to squint at her. 'I thought you wanted a cuddle.'

'I'm OK, thanks,' she said.

She took a sip of the beer. She felt her mouth screwing up around it. 'I need some orange juice,' she said, and she stood up, glad not to be touching him.

'Oh. Yeah. Not beer. I forgot.' He stood up too, unsteadily. 'Stay by the fire. I'll get it.'

She thought about telling him she could do it. But she was still racked with cold, and the fire was the one warm point. She sat again and hunched in front of it, as close as she could get without her skirt catching the embers. She blew on it once more to bring the heat back. She'd coaxed a few of the sticks into flame by the time Brett reappeared next to her.

'Here.' He waved a carton of orange juice at her, and she took it gratefully. She put the opening to her mouth and drank.

The beer must have left a strange taste in her mouth, because the orange juice seemed bitter.

She was too thirsty to stop drinking it, though. She chugged and chugged at it, swallowing quickly until it was drained dry.

She was breathless by the time she had finished. Breathless and sticky with juice. But no longer thirsty. Her mouth wasn't dry now. It was . . . tingly somehow. A little numb.

Brett crouched next to her, and gave her a strange smile that she didn't think she liked. 'How do you feel now?'

He put a hand out towards her, and she moved her head back instinctively.

'Don't be silly,' he said quietly. His hand reached further until he had her neck and the bottom of her jaw in a gentle grip.

'Please don't,' she said. Something felt wrong. Him. The campsite. Something in her. 'Please don't.'

'You need to learn when to stop fighting,' he said, and with his other hand pushed her skirt up towards the top of her thighs.

'Brett,' she said, pushing it back down.

In a lunge, he jammed his mouth over hers and shoved her backwards on to the ground. Her elbow ended up in the embers, and she pulled it away sharply. She could feel sticks digging into her back. He was pressing down hard on her, and her first kiss, which she had imagined over and over, was not gentle and tender. It was a forceful, inescapable, painful thing.

She tried pushing at him, but he was stronger than she was. And the more she pushed, the weaker she felt. The dizzier.

He pulled his mouth away, and knelt up. He was tugging at the belt of his jeans.

Aurora tried to roll over. To stand up and move away from him. But she felt weak. Shaky. She made it to her hands and knees, the ground looking strange and out of focus to her as she tried to move over it.

And then she felt a sharp pull on her ankle, and she was sliding backwards, her face in the fallen sticks and leaves and being scratched and cut by them.

'Come on, Aurora,' he said, and leaned over to breathe in her ear. 'All you need is a good fucking.'

40

After Jonah hung up, O'Malley was immediately full of questions.

'Why do you think it was young girls?' he asked.

'Partly because Brett resisted Topaz but kissed a younger girl the week before, and partly because of the connection with Matt Stavely,' Jonah answered. 'I think Matt Stavely really was supplying Rohypnol, but to Brett Parker instead of Mackenzie. I think Stavely found himself dragged into a lot of things he didn't really want to be involved in.'

'So, what ... he led us there to get free of Brett Parker's shit?'

'I'd guess so,' he said.

'What about Aleksy Nowak?' the sergeant asked. 'Why didn't he report Brett to the police when he found whatever he found?'

'I don't think he knew what he'd found at first,' Jonah replied. 'I'd lay money that it was a phone full of text messages to and from some of these girls. If you saw that stuff, you wouldn't know their ages; you'd just think he was a cheat, wouldn't you?'

'Yeah, true,' O'Malley said thoughtfully. 'But if he went ballistic at me, I'd probably start to wonder ...'

'Yup,' he said. 'I think he'd been worrying away at it for two weeks, and wanted Jojo to support him in going to the police. Hence the message he sent asking to talk to her. Brett must have realized how bad he'd made himself look, so he used one of his other phones to message Aleksy.'

'Jesus,' O'Malley said. 'It's . . . it's Machiavellian, isn't it? Everything planned for.'

'Yes,' Jonah said slowly. 'Except for Stavely turning on him.'

There was a pause, and then O'Malley said, 'The original crime. Killing Aurora. It wasn't deliberate.'

'Yes,' Jonah agreed. 'The other kids were regular drug users. They knew damn well how much would be deadly. It was Brett, who'd never tried anything before, who looked at that bag and thought it was only a small amount, and who was too unaware of the effects of an overdose to recognize them in Aurora. The morning after, Jojo and he went to hide the stash. But Jojo sidetracked to get a dead animal, and Brett went on to start covering the hideaway up. He was the one person who had the opportunity to find Aurora that morning. By the time Jojo came back, he'd realized what he'd done. That Aurora had crawled into the hole while overdosing, and died there. And he vomited. Not from the smell of the animal, but because he'd realized that he'd killed her.'

'So do we wait until crime scene have looked at that computer,' O'Malley asked, 'or do we pick Brett up straight away?'

'Hopefully he'll arrive home to see his perfect plan in tatters,' Jonah said, with a small smile. 'All thanks to a two-bit drug dealer he thought would do anything for him.'

He wondered whether Stavely would resurface, or if he'd set up an escape route for himself. He badly wanted to ask him some questions.

But as he thought back over Stavely's actions, he found himself troubled. Why the knife? Why would he turn up to Brett's armed with a knife? Stavely must have known that Brett wouldn't be there, or he wouldn't have tried to create a crime scene. In fact, he must have known that he was being followed by Hanson, too. So why go armed, and make it much more likely that he would be forcibly arrested?

Perhaps to get Hanson's attention, he thought. A man armed with a knife setting off somewhere was a fairly attention-grabbing thing. And then he felt a twinge of unease. Maybe that had been the point, but maybe it wasn't Stavely who had thought of it.

What if Brett, who had clearly been directing his actions for a long time, had told him to pick the knife up? And if he'd told him to do that, it had been to make sure that he was getting a lot of attention.

There was a feeling of wrongness spreading through him. Whatever Stavely had done in the end, it looked like he had waited until he saw Hanson watching his flat, and then drawn her – and, by extension, Jonah and his team – off on a wild-goose chase. He hadn't needed to go to a phone box to make a call. He could have taken a call on his mobile, which was probably how Brett had got in touch with him for years. But taking a phone call was a good way of making his next actions seem significant.

He put another call through to Hanson. 'Juliette, do you have Anna there?'

'Yes,' Hanson answered in a light voice. 'Yes, she's just here, and she's doing fine.'

'Great. Can you just find out from her where her husband might be? We'd better warn him about the break-in.'

Hanson passed that on, and then there was a muttering from Anna.

'She says he's gone for some trail running somewhere,' the constable told him. 'She says she can try calling . . .'

There was a sound from Anna, followed by some talking, and the constable said, 'There's no reply, but she says she can use Find My Friends on her iPhone. He's got her added, which means she can see him too, if she needs to.'

Jonah waited with his heart doing strange things in his chest. After a few seconds, Anna's voice came again.

'He's off in the forest, she says, near Burley.'

His heart definitely skipped. He could hear Jojo at the end of their interview, a few hours ago.

Maybe an hour? It's near Burley . . .

'Thank you,' he said mechanically, and ended the call. And then he switched the siren and lights back on, trying to ignore the awful feeling that they were way, way too late.

Brett was smiling to himself as he jogged along the path. This was glorious. The sunshine; the trees; the view. His body felt like a living machine. It felt powerful and perfect.

He was looking forward to seeing Jojo. He felt such a strange mixture of affection and hatred towards her. Though maybe hatred wasn't the word. Disappointment, perhaps.

He'd warned her so many times. With her garden, and with Aleksy. In so many subtle statements.

And after years of being obedient and helpful to him she'd suddenly turned on him. The private chat with the detective at the climbing wall that Stavely had reported back on. How she'd trekked into the station the next day to give a statement, and then when she'd come over with the others. He couldn't get over that, how she'd sat in his house, defiantly looking him in the eye and saying that it was time for everyone to tell the truth.

She hadn't listened to his warning. The questions Sheens had been asking them all told him that loud and clear. She'd been leading them towards him.

He wondered what had changed. Was it Sheens? Had

he manipulated her more cleverly than he'd given him credit for?

He felt a keen sense of pain all over again at the betrayal. That long-ago morning, when they'd hidden the stash together, and she'd used the dead stoat to hide the scent, she'd been definite. She'd told him that she was going to cover up for him. And she must have seen Aurora in there. She must have known that was why he'd puked.

She'd already covered up for him before that, anyway. She'd said nothing when they all discussed whether anybody had seen Aurora after she'd gone to bed. Even though Jojo had seen not only Aurora, but him, too. She'd stood blinking across the fire at him.

Of course, at that point, Brett had thought it was just his coercion of Aurora she was covering up. A slightly awkward situation, and a vanished girl he needed to find first so he could talk her round.

But Jojo had told him that she'd hide it for him, or as good as. She'd been on his side. And she'd stayed on his side even when Aleksy had realized that something was wrong.

It had been utterly stupid, Brett knew, keeping the phone in his study when he wasn't using it. He was still angry with himself about it. So much careful planning, and he'd been tripped up because he hadn't thought anyone would be looking in the desk drawers.

He'd moved it after Aleksy found it, and kept it behind some of his books in the den. And, in fact, he'd swapped to a new phone pretty soon after that, and hidden the old one in the attic. He'd started locking his study, too, because there was still the computer to worry about.

The strange thing to Brett was that Jojo seemed to be charmed by him, but didn't want anything sexual from him.

370

He'd made offers to her, even after Aleksy had died, and she'd always declined. Perhaps he should have realized that meant she wasn't really on his side. Though she'd laughed and smiled at him, accepted his hugs and his compliments, and listened with that steady gaze whenever he had a small gripe about Anna to share.

She'd even listened when she'd been raw with grief over Aleksy's death, and had confided in him that her boyfriend had been planning on leaving her. He'd held her when she sobbed that she'd hounded him, and it was her fault he'd died.

'It's not your fault,' he'd said quietly. Which had been a lie. It had been all her fault. She shouldn't have brought Aleksy into this.

He wasn't sure whether he liked the symmetry here. That Jojo was going to die just as Aleksy had. He had the smallest of doubts: that it would be too similar. That Sheens would see through it. That everything would unravel.

But that feeling of anxiety fought with decades of getting away with this. He'd planned it all carefully, and they wouldn't be able to connect him. Not with Stavely off laying a confusing scent to Daniel Benham's house.

And besides that, Jojo had let him down. In the end, she'd turned on him. And she had to be punished for that.

O'Malley googled the Dagger-Edge climb, and checked through climbing club sites until he'd found directions for getting there. Then they called the switchboard and told them to send the closest squad car.

Jonah put the call through himself. 'You need to park in the car park off Station Road,' he told the operator, 'and follow the central path. It forks right. Take that, and then ignore any turn-offs until you're at a signposted fork towards Burley Ridge. They'll be up there.'

'How long ago did he leave?' O'Malley asked quietly.

'I don't know,' Jonah said. 'But Jojo must have been there for more than an hour by now. Maybe two.'

Jojo had left Dagger-Edge till last. It was still her nemesis, this climb, with its final lunge on to a hold that should be easy, but which was just too high and too far. Even with a rope, she had never managed to make herself do it.

And today, she didn't have a rope. It had been Aleksy she'd been thinking of on the drive here. Aleksy, who she was beginning to think hadn't betrayed her, and who hadn't fallen because of her. Aleksy, and his ability to fling himself without any support at climbs that would make other people blanch.

Sometimes I think I only make it because I don't have a choice, he'd said to her.

Well, today, she wasn't giving herself a choice.

Her hands found the jug that started the route. They closed on it and her feet swung into place on the ridge below it. She knew this. She was at home on it.

The next move was another quick one. She pulled her left foot up and dug her toe into a narrow depression. The toe-hold felt like nothing, but she was light with adrenalin and she pushed up on it anyway.

She had her weight set for the next move when she heard a noise behind her. Shifting slightly, she looked down and to her left, and saw Brett below her, pausing for breath with his hands on the back of his head, elbows out to each side. He was in running gear, and there was sweat on his forehead.

'Hello, Jojo,' he said, and despite the fact that it was Brett

speaking – Brett, who had been kind to her for thirty years –
a chill ran right through her.

She was aware that she was only just out of his reach as she
called, 'What are you doing here?'

'You brought me here,' he said with a sad smile. 'I warned
you not to, Jojo. Why have you been talking to them? Why
are you no longer my ally?'

Jojo looked at him for a moment. 'Your ally?'

She had found the next hold with her left hand – a sloper
with a good grip to it – and she pulled her right foot up to a
crack and pushed upwards. She was definitely out of his
reach now, but he was stepping closer.

'You know I didn't mean for her to die,' Brett said, looking hurt. 'You knew that then, but now you seem to have
forgotten it.'

He was talking about Aurora. Of course he was.

Jojo had the sudden sick feeling that this was how Aleksy
had died. That Brett had spoken to him like this, with disappointment and a little anger, and had then killed him. Had he
climbed up below him and pulled him off? No, he had been
at the foot of Mechanical Vert. Brett had probably walked up
the easy way and waited at the top, then pushed Aleksy off.

'I haven't forgotten anything,' Jojo said. She took the next
move with less certainty. She couldn't stop imagining Aleksy's cry as he'd fallen. 'I've just realized a lot of things. You
killed him, didn't you?'

She knew she ought to be mollifying him, but she had a
burning need to hear him say it.

'Aleksy?' he asked. 'Of course I did. The stupid prick went
snooping when he should have kept his nose out. It wouldn't
have taken him much to join the dots.'

It was something between fear and rage that took her

through the next three moves. She looked down past her feet at a scraping sound, and saw that Brett was on the wall. He was clumsy and inelegant, but he was strong, too. He was making easy work of that first jug.

He was coming up to get her, presumably planning on catching up with her and pulling her off. The sick feeling in her stomach increased.

'Jojo, please understand that you've made me do this,' he said, his voice a little breathless as he shifted round, preparing to make another move. 'Just like Aleksy did. I have never wanted to harm anyone.'

'You didn't want to harm Aurora when you raped her?' Jojo asked.

'Harm her? She enjoyed it. She wanted it. I saw how she looked at me all evening . . .' He paused as he made another effortful move, and then went on. 'You know I never meant her any harm. When I saw she'd died . . . it was awful. And I've been protecting all of you –' he shifted again – 'for thirty years. I could have framed any of you easily. But I didn't. I kept you all safe.'

Jojo moved up once more, and now had reached the furthest point in this climb she had ever made. The point beyond which she had never gone. She was nine metres up, and the next move was the one that meant launching herself into space and hoping. The last move before she could grab the upper lip and top out. One more move before she could pull herself up on to the grassy top of the sheer face.

She'd bottled it every time, even with a rope. It had been too high. Too far. She'd abseiled back down, angry with herself. But now she had no way of abseiling, and doing some of those moves in reverse was going to be gnarly. The simple thing – the safer thing – would be to go for the top.

'Are you frightened, Jojo?' Brett asked, in a voice that was suddenly very different. He wasn't trying to explain. He was trying to scare her.

It gave her a cold feeling realizing that it would be a lot easier for him if she simply fell.

'Why would I be frightened?' she asked, though she could feel adrenalin pulsing through her. Her left leg had started to wobble slightly, and she had to breathe consciously to stop it getting worse.

'Everyone's scared of dying,' Brett said. 'Even Aleksy. You should have seen his face as I shoved him off backwards. He thought he'd made it to the top.'

Jojo closed her eyes against the image of him falling, but it was still there. The vision of his long, slow descent to the ground. It made her feel as though she was falling already.

'I guess Aurora . . . must have been frightened, too,' she said.

He'd made another move. He was closer to her. Feet away. What if he got close enough to grab her foot while she was there, frozen? Would she be able to hold on?

'She should have gone for help, instead of crawling away,' he said. 'But I suppose she was confused. She thought it was safe in there. And instead, she died there, all on her own.'

Jojo shook her head. She thought of the brilliant, kind-hearted girl, and it made her heart ache. But it made her furious, too. That he'd cut her life short for the sake of a gratuitous shag.

'Fuck you, Brett,' she said, and without thinking any further, she launched herself at the final hold.

The moment of hanging in space was vast. There was a seemingly minute-long delay before some kind of contact.

The feeling of her hands closing on the final jug-like hold

was almost unexpectedly easy. It was only instinct that made her close her hands on it, while her brain caught up and realized that she had made it.

Her right foot kicked something and she scrabbled at it. She found a large bulge beneath her. It was like standing on a step.

She smiled to herself. It really had been as easy as everyone kept saying.

She found another, smaller hold with her left foot. She pushed up off it until she could put her right hand over the lip. She dragged and kicked herself upwards until she had her right toes on to the edge, too.

With a shaky last push, she stood up, and turned to look down at Brett.

He was doing well for a non-climber. And particularly so for someone wearing running shoes. He had the kind of body tension a lot of climbers trained a long time for, presumably from decades of running and cycling and swimming.

But the next move was harder, and he was still one short of the crunch point.

'How's it going, Brett?' she called down, buzzing with triumph.

He glanced up at her. She couldn't tell from his expression if he was concentrating on keeping hold of the rock, or if he hated her right then. She hoped it was the second one.

'Shall I give you a hand?' she asked, with a grin.

She wondered if he would screw this one up. His body weight was all wrong, his weight too far over his left leg when he needed to free it up. But he made a lunging jump upwards and made it anyway, his height paying off.

He was one move away from her.

'All to play for now,' she said. 'One last move.'

She saw him pause and take his right arm off for a moment. He flexed his fingers and then quickly replaced them on the rock.

'Ah, yeah. That's the trouble with not being a real climber. Your hands give out first.'

He laughed. It was a short, breathless bark.

'They'll last long enough to shove you off this fucking cliff, Jojo.' Despite the sweat on him, he still gave her a smile. 'You should have stood by me and kept quiet about seeing me with her.'

Jojo gave a laugh. 'That's the thing, Brett. I didn't see you. I was staring into a fire, and you were past it. You were bloody invisible to me. And you've stayed that way. Whatever games you've thought we've been playing for thirty years were all in your head.'

She could see that had unsettled him. He was looking up at her, trying to work out if she was telling the truth. But then something hardened in his expression and his gaze fell on the rock again.

'It doesn't matter,' he said. 'You're going to die either way.'

She couldn't help grinning again as he looked around for a close-by hold. He scanned and scanned for something to grab on to, before eventually fixing his eyes on that final jug, separated from him by three and a half feet of clear space. And, of course, a full three feet higher up.

'That's the one,' she said cheerfully. She moved a little until she was standing right above it. 'All the way over here.'

Brett took his right hand off and reached out a little, before putting it quickly back on again.

'Is Brett a little scared?' she asked.

'Shut your fucking mouth,' he said.

He didn't look up at her again. He was too busy preparing

377

himself. Shifting his weight further to his right, and pulsing slightly. He was counting down to himself.

'Jesus, will you hurry up, Parker? I've got things to do.'

He didn't say anything. He was primed for that move, and Jojo felt herself tensing with him. She crouched slightly, willing him to move for it. Willing him to jump.

He sprang suddenly. But she could see as he did it that he'd doubted himself even as he'd jumped; that he hadn't really committed to that leap.

He'd gone barely a foot upwards and across. His right hand reached out, but he was nowhere near the hold.

A strange sort of spasm ran through his body as he started to fall. When she had time to think about it later, she wondered if it was disbelief.

He fell quickly, and she watched him all the way to the unforgiving stone and hard mud of the ground.

Jonah's phone rang as they were pulling up along the roadside. There were two squad cars there too, but the officers were only just climbing out. They'd been no more than seconds ahead of him.

'Jojo,' he said sharply, as he answered. 'Are you all right?'

'Don't stress,' he heard her say, in a voice so sarcastic and laid-back that he felt like he might have been tricked into coming here. 'Brett Parker is dealt with.'

'What do you mean?'

'He chucked himself off the cliff-face,' she said. 'Not deliberately, I should probably add.'

He still ran the whole way to the climb.

O'Malley was just behind him, and the uniforms followed behind the sergeant. When they cleared the trees, and came into view of Brett Parker's body, he slowed, and O'Malley bumped into him and then apologized.

Jonah found it hard to look away from the strangely angled pile of limbs, and the large spread of blood. But he was aware that he needed to find Jojo.

He shielded his eyes and looked upwards. Jojo was sitting right on the edge of the cliff, swinging her feet gently. She waved at him.

'Are you all right?' Jonah called.

'You already asked that,' she shouted back, and clambered to her feet. 'I'm fine. Really. I'll come down. It's a bit of a scramble down the back. Give me a minute.'

Jojo disappeared, and then reappeared a minute later round the right-hand side of the cliff.

She nodded to the other officers, who were now standing somewhat lamely around the body. She gave Jonah a slightly crooked grin. 'I made the last move on the bloody climb,' she said quietly. Triumphantly. 'Seems like it's easier when you think someone's going to kill you if you don't.'

'Well done,' Jonah said, a little wryly. 'I take it Brett failed, then?'

'Yeah. Probably for the best,' Jojo said thoughtfully. 'If he'd made it, I'd have kicked him off the edge.'

41

Jonah called the Jacksons on the way back to the station. There was a feeling of victory at finally having an answer, but it was more than usually marred by the pain they were going to feel at how their daughter had died: alone, overdosing on drugs she hadn't wanted to take, having been raped by a boy she'd probably trusted.

Joy answered this time with the rather endearing, old-fashioned habit of reciting the phone number.

'It's DCI Sheens,' he said. 'I'm sorry I've left you waiting, but we've got some very important developments to tell you about. Would you and Tom be able to come into the station? I think it would be best if you came and talked to me here.'

'Oh,' Joy said breathlessly. 'Tom, can we . . . can we go to the station? I'm sure we can. They've got something important to tell us. Do you . . . do you know who killed her?'

'Yes,' Jonah replied. 'Yes, we do.'

'He thought I saw him.' Jojo's voice was unusually straightforward. It was strange listening to her without any sarcasm; without seeing any half-smiles or mockery. But he was fiercely proud of everything she was saying, and of how well she would come across in her statement. 'He saw me looking over, and didn't realize that he was too far outside the firelight. He thought I was keeping it quiet for years.'

'Why would he think you would cover for him?' O'Malley asked, being the thorough copper.

'I think he connected my willingness to go and hide the stash with my silence about seeing him. And he told me today that he thought I'd seen her in there, too. You know he puked, when I was dragging a dead stoat around to mask the scent? I thought it was the smell, but he'd just seen her body and realized what he'd done.' She gave a very slight shiver. 'He kept repeating that he'd never meant to kill her when he was climbing after me. And he really thought she'd enjoyed it when he'd raped her . . .'

'He never talked about you seeing him after the murder?'

'No. I think there was a lot going on in his head that had nothing to do with reality. He claimed he'd been keeping us all safe for thirty years by not framing one of us. He'd taken on this role of keeping us together for some reason. It was . . . controlling, I think, but maybe he really did think he was the good guy. When I got together with Aleksy, he made a huge effort to be friends with him, too. To keep him onside.'

'So that friendliness,' O'Malley asked. 'It was maintained right up until recent events?'

'Yeah,' Jojo said. She stopped looking at O'Malley. She glanced over at Jonah and then away from both of them. 'I thought so. But there was . . . there was a row with Aleksy. I told you about that, didn't I? I could tell something was wrong, but I didn't guess that he'd figured out Brett's dirty secret.'

'Did anything else come of it?'

'No,' Jojo said. 'Well . . . yes, actually. Brett was quiet for a bit, and a few days later, my sheds, and most of my garden, were burned down. And then, straight afterwards, suddenly Brett was my best friend, and all charm. Flirting. Making me feel . . . like he cared more than Aleksy, who had barely helped me with the clear-up. It all got a bit messed up.' She paused, and then said slowly, 'It seems obvious now that he thought I knew something. He was warning me to keep my mouth shut, with that fire. And then, once he'd warned me, he wanted to reel me back in, didn't he? To say "Here's how bad it is when we're not friends, and here's how good it is when we are."'

She let out an unsteady breath. 'He told me he killed Aleksy. And he tried to say that it was Aleksy's fault, because he shouldn't have snooped. I don't even know . . . I don't know what he found.'

'Did he tell you how Aurora died?' Jonah asked quietly.

'Yes. Well . . . he said she should have gone for help instead of crawling into that hole. Was she . . . was she definitely dead when we filled it in? He thought so, but . . .'

'We're still looking at tox reports,' O'Malley said.

Jojo shook her head. 'I can't believe he could be so stupid. Giving her drugs he didn't understand and leaving her to die without even realizing it . . . And then in the morning he was raging at everyone because she'd vanished.' She nodded bitterly. 'Raging at us because he couldn't get to her and mess with her head.'

Later, once they were done, Jonah offered to show her out. They walked silently out of CID and down towards the street, Jonah very much aware of her bare arms and legs, and of her closeness.

At the entrance, Jonah paused: a signal for her to wait, too.

'If it helps,' he said quietly, 'forensics are positive she was dead long before anyone woke up. The Dexedrine was in five-gram bags, and it looks like Brett fed her the whole thing. That's between five and twenty times the typical amount to overdose, and she can't have weighed more than sixty kilos. The pharmacologist thinks death would have been well within an hour.'

There was a silence while Jojo looked towards her feet. She nodded, then lifted her head once again and gave him a faint smile. 'I suppose all of this will take a while to tie up,' she said.

'It usually takes a bit,' he said, nodding. 'But not for ever.'

Jojo's smile warmed a little. 'I'll see you soon, then.'

Topaz climbed the stairs away from Connor, hoping that he would understand. It was Aurora's room that she went to, once again, instead of her own.

She felt like Aurora had walked in there with her. She was seeing her sister's pale, smiling face; her gold hair; her quick, shy movements.

She sat carefully on the bed, remembering what Connor had said to her when she had let herself back into the silent kitchen.

It was Brett. Brett killed her, darling. Your parents have been trying to call you.

She'd reached her father on his seldom-used mobile, and he'd told them what the police thought: that it had been a sexual assault turned into an accidental murder. That Brett had drugged her, and killed her.

'But he's paid for it,' Tom had added. 'He tried to have a go at Jojo and fell off a cliff.'

She'd rung off, and felt a wave of desperate guilt. She had laughed with the man who had killed Aurora. Had hugged him. Had, thirty years ago, slept with him, on the night that he'd killed her.

But as she had sobbed bitterly on to Connor's shoulder, another feeling had stolen in. One of release.

For the first time since Aurora had vanished she found that she could think of her sister without that burning lack of resolution. Without having to wonder what she'd suffered.

Sitting in her sister's room, surrounded by its girlish butterflies and flowers, she could picture her infuriating, beautiful, spacy, wonderful sister sitting next to her. And it made her smile.

It was the conversation with Anna that had been the hardest. As Jonah had softly explained her husband's crimes, her breathing had become shallow and she'd tried to stand up. To leave the room.

Hanson had accompanied her to find water, and to get fresh air. It had been a good twenty minutes until Jonah had been able to tell her that her husband was dead.

When she finally spoke, her story had been one of the most painful accounts he'd heard. It had swung wildly between fierce protection of her husband, and admissions of his bullying; of the way he had constantly checked up on her, and picked holes in everything she did. How he would look at her phone constantly and rage at her for saying things to her friends, and how she'd stopped saying anything to anyone in the end. How he had refused to talk to her for three days when she'd read his emails, as a form of payback, and how he'd frequently said the harshest possible things to her before suddenly apologizing and telling her how much he loved her – and how good she was for standing by him when he was so damaged. How he had used the tracking on her phone to keep tabs on her.

Jonah felt a sense of satisfaction that that, at least, had been used against him in the end, because it had let her track him, too. That if he had managed to harm Jojo, they would have been right there to pick him up.

After the interview with Anna, there had been one with Stavely, who had handed himself in late that night. He had given Jonah a slow nod as he had been brought up to CID, and Jonah had almost smiled back at him. The drug dealer who had taken thirty years to do the right thing.

In fact, Stavely proved to be a godsend. They made an early agreement to waive charges against him for obstruction of justice and breaking and entering in order for him to give them everything he had on Brett Parker. His account had been succinct and convincing, and had told Jonah a great deal.

Matt Stavely had been drawn into Brett Parker's world a few months after Aurora's death. Brett had turned up at Stavely's old flat on a drizzly November evening, and told him that the drugs Daniel Benham had bought were sitting in a hole in the ground, almost all of them still there, and that Benham was never going to go and get them. He told Stavely that he could take the lot, and that Brett would pay him to do it, too, if he retrieved them.

'I want them gone,' Brett had told him. 'And, ideally, if any traces remain, I want them to very clearly be someone else's.'

He'd handed Stavely a crushed can of beer in a plastic bag, which he'd told him had Connor Dooley's fingerprints on it.

'If you leave it there, then I'm safe, even if they do realize there were drugs there.'

Stavely, who had made bad decision after bad decision over the preceding months, and who had owed his supplier a terrifying amount, even with Benham's money, had agreed to it. Thousands of pounds' worth of Dexedrine and a couple of hundred upfront had been lifeblood to him.

So, with a series of directions and on Brett's suggestion, he had waited until the early hours of Christmas Eve, when there would be nobody out in the forest, and when the roads were utterly dead. He'd taken a series of lights and a shovel, and had made his way to the riverbank, where he had begun digging until he'd found the first packets.

It hadn't taken him long to find Aurora.

He'd spent an hour wondering what the hell he should do. He'd paced around the freezing woodland and thought that he should go and call Brett Parker, or the police. But how could he explain this? This midnight drug recovery? He'd be in total shit.

As, he realized, Brett Parker had known.

It had been a nightmarish experience, the rest of that night. He had dug around her decaying remains, saved from full exposure to the smell only by the frozen ground. He'd loaded packet after packet into a holdall, and tried not to touch her. Some of them had fluid on them, part of her. He couldn't even think about it now without feeling sick. He'd broken the ice in the shallows of the river and washed them, and put them in the bag anyway.

As the sun came up, he'd tipped the beer can out of its bag into the hole, and then shovelled the soil back over it until there was only a heap of earth to see. He'd left, and driven home without even remembering the journey.

He'd called Brett, who had told him coldly not to be an idiot. That he was part of this now, and that Brett wasn't going to let him suffer. That Brett could do him a lot of good if Stavely was on his side.

He'd been terrified of discovery, and hungry for the funds Brett was offering him. And so he had become a periodic employee of Brett Parker, and had become more and more entangled in the terrible things that he did. He had supplied him with coke, with some of the Dexedrine, and then, later, with Rohypnol.

'Did that worry you?' Jonah had asked him.

'Of course it fucking did,' Stavely had said furiously. 'But I was part of his dirty game. I was deep in it, and I was afraid of what would happen if I said no. So I kept quiet and I did what he told me.'

Which, it turned out, had included setting two fires at Jojo Magos's house eight years apart. Brett had been careful not to do anything himself from start to finish.

But, as careful as he'd been, he had made a few mistakes along the way. He'd let Stavely into his study when he'd showed up for payment, in order to pretend to Anna that it was normal business. And in a moment of bizarre pride some years later, he'd showed off some of the messages he was exchanging with one of the girls he was grooming. He'd thought they were on the same side. He hadn't recognized the loathing in Stavely's face.

Stavely had eventually seen his opportunity to reveal the truth when he'd been told to provide a distraction. He had to check that Hanson was out there, watching him, and then go through a series of actions. Except that he'd told the cab driver to take him to Brett's house, instead of Daniel Benham's, where he was supposed to pretend to be trying to sell him drugs. He'd been told to play the innocent about the kitchen knife, which would stay in its packet, having done its job in luring Hanson in.

'I thought about that girl, under the ground, and the other girls being raped and all, and . . . well, I may be a fuck-up and a dealer, but I'm not a murderer or a fucking rapist, and I couldn't let him do it any more. I've got a niece the age of some of those girls. Jesus.'

He offered them all his communications with Brett Parker to help them, and Jonah was grateful. They needed to begin the hunt for the other rape victims.

They could start, he thought, with Zofia Wierzbowski. And there was Coralie Ribbans, too. He was dreading talking to Coralie, who he believed had been Brett's victim for decades, and who had been so entirely influenced by him that she had never realized it.

It was one a.m. before everything had been wrapped up for the day. Before going home, Jonah returned to his office and very gently pulled Aurora's picture off the board, removed the Blu-Tack, and opened one of the evidence boxes. He laid the picture in it, and pushed aside thoughts of Aurora curling up underground to die alone. She deserved to be remembered differently.

There would be more to do in the morning, and for a lot of mornings after that, but sleep had to happen, too. And families and friends and normal life. It was time to make the promised visit to his mother.

42

The sun had showed up for Aurora, and it seemed appropriate somehow to Topaz. She often remembered her sister haloed by sun, a dreamy expression on her face. And so Topaz had dressed for her sister, too, in a gauzy, floral dress that buttoned down the front, all white and red and green. No black for her today.

Connor took her hand as they walked from the church to the grave. They followed her parents, and the coffin that was being carried by four professional bearers. It must have been feather-light, with so little left of her now. Topaz tried not to think about that.

She squeezed her husband's hand, and after a pause he squeezed back. She wondered whether they would ever be like they had been, before it had all been dug up and she had come to doubt the one person she had always trusted. And whether Connor could ever forget that it had been Aurora's killer that she had chosen to sleep with instead of him.

She glanced over her shoulder at the trio behind them. Jojo and Daniel were either side of Anna, almost supporting her as she walked. There were tears cascading down her face. She wouldn't have been here at all if Jojo hadn't driven to her house and told her they wouldn't hold the funeral without her.

How the hell they were all going to deal with Brett's funeral was a question for another day.

Jojo looked so strong as she held Anna and soothed her. Topaz found herself envying Jojo's strength, and then decided that she would just have to imitate it.

Behind the trio came Mary and Polly Benham, who were arm in arm and talking in low voices, flanked by Aurora's only real friend, Becky, who was as round and as shy as she had ever been at school, and whose eyes were raw and red.

And half hidden behind all of them was Coralie. Her head was bowed under a small black hat, but Topaz could see dark smudges of mascara underneath her eyes.

'Wait,' she said to Connor suddenly, and moved aside to let the others past.

As Coralie drew level, Topaz let go of Connor's hand, and reached out to her oldest friend. 'Coralie,' she said. 'Here.'

Coralie stepped towards her, and Topaz wrapped her in a fierce hug. Her friend's silent tears became all-out sobbing. Topaz held her and swayed, knowing that Coralie was crying as much for the loss of the man she had thought loved her, who had carried on a long-distance affair with her for thirty years in order to control her, as she was for Aurora or anyone else.

'He's gone now, but that means there's nobody in the way of us,' Topaz said.

And to her surprise and intense gratitude, Connor came to join the hug, putting an arm round each of them and rubbing Coralie's back gently.

So the three of them had been the last to arrive at the graveside, as strange a trio as Anna and Daniel and Jojo were. The minister had nodded to her, and then began to consign Aurora to the earth.

The earth had had her for a long time, Topaz thought. It didn't have any right to have her again. She should have been with all of them. With her family, and maybe with children of her own. She imagined how Aurora would have been as a mother, and knew that she would have been wonderful.

There was a tightness in her throat as Aurora was lowered back into the ground, a bare two weeks after she'd been lifted out of it. Topaz looked up and away, and then, in her turn, lifted a handful of earth from beside the grave, and held it over the chestnut coffin.

'I'm sorry,' she whispered, and let it go.

Acknowledgements

A debut is always going to be the result of an awful lot of help from an awful lot of people. I have so many to thank, but some having been total, shining stars in the process.

First and foremost amongst those is my loveliest agent, Felicity Blunt, who recognized something to champion early on, and then stood by me through all of the difficult and the fun times, and whose wonderful eye for editing made this book ten times better than it would have been.

And the amazing Joel Richardson, kick-ass editor, who is probably responsible for most of the other good stuff you see in here and to whom I owe being able to devote myself to writing.

To Rufus and Paul, who have been amazingly supportive and understanding at least some of the time when their mummy/girlfriend was busy writing, and who have also been massive procrastination aids in fun ways. And one of whom even error-checked for me at a crucial time.

To Kyn, who proofread and pointed out any time I'd been profoundly confusing.

To the Penguin editorial team for all their hugely valuable help, and to the rights team for getting the book out to countries I never would have dreamed of.

And then there are all the others who helped in various ways. There are so many resources I found invaluable in researching this book, and I should have been better at recording them all. It's been utterly fascinating to get to know the world of policing – even a little – and to realize how different it can be from some fictional versions. I can cite Clare Mackintosh's fantastic (and heartfelt) threads on what annoys her about fictional presentations of policing as one very eye-opening source. And thanks must go to those officers of Cambridgeshire Constabulary who were patient enough to answer some very stupid questions from me. I just hope I haven't let any of you down.

Finally, I have to apologize to Hampshire Constabulary for inserting Jonah's team into Southampton Central Station, and for structuring my own CID there. I hope I can be forgiven for that, and for all other crimes of invention on top of reality.

Enjoyed SHE LIES IN WAIT?

Jonah Sheens will return in 2020 in a new thriller.

Pre-order now, or follow Gytha Lodge for all the latest updates.

thegyth

GythaLodge

8